The Linen Queen

A NOVEL

PATRICIA FALVEY

CENTER STREET

New York   Boston   Nashville

Copyright © 2011 by Irish Books LLC

All rights reserved. Except as permitted under the U.S. Copyright Act of 1976, no part of this publication may be reproduced, distributed, or transmitted in any form or by any means, or stored in a database or retrieval system, without the prior written permission of the publisher.

Center Street
Hachette Book Group
237 Park Avenue
New York, NY 10017

www.centerstreet.com

Originally published in hardcover by Center Street.

Center Street is a division of Hachette Book Group, Inc.
The Center Street name and logo are trademarks of Hachette Book Group, Inc.

The publisher is not responsible for websites (or their content) that are not owned by the publisher.

Printed in the United States of America

First Trade Edition: February 2012
10 9 8 7 6 5 4 3 2 1

The Library of Congress has cataloged the hardcover edition as follows:
Falvey, Patricia
    The linen queen / Patricia Falvey.—1st ed.
      p. cm.
    ISBN 978-1-59995-200-0
    1. Young women—Northern Ireland—Fiction. 2. Women textile workers—Northern Ireland—Fiction. 3. World War, 1939-1945—Northern Ireland—Fiction. I. Title
    PS3606.A49L56 2011
    813'.6—dc22
                        2010032786

ISBN 978-1-59995-199-7 (pbk.)

The Linen Queen

"THE LINEN QUEEN takes the reader through an emotional ride as World War II transforms the lives of those in Northern Ireland." —*Irish America Magazine*

"THE LINEN QUEEN is a romance in the truest sense; it knows that love can't conquer every ill, but if you make the right choices...Falvey's young heroine discovers that happiness becomes a distinct possibility." —*The Irish Voice*

"Falvey's characters balance each other nicely. While set in Ireland, the story's location is not the main focus. The difficulties of life during wartime and balancing one's desires and responsibilities are the main attraction." —*Romantic Times Book Reviews*; 4 out of 4 stars

"I loved the book and look forward to the next from this great author. I think this book would be enjoyed by the fans of World War II—and Ireland—themed stories. I highly recommend both of Patricia Falvey's novels." —Celtic Lady's Blog Reviews

"Lush scenes, filled with all the emotions of a war that beckons with no horizon in sight, this novel creates its own Irish lilt through Sheila McGee. Lovingly written, and just as poignant as *The Yellow House*." —TheReviewBroads.com

"Falvey is an outstanding and evocative storyteller; would recommend this to anyone who loves historical fiction. I even believe she's giving Maeve Binchy a run for her money for my favorite Irish author." —Read-all-over.net

The Yellow House

"*The Yellow House* is that great rarity, a book about Ireland written by an American who knows what she's talking about. Intelligently plotted, with engaging characters, the novel offers a fresh view of the highly dramatic Revolutionary Period in Ireland. The well-researched history illumines but never smothers the story line. Small details bring the era to life with stunning clarity. The writing is lucid and accessible, occasionally even lyrical. This is a very rewarding first novel and I look forward to reading more from Patricia Falvey."

—Morgan Llywelyn, author of *Lion of Ireland*, *Pride of Lions*, *Grania*, *The Last Prince of Ireland*, and The Irish Century series

"*The Yellow House* is an eloquently written story of the emergence of hope and love in a time of struggle and confusion in Ireland. It avoids the ever-present pitfalls of drowning us in a history lesson while not ignoring the richness of that very history. With her debut novel, Patricia Falvey breathes life back into an Ireland that has nearly vanished from memory. For that, I am grateful."

—Robert Hicks, *New York Times* bestselling author of *The Widow of the South* and *A Separate Country*

"You can often tell where a book's plot and characters are going. But so many times I was astonished to find that what I expected on the next page was a complete surprise to me. Falvey held my attention with suspenseful events that constantly amazed me…*The Yellow House* is a powerful book, full of strongly drawn characters that exemplify vitality, humanity, and passion for life. They are so realistic, that early on I felt like I knew them."

—Frank West, *Irish American News*

"Patricia Falvey draws on her North of Ireland roots to put a human face on the turning point in twentieth-century Irish history. A moving novel and singular achievement."

—Mary Pat Kelly, author of *Galway Bay*

"This novel delivers the best of both worlds: secrets, intrigue, and surprising twists will keep readers flipping the pages, while Falvey's insight and poetic writing tugs at the heartstrings of the most cynical audiences."   —*Publishers Weekly*

"*The Yellow House* was extremely interesting from an educational perspective. It brings to life the struggles of individuals and communities seeking freedom."

—Cecie O'Bryon England, *Washington Times*

"If you like historical fiction, with great flourishes of families destroyed and remade, this is a classic." —*The Review Broads*

"Falvey tells a good story along the way. A host of interesting characters, surprising but plausible plot developments, and deftly incorporated details of the Irish struggle for independence add up to a debut novel sure to please fans of historical romance."
—Kathy Piehl, *Library Journal*

"Falvey very successfully weaves together the politics, history, and landscape of Ireland in this period...Falvey brilliantly illustrates the cultural, political, and economic conflicts that result in erecting Ireland's North/South dividing border. The well-researched history of the period emerges through the characters, their conflicts, and their choices. The story is absorbing and satisfying historical fiction."
—*Sacramento Book Review* and *San Francisco Book Review*

"The early scenes of Eileen's and James's lawless exploits for the Catholic resistance make for thrilling reading...The book serves as a provocative reminder of the tangled strings of family, war, and familial war, and also...as a splendid example of old-fashioned, minimal-bodice-ripping romance."
—Joy Tipping, *Dallas Morning News*

"The characters are full, rich, and real and the history of Ireland feels authentic. The author refrains from delineating clearly between the good guys and bad guys. She allows the reader to make their own decisions and I liked that. *The Yellow House* is a winner. I just can't shake the memory of it and that's a good thing." —Andrea Sisco, *Minneapolis Insight Examiner*

"[O]ne of the best historical fiction novels I have read in years...I simply could not pull myself away from this book. It took me back to classics such as Gaskell's *North and South* and the heroine Eileen had so many of the qualities that I have always loved in dear Tess of Hardy's *Tess of the D'Ubervilles*. When one book can bring me back to two of my favorite books of all time that are both absolute classics, I am in awe. This book kept me emotionally invested until the very end...Wonderfully written, magically created, it could only come from a true Irish lass and to be her debut novel...amazing. I loved it...every page."

—*Stiletto Storytime*

"It is rare for a first-time novelist to tackle historical events in as refreshing a manner as Patricia Falvey does in *The Yellow House*...Falvey controls the story, weaving her characters through the First World War and the Troubles, allowing the characters to be the masters of their own fate rather than falling back on history to guide the plot...Readers will be inclined to gluttonously scarf down this novel in one sitting as I did. Take your time reading *The Yellow House*; you'll be sad to see the last page."

—*Irish America* magazine

"Religious intolerance, political strife, and personal drama combine well in this historical novel whose themes are still relevant today."

—*The Hartford Courant*

"Set in the tumultuous years before and after World War I, *The Yellow House* is an impressive debut that will appeal to readers of Irish family sagas. Falvey skillfully takes major events and reduces them to a personal level, focusing on the effects of World War I and religious unrest in Ireland on one woman and the people around her...Falvey steers clear of the stock characters that often plague novels set in Ireland. The love triangle between Eileen, Owen, and James, combined with the historical context, provides plenty of tension and keeps the story moving quickly...it's hard not to root for [Eileen] as she fights to reclaim her birthright."

—*Historical Novels Review*

ALSO BY PATRICIA FALVEY:

The Yellow House

Available from Center Street wherever books are sold.

For

Lizzie, Ellen Jane, Nellie, and Angeline

yarn spinners, all

ACKNOWLEDGMENTS

I would like to thank my agents, Denise Marcil and Anne Marie O'Farrell, for their support, enthusiasm, and encouragement throughout the writing of this book, for keeping me on track, and for cheering me on to the finish line. Thanks to my editor, Christina Boys at Center Street, for her faith in me, and for her patience and invaluable insights. The time and effort she put into the editing process were generous beyond my expectations. Thanks also to her assistant, Angela Valente. Thanks to Amy Ryan, Shanon Stowe, and to all the great staff at Hachette Book Group. Also thanks to David Hancock of Dallas for his insightful website design, and for his friendship.

I would also like to thank my friends everywhere for their ongoing support and enthusiasm for this new career of mine. Thank you for your gentle inquiries as to progress, your encouragement, and your words of support as I made my way through the sometimes perilous territory of a second novel. Thanks especially to the Good Eats Gang in Dallas for patiently listening while I talked nonstop to "real people" after I had spent many hours talking only to my fictional characters.

My special thanks to the Joel Silverman family of Akron, Ohio. They welcomed me into their midst with joy and love. They included me in their rituals and gave me insights into their culture that proved invaluable in writing this book. Thanks also to Bernard for introducing me to them, for his constant support, and as always for all the jokes that brought me laughter when I really needed it.

Thanks also to Pat O'Keefe of Newry, son of a sea captain, for his stories about the boats and sailors of Newry. Thanks to the many women in my family whose memories of the spinning mills were passed down to me, and to the women everywhere who have toiled in the mills.

And as always special thanks to my dearest sister, Connie, whose pride and love bring me amazing joy, and who, along with her sons, Noel, Colin, Shane, and Don, continues to keep the gift of my Irish heritage alive and well in me.

Chapter 1

From Monday to Thursday we sang to break the monotony; on Friday we sang to celebrate. In the four years I had worked at the Queensbrook Spinning Mill in County Armagh in the North of Ireland the singers were mute on only three occasions—the day Bridie McCardle's child was buried; the day Lizzie Grant caught her hair between the rollers of her spinning frame and was carried out on a stretcher; and the day after England declared war on Germany.

On this particular Friday in late March of 1941 we sang as usual to celebrate the upcoming two days of freedom from the mill. I stood barefoot, just as I had every weekday since I was a fourteen-year-old doffer, the water from the condensing steam swishing around my ankles, and forced a hank of flax through a trough of hot water to soften it. As I guided the flax down through the eye of the flyer and onto the yarn bobbin we finished up "My Lovely Rose of Clare" and paused for breath. My friend Patsy Mallon called out to a young lad who stood in the aisle near her frame.

"Would you ever come over here and piece me threads together, Danny? There's a good lad."

I looked up, wiping the sweat from my forehead with the back of my hand. Patsy was a big, bold girl with a large bosom and a salty tongue. She scared the wits out of young part-timers like

Danny who went to school in the mornings and worked in the mill in the afternoons. Patsy would lean over them, pressing her breasts against them as they worked to tie the threads or replace the empty bobbins on her machine. I shot a glance at my other friend, Kathleen Doyle, who worked two spinning frames at the stand next to mine. Kathleen's face reddened as much as Danny's had done and she bowed her head. Kathleen was the most innocent girl on the floor.

The late March day was drawing in. Soon darkness would sift through the grimy windows, which were set so high up on the walls you couldn't see out of them. I looked over the enormous room with its dim light and orderly rows of wet spinning frames extending the length of it, separated by narrow aisles called passes. I felt small in here, dwarfed by the room's size and timid in the face of the rows of bobbins that grinned like misshapen teeth and spat and hissed like devils. I sighed. At least it was Friday. I would have two days off before I had to return to this cave.

Just as the Friday afternoon singing resumed—a rough chorus of spinners and doffers murdering the gentle, plaintive notes of "The Croppy Boy"—the doffing mistress, Miss Galway, marched down the middle aisle between the rows of spinning frames and blew her whistle louder than a banshee's scream. Miss Galway was an ancient woman—some said she'd been there as long as the mill itself—but she still had a fine set of lungs. Every time she blew her whistle to get the attention of the young part-timers we all winced. Today she blew it longer and louder than usual and we knew something was up. Without a word we all pulled the handles on the side of our frames and our machines shuddered and fell silent.

"Ladies, we have a visitor today. Mrs. McAteer wishes to make an announcement of some importance."

We all turned towards the door as Mrs. Hannah McAteer entered on cue. She was a tall, grim woman with a long, narrow face and black hair flecked with gray. She was the widowed sister of Mr. Carlson who owned the mill, and the mother of Mary McAteer who worked in the mill office. Patsy said the *craic* was that Hannah, a Quaker, had married a Catholic farmer who'd been killed in the First World War and left her penniless. She and her daughter were at the mercy of her brother, Patsy said, and that was why she always looked as if she'd just smelled shite.

"Good afternoon," Mrs. McAteer began, looking around as if she indeed smelled something bad. Well, who could blame her for that? The smell of oil and grease and sweat in the room would choke a horse.

"I have some very good news for you."

We left our machines and edged closer to her.

"I assume you have all heard of the Linen Queen competition that takes place every year at a linen mill in Northern Ireland. Well, this year it is Queensbrook's turn."

She attempted a smile as a cheer went up from the spinners. She raised her hand for silence. "Now, this is a very important honor for us here in Queensbrook. Mr. Carlson has asked me to head the committee to choose those girls lucky enough to be asked to enter the competition. I shall take this responsibility very seriously in order that Queensbrook may stand the best chance of winning. Six girls from Queensbrook will be given the chance to enter. That's four more than usually allowed, since we are the host mill. To be fair we will choose three from the weaving shed and three from the spinning mill."

Kathleen and Patsy stood on either side of me, each one clutching my arm.

"Well, no harm to the weaving girls," Patsy said, "but they all look like ghosts over there what with the heat and the noise and the dust. They'd be no competition at all. At least the spinners all have great complexions on account of the steam."

"Can you believe this, Sheila?" whispered Kathleen.

I wanted to believe it. A strange flutter took hold of my heart. I had heard about the Linen Queen competition in which girls from mills all around the North competed for the title. Talk was that the winner was awarded prize money as well as a crown and sash. Winning the crown would be nice, I thought, but the money might be enough to buy a ticket to England. My throat went dry.

"Of course you must understand that the Linen Queen competition is not merely a beauty competition."

Was Mrs. McAteer looking directly at me, or was I imagining things?

"A girl's fitness to represent the mill—good attendance, solid work habits, a respectable family, and, above all, good character—will be considered above looks. And of course she must be between eighteen and twenty-one years of age."

This time I was sure she glared at me when she spoke of character. True I had mocked her daughter, Mary, more than once and Mary had caught me at it. Well, Mary had deserved it. She'd called me names to my face and accused me of being loose with boys. How could I help it if the young eejits followed me out of the mill every day calling foolish oul' blather after me? It was Patsy who asked for that kind of thing, not me. But I was sure Mary had told her ma all about it. I hadn't cared until now. As if she read my thoughts, I turned to see Mary, a plump girl with black hair, standing in the doorway taking everything in.

"The competition will take place on Saturday night, April twelfth."

Mary's ma continued speaking to the hushed crowd. "The entrants will be announced one week from today, which will give the lucky girls a fortnight to prepare. Frocks will have to be festive, but modest. Those chosen will be given a list of rules. Good luck to all of you."

A festive frock, I thought. How in the name of God would I ever afford such a thing? The earlier flutter in my heart turned heavy.

Mrs. McAteer swung around and walked towards the door. No one moved. Then as if she'd suddenly had an afterthought she stopped and turned. "Oh, and the prize money this year is two hundred pounds."

A gasp went through the room.

"Jesus, Mary, and Joseph, that's a fortune of money," shouted Patsy. "I could move out on my own, and I could buy as much finery as I liked, and I wouldn't have to give that tight-fisted bastard another penny."

Patsy was talking about her da, who took all her money off her and had been beating the daylights out of her since she was a child.

"It would be like a miracle," Kathleen whispered. "Think what my ma could do with the likes of that."

Kathleen was the oldest of ten children. Her da was disabled and her ma had taken the consumption after years working in the weaving shed. The family depended on Kathleen's wages.

I said nothing. Thoughts collided in my brain. If it was based on looks I knew I'd stand a fair chance. And I hadn't missed a day's work since I started at the mill. I'd even fought off the mill fever that most youngsters suffered from when they first started. I'd kept going in those first few weeks even though I was hardly fit to stand. My attitude could be better I knew, but it was hard to smile all the time when you hated the mill as much as I did. And I had turned eighteen since the previous competition had been held in Lisburn and so now I could qualify for the first time. As for character—well, I realized that was in Mrs. McAteer's hands. Would she hold me back on account of the gossip that surrounded me?

A twinge of guilt crept over me when I thought of Patsy and Kathleen. We'd been friends since our schooldays and to tell the truth they were the only friends I had in the mill. They each deserved to win the prize. What if I was picked to enter and they weren't? I pushed the thought aside.

As we left the mill that night, all the talk was about the competition. I'd never witnessed such excitement. Even the older women who would have no chance of being picked encouraged the young ones. They were all delighted for us. I couldn't wait to talk to Ma.

ༀ

I said good-bye to Patsy and Kathleen at the tram station. They both lived out in the country and came and went every day on the electric tram that the mill had laid on for workers from outlying towns. I lived in the mill village itself and had only a short walk to my house on Charlemont Square, one of two squares in the village with identical houses built around a green, all of them occupied by mill workers and their families. Well it wasn't my house, exactly. It was the house where my ma and I lodged with my father's sister, Kate, and her husband, Kevin. We had lived there since the time my da left on his boat when I was ten years old and never came back. Aunt Kate had taken us in, but she never let us forget her charity. Kevin was a big, burly customer with a bad temper. I stayed away from him as much as I could, particularly when he was on the drink.

My ma and I slept in the granny room at the back of the scullery in an old iron frame bed covered with four sacks. It wouldn't have been so bad if it hadn't been for the fact that there was a perfectly good bedroom up the stairs that had been standing empty for years. It had belonged to Kate and Kevin's only child, Donal, who had left home five years ago when he was seventeen and had not been seen since. I was at school when it happened, but according to the neighbors, when he left he had said he was never coming back. He'd fought with his parents for years and was always saying he couldn't wait to get away from them. I completely understood his need to escape. But Kate refused to believe he was gone for good and so she kept his room like a shrine—his clothes clean and pressed and hanging in the wardrobe, his copy books laid out on the small desk, his bed made up every week with fresh linen sheets. It was comical and eerie at the same time.

I slowed my step as I neared the house. Doubt began to taint my earlier excitement. Could I dare to hope that I'd even be picked to enter, let alone win? Maybe Ma would be in one of her good moods and would encourage me the way the other women in the spinning mill had done—but I was no sooner in the door when I realized it was a foolish hope. Ma was in one of her desperate bad moods. I could tell by the fact that she still wore her stained work apron and hadn't bothered to comb her hair. Ever since I was a child I never knew which Ma I was going to find when I walked into the house. There were days when she sang like a lark, all smiles and kisses. And there were days like this when she looked like an old woman with the life drained out of her.

"Don't go getting any ideas in your head!" she began. "There's girls all over the country better looking than you are, miss," she said. "And we've no money for fancy frocks and all the rest of it."

"Don't start, Ma," I said wearily. "I haven't even been picked yet."

"And you won't be!"

Ma worked in the weaving shed as a cloth passer, where she checked the woven cloth for faults. It was a good job, but a hard one. Most of the weavers hated her because she was so critical. It didn't seem to bother Ma. She was only forty years old, but sometimes she looked twice her age, as she did now. I felt a rush of sympathy for her. She'd had a hard time of it since my da had left. And it was no easy matter for her living in another woman's house and having to slave at the mill like the rest of us. But I shook the feeling off as quickly as it came. None of this was my fault. Why should I have to suffer as well?

Ma sat in the armchair beside the fire.

"I know what you're thinking, miss," she went on, her voice ragged from coughing and cigarettes. "You'll win this competition and then you'll be too good for the rest of us. You'll forget where you came from. And you'll go off gallivanting and forget about your duty to me. And me not a well woman."

Ma always added the last part to nail my guilt securely in place. I sighed.

"I don't want to talk about it, Ma."

I tried to push past her towards the scullery, but she reached over and grabbed my arm. "I don't know where you got this notion that you're better than the rest of us," she said, "but you're not. If it wasn't for me you'd be out on the street."

"If it wasn't for you I'd have finished school by now, and I'd have a good job and we'd both be better off!"

Ma's grip tightened on my arm. "We needed the money," she said. "And you needed to find a husband to support us. How were you going to meet a chap locked away in that convent school?"

I sighed. There was no talking to her when she got like this. I waited for the rest of it.

"What about Gavin O'Rourke? He's a fine chap and he makes a good living with that boat of his."

"He's a sailor," I said. "I thought you'd no time for sailors after what Da did to us? Besides," I finished, "it's just not like that between us."

Ma swore under her breath. "Love," she said. "What good does it do you? You can make a marriage without it. I never loved your da."

"And look how you ended up," I said. "I'm tired. I'm going to lie down."

I pulled my arm away from her and went into the granny room and lay down on the bed. All the earlier pleasure of possibility had drained out of me. Ma always managed to do this, I thought. Why did I even listen to her? I sighed. Well, when you lived together and slept together, it was impossible to escape. I closed my eyes and welcomed the darkness.

ତ୍ୟୁ

The next morning, Saturday, Ma refused to get up out of bed. When she was in one of her down moods she would lie there all day, refusing to open the curtains to let any light in. If I moved, she complained I was keeping her awake. After a while I could stand it no longer. I jumped out of the bed and drew back the curtains.

"You can't stay there all day, Ma," I said.

Ma turned over and hid her head under the four sacks.

"I'm not well," she moaned. "Why don't you go down to Mulcahy's later and get the bread."

"Och, Ma," I said, "you know I hate being around that man."

"It's your imagination," Ma said. "You think every man is after you. You've got a quare bob on yourself, my girl."

Ma turned over to face me. "There's money on the dresser— what few shillings we have left—and it's our turn to buy the bread. So go on now and get in the queue early."

It was twelve noon when I left the house. To tell the truth I was glad of an excuse to get out. The place smelled so musty I could hardly breathe. I took in a few gulps of fresh air the moment I closed the door behind me. I buttoned up my coat and walked back down the hill to wait for the tram into Newry, the main town in the area.

At four o'clock I was still stuck in the bread line outside Mulcahy's bakery on Hill Street. Myself and the other women there had been queuing up for hours. Just before closing time on Saturdays the bakery sold off the leftover bread and scones for next to nothing. They would be stale by Monday, so better for Mulcahy to get a few pennies for them than throw them out. The women with money would never have been caught dead in such a queue—those well-dressed ladies with their baskets had come and gone by now—hurrying away for fear they would catch a disease from the rest of us. I was mortified to be seen there, but today it was better than being stuck in the Queensbrook house.

I stood now, shivering in the chill March air. The other women wore coats and mufflers and old boots, but I wasn't going to be caught dead in a getup like that. Instead I wore my best coat, thin as it was, my bare legs freshly stained with tea, and high-heeled shoes. And, as usual, I had forgotten my gloves. I was freezing. I recognized many of the women from Queensbrook. The young ones chatted away, but the older ones looked dreary and defeated like my ma. We all carried empty canvas bags, hoping to fill them up with bread.

"What passes for bread these days is a disgrace," said one.

"Aye, nothing but water in it. No good for the children."

"And still they make you queue up and beg for it like dogs."

The line moved slowly. Darkness fell, and the wind picked up. I wrapped my coat tighter around me. Just as I reached as far as Mulcahy's the shutters came down on the windows and door. Mulcahy himself, an oul' boy with a red face, came out to confront us.

"Sorry, ladies. We're closed. You may go home now. And come back on Monday."

Groans and curses erupted from the line. Some of the women turned and left, a look of resignation on their faces. Others pleaded and coaxed, but Mulcahy shook his head.

"Go home now," he said again. "The bread's all gone. And I haven't all night to be arguing. Why hello, Sheila, I didn't see you in the crowd."

His voice turned sweet when he saw me. He grinned broadly, exposing yellowed teeth. "And how's your mammy, love?"

"She's not well at all," I lied. "She'll be desperate when I arrive back with no bread for the tea."

I knew exactly what I was doing. Some of the women watched me with mouths open. Mulcahy came over and put a hairy arm around my waist.

"Och, I'm sorry to hear that, love. Come with me now, sure I might be able to find a bun or two for your poor ma. Lovely woman, lovely woman."

I didn't know which of us was the bigger hypocrite. We both knew Mulcahy wanted to get me in the shop so he could press himself up against me and blow his hot stale breath on my cheek. I shrugged. I could tell him to feck off, or I could go in and put up with him so I could get the bread and not have to listen to Ma complain. I tossed my head at the women who were gaping at me.

"See youse Monday, girls," I said. "Safe home."

"So I hear the Linen Queen competition is at Queensbrook this year," Mulcahy said as he shoveled the bread into my bag. "A pretty girl like yourself should stand a grand chance of winning."

I shrugged. "I haven't been picked yet," I said.

"Och you will, love," Mulcahy said.

I thought if I kept the conversation going I could keep him at his distance.

"Besides," I said, "even if I'm picked, I have no money for a frock, so there's no point getting my hopes up."

It was the worst thing I could have said. Mulcahy laid down the half-full bag on the counter and pressed in close to me. "If it's just a matter of a frock," he whispered, "sure I'll be glad to see you right on that, love. I'd be happy to do you the wee favor."

I felt his heavy breath in my ear and the weight of his thick body pressing against me. I swallowed down the bad taste that rose in my throat. Soon his lips moved across my cheek and found my mouth. I stood paralyzed while his tongue slobbered over mine. He pulled back. "I'd want nothing for the favor, except for you to be nice to me, love."

He pulled away and winked. "Now let's fill up the rest of this bag."

He finished pushing in the bread and buns and scones and handed the bag back to me. "You just let me know when you need the money, love."

I backed out of the shop without answering him and hurried down Monaghan Street in the direction of the tram to Queensbrook. I let one tram go. I wasn't ready yet to go home and face Ma. I sat down on a bench and leaned forward, my elbows on my knees and my palms on my cheeks. I thought over what Mulcahy had said. What if I was picked and needed money for the frock? Would I take his offer? The thought sickened me. But there again, how badly did I want to get out of this place? Shouldn't I be willing to do anything? The thoughts gave me a sore head and I closed my eyes.

It was well after seven in the evening when I stepped off the tram in Queensbrook. A cold, spitting rain hit me in the face like needles. My hands and feet were freezing. I opened the door quietly, hoping Ma was still in bed and that Kate and Kevin were out. But Ma was waiting for me in her armchair beside the fire.

"It's about time, miss," she said.

"I'll put the bread in the scullery," I said, ignoring her bad temper. "I got the last of it."

"We were all waiting for it for the tea," Ma complained. "It's probably stale by now."

"Well, we have some now," I said wearily, "and don't ask me what I had to do to get it."

Chapter 2

༄

The atmosphere at the mill on Monday morning was giddy. The spinners could talk of nothing but the Linen Queen competition.

"I saw some lovely material in Foster's on Hill Street. It would make a gorgeous dress," Patsy said.

"Well for you has the money to be dealing with Foster's," I said.

"Sure I'll take the price out of me winnings!"

"But material is rationed." Kathleen was always the cautious one. "After all, there's a war on."

Patsy laughed. "Well, if we can't get it here there's nothing to stop us smuggling it up from the South."

"Except the customs men," said Kathleen.

Patsy laughed louder and grabbed her breasts. "Sure they'll be too busy looking at these to bother about what's in me bag!"

Kathleen reddened. "You're an awful case, Patsy, so you are."

The week dragged on as slow as a funeral march. My thoughts swung between tipsy hope and sober despair. I fought to reason with myself. If I wasn't picked it would all be for the best. I wouldn't have the worry about the frock and all the rest of it. And to be picked and not win would surely be worse than not to be picked at all. But a faraway voice would always cut in. What if I was picked? And what if I won? The possibility of it sent me into a state of fever just like the one I suffered when I first came to the mill. I was so weak I could hardly stand, and I wanted to vomit. I found myself praying for Mrs. McAteer to appear and put us all out of our misery.

Our singing had reached a crescendo on Friday afternoon as we repeated the chorus of "The Boys from the County Armagh" for the third time when Miss Galway reached for her whistle. She wouldn't even have needed to blow it—we all stood immediately at attention. But blow it she did and clapped her hands. We turned off our machines without bidding and crowded around her. Mrs. McAteer appeared, carrying a paper in her hand. You could have heard a mouse in the room it was so quiet.

"Hello again, ladies," she began. "This is the moment you've been waiting for all week."

Get on with it, I thought. I had no patience for any rigamarole and nor did anyone else.

"Well, I won't keep you in suspense any longer."

She raised the paper in front of her and cleared her throat.

"As I had mentioned last week, our plan was to choose three girls from the weaving shed and three from the spinning mill." She paused. "Alas, we did not find any eligible girls in the weaving shed."

Patsy elbowed me. "Didn't I tell you? They all look like fecking ghosts over there. All the more chances for us!"

"And so that means we will have six from the spinning mill."

A cheer went up and Mrs. McAteer put up her hand for silence.

"The first girl chosen is Miss Eileen O'Hare. Where are you, Eileen?"

We all swung around. Eileen O'Hare had only been at the mill about a year. She was a pretty enough girl with red hair and white skin, small and slender, and quiet. We didn't know what to make of it. But we clapped politely as she blushed and nodded. I took in a breath. One down, I thought.

"Congratulations, Eileen, we all wish you the best of luck," Mrs. McAteer continued.

For the love of God would she not hurry things up?

"I'm dying to pee," whispered Patsy.

"Next, we have Abby Smith. Congratulations, Abby."

Abby Smith was one of the few Protestant girls on the floor. She kept to herself and none of us knew much about her. She was pale and fair-haired, with a long nose and thin face. We applauded halfheartedly as she bowed her head and uttered a muffed thank-you.

I couldn't understand what the logic was. Both Eileen and Abby were quiet girls, pretty enough, but no oil paintings. My heart began to sink. If they weren't taking looks into it at all, then what chance did I stand?

The third girl, Celia Foye, was called. Like the other two, she was quiet and tidy, with wide eyes and the look of a frightened rabbit.

Three to go, I thought to myself. My fingers had turned to ice. I could scarcely breathe. If I did not get this chance, I thought, my life would be over. I would be doomed...

"Kathleen Doyle," I heard from far away. Could I have heard right? Kathleen was my friend, and a lovely girl, but she was hardly ft for a beauty competition. She was plain and stout and...och, Jesus...

Kathleen gasped beside me. She threw her hands to her mouth. "Oh...oh," she cried. "I don't believe it. Oh, wait 'til I tell Mammy."

I shot a look at Patsy. Her mouth was open in shock. I swallowed hard and gave Kathleen a hug. "Well done, Kathleen," I whispered, even though it took everything I had to get the words out.

"And now, last but not least, Miss Patsy Mallon."

I was struck dumb. Patsy? Of all people—Patsy? I could get no words out. Patsy let out a yell that would have wakened the dead.

"Jesus, Mary, and Joseph," she screamed. "Can you believe it at all?"

The young part-timers shouted and whistled and clapped. Patsy was very popular with all of them. Kathleen broke into a broad smile and hugged Patsy. Then she turned to me, jiggling with excitement. "You're next, Sheila," she said. "I know it."

When Mrs. McAteer began to fold up the piece of paper bearing the names of those chosen, it suddenly struck me. She had said "last but not least" before she called Patsy's name.

"But that's only five," I cried out.

Everyone swung around to look at me. The room fell silent. I trembled with fear and passion and anger. Mrs. McAteer pinned me with a stare, a faint smile on her face.

"You are correct, Miss McGee. I have only called five names. The sixth girl chosen is Mary McAteer."

"But that's not fair," I cried again. "She...she doesn't even work in the mill."

"Oh, but she absolutely does," said Mrs. McAteer in a sweet, calm voice. "Mary has worked diligently in the mill offices for the last three years. Without her you girls would not get your pay packets accurate and on time every Friday. I would say that more than qualifies her to be considered for the competition."

I did not have to turn around to know that Mary McAteer was watching from the doorway—all the spinners were staring in that direction. Instead I stood rooted to the ground.

"Aren't you going to congratulate me, Sheila?" boomed Patsy.

I wondered if Patsy would have congratulated me had the situation been reversed. I said nothing. Kathleen came up and put her arm around my shoulder.

"I'm sorry, Sheila," she said. "You should have got a place instead of me. You deserved it."

Anger raged through me. "Why? Why do you think I deserve it, Kathleen? It's only looks that would have got me through, and apparently that's not enough in Mrs. McAteer's books. I did nothing else to deserve it."

"She was afraid you would beat out Mary," said Kathleen, ignoring my outburst. "You're the prettiest girl here; we all know that, don't we, Patsy?"

Patsy shrugged. "I'm told beauty's in the eye of the beholder," she said, and walked away.

The singing began again. In honor of the contestants "The Boys from the County Armagh" became "The Girls from the County

Armagh" and was sung again with gusto. I put my head down as I started up my spinning frame and with every ounce of strength I had I held back the tears that threatened to erupt. I doubted that I would ever join in the singing again.

ഇൻ

Ma's bad mood lifted the minute she heard I wasn't picked.

"Didn't I tell you?" she said, beaming as if she'd just won the prize herself. "I knew you didn't have what it took. If it had been me now—ah, I'd have been the first one picked. And I'd have won it too, no bother. There wasn't a girl in the North could hold a candle to me when I was your age." She paused and sighed. "And to think I threw it all away on the likes of your da!"

I tried not to listen. I'd heard it all before—how Ma was beautiful and all the boys wanted her and she married my da only because she got pregnant with me. Ma lit a cigarette and inhaled deeply.

Aunt Kate sniffed. "Patrick was no slacker, either," she said, referring to my da. "Every girl in the county was after him. He could have had his pick. And who knows what women in foreign parts had their eye on him."

Kate glared at Ma, but in turn Ma winked back at her. "At least the man had good taste," she said.

"I can't get over them picking that Patsy Mallon though," Ma went on, ignoring the look of pain on my face, "nor that wee mouse Kathleen Doyle."

"I hear that Patsy one's a bad article." Kate raised her eyes and blessed herself. "The stories I've heard!"

"Och, she's just out for a bit of *craic* like the rest of us," I put in. I didn't fully understand why I needed to defend Patsy just then, except that I knew Kate felt the same way about me.

"At least Kathleen's a lovely girl and devoted to her ma," said Kate, looking directly at me.

"Aye, not like this selfish wee bitch here," said Ma. "This one can't wait to run away. Am I right? Well the wind's been taken out of your sails now, miss. Maybe this will knock the nonsense out of your head and you can start looking for a husband."

I ran to the front door and opened it as Ma's words taunted me from behind. I stepped out into the street and took in gulps of fresh air. Would I ever hear the end of this? By even trying to join in the competition had I succeeded in making my life even more unbearable? Rain fell as I stood outside the Queensbrook house. I let it soak through me, praying it would wash out my pain.

ശ

On the following Sunday I refused to go to Mass with the family, claiming I was too sick. When everyone had left I hurriedly dressed and went outside and lifted my bicycle out of the back shed. I didn't even have to think where I was going. I always went up to the Flagstaff when I was feeling sad. The place gave me a comfort that no other place did.

I sat now on a stone bench. The view across the shining water of Carlingford Lough towards the Mourne Mountains beyond would lift the spirits of a drowning man. Even on rainy days, the place had a mournful beauty. But the rough weather of the last days had passed, and the sky was a bright, clear blue and filled with fresh white clouds. From the top of the hill I could look out and see the three counties of Armagh, Down, and Louth. "The place where the three counties meet" was the saying of the locals. Gulls wheeled overhead and the wind rustled the bushes. The grasses, still damp from the rain, bore the lush, fresh look that always followed a storm. In the far distance the sound of church bells mingled with a ship's horn. I sighed. Would I ever be on board one of those ships? Would it ever happen now? I rested my elbows on my knees and put my chin in my hands and gazed out at the horizon.

I didn't bother to turn around when I heard the noise. Instinctively I knew it was Gavin O'Rourke wheeling his bicycle over to where I sat. We often came here together on Sundays after Mass when his boat was in port. We didn't usually talk much. There was no need to. We drew a comfort from each other and from the silence. Sometimes he would read aloud to me from a book of poetry he kept in his pocket. Other times he would read silently to himself.

As children Gavin and I played on the Flagstaff often. We used to climb to the summit from Upper Fathom Road where we both lived and lie down on our stomachs to watch the cargo boats coming and going up and down the Clanrye River on their way to and from the port of Newry. Gavin's da and mine were both captains and we loved it when we recognized one of their boats coming in from the Irish Sea by way of the lough. As they came up the river they would blow their horns and we knew it was a signal meant just for us and we would stand up and wave like lunatics.

Gavin threw his bicycle to one side and sat down on the grass at my feet. He pulled out a packet of cigarettes, lit one, and inhaled deeply. He followed my gaze out towards the horizon.

After a while he said, "You weren't at Mass."

Something in his voice and manner seemed unsettled. Normally he would lie back lazily on the grass and blow rings of smoke into the air as if he didn't have a concern in the world. It was what I liked about being near him—the comfort of his calm spirit. But today something was not right.

"So what's the *craic*?" he said at last.

I shrugged. "Some *craic*," I said. "I wasn't even picked to compete in the Linen Queen competition, and the prize money would have been two hundred quid, and Patsy and Kathleen were both picked, and Ma is delighted I was passed over, and..."

I stopped when I realized Gavin was paying no attention to me at all. He had turned his back and was gazing out to sea. His whole body appeared alert as if he were bracing for an attack.

"What's got into you?" I said.

He turned around. "Sorry. What were you saying?"

"Oh, just give us a fag," I said.

He handed me a cigarette and lit it for me. I inhaled deeply and sighed. There was no point going into all of it again.

"I should have known," I said. "Nothing good ever happens to me. If I'm not careful I'll be stuck in this bloody oul' place for the rest of my life."

"Why, what happened?"

"I just told you. I got passed over for the Linen Queen competition."

Gavin turned to fully face me. He shook his head in disgust.

"Is that all's on your mind, Sheila? For God's sake will you just forget about all that nonsense."

"It's not nonsense," I protested. "It's the only way I can think of to escape from this bloody place."

"There's worse places."

"Easy for you to say. You get away from here anytime you like. You've seen the world."

Gavin had inherited his da's boat after he died. At twenty-two he was the youngest captain in the feet.

"And yet I always come back. This is home. And to my mind there's no place can beat it."

"It may be home to you, but it's a prison to me."

"And you think escaping justifies you being the puppet of the English Crown?"

"What in the name of God are you on about?"

"You know fine well. Putting a crown on your head and parading around the country representing the English owners of the linen mills. You don't think that's selling yourself out to them?"

"Och, Gavin, I think you're astray in the head. It has nothing to do with the English." I paused. "And anyway, I'd represent the devil himself for two hundred quid."

We lapsed into silence. The boat I had heard blowing its horn in the lough now appeared in the river. Gavin peered down at it.

"There's the *Elm* now. Danny's made it back alive, thank God."

"Why wouldn't he?"

"At the rate the German U-boats are torpedoing the merchant ships it's always a miracle when we arrive home in one piece. Look at what happened to the *Athenia*."

The *Athenia* was a passenger boat out of Belfast that had been torpedoed on the very first day of the war. I straightened up. "Is that what you're thinking about every time you go out?"

"Aye, it's always at the back of your mind."

I shrugged. "Bloody morbid, so it is."

I looked at Gavin's broad, open face, his hazel eyes, and the mop of unruly chestnut hair. He was the only real friend I had—someone I could talk to without having to put up a front. We could fight all we liked, but we were always honest with each other. I never let others see when I was frightened or lonely. To them I was Sheila McGee the belle of the ball, Sheila who's full of the devil and sure of herself, Sheila who'll get what she wants from this life. I chuckled at the thought of it. I had them all fooled, so I did.

"D'you ever miss your da?" Gavin said suddenly.

"Aye," I said without thinking.

"He always loved you, Sheila; anybody could see that."

"Fine way of showing it," I muttered.

I thought back, as I had done a thousand times before, to the day when Da had taken me into Newry with him. We often rode our bicycles down to the *Sheila Rose* before he went out on a voyage. Most of the boats around there were named after trees, like the *Walnut* and the *Elm*. Gavin's da's boat was called the *Ashgrove*. But my da had named his boat the *Sheila Rose* after me. I played on the boat, and the men gave me sweets and patted me on the head. Da would describe to me the places he was sailing to and promise to bring me back something special. But that one day was different. He wasn't smiling the way he usually did. When it was time to sail and he lifted me off the boat and set me on the pier there were tears in his eyes. He knelt down beside me.

"I won't be back this time, Sheila love," he whispered. "You see, I can't live with your ma anymore. I suppose she can't help the way she is, but I can't stand any more of it. And she's not going to change. I'm sorry, love. This isn't your fault. I'll always love you, Sheila Rose."

Terrified, I grabbed on to his arms. Tears stung my eyes. "Take me with you, Da," I cried. "I'll be good."

Da shook his head. "No, love. Your ma still needs you. I'll try to send money when I can."

He reached into his pocket and took out a tiny carved mermaid. He had always called me his "wee mermaid," saying I belonged on the sea, just like he did.

"Here, love," he said. "I made this for you—to remember me by. It's a wee merrow. Here, take it."

In Ireland we have legends about sea creatures that are half human and half seal. Some call them selkies. Others call them merrows. "Merrow" was Da's pet name for me. He thrust the tiny figure into my hands and pushed me away from him. "Go on home, now, there's a good girl."

He jumped back on the boat. He never turned around to look at me, but disappeared below the deck. I sank down on the pier, confused, tears blinding me. I sat there until the sailors untied the ropes and the *Sheila Rose* pulled away from the dock. Eventually a sailor, a neighbor of ours who had just come off another boat, reached down for me and pulled me to my feet.

"Come on, daughter," he said kindly. "It's time to go on home. Your da's boat is long gone. Your ma will be worried about you."

In the years that followed I came to understand that Ma, when in her high moods, spent all our money and, worse, flirted with men when Da was out to sea. She'd said having to marry Da because she was pregnant with me had spoiled her chances with other, richer men. No wonder Da left her. No wonder I wanted to leave her too.

Money came sometimes in envelopes with foreign stamps, and Ma managed to spend it all. Eventually the money stopped coming, and we never heard from Da again. Word came later that he had drowned when the *Sheila Rose* sank in a storm somewhere off the coast of Africa. I often thought about how Da had said I belonged on the sea. He told me stories of how the merrows used to come up on shore and shed their skins to sun themselves. If a human stole a merrow's skin and hid it, she could not go back to the sea. When Da left me, I thought, he stole my skin too and left me marooned on dry land.

Gavin's voice brought me out of my trance. "I miss my da too," he said as if he knew what I had been remembering. "Today's the fourth anniversary."

Of course, I thought. That's what had him in the strange mood. Gavin's da had been shot and his body brought to the doorstep of their house when Gavin was just eighteen. I didn't know the circumstances of his da's death. My ma said he had been with the Irish Republican Army and it was Unionists killed him in reprisal for things he had done during the Uprising. It seemed to hit Gavin hard. He was changed after that in ways I never understood. That's when the dark moods started, and the anger at the British, and all the rest of it. Gavin gave up all plans to train as a teacher, took over his da's boat, and moved away.

"I won't live in the North," I recalled him saying, "after what those bastards did to my da."

I looked at him now. "I'm sorry," I whispered. "I forgot."

I felt awful blathering on about my own problems. No wonder he was in no mood to hear them. He stood up and put on his cap and tightened his muffler around his throat.

"Time to go," he said. "It's getting cold." He studied me. I was blowing on my hands, which were suddenly freezing. He grinned. "Forget your gloves again, miss?"

"I don't suppose you have an extra pair, do you?" I said.

He removed his own and handed them to me. "I suppose some things never change."

He lifted his bicycle and began to walk it back down the hill. He looked over his shoulder. "Coming?"

I shook my head. "No, I'll stay a wee bit longer."

"Don't be too hard on your ma," he said, "nor on yourself either. If you're meant to leave here, another chance will come along."

I watched him disappear down the hill. I shivered. An odd feeling came over me as it always did when I watched Gavin leave me—a tiny fear, like the prick of a needle. "Safe home," I whispered.

Chapter 3

❧

If I'd thought the mill fever was bad during the early days at the mill, it was nothing compared to the torture I suffered during the two weeks following Mrs. McAteer's announcement of which girls had qualified to enter the Linen Queen competition. If anyone else had been disappointed about not being chosen, they didn't seem to show it. Instead, everyone joined in the enthusiasm of the qualifiers. The talk was of nothing but frocks and shoes and hairstyles—and, of course, the prize money. The list of rules had been handed out and was the cause of great merriment.

"Skin must be covered at all times! For God's sake you'd think we were competing to join the convent!"

"Did you ever hear the likes of it? Judges' questions must be answered in a polite and modulated tone! Well, that's the end of the road for Patsy!"

"All entrants will show each other courtesy and respect."

"In other words we're not to be tearing the frocks off them nor calling them whores!" crowed Patsy in delight. "Och, it's going to be a great night altogether!"

I tried to smile and join in, but I couldn't. I was sick over the whole affair. I just wanted the competition to be over and done with. Despair threatened to drown me when I thought about the future. Was I to be stuck here in this place for the rest of my days? The monotony of the work was enough to drive you astray in the head. How long would it take for the brains to be sucked out of me altogether? It had been years since I'd read a book, even though I had loved to read, particularly stories of adventure and faraway places. I loved to imagine sailing away to foreign lands with my da on his boat. I sighed. How long would I be able to keep my dream alive?

On Friday morning—the day before the competition—I stood at my spinning frame thinking about what Ma had said about finding a husband. I was beginning to think it was my only alternative. I had no time at all for the lads in the mill—most of them hadn't the sense they were born with. Gavin O'Rourke's face floated in front of me. I loved Gavin like a brother—but marry him? It wasn't like that between us. Ma was always harping about him. I gritted my teeth. Well, that was reason enough not to marry him. I wouldn't give her the satisfaction.

"Miss McGee!" Miss Galway's voice shocked me so much I dropped the yarn I was holding. "You're wanted in the office."

The spinning frames around me slowed down as girls turned to see what was happening.

"Now, Miss McGee!" Miss Galway shouted. "Mr. Carlson is not to be kept waiting."

I pulled the handle on my frame to stop it and wiped my hands on my apron. By the look on Miss Galway's face I could see she was in no mood to be answering questions. So I backed away from my machine and walked down the aisle towards the office.

When I opened the office door I was met by glares from Mrs. McAteer and her daughter, Mary.

"Mr. Carlson is waiting," said Mrs. McAteer through tight lips.

My heart began to pound. What now? What in the name of God did they want?

I knocked on Mr. Carlson's door and opened it when I heard him grunt.

He sat behind a big, cluttered, dusty desk. He was a grim-faced man with features like the rocks in the Queensbrook quarry. I'd hardly ever seen him since I'd come to work at the mill. I stood, my knees threatening to give way under me.

He stared at me as if he were inspecting me, and I felt uneasy, and embarrassed by my bare feet.

"Sit down," he said at last.

He leaned back in his chair. "I have called you in, Miss McGee, because I have just discovered that my sister, Mrs. McAteer, may have erred in her selection of the girls for the competition."

I waited. I had no idea what he meant. He cleared his throat.

"I have seen you from time to time about the mill and the village," he said.

I stiffened. Had the oul' bugger been spying on me?

"And now that I have taken a good look at you, I know I am right in my assumptions."

He sat forward, gazing at me with pale blue eyes and stretching his mouth in what I supposed was a smile. I thought I might faint. I gripped the seat of the chair with both hands.

"The Linen Queen competition is very important to our industry, Miss McGee. The mill that is represented has the opportunity to promote its products all over Northern Ireland, and sometimes beyond. And since we at Queensbrook are the hosts, it seems ft-ting we should do everything we can to win."

I sat rooted to the chair. My heart began to race.

"It is in our best interests, therefore, to put forward those girls who stand the best chance of winning." His smile faded. "You, Miss McGee, are the most attractive girl in the spinning mill and you should have been chosen."

I found my tongue. "Mrs. McAteer said it wasn't based on looks."

"She was wrong," he said sharply. He stood up. "Come with me."

My heart was hammering to beat the band as I followed him to the outer office. Could it be true? Had my prayers been answered? Hannah and Mary McAteer stood there, along with Patsy, Kathleen, and the other girls who had been picked to enter the competition. Only Kathleen smiled.

"Hannah, please add Miss McGee to your list."

"But, Charles," she began, her face crimson, "there is no time.

The girls have already been chosen, and the competition is tomorrow evening—"

Her brother held up his hand to stop her. "I said add her to the list. Did I not make myself clear?"

He turned and went back into his office and banged the door behind him. The rest of us stood stock-still. Mrs. McAteer's bosom heaved up and down as she fought for words.

"There are still only six places," she said. "One of you will have to drop out to make room for her." She sneered the word "her" as she looked at me.

A sigh of protest went up. I wished the ground would open up and swallow me whole. I had wanted to be chosen more than anything in the world, but not like this. I hated Mrs. McAteer at that moment more than I had hated anyone in my life.

"It's all right," I murmured. "None of you should have to give up her place. Besides—it's too late to get ready, and," I finished lamely, "I have no money for a frock."

Each of the girls looked from me to Mrs. McAteer and back again. Patsy's face was dark with fury. She was my friend, but she wanted the chance as much as I did. I couldn't blame her for her anger. The room was silent.

"Well hurry up," Mrs. McAteer said. "We don't have all day!"

"You can have my place, Sheila." Kathleen's solemn face peered into mine. Before I could answer, she went on, "I don't stand a chance, anyway. We all know that. Just look at me. And besides, I'd be so nervous I'd probably make an eejit of myself in front of the whole county."

"No, Kathleen," I began. "It's not fair."

I threw a daggers look at Mrs. McAteer. How could she have put us all in this position? If she hadn't resented me so much she would have picked me in the first place and we would have been spared all this.

"You can have my frock, Sheila," Kathleen was saying. "I'll go home at the dinner break and get it. It's not much, but the material's a lovely blue that'll match your eyes." She paused and smiled. "You'll have to make some alterations on it. It's big enough to drown you. But I know you're handy with a needle..."

I put my hand on Kathleen's arm. I fought back tears that pricked at my eyes. "No, Kathleen," I whispered. "It's not fair," I said again.

"It's settled," Mrs. McAteer's sharp voice cut in. "I will strike Kathleen's name from the list and substitute yours. I hope you are satisfied, miss!"

Satisfied? How could I be satisfied? The oul' bitch was making it sound like it was my fault. But I hadn't asked for it. I gave Patsy a pleading look, but she turned away. I sighed. I supposed all the spinners would get the wrong end of the stick. They would think I had deliberately gone to Carlson and ended up getting Kathleen disqualified. The brief sweetness I had tasted when Carlson told me I was picked turned sour. This was not how I had wanted it.

ගග

I worked until all hours Friday night and most of Saturday altering the frock Kathleen had given me. Poor Kathleen—she had followed the rules so strictly that the frock would have better suited a nun than a beauty queen. It fell down to my ankles and was cut so high on the collar that it could have choked me. She was right about the color, though. It was a lovely shade of deep blue that matched my eyes exactly. The material was flimsy and needed lining in order for it to sit well. Its only adornment was a row of shiny glass buttons down the front and a wide, stiff belt covered in the same material with a shiny buckle. It would have looked a show on Kathleen. It was merciful, I thought, that she had given it to me and spared herself the embarrassment.

Ma had heard the news.

"Disgraceful!" she pronounced when I walked in the door. "Pushing that lovely wee girl aside so you could have your own way. And then taking her frock off her. I don't know how I'm going to hold my head up at the mill."

"I didn't push her out," I protested. "It was Carlson ordered that I be entered, and Mrs. McAteer said somebody had to give up her place for me."

"You could have acted like a lady and refused," said Ma. "But you were too selfish."

She sat back in her armchair and lit a cigarette. "Well, no matter. You'll never win anyway. Once people find out what happened they'll all be against you—even the judges. Your pretty face will do you no good, miss."

"We'll just see about that." I walked on into the granny room and banged the door shut behind me.

I didn't really expect Ma to be happy for me, but still her words hurt. I stooped down and dragged the old sewing machine out of the cupboard. I hadn't touched it in years and it was covered with dust. I prayed it would still work. As I hauled it out into the parlor and set it on the table, I thought about Mulcahy the baker. It might be easier to go and see him early on Saturday and get the money to buy a dress. I knew Ma would be harping at me all night, but when I imagined Mulcahy's lips slobbering over mine I shook my head. I'd take Ma's insults over that any time of the day.

I tried to ignore Ma as I laid Kathleen's frock out on the table. I turned it over and back and then I took up the scissors.

"What in the name of God are you doing?" said Ma from behind.

"I'm altering it to fit me," I muttered through a mouthful of pins.

"You can't go destroying the frock that the girl's after lending you."

"She said it was all right," I said.

I hesitated, scissors in hand. Ma had struck a nerve. What if Kathleen wanted the frock back? Did I have the right to cut it up? I lifted it and held it up against me. It was like an enormous billowing blue sail. I couldn't wear it like this. I took a deep breath. Oh well, in for a penny, in for a pound, and I began to wield the scissors.

I worked late into the night. Ma eventually fell asleep in her chair. Kate came in from visiting a sick neighbor, nodded at me, and went straight up to bed. Kevin was away out to his favorite pub in Newry. For once the house was quiet. I cut the dress shorter and used the material saved to make a frill to go around the neck and around the hem and a sash for the waist. I cut the top of it into a V-neck—not too low, but low enough to expose my neck and upper chest. So much for modesty! I removed the glass buttons and sewed in darts to take in the bodice and give it some shape. I tore up an old skirt and used the lining. It was beginning to look like a real frock, almost like something you could buy in Foster's in Newry. I was pleased and exhausted when I finally went to bed.

On Saturday morning I woke to rain lashing against the window. I groaned. The frock would be ruined before I even got to the competition. So would my hair and my shoes and all the rest. I decided I'd just have to wear any old thing over to the Temperance Hall and carry all I needed in a bag. The thought cheered me up and I hopped out of bed and went back to my work on the dress.

I was trying it on when Ma came shuffling out of the granny room.

"You look like a tart," she said. "That neckline is a disgrace."

I swung around. "It's not," I said. "Wait 'til you see what Patsy Mallon's going to be wearing."

Ma grunted. "That one's no better than a tinker. She's hardly one to copy."

Suddenly tears welled in my eyes. I turned away so Ma would not see them.

"Och, Ma, would you not say something nice to me for once?" I said over my shoulder.

Ma grunted in reply. I wiped the tears away and began furiously ironing the blue frock. Da would have been proud of me, I thought. Da would have told me I was beautiful.

It was late afternoon when the frock was finished to my satisfaction. I folded it carefully and placed it in a large cloth bag. I had washed my hair that morning and wound the wet strands into small curls and secured them with clips. I looked out at the rain and decided to put on a scarf and then brush it out when I got to the hall. I put my rouge and powder and lipstick in another bag and looked around. I needed shoes and some jewelry.

"Ma," I said, without thinking, "could I borrow that wee necklace? You know the silver and blue one Da gave you when I was born?"

Ma glared at me. I bit my lip. It was too late to take the words back—I didn't know what had made me ask. I waited. After a minute or two, Ma stood up and went into the back room. She came back with a small black velvet box and roughly pushed it at me.

"Your da always said it was lucky, but a lot of good it's done me."

"Thanks a million, Ma," I said and leaned forward to kiss her cheek, but she pulled away. "I'll take good care of it."

I went into the scullery and lifted a pot of cold tea and poured some into a bowl. I took a cloth and dipped it in the tea and rubbed it up and down my legs. Because of the rationing we could not buy nylons in the shops, but the tea gave our legs a bit of color. Then I took a black eyebrow pencil and carefully drew a line down the center of my calves to resemble a stocking seam. I prayed the rain wouldn't make it all run.

"How do I look, Ma?" I said as I made for the front door.

"Like a gypsy," said Ma.

I looxked down at my old raincoat and boots and touched the scarf on my head and laughed. "Aye, well wait 'til you see me later. I'll be dazzling!"

Ma rolled her eyes. "You're as mad in the head as your da was," she said. Her face softened although she did not smile.

"Watch yourself," was all she said, but to me it was as if she had wished me all the blessings a mother could wish for her daughter.

The rain soaked me as I rushed down the hill towards the Temperance Hall where the competition was to be held. Water from puddles splashed the back of my legs but I was in too much of a hurry to try to avoid them. I was already very late. When I reached the door of the hall my heart was pounding and I couldn't catch my breath. I paused and bent over in the doorway until the sharp pain in my chest eased.

Crowds pushed past me—men and women from the mill and people I'd never seen before. Tweed jackets smelled like damp sheep and pockets bulged with flasks and paper bags. There was no drink served in the Temperance Hall and so the men smuggled in whiskey and porter. I supposed plenty of the women had wine and spirits hidden in their bags and baskets too for they were no strangers to smuggling since the war rationing had begun.

I straightened up and pushed my way into the main hall. Thank God nobody seemed to recognize me in the getup I wore. I rushed up the side of the hall towards a big stage. A banner reached across it that read "Linen Queen, 1941" in big blue letters on a white background. Chairs and tables had been set up for the judges and behind them, at the back of the stage, Paddy Moloney's band was tuning up. I swallowed hard and pulled open a door behind the stage that led to a side room. And then I stopped dead in my tracks. The room was bursting with girls of every size and shape. The noise was deafening as they shouted and screeched and cursed and cackled. Clothes few everywhere: corsets and petticoats and frocks. And in the thick of it all towered Mrs. McAteer like the circus master in the middle of the ring. She scowled when she saw me.

"You're late!"

Sure I know that well enough, I thought, but I said nothing. I pushed my way to a corner of the room and dropped my bag on the floor. I bent to take out my frock and was knocked on my knees by an ignorant big girl.

"Will you watch yourself," she said. "I nearly fell over you, you eejit."

"You stepped on my frock," I said.

I pulled off my wet garments and carefully stepped into the frock. The girl who had knocked into me was still raging. She was not from Queensbrook.

"Fecking country girls are as ignorant as pigs," she said to a group of girls beside her, "worried about their *frocks*. They don't even know the proper word is *dress*!"

"Who are you calling pigs?"

It was Patsy. I looked over. She stood facing the girl, her hands on her hips. She wore only a brassiere and a tight corset that was riding up her behind. She looked so comical I almost laughed. But I stopped short. I realized she was not defending me. When she swung around the shock on her face was obvious.

"I thought you weren't coming," she said. "I thought maybe you'd changed your mind and taken pity on poor Kathleen." Then she threw her hand to her mouth. "In the name of God what have you done to Kathleen's frock?"

"I altered it," I said.

"You cut it to ribbons, you wee bitch."

Mrs. McAteer walked over when she heard Patsy shouting. She looked me up and down. I was just tying the sash around my waist.

"Didn't you read the rules, Miss McGee? That frock is much too vulgar. You will pin that neck closed immediately."

I glared at her. "There's plenty here with necklines lower than this," I said, looking around the room. "Why don't you tell them to pin it up?"

Her face turned crimson. "Those girls are from other mills and I am not responsible for them. You will do what you are told."

She turned on her heel and marched away. "Oul' bitch," I muttered under my breath and searched for a safety pin.

I squeezed in front of a mirror beside a tall, thin girl wearing a shiny emerald green frock. She was pretty with long black hair, much like my own, and pale skin and deep emerald eyes, the color of the frock. Och, but the frock! It was so old-fashioned it must have belonged to her ma. Even my own ma would not have been caught dead in it. She smiled at me.

"It's mad in here isn't it?" Her accent had a sharp Belfast edge.

"Aye. Where are you from?"

"Ballymena. Me ma made me wear this. She won the prize herself twenty years ago in this very dress. She thought it would bring me luck."

I reached up and secured Ma's blue and silver necklace around my throat.

"Your dress is lovely," she whispered. "It must have cost a fortune of money."

I shrugged. "Not really." I was not about to confess I'd made it myself from a friend's hand-me-down.

I concentrated on putting on my makeup. I drew a thin black line along my eyebrows, rubbed on rouge, and painted my lips with bright red lipstick I'd lifted from Ma's bedside table. I took out the clips and let my hair fall down. Thank God it had dried. Then I realized I'd forgotten my brush. I swore under my breath. I called out to Patsy.

"Can I get a lend of your brush?"

"No," said Patsy, "I might need it."

"You can borrow mine," said the emerald green girl.

I took it from her. I supposed all the ones from the cities weren't so bad after all—better even than your own friends. I brushed my dark hair into waves and secured it at my right temple with a small silver clip.

"Are you nervous?" the girl asked.

"Not at all," I lied.

Mrs. McAteer clapped her hands. "Girls, finish up now. We will be marching into the hall in five minutes. Finish what you're doing and clean up this mess!" She looked around the room in disgust. Discarded clothes littered the floor, while hairbrushes, powder puffs, makeup, pins and sewing needles and thread were scattered on the tables. She clapped her hands again. "Come along now," she trilled, "line up now, single file please. Mr. Carlson is about to speak. Silence, please."

"Welcome to the twenty-fifth Linen Queen competition," Mr. Carlson began from the stage. We heard a cheer go up from the crowd.

"We are honored to host the event for the very first time here in Queensbrook. It is especially gratifying that we can still hold such a happy event while England is at war." Muffed groans greeted his words. "Hopefully, Northern Ireland will be spared," he continued, "but Queensbrook Mill and its workers stand ready if called upon to do whatever is necessary to aid our mother country in her time of need..."

He blathered on for a while as we all grew impatient. I tried not to notice my nerves. In my haste to get to the hall and get ready I hadn't had time to think about the competition itself, let alone about how badly I wanted to win the prize. I tried to distract myself by looking around at the other girls. Mary McAteer had not appeared yet. Her ma must be hiding her in a private room somewhere, I thought. Too good to mix with the rest of us. Our other Queensbrook girls—Eileen, Abby, and Celia—all looked well enough but would not be much competition. I had to admit some of the out-of-town girls were beautiful though, and my confidence began to plunge. I stole a look at Patsy. She wore a tight scarlet dress with a neckline so low her white breasts were almost jumping out of it. Her blond hair was brushed back in a bob, and she wore big glass earrings and a necklace to match. She looked cheap, I thought, but maybe the judges would love her. Men liked that kind of boldness. I reached for the pin I had put at the neck of my own dress and in one movement pulled it out.

Finally, Mr. Carlson introduced the judges. The band struck up with "The Star of the County Down" in honor of the previous year's winner who was from Bangor, and all twenty-four of us fled out to the cheers and clapping of the audience.

Mary McAteer appeared from nowhere to lead the procession onto the stage while I was the last one out. The bright lights almost blinded me. I waved to the crowd the way I imagined a royal princess might do. Camera bulbs flashed and the audience became a blur. I could hear the spinners though, singing away and catcalling to some of the girls as they walked across the stage.

"Hello, Eileen. Does your mother know you're out?"

"Good girl yourself, Patsy Mallon!"

No one called out to me.

We paraded past the judge's table and gave a slight curtsy as our names were called. My legs shook under me but I kept a smile on my face and looked the judges straight in the eyes. We marched off the stage again and waited in the wings while the judges huddled with one another. The rules called for five girls to be selected and the winner and runner-up would be picked from among them. They were each to be asked a question, and supposedly the results would be based on their answers.

Mary McAteer was called first. She let out a squeal when she heard her name and threw her hands to her mouth as if she couldn't believe it. Hypocrite, I thought. Of course Carlson's niece was going to be recognized; we all knew that. But she'd hardly win. True, Mary looked better than I'd ever seen her. The glittery silver dress she wore was gorgeous, and she'd had her hair done in an expensive shop. But she was still plump and shapeless, and no amount of money could change her into a silk purse. She pushed past me, her eyelids fluttering. But when they asked her to describe a visit to the biggest city in Northern Ireland she stammered like an eejit and began talking about London.

The rest of us squealed with laughter, and Mrs. McAteer threatened to throw us out. Three more girls were called, all of them from other mills. They were the good-looking ones I had noticed before. I felt a grip on my arm. The girl in the emerald green dress stood beside me.

"Pray for luck," she whispered. "Me ma will kill me if I don't win."

And mine will kill me if I do, I thought to myself.

Whatever confidence I had was beginning to slip. There was only one place left. Was it possible I would not even get called? Would I have to go home with one hand as long as the other? Would this one chance to make something of myself pass me by? I was sinking into such despair that I didn't even hear my name called until Mrs. McAteer roughly shoved me out onto the stage. Cheers roared up from the men in the crowd, although there was only polite applause from the women.

One of the judges beamed at me and said, "Miss Sheila McGee, is it?" I nodded. "Tell me, Miss McGee, and what would you do with the two hundred pounds prize money should you win this competition?"

Inwardly I did a little jig. I had rehearsed my answer to such a question for years before I ever dreamed I could be standing here. It was the biggest lie of my life. I bowed my head and smiled my most angelic smile. "Well, sir," I said, "first of all I did not enter the competition for the money, but for the privilege of representing my mill, my town, and Northern Ireland as the Linen Queen. As for the money, I shall give it to my mother who has worked her hands to the bone all these years to care for me."

There was a silence in the hall. The judge who had asked the question stared at me, then broke out into a smile that was more of a leer.

"Thank you, Miss McGee," he said. "That was a splendid answer."

It took them less than two minutes to declare me the winner. Cameras flashed, and the band played "When You Wish upon a Star" as Mr. Carlson placed the linen sash on me that proclaimed "Linen Queen, 1941" and awkwardly set the silver tiara on my head. "Well done, Miss McGee," he whispered, obviously more pleased for himself than for me. Last year's winner shoved a bouquet of flowers into my hands and flounced off the stage. I took a moment to arrange the tiara more securely on my hair and fix a broad smile on my face and I walked back and forth across the stage and the band struck up "God Save the King." The night was mine. I had won.

෨෮

By the time I returned to the dressing room most of the girls had gone. Only Mrs. McAteer and Mary remained. Mary had been picked as the runner-up. None of us were that surprised, given who she was. At least the judges and Carlson hadn't been shameless enough to declare her the winner. Mary and her ma stopped talking when I walked in. I picked up my things in silence, put my coat on over my dress, and walked out. The crowd was emptying out of the hall as I stepped out into the rain. Mill lads came up to hug me and for once I was glad of their attention. Some of the spinners muttered congratulations but I could tell the word had spread about me and Kathleen and I was probably the last girl they wanted to see win. Kathleen herself came up to me.

"Congratulations, Sheila," she said. "And the frock was lovely on you."

Guilt seized me. "I'm sorry, Kathleen, but I had to cut it down; it was—"

Kathleen put up her hand. "It's all right, Sheila. It looked so lovely on you I want you to keep it."

"Och, Kathleen—" I began, but just then Patsy came up behind us.

"C'mon, Kathleen," she said, ignoring me. "Some of the lads are going to Newry for a drink—they've offered us a lift."

"Oh, you go on, Patsy," said Kathleen. "I have to be getting home." She turned to me. "Aren't you going to celebrate, Sheila?"

"No," I said. I realized then that I had no one I cared about to celebrate with. Patsy had turned against me, Ma was at home nursing her misery, and Gavin wasn't anywhere to be seen. I had vaguely hoped he would come, even though he didn't approve of the competition.

As I walked slowly home in the wet darkness I tried desperately to warm the cold thing that coiled inside me. I clutched the envelope that held the two hundred pounds. I had wanted this prize more than anything else in the world, but I had not realized the price I would have to pay for it. I was special now—set apart from family, friends, and neighbors by status and envy. I realized that tonight I had not just won a title, a tiara, and money. The real prize was my discovery of the raw power of beauty.

Chapter 4

❧

The house was in darkness when I arrived. I breathed a sigh of relief. I wouldn't have to face Ma and all her questions. She would have her hand out for the money too. Up until now I'd thought I would give her a few pound, and maybe a few pound to Kathleen, and I would keep the rest. I would set it aside until I could make my arrangements to sail to England. After all, I still had a week's wages coming from the mill, and it would take time to get my papers in order and pack my belongings. I realized now I had not thought the plan through very well. I supposed I had never really believed I would win. Well I had! And the money was mine. Ma had taken every penny of my wages from me for the last four years. If it hadn't been for the savings club at the mill I would have had no money to buy a stitch of clothes. No, she was not getting this!

I crept around the back of the house to the shed. The rain had stopped but the ground was muddy and soft. I stooped behind the shed and with the pair of scissors I'd had in my bag I scooped out a hole in the ground. I tore the plastic cover off the linen tablecloth that had been part of the prize and wrapped it around the envelope. I scooped the earth over the hole and stood up.

❧

The next morning, as if on cue, Ma sat up in bed.

"Where's the money?" she said.

"Thanks for the congratulations, Ma."

"Don't be cute. I heard you won. Now hand it over."

I wanted to cry out that the money was mine and that I deserved to keep it, but I knew it would do no good. Aunt Kate and Kevin would hardly take my side in the argument. No, it was best to keep it hidden until I could get away.

"I didn't get it yet," I said casually.

"I don't believe you."

"Believe what you like, but the fact is the money had to be approved in Belfast and they were not going to release it until the winner had been certified and all the rest of it."

"Sounds like bollocks to me," Ma said.

I shrugged. "I'm tired, Ma. Leave me alone."

I pulled the covers up over my face. I prayed Ma would believe my story.

"I heard they gave you an envelope," she persisted. "Kate was there and saw the whole thing. She said you looked like a trollop."

"The envelope was just for show. There was nothing in it. And tell Kate to keep her opinions to herself."

Ma sat up suddenly. "Did you bring back my necklace?"

"It's on the table," I said sleepily. "It brought me luck, Ma."

An hour later Ma poked me in the side. "Get up out of that bed and get ready for Mass," she said. "It's Easter Sunday, so it is."

I groaned. "I told you, Ma, I'm wrecked after the last few days. I'll go with you to the Missions on Tuesday night, all right?"

"Suit yourself. It's not my soul that's going to hell."

ഇ൦

Early on the following Tuesday morning I struggled up the road to the mill along with the other workers. We looked a desperate crowd altogether, huddled against the cold, our lunch boxes under our arms. The mill horn blew like a siren from hell. An odd feeling came over me as I looked down at my coat and muffler and old boots—drab compared to the finery of Saturday night. Had it all been a dream?

The mill had been closed for the Easter holiday on Monday. I had been glad of the delay. It had given me time to adjust to having won the competition and to prepare myself for what I knew would be a difficult day. It was cold as I climbed the stairs to the spinning room and I pulled my coat tighter around me. I shrugged. In a few hours the place would be as hot as hell from the steam thrown off by the spinning frames. The smell of oil and damp flax would turn our stomachs, and our feet would be soaked from the water that collected on the floor. It was a wonder we all hadn't caught our deaths of pneumonia or pleurisy. But soon I would be far away from here. The thought cheered me.

I clocked in and went to a room in the corner of the spinning floor to take off my coat and shoes and put on my apron. The spinners were already cranking up their machines—the clack-clack of the moving frames beating a rhythm in my ears. This morning everyone laughed and joked, sharing stories about their weekend doings, enjoying the camaraderie they always did. They quieted down when they saw me approach.

"Well, if it isn't Sheila McGee," said Patsy. "I thought you'd have sailed away on the *Queen Mary* by now."

Patsy had not even been picked for the top five. Her anger hurt me but I wasn't going to let it show. I waved my hand in the air.

"Och, Patsy, no. Sure there's so much I still have to do to get ready. And I didn't want to leave me poor ma alone for Easter. Next week will be time enough."

Patsy raised a penciled eyebrow.

"Oh, and here I thought you couldn't wait to get away from us." The other girls joined in along with her.

"Aye, sailing away and leaving poor Kathleen here with the rest of us."

"And not a second thought for any of us."

"No bother," I said as cheerily as I could. "Sure I'll let you know when it's time. Then you can all throw me a grand party." And with that I marched off to my machine and cranked it up.

Seeing they couldn't get a rise out of me the girls changed the subject. Rationing, as usual, was always good for plenty of talk. Since the war had begun, goods in the North had become scarce. It was worse in England, we were told, but that didn't stop our complaints. While our mothers were worried about the lack of bread, milk, butter, and sugar, we were more concerned with the shortage of nylon stockings and perfume and cigarettes.

Times had not been good in Northern Ireland ever since the border had been drawn almost twenty years before. People were still weary from the Uprising. England, going through hard times herself, hadn't much money to spare, and her promises of welfare payments and money for education never came through. The people in the twenty-six counties to our south, which we still referred to as the Free State even though it was now officially called Eire, were busy taking care of themselves and had no time left for us. We weren't part of Ireland anymore. But it seemed to us we weren't part of England either. We were like orphans that nobody wanted, and the weariness and lack of national pride was starting to wear people down. I usually didn't bother my head with such things, and I always told Gavin to shut up when he started talking about politics. But since the shortages had begun, and the fear of war started creeping into conversations, I had become more and more annoyed and impatient. This war could interfere with my plans. I prayed I could get away before the war came to the North.

Patsy turned the conversation back to me. "Sheila, now you're the queen maybe you can marry some rich oul' bollocks and you won't have to leave your ma after all." Jesus, would she ever shut up?

"Aye," said Kathleen Doyle, a wistful note in her voice. "Sure you'll have plenty of chances now, Sheila, to meet rich chaps. Maybe one of them will take a fancy to you."

There was no malice in Kathleen. I used to wonder if she wasn't a bit simple, or false like my aunt Kate. But much as I looked for flaws in her, I found none. She was the genuine article. And for all their blather, I knew the other girls deep down wanted to believe that what she said was true. Just like me, they all needed a bit of hope.

The talk died down as the day went on although the surly looks continued. I prayed the worst of it was over. It would be better tomorrow, I thought. And besides, I only had to stand it for a few days until I had my plans made and I was on my way. I was smiling at the thought as I reached for my coat. It felt heavier than usual and I wondered for a minute if I had the right one. But it was mine all right. As I pushed my arm into the right sleeve I heard giggling behind me. I ignored it as I wrestled with the sleeve. Something was catching my hand. I tried the left sleeve and the same thing happened. It was then I realized someone had sewn the sleeves shut and had filled the pockets with bobbins. It was the sort of thing the spinners did when a girl was leaving the mill to get married. As I turned around to protest, hands lifted me up and carried me down the stairs to where a wheelbarrow stood with a banner floating from the handle that read "Linen Queen, 1941." I struggled as they plunged me into it and shoved a paper crown down on my head. They gave the barrow a mighty push and set it rolling down the hill from the mill, as they ran after it shouting at the tops of their lungs.

"Good luck, now, Sheila, may you get the man of your dreams!"

"Remember us, Sheila, when you're living in the lap of luxury!"

The barrow moved at dizzying speed and the workers who were streaming out of the mill stepped aside and laughed and cheered as I rolled past. There was nothing I could do to stop it. It would have been comical if it was not for the fact that the spinners had done this deliberately to disgrace me. I was sure Patsy had put them up to it—not that they would have needed much coaxing.

I was light-headed when the barrow finally stopped. I glared at the mill lads who helped me out of it. Eejits. They were no better than the rest.

"Och, it's just a bit of *craic*, Sheila." They laughed.

"*Craic* my arse," I muttered.

I ran towards the house fighting back tears. I was angry and embarrassed at the same time. I pushed through the door and banged straight into Ma.

"Hurry up," she said, "we want to get a good seat at the Missions."

I swore under my breath. I had forgotten all about my promise to go with her to hear the missionary priest who was preaching in Newry.

"Hurry up," said Ma again. "And where in the name of God's your coat?"

ೞ

The missionary priest was speaking at a special evening Mass in Newry Cathedral that Tuesday and my ma was mad to go. She loved the missionary priests. We all did, for that matter. It was like going to a show, instead of an ordinary Mass. The missionary priests burned with a special kind of fire that was seldom found in our local priests. They were full of great stories of famine and plague and wars in foreign, faraway places. Whether the stories were true or not mattered little to us—we just enjoyed hearing them. The really good ones made us feel so guilty about our own cushy lives that we filled the collection boxes to overflowing—money for the black babies in Africa, for training of more missionary priests. We would give them anything they asked for. I'm sure the local priests were jealous even though they probably got a cut of the collection to make it worth their while. And besides, it brought out people who had not set foot in a church for years—maybe this experience would coax them back into the fold.

I was still shaking from the wheelbarrow experience as I genuflected before the altar and pushed my way along with Ma and Aunt Kate into one of the pews near the front. Uncle Kevin said he was too sick to go. Too sick from the drink over the Easter holidays was more like it. The church was full to bursting. The weather had been cool but many of the parishioners had followed the old saying "Cast ne'er a clout 'til May is out" and still wore their heavy winter coats, scarves, and boots. The sweat was pouring off them. Some of them didn't have the sense they were born with. I'd had no choice in what to wear—my only coat was still back at the mill, sewn up and filled with bobbins.

Father Toner, the head priest, stood up to introduce the missionary. My mind wandered as he droned on about the good these traveling priests do in the world and all the rest of it. Noise and shuffling rose from the pews behind me. The rest of the people were as bored as myself. We came to hear the missionary, not Father Toner. But as the noise grew louder I turned around. Something was not right. A buzz of conversation had arisen at the back of the church, and the doors had been opened wide. It was then I heard the faint sound of sirens. There must be a fire somewhere, I thought. But the sirens grew louder. I had never heard so many of them at one time. As I watched, people began to move towards the front doors. Something was going on. Curiosity overcame me and I grabbed Ma by the arm.

"Come on," I said, "let's go."

Aunt Kate gave me a fierce look and put her finger to her lips the way the nuns always did in school. But I ignored her and fought my way past her, pulling Ma behind me. The sudden look of terror on Ma's face made the hair on my skin stand up. I pushed my way down the main aisle, carried now in the tide of people who were bent on finding out what was going on outside. The sirens screamed nonstop, so loud they drowned out Father Toner's plea for calm. Eventually we reached the cathedral doors and a burst of air slapped me in the face. The weather had turned colder. Ma stuck close to me, her fingers gripping my arm like a vise. We said nothing as we followed the crowd up Hill Street in the direction of the Belfast road. As we approached, the wail of sirens grew deafening. A strange excitement filled me—anticipation tinged with fear. It was unlike anything I had experienced before—not even when I won the Linen Queen competition. Something new and strange was happening. I could hardly wait to find out what it was.

As we reached the main road, we witnessed dozens of green fire engines speeding hell for leather towards Belfast. Green fire engines! They were from the Free State. What was happening? Then, as if in answer, a low whine sounded in the distance. The crowd turned as one towards the horizon, where small black dots the size of pencil marks appeared against the evening sky from the direction of Carlingford Lough. As they few closer they became a swarm of droning insects. A whole flock of planes was heading towards us. And then they were overhead and we could almost reach up and touch them. The noise deafened us and we covered our ears. We stared helplessly into the sky. No one spoke. Even the policemen stopped shouting at us to disperse. We all stood frozen in place. Then we turned as one and watched them fly on north towards Belfast.

A hand on my left arm made me swing around. It was Gavin. His sudden appearance brought a sense of relief. I turned to look at Ma. Her face was ashen and her eyes wide with fear. I looked back at Gavin.

"Thank God you're here," I said.

Gavin carried his kit bag over his shoulder. He had just got off his boat.

Ma found her voice. "What's happening, Gavin? For God's sake what's happening? Has the world come to an end?"

Normally I would have been embarrassed by this outburst, but this evening I realized I was as frightened as she was.

"It's the Germans, Mrs. McGee," he said quietly. "They're bombing Belfast."

A split second of horrified silence greeted his words, and then the questions began. People surrounded us, pressing in to hear what Gavin had to say.

"There was a dispatch on the ship radio," he said, "just as we were coming into port. The Germans are dropping bombs on Belfast. The whole city is on fire."

"Mother of God."

"Have mercy on us."

Some people began reciting the rosary. Several young chaps cheered. "It's started. At last we'll see some action." Some of the girls cheered too, giddy with excitement, while others sobbed. The police, having recovered from the shock of the planes, began shoving us back down towards Hill Street.

"Go home," they shouted. "There's nothing to see here. Go on home."

"So it's finally come. Bloody England's war is in Ireland." Gavin's voice was rough behind me. "Are you satisfied now, Sheila?"

"Satisfied? Why would I be satisfied? I never said I wanted the war here."

"But you didn't care."

"No, I never cared before. And I don't now," I said. "No bloody war's going to interfere with my plans."

Suddenly Ma let out a wail like a banshee. I swung around to look at her. There was a wild look in her eyes that reminded me of the missionary priest. The fear seemed to have left her and something else had taken its place. She was almost giddy—wilder than I'd ever seen her. She frightened me.

"Ma," I said. "It's all right. We're all right. We'll go home now."

But she shook her head violently. "Didn't I say they would come? Wasn't I always telling you they would? And nobody believed me. Well, they're here now, daughter. They've hit Belfast. And Newry will be next. And they'll destroy the mill and then what will become of us?"

As I stared horrified at the changing expressions on Ma's face— fear, anger, glee, and fear again—I realized I had been wrong. The war *was* going to interfere with my plans. I looked past Ma and I saw my dream of escape led away like a prisoner and a heavy gate slam shut behind it.

Chapter 5

℘

There was no singing at the mill on Wednesday or for many days after that. We were all in a state of shock. If there was any consolation in it at all, it was that the Linen Queen competition and wheelbarrow incident had been forgotten. The talk was only of war, and whether the bombers would come again, and whether they would strike Newry next.

I could hardly leave Ma now given the desperate state she was in. She cried morning, noon, and night. The slightest noise sent her diving under the bedclothes. She began to lose weight and her face grew pale and drawn. A couple of times I went out at night to the backyard to make sure my envelope with the prize money in it was still buried there. It was all I had to hold on to now—the faint hope that soon the war would be over and I would be on my way. It was all that kept me going.

The only one who had not forgotten the Linen Queen competition was oul' Mr. Carlson. To my shock his secretary appeared beside my spinning frame one Friday afternoon, less than two weeks after the Belfast Blitz, and handed me an envelope.

"Your instructions for the first Linen Queen appearance," she said, and turned on her heel and marched away.

I stared at the envelope and then thrust it in my pocket. I would have to wait until my shift was over before I could stop and open it. While I threaded the yarn around the bobbins I let my mind wander. Maybe I had been called to the mayor's house, or maybe to a party at some rich oul' feller's mansion, or maybe a reception at Derrymore House where Carlson himself lived. I was so away in my imagination that I jumped when the closing horn blew.

I raced down the stairs with the rest of the spinners. Their spirits had lifted. It was Friday. They would be off for the weekend.

"May as well enjoy it," one woman called. "Sure the rumor is we're going to be working our arses off soon now that the war's come home to us."

She was right. The mills would be called into service making supplies for the troops.

I sat down on the stone wall beside the wee river that ran past the mill grounds and ripped open the envelope.

"Och, Jesus, Mary, and Joseph," I cried aloud. "It must be a joke."

בר×

The next morning I climbed down from the tram in Mullagh-bawn, a small country town not far from Newry, to be greeted by Billy Taylor, a manager at the Queensbrook Mill. I looked around for Mr. Carlson, but there was no sign of him. Instead I came face to face with Mrs. McAteer. She looked me up and down. I hadn't been sure what I was supposed to wear so I wore the blue frock I had worn the night of the competition, and the same high-heeled shoes. I carried the sash and the tiara in a cloth bag, along with a linen tablecloth and six serviettes in a plastic wrapper, which had been left for me to pick up in the mill office. Mrs. McAteer gave me a smirk and said nothing.

As I walked with Billy Taylor up the winding road from the tram station I breathed in the fresh air. I looked up at Slieve Gullion, the mountain that dominated much of the landscape in the area. It was green and fresh and was dotted with wee white cottages and sheep grazing on the slopes. How different it was from the mill or

Queensbrook itself. I briefly envied the people who lived out here. But the thought was short-lived. We reached the top of the road and came to a white wooden gate that led into a feld where they were holding the annual Armagh County Pig Fair. As we entered, the smell of swine and manure nearly choked me.

"Put on the sash and the tiara," Billy Taylor said, "and smile."

A group of older men came rushing forward to meet me— farmers in suits they probably only ever wore to Mass and to funerals, and the mayor himself with a gold chain big enough to strangle a horse hanging around his neck. I shook their rough hands, smiling as best I could. Out of the corner of my eye I saw Mrs. McAteer. The oul' bitch had come to spy on me. If I put one foot wrong, I knew, I'd have my title taken away sooner than I could spit.

The men led me to a pen containing about a dozen huge, noisy pigs.

"The judging is about to start," cried one of them. "We'll have a winner soon. Would you like a drink, love—or something to eat?"

The idea of eating or drinking anything in this place sickened my stomach so I refused as politely as I could.

"Ah, she has to keep the lovely figure, you know," said one oul' feller in a cloth cap as he slapped me on the behind.

I gasped and tried to step away from him, but my heels sank farther into the mud.

"Let's walk around," said Billy Taylor, and he took me by the arm.

A large crowd had assembled. Children ran about with balloons and toffee apples while their parents sat at picnic tables eating and talking and laughing. A brass band played in the background. A pair of young boys pointed at me and laughed. Several wee girls with sticky hands surrounded me, touching my arm and my sash and looking up at me with wide eyes. I felt like an eejit.

"How long do I have to stay?" I muttered to Billy Taylor.

"Long enough to tie the ribbon on the winner." He laughed.

"What?"

He was right. A half an hour later I was struggling with a huge, angry pig, trying to tie a blue ribbon around her neck. Her hooves scraped my dress, leaving muddy rings all over it. Finally I had to get down on my knees while two of the farmers held the pig steady enough so I could tie the bow. As I finished, a flash caught me in the eyes. I looked up and there stood a boyo with a camera grinning at me.

"Merciful God," I said aloud. "You're not going to print that, are you?"

"I am indeed," he said. "You looked lovely. Far better looking than herself." He nodded towards the pig.

I wanted to take his camera and push it into his face. Instead I stood up as gracefully as I could and smoothed out my dress. I reached into my bag and presented the pig's owner with the linen tablecloth and serviettes. I waved at the crowd and grabbed Billy Taylor's arm.

"He seemed to appreciate the linens," said Taylor.

"Aye, much good it'll do him beyond in the mud hut where he lives."

I knew it was a mean thing to say, but at that minute I didn't care. All I wanted was to get back on the tram and go home to Queensbrook and pray no one I knew would ever see the photo of myself hugging a pig.

 confused.

If I'd thought that time moved slowly while I had waited for the Linen Queen competition to come to Queensbrook, it was like a speeding train compared to the snail's pace at which my life crawled by afterwards. There were days when I thought I would go mad. I worried that I would fall into a depression like Ma but, unlike her, never climb out of it. I tried to put a brave face on matters, but hope threatened to slink away like a fox after a kill. I fought to hold on to it.

And now, as if to add insult to injury, I was stuck with the obligations of the Linen Queen title with no end in sight. Ever since the pig fair, I'd been called upon to attend every kind of function you can imagine. I smiled as fat-bellied men cut ribbons in front of new shops, I smiled as mud-booted farmers paraded their prize cows at market fairs, and I smiled as petty officials presented one another with medals and plaques. And all I got out of these events were leers and foul proposals, and the occasional slap on my behind.

"My bloody face is sore from all the grinning," I complained to Gavin one afternoon in March as we sat in our usual place up on the Flagstaff.

Gavin shrugged and lit a cigarette. "I thought that's what you wanted," he said. "To be the center of attention."

"I wanted the money," I said, cadging a fag from him and lighting it.

"Oh, come on, Sheila, you wanted the attention too. You know you did."

I took a long pull on my cigarette and slowly let out the smoke.

"OK, you're right, I did," I said. "But this isn't what I bargained for. I thought I'd be going to glamorous dinners and dances and not feckin' pig fairs out in Mullaghbawn."

Gavin laughed. "You're the queen," he said. "You have to be gracious to all your subjects wherever they are."

"Feck off !" I said.

Gavin leaned back on his elbows and looked out towards the lough and then back down towards Newry port. I followed his gaze. A boat sat in Victoria Locks on the Lower Fathom Road waiting for the tide so she could sail out.

"Who's that?" I said.

"Danny Boyle. The *Elm*'s waiting for the tide." He smiled and took a puff on his cigarette. "I remember when I was young and my da's boat had to wait at the locks," he said. "I used to run down and bring him cigarettes, and maybe some soda farls Ma had just made. He'd be there for hours. Sometimes when he knew it would be a long delay, he'd climb up the hill and surprise us."

I said nothing, just let him enjoy his memories.

"Seems a long time ago, doesn't it, Sheila. We were innocent then."

"Aye." I smiled.

"Remember the night you saw your da's ghost up on this very hill, and you followed him all the way home?"

I stubbed my cigarette out on the grass and lay back. "Gavin, you know I don't believe in all that palaver of ghosts. It was my imagination, that's all."

"It was the night the *Sheila Rose* sank all the same," said Gavin.

Gavin believed in ghosts, and the fairies, and signs and pre-monitions. It was strange how different we were—after all we'd both been reared out in the country listening to sailors tell stories around the fireplace on dark nights. All the sailors were superstitious, including my da. I used to love the stories though. And I know I believed them at the time. But somewhere over the years my innocence had leached out of me along with my trust in other people.

"D'you remember the wee dog you found, Sheila? The one that had its paw caught in a rabbit trap?"

He was in a strange mood today. "Aye, the one my ma poisoned!" I said.

Gavin shrugged. "You have no proof it was her did it. But I remember how you cried over that wee thing. It wasn't long after your da died." Gavin reached over to touch my arm, but I pulled it away.

"Of course it was her that did it!" I said. "You know rightly it was. She was always jealous of anything or anybody that took attention away from her. Just like she hated me for all the attention Da used to give me."

I didn't like thinking about the past. A pain always bored into my stomach like a screwdriver when I did. I had to concentrate on the future, I told myself. I had only myself to rely on. I hoped the war would be over soon. Then I would be on my way. I wasn't going to let the weight of old memories paralyze me.

I pulled another cigarette out of Gavin's pack and lit it.

"Can we change the subject?" I said. "This is bloody morbid."

Gavin sat up. "Not much good news about the war," he began.

I sighed. "Can you not talk about something happy for once?"

"There's not much to be happy about. The war isn't going well."

"Well, I for one wish they would either bomb us and get it over with, or that one side would win once and for all. This bloody limbo is giving me the pip. And the rationing is driving me mad."

"Be careful what you wish for, Sheila," said Gavin.

ᕪ

The priests always told us that there was a place between heaven and hell called purgatory where you were sent if you had not lived a good enough life to go to heaven, but had not sinned badly enough to go to hell. It was a limbo where you had to wait for something to happen—good or bad.

As the summer days of 1941 crept by one by one we all waited in such a limbo. Was the Blitz of Belfast a one-time event? Would Hitler not bother again with the rest of us? Would we be able to go on about our business? Or would we be caught in the hellfires of more bombings? Every noise made us jump out of our skins. Every wail of a siren, every whiff of smoke made us clutch our chests and hold our breath. The York Street Flax Spinning Mill in Belfast had taken a direct hit the night of the blitz, and Ma was convinced all mills in the North would be targets. But so far, no danger had come to Queensbrook. Belfast had been bombed several more times. The stories of the dead and wounded were awful to hear—bodies unrecognizable from burns thrown in unmarked coffins, orphaned children wandering the streets, people numb with the shock of it all. Dublin was hit once, and then Dundalk, but the Germans said both were mistakes—after all, the Free State was neutral. Everybody believed they had meant to hit Newry instead. We craned our necks every night of the week, searching the sky for Jerry bombers.

But besides the dread, there was also a thrilling sense of excitement. New rules had been ordered and auxiliary brigades set up to enforce them. We were to cover all windows at night with black curtains or shades so that the Jerries would not be able to see any lights. We had to cover the lamps on cars and bicycles and inch our way along the ink-black roads at night. Auxiliaries patrolled the roofs of buildings. In case a bomb dropped and started a fire they were ready with sandbags to douse the flames. To many of the young ones, like myself, it was all great *craic*, while the old people blessed themselves and prayed and recalled stories of the Uprising. Those in the auxiliary took it all very seriously though, puffing out their chests at the importance of their jobs. Chaps whose life had never amounted to more than signing on at the dole when they were out of work suddenly had a new meaning in their life. Others of them simply liked barking orders at the rest of us. I shrugged and laughed at them.

Besides the heightened sense of excitement the war brought, it also heightened my recklessness. If I was going to be bombed to kingdom come I might as well have a good time before I went. I began going out more, dancing and carrying on flirting with the lads. Ma and Aunt Kate gave me no peace about my attitude. One Friday night in the late summer I was decked out ready to go to a dance in Warrenpoint when Ma started in.

"Oh, no you don't, my girl," she said, puffing away on her cigarette. "You've no call to be gallivanting tonight. We have a full day's work tomorrow and we should be grateful for the overtime. We need to save what we can before the bombs fall on us. Look what happened to the York Street Mill."

It was her same old blather. She moaned every day about the mill being destroyed. My patience was stretched thin. I had stayed behind because she was so afraid the night of the Belfast Blitz. Now it almost seemed to me as if she were taking a queer pleasure in the thought we could all be blown up. I didn't want to believe she was astray in the head, but I sometimes wondered. It was only when she put her hand out for my wages every week, figuring the amount to the exact penny, that I realized she was cute as a fox.

"Where's the rest of it?" she said tonight.

"What rest of it? That's the lot."

"I heard you girls got bonuses."

"Well you heard wrong."

"They're after bombing Dublin by mistake," said Ma. "It could be us next. And how can you be out enjoying yourself when there's young ones being killed up in Belfast every night of the week? And if they're not bombed, sure they're crouching in air-raid shelters afraid for their lives."

I had heard the same line over and over again for months.

"You know you could be doing some good instead of going to dances, Sheila." Saint Kate was on her soapbox again. "You could volunteer with the auxiliary. Many of the young ones are doing it. Mrs. McAteer tells me Mary and her friends spend all their free time making bandages for the soldiers and—"

My temper got the better of me. "Will you look at who you're talking to, Kate?" I cut in. "Can you see the likes of me making fecking bandages?"

"Selfish!" cried Ma. "Always was. The father spoiled her, you know. Ruined her. She'll always be a selfish girl."

My cheeks began to burn. "Selfish, is it?" I cried. "And what's that money in your hand this selfish daughter is after giving you? And why did this selfish daughter stay here to look after you when she could be long away from here?"

Ma flicked her cigarette ash into the fire. "It's your duty to look after me, and me not a well woman. It's—"

A fit of coughing silenced her. I turned for the door. Kevin staggered up behind me and the smell of his breath almost knocked me over. He put a rough hand on my shoulder. "You look nice, darling," he slurred. "I'll bet the young lads will be all over you tonight."

⁊ඏ

We rode along the shore road towards Warrenpoint. Tommy Markey, a Newry lad, had borrowed his da's car. Tommy was good-looking and he had a big notion for me. If I hadn't my mind set on going away I might have taken him more seriously. As it was, he was just one more boyo with a crush on me. Patsy and Kathleen were with us along with a couple of lads from the mill.

Patsy acted as if there'd never been any trouble between us, and I went along with her. But deep down I knew I'd never feel the same about our friendship. We hung out of the windows singing a chorus of Vera Lynn's "The White Cliffs of Dover." You'd not have thought there was a war on at all the way we were carrying on. I breathed deeply, inhaling the fresh sea air, glad to be away from the stifling house in Queensbrook.

We drove alongside the Clanrye River and down past Narrow Water Castle, an old ruin that was now a private house owned by some rich old fellow. Eventually the river opened out into Carlingford Lough, a stretch of water that divided the North of Ireland from the Free State. Across the lough we could see the Cooley Mountains as we passed Omeath and Carlingford, both towns in the Free State. Our excitement grew as we entered the small beach town of Warrenpoint. At eight o'clock in the evening it was still light as day, and the August air was warm. In the North of Ireland summer days were long and nights were short. I loved the long, light evenings. A carnival was set up on the beach, with roundabouts and music and stalls selling toffee apples and ice cream. People strolled on the promenade or sat along the sea wall. The mood was festive, as it always was during the summer. I felt a stone weight leave my shoulders. I loved the excitement of this town, and I loved the smell of the sea.

Tommy drove along the Sea Road looking for a safe place to park the car. Three-storied white terraced houses, known as the Seven Sisters, lined the road overlooking the lough. As I looked on down the road towards Rostrevor, the Mourne Mountains came into view on my left-hand side. We were bound for the Castle Hotel for a big Friday night dance. It was going to be a great night altogether. We tumbled out of the car, Patsy and Kathleen and I smoothing out our skirts and our hair as we waved to bands of young people who milled outside the hotel. I dragged my feet following the rest of them inside. Instead I turned and looked out over the water. How I loved being beside the sea. It reminded me of the good times with Da. I walked over to the sea wall and lit a cigarette. I lingered for a minute, remembering, then shrugged and turned and walked on in after my friends.

The high-ceilinged ballroom in the Castle Hotel was packed with young people. A stage was set up at one end and soon a band would be in full swing playing the top hits of Glenn Miller and Artie Shaw and the other popular American bands. I couldn't wait to get out on the dance floor. I'd have no shortage of partners, and I planned to dance the feet off myself all night. As I looked around, I saw Gavin at the bar, sitting by himself drinking a pint. I went over to him.

"Hello, stranger," I called as I touched him on the shoulder.

He swung around, startled, as if I had woken him up out of a trance.

"Oh, hello, Sheila," he said.

Every now and then Gavin seemed to go away into himself, as he did now. I shrugged and went back to the dance floor. At nine o'clock the band struck up with "In the Mood" and Tommy pulled me out on the dance floor. I was a good dancer, light on my feet, and I twirled my skirt around me as I moved. I always attracted plenty of attention. As the night went on I had no end of lads dying to dance with me. I hardly sat down. Once in a while I glanced over at Gavin. He had not moved from his stool. Well, it was his loss. I was here to have fun.

I was in the middle of a dance with a good-looking chap from Camlough when all of a sudden all the lights in the hall went out. Everybody screamed, more in excitement than fear. What was happening now? We pressed together in the dark, our bodies sweaty and breaths ripe from drinking. People struck matches to give them a bit of light. All of a sudden I did not want to be in this crush. I began to push myself towards the door. As I did so, Gavin caught up with me and took my arm.

"Come on," he said.

At first I shook him off. "I can find me own way out, thank you very much," I said.

I realized I was angry with him for having ignored me all night. He paid me no mind and firmly escorted me out of the hall. When we reached the street, the sound of air-raid sirens was deafening. Blackout blinds were pulled down in all the windows. Even the carnival was black and silent. I shivered and moved closer to Gavin. The rest of the dancers spilled out onto the street, their earlier merriment silenced. Tommy Markey found me. He staggered over, unsteady on his feet.

"Come on, Sheila, let's find the car."

"Aye."

I turned to go with him but Gavin held on tight to my arm.

"That's not a good idea," he said, looking straight at Tommy. "It's not safe driving a car with no lights on these black roads. You'd be better off coming across the water with me to Omeath. It'll be safer."

I began to protest, but the look on his face silenced me.

I turned to Tommy. "It's all right, Tommy. I'll go with Gavin. Safe home."

Tommy hesitated. "But you came with me..."

I was afraid Tommy would start something with Gavin. Tommy got very jealous when he had taken drink. I walked over and put my hand on his arm.

"I had a lovely time, Tommy, but my ma's waiting for me in Omeath," I lied. "She gets awful afraid of the sirens. Go on home now, there's a good lad."

I leaned over and kissed him and gave him a gentle shove towards his car.

"If you're sure then," Tommy muttered. "Safe home."

"And you," I called.

The whine of airplanes sounded overhead. They were flying up the lough again towards Belfast. Or maybe this time they were aiming for Newry. I imagined Ma standing outside the door looking up into the sky. Would she be alarmed? Or would she be happy that maybe she was right and they were coming to bomb the mill? I put the image out of my head.

"Let's go," said Gavin as he led the way down to the pier, where a few boats were docked.

We climbed into a small motorboat and Gavin started up the

engine. We could hardly hear the growl of the motor over the sirens, which still wailed like banshees. It was after eleven o'clock at night but it was still not quite dark. I looked back at the Sea Road. All lights were out as if the place were in mourning. I shuddered. In front of me, across the lough, lay the village of Omeath, which was in the Free State. Lights flickered here and there in the windows of small cottages scattered along the shore and up in the hills beyond. It looked peaceful and comforting, although I knew there were some who would see the lights as defiance. Gavin was looking in that direction as well.

"Thank God the southern people don't have to put up with that blackout shite," he muttered.

"No, I suppose they prefer helping the Germans see where they're going."

"You sound like a Unionist. I thought you didn't give a tinker's curse what people thought about the war."

"I don't," I said. "I just said it to annoy you."

He smiled in the dusky light. The little boat plowed her way across the lough, her motor humming. Gavin had his hand on the tiller and he looked easy and relaxed, unlike the cut of him earlier in the evening. Gavin belongs on the sea, I thought.

"You know I was watching you tonight," Gavin began, and I stiffened. I knew what was coming—another lecture on my behavior. All sense of peace left me. "Sheila, why do you let the drunken louts paw you the way they do?"

I turned and faced him, ready for battle.

"First of all it's none of your bloody business," I said. "And second of all, I'll dance with whoever I want to—and I have plenty of choice. Any one of them is better than a wet blanket that sits at the bar with a face on him would frighten the devil himself."

"That's not the point." Gavin's voice had grown cold. "It's your reputation I'm talking about. You seem to have gone wild ever since the war came. There's them that thinks you lie down with any Tom, Dick, or Harry." He paused. "There's them that says you're just like your ma was."

"And who's them?"

"Respectable people."

"Nosy oul' bastards," I cried. "Jealous oul' women or ugly young ones who couldn't get a man to look at them. Or oul' men who would like a go at me themselves."

Gavin and I had had this argument before. He said it was because he cared about me and didn't want to see me come to any harm. I said that was all shite and he was just an interfering bastard.

"You're not my da," I shouted at him, as I had done many times before. "You've no call to be telling me what to do. I'll live my life as I please."

We were quiet then, each of us lost in our own thoughts. Part of me was still livid for having my fun cut short by the bloody sirens, but part of me was glad to be away from the crush of the crowd and the sweaty hands of fellows I didn't even know. It was always the same. Sometimes I enjoyed the game of teasing them—leading them on—and then slapping them down when they went too far. And other times—well, other times I was disgusted with all of it. I felt clean out here on the water, pure and innocent in a way I could never feel in a pub or at a dance or even at home.

While I knew Gavin was right in what he said about how people talked about me, I was never going to admit it to him. And the truth was as time went on I really didn't care what they thought. I had begun to enjoy the reputation I had. It made me feel important. It would have been far worse if nobody had noticed me at all. But every time Gavin brought it up, a spike of pain bore through me. I tried to ignore it. Why would I care what he thought of me? And so I always changed the subject as fast as I could, or walked off without answering.

I could hardly walk away now. I was trapped in the bloody boat with him. When we reached Omeath, Gavin turned off the motor and tied the boat up at the pier. We climbed out. I stumbled in my high-heeled shoes and Gavin caught my arm. I shook him off. He went over to a shed beside the pier and took out a bicycle, which he must have left there earlier.

"Let's walk to my house," he said, "and we'll pick up my spare bike. Then I'll ride over to Queensbrook with you."

I didn't answer, just walked on ahead of him as he wheeled his bicycle up the road from the pier. His house was not far from the shore. It was a small cottage that he had found some years before.

When we reached his house he laid his bicycle down on the ground.

"I'll just go and get the spare one," he said. And then, "Would you want to come in for a cup of tea?"

"No," I said firmly. "I'll just wait here."

"Suit yourself."

I folded my arms in front of myself and looked away from him. I stood there tapping one foot on the ground while he went around the back of the house to fetch the other bicycle.

I could have told him I would see myself home, but I wasn't that stupid. In fact, I was a bit afraid. The roads up here in Omeath were very dark, and although I ridiculed him when he talked about ghosts and fairies and other spirits, still I hated being out on dark country roads by myself. So I let Gavin ride alongside me until we came down out of Omeath and reached Queensbrook. At the bottom of my street, I stopped and turned to him.

"Thanks," I said. "I'll be seeing you. Safe home."

"You're welcome," he said. I couldn't read what was in his voice, but I wasn't concerned. No matter how much we fought, Gavin and I never fell out for long. I would see him again on the Flagstaff, and we would talk as if nothing had happened.

I pedaled up the rest of the hill. My feet were tortured in my fancy shoes. I couldn't wait to get home and get them off me. But then I thought about Ma sitting by the fire waiting for me and I slowed down. On one hand she would be gleeful that the bombers had come again and proved her warnings right. On the other hand, she'd be clinging to me in fright. Not for the first time I hoped the bombs would drop on us soon and put us all out of our misery.

Chapter 6

ᴄ

As summer gave way to autumn I went to work in the mill every day, working the overtime shifts and trying to hide some of my wages from Ma. Production was going full tilt. There was great demand for supplies for the troops—canvas sheeting, cotton for uniforms, linen for parachutes. We were paid in cash and I carefully opened up the envelopes, took out any bonus money and a few extra coins, and sealed it shut again. If she knew I was hiding some, there was nothing she could do. I was a good liar. I was entitled to what I kept, and more. I had a fair bit of money saved now, and along with the prize money I still had buried in the backyard it would be more than enough to pay my fare to England and get me settled. Whenever Ma asked about the prize money I told her that it had been delayed again because the offices in Belfast had been bombed in the blitz and all the records destroyed. She gave me a suspicious look, but said nothing.

The Belfast bombings had slowed down, and Newry had still not been hit. By winter I had begun to think again about my decision to stay behind with Ma. What did she need protecting from now? The Jerries were clearly occupied with their doings in the rest of Europe, and while the auxiliary in Newry still went about the business of test air raids and blackouts, nothing bad happened. Everybody remained on alert—after all it would only take one

bomb to blow us all to kingdom come. But I was growing bored
with the whole lot of it. Some local girls had gone off to work in
factories in England—Liverpool and Birmingham and the like.
I didn't fancy the thought of that too much. I had never imagined going across the water just to work in a place that was no
better than the oul' mill. I had imagined a much grander life-
style altogether—although as I thought about it now I realized
I had never really developed a plan. I had never sat down and
thought about what in particular I was going to do when I got
there. My whole focus was just on getting away. But now, even
factory work sounded more appealing than living in the cramped
house in Queensbrook with a sanctimonious aunt, a drunken
uncle, and a mother who changed personalities as often as some
women changed their knickers. I could sense feelings of unease
and resentment grow in me. They burst out one Saturday afternoon when I came home from an extra shift at the mill and found
a strange girl sitting in the kitchen.

"Who're you?" I said sharply. The girl had done nothing wrong,
but something about me ma's smug smile and the girl's surly look
set me on edge.

"Who's asking?" she said, just as sharply. Her accent was
unmistakable—Belfast—and low class at that.

Ma stood up, still smiling, and came over to hug me. She was
in a good mood. "This is Grainne, love. Grainne Malloy. Isn't she
a lovely wee thing?"

I stared at the girl. She looked to be about twelve years old. She
had frizzy red hair and a face full of freckles. She was scrawny
looking, as if she had not had a good meal in a dog's age. Her eyes
were green, and they stared right at me without blinking. Her
gaze had no malice in it—but it had no apology and no shame
either, and certainly no innocence. It gave me the creeps.

"Grainne's from Belfast," Ma said. "She's an evacuee from the
war. There's loads of them being billeted down here in the country. I told Mrs. McAteer we'd take a wee girl." She turned and
looked at Grainne. "She's a bit older than I expected, but och
well, she needs a safe place to stay as much as the rest of them."

"And where's she going to sleep?"

"In the granny room with you, darlin'. I'll be sleeping in Donal's room."

"In the shrine?" I said. "Kate's let nobody near that room since Donal left." I paused. "There must be money in it for her."

Ma smiled. "Ah well, there's the best part of it. We get ten shillings and sixpence a week as long as she's here."

I laughed. "I should have known," I said. "Aunt Kate would hardly take in a charity case out of the goodness of her heart."

"Oh, no love," said Ma. "She'd have taken her in anyway, I'm sure of it. Your aunt Kate is a very generous woman."

Generous my arse. Aunt Kate was an oul' skinflint, and Ma knew it. Ma was just in one of her flying moods. Times like these she was delusional. An odd feeling came over me. I had expected anger, and indeed it was there, gathering beneath the surface. But I was surprised that another emotion beat anger to the punch. Why I should give a tinker's curse that Ma had a new girl in the house, I didn't know. Was I afraid this Grainne would take my place? And if she did, wouldn't that be a good thing—wouldn't that set me free to go my own way? And yet the feeling seeped through me, sickening me. Jealousy. I fought it off and seized on the anger instead.

"You expect me to share a bed with this tinker?" I shouted. "Is it astray in the head you are? I'll sleep in the outhouse before I'll do that. Who knows what she's carrying—lice, disease, scabs? How dare you? I pay my own way here—I'm entitled to my rights."

"Och now, Sheila," Ma began.

"Och, nothing!" I was raging now. "I'll not stand for it. You'll have to send her back. It's her or me."

The girl watched us without a word. There was a hint of a smile on her face as if she were enjoying it. She had an old head on her shoulders this one.

I went over to Ma and took her by the arms. I shook her hard. "It's her or me," I said again. "Make up your mind."

Ma put up her hand to smooth my hair. "Ah now, Sheila, she's just a child. And sure you'll get used to her. You might even become friends..."

I pushed her away and ran through the scullery to the back room. Ma was still calling after me but I ignored her. I swore aloud as I tripped over a battered oul' suitcase that lay open on the floor in the middle of the granny room. So she'd moved in already! Bloody cheek! I reached into a drawer and pulled a small biscuit tin from underneath a pile of knickers. I had been hiding my bonus money in there. I didn't even open it. I grabbed a big canvas bag and threw the box into it along with clothes, flinging open drawers and the wardrobe and snatching a few things off the dressing table—a brush and comb set, some perfume, and the wee carved mermaid Da had given me years ago. I zipped up the bag and came back out through to the parlor.

"Suit yourself," I said.

Tears stung my eyes. Tears of anger, or hurt, I didn't know rightly which. I blinked them back. I had no time for crying.

Ma and the girl watched me in silence. I opened the front door, and then I hesitated on the step, waiting to hear Ma's pleas to come back. But neither of them spoke. I pulled the door closed behind me and waited. When there was no sign of Ma coming after me I slipped around the back of the house and hurriedly dug up the prize money envelope with my hands and threw it in the bag. Then I set off down the hill to the tram.

The tram came quickly and I got on, ignoring the shouts of some local lads who raced down the hill and hopped on at the last second.

"Hello, Queen Sheila. What's the *craic?*"

"What d'you have in the bag? Are you after robbing the bank?"

"Are you up for the Ceili House later?"

I ignored all their questions. I gave them a look would turn them to stone and eventually they shrugged and started talking about football. My heart was beating a mile a minute. I had pictured this moment in my head over and over since I was fourteen years old. I was finally running away—bound for the train to Belfast and then the boat to England. Off to seek my fortune.

But in my fantasies I had been giddy with delight, laughing and singing, and everybody congratulating me and wishing me luck. Now, all I felt was sadness. I was as depressed as Ma on her worst days. I felt cold inside as if a part of me had died. I stared at my hands as they held the bag on my knees. They didn't even seem like my own hands. Nothing felt like me. It was as if the real Sheila had disappeared somewhere and only this shell was left. I moved around on the seat, trying to snap myself out of it. But still the feeling remained. I realized I felt the same way as when I was ten years old and I sank down on the pier after Da's boat had pulled away to sea. I felt abandoned. I shook my head. Abandoned! Even though I was the one running away from this bloody place, still I had the awful feeling that it and everyone in it had abandoned me. I didn't understand it one bit.

I left the tram and made my way to the train station. There was a train to Belfast leaving in two hours. All I could afford was a third-class fare.

"Such a pretty girl should be traveling first class. Have you no man to buy your ticket for you?" the shrunken oul' clerk said as he handed me the ticket.

I ignored him and grabbed it from his hand. I walked away and sat down on a bench farther up the empty platform. I pulled my coat around me as the wind blew through the station. As usual, I had forgotten my gloves. I shrugged, thinking the girl, Grainne, could have them now. I looked out at the empty railway lines, which stretched away to eternity. I tried to shake off the bad feeling.

Eventually, the platform began to fill up. Three young lads in army uniform arrived, laughing and shouting at one another. They must have been home on leave and were going back to the front, I thought. I didn't recognize any of them. One caught me looking at them and nudged the others. They all turned and one of them whistled while the others grinned. They really got my goat.

"If you're going to stare at me all day," I snapped, "the least you could do is buy me a bloody cup of tea."

They elbowed one another again. The one who had whistled

came over and helped me up off the bench and took my canvas bag in his hand.

"Grand idea," he said. "C'mon lads."

They escorted me into the station cafeteria. It was a dismal oul' place with dim lighting and a high, dirty ceiling. But it was warmer than the platform. I sat down at a rickety table trying to look like I was too good for this place and everybody in it. The army lads fell over themselves to get to the counter to buy me tea.

The teacups were so dirty you were almost afraid to drink out of them, and the tea was black and strong. They had run out of milk and sugar. Rationed. I cursed wartime but I drank the tea anyway and it warmed my insides. I munched on a bun they had brought me, and slowly I began to feel better. I was almost my old self. I tossed my hair and smiled my best smile and pretended to admire the bravery of the chaps who sat around me. Each one was trying to best the others with some story of his brave doings in the army, and although I knew most of it was shite I nodded and sighed and tried to look impressed. I was back in form.

Eventually I got bored with their stories. I looked around the cafeteria. At the table next to us were two dark-haired young women who looked like sisters. They had rosy, fresh faces—certainly not mill girls. They had been eyeing me and the soldiers and exchanging looks with each other. They didn't bother me—I was used to those looks from other women. Normally, I would have ignored them—or played up in order to scandalize them even more—but I was interested in these two. I wondered if they were going to England. Maybe if I was nice to them they might have some suggestions for me. So I picked myself up and excused myself from the boys.

"Thanks for the tea, lads," I said as I got up, ignoring their disappointed faces, "and good luck to you at the front."

I approached the table where the girls were sitting. I pointed to a chair.

"Is this seat taken?" I asked in a sweet voice.

They looked shocked, but I supposed their good manners would not let them refuse me. I sat down and sighed. I indicated the lads over my shoulder.

"Poor lads," I said. "They begged me to sit with them, and I thought they deserved a little female company given what they're facing. And so, even though it's not something I'd normally do, I let them buy me a cup of tea."

I smiled at the girls, innocent as the day is long. "Are you two sisters?" I asked brightly. "You look so much alike."

They hesitated for a moment as if weighing me up, and then one said, "Yes, we are. We're a year apart in age, but we're often taken for twins."

I nodded. "I wish I had sisters," I said. "By the way, I'm Sheila McGee."

They introduced themselves as Anne and Mary McTaggart from Mullaghbawn.

"Oh, I know it," I said. "Lovely place. I appeared at the county fair there once. I'm the reigning Linen Queen, you know."

They said nothing. "Are you going to England too?" I continued. They nodded.

"Whereabouts?" I asked, hoping to get the conversation started.

Anne, the one who had spoken first, smiled. "Bristol," she said. "We're on our way to join the WAAFs."

I spluttered. "The WAAFs? The Women's Auxiliary Air Force? Youse are bloody joining up?"

The one called Mary winced at my language, but Anne nodded. "Yes. We don't think the lads should have all the fun." There was a bit of mischief in her eyes. So they weren't as prim as I first thought. But I still couldn't get over it.

"But joining up!" I said again. "Youse could get yourselves killed."

"Aye," said Mary, finding her voice, "or die a slow death growing old on our farm in Mullaghbawn."

So they were escaping too. I stared at them with sudden respect.

"What about yourself?" asked Anne.

"I don't have any real plans yet," I said, ignoring Mary's comment. "I'll probably start off in some factory—I have experience at that—until I find my footing and get something better." It sounded pathetic even as I said it.

"But you said you're the Linen Queen," said Mary. "Why would you leave all that?"

I ignored her question.

"So you have someone sponsoring you," said Anne.

"Sponsoring me?" I looked at Anne, confused. "No, I'm by myself."

"So how did you get your papers?" said Mary, leaning forward.

"Papers?"

"Aye, you'll go nowhere without papers. We looked into it, didn't we, Anne? And we were told without a sponsor and the proper papers our only choice if we wanted to leave Ireland was to join up. Isn't that right, Anne?"

Her sister nodded. "Right enough."

I was dumbfounded. I looked around the cafeteria, which had filled up now, but everything was a blur. This couldn't be true. They would have to let me out of here. Surely I could persuade some official to let me on the boat to England. I remembered the lesson from the night of the Linen Queen competition. Beauty is power. I had become very good at getting my own way.

As if reading my mind, Anne said, "And they'll not be letting you through on your good looks either, Sheila. Since the bombing started in Belfast, they've tightened up all the rules." She looked at Mary. "We've already tried persuasion, haven't we, Mary?"

Mary blushed and nodded.

I stood up suddenly and grabbed my bag. "Well, we'll just see!" I said.

I rushed out onto the platform. The Belfast train was due in ten minutes. I found the stationmaster, an arrogant-looking customer in his forties. I had noticed him eyeing me earlier as I sat on the bench. I marched up to him.

"Excuse me, sir," I said as sweetly as I could. "You look like a man knows everything that's going on."

His face flushed with pleasure. Och, it was always so easy!

"I'm told I might need papers to go to England. Do you think there would be any way for me to get something from you that might let me pass through? I'm sure they would listen well to an important man like yourself."

He stared down at me to be sure I wasn't just taking the mickey out of him. I made my face as serious as I could. "I would be ever so grateful," I murmured.

After a minute he shook his head. "I'm afraid, darling," he said, "they're very strict on the other end. You're not the first pretty girl who has thrown herself on their mercy only to see the same girls back again in Newry on the next train with their tails between their legs." He sighed. "Hearts of stone, those boyos. Hearts of stone."

I opened my mouth to speak, but I realized I was getting nowhere. I turned to leave but he wrapped his big fist around my wrist. "But if there's anything else you need, love, I'd be happy to oblige."

I jerked my wrist away from him. "Go to hell!"

A train from Belfast on its way to Dublin steamed into the station, its big engine belching black smoke. It shimmied to a stop and the carriage doors began to open. The first passengers off were a group of young children. They were ragged and white-faced. They clutched small suitcases, most of which, like Grainne's, had seen better days, and wee boxes containing gas masks. I guessed they were evacuees. I felt a sudden rush of pity for them, but I shook it off as quickly as it came.

Just after the train pulled out, the whistle of another train approaching from the opposite direction made everyone turn around. The train to Belfast was arriving. I watched it in horror. What was I to do? The train lurched to a stop. No one got off. Nobody on the train was interested in Newry, I thought. They all wanted to go to Belfast—and beyond. The crowd on the platform thinned out as people climbed aboard, pushing and shoving one another to get the best seats in still-empty carriages. Once the doors slammed shut, windows were pushed down and heads came out. Passengers waved to the few friends and relatives left on the platform, while the stationmaster strode up and down yelling, "All aboard. All aboard for Belfast."

I shrank back as he passed me. He turned around and glared.

"All aboard!" he shouted again. "Last chance for Belfast."

I backed up even farther as the big steam engine belched out smoke and carriage doors slammed and windows clattered shut. I stood watching, my brain in turmoil. What was the point of going only to be turned back and all my money used up on the tickets? But how could I go back to Queensbrook after this—wasn't I better off taking my chances in Belfast? As I struggled with my thoughts, I watched the train pull away as if in slow motion. I watched it chug up the line towards the green hills that lay outside the station. The shriek of the whistle grew fainter, ebbing away, just like my dreams. I stood watching long after the train was out of sight leaving the tracks empty and silent. Eventually, I picked up my bag and walked over to the ticket office. I thrust the unused ticket at the oul' clerk behind the caged window.

"Give me a refund," I said.

"So you've decided to wait and let some Prince Charming buy you a first-class ticket after all? Good for you, girl. Good for you."

I grabbed the change, ignoring his blather. Prince Charming, indeed! Oul' eejit.

I was in such bad form when I arrived back in Queensbrook that night I didn't even bother burying the prize money envelope again. I just wanted to go into the granny room, climb into bed, and pull the flour sacks up over my head. But there was no chance of that. The bloody place was so small we were tripping over one another. I bit my lip and said nothing as I shut the front door behind me and dropped the canvas bag on the floor. Ma eyed it and lit up in a big smile. She ran over to me and tried to hug me.

"Och, love, you've come back to me. Sure I knew you would. Under all the proud talk, sure you love your ma, don't you pet."

I shoved her away. I could hardly stand her when she was in this stupid mood—all sweetness and kisses and hugs as if we were long-lost friends and not mother and daughter at all. I said nothing. I ignored Aunt Kate as well, who made the sign of the cross when she saw me and thanked God out loud for my return. But the worst part was the girl, Grainne, who sat by the fire watching me, a knowing oul' look on her young face. I wanted to swing out my hand and slap her. How was I going to be able to stand this? Suddenly joining up sounded like a small price to pay to get away from here. The McTaggart sisters might have been right. A surge of regret filled me for letting the train go to Belfast without me. Ah well, there'd be more trains. Right now, I just wanted to sleep.

I picked up my bag and pushed past all of them and back into the granny room. I sat down on the bed and slowly unpacked my bag. I shoved my clothes and the biscuit tin containing my money back into the drawer along with the prize money envelope. I put the perfume and the brush and comb set back on the side table. Then I took out the wee carved merrow that Da had given me and I held it in my two hands. Part of me wanted to crush it until it was in pieces, but instead I held it to my chest and tried to fight back the tears.

I heard a noise behind me and I swung around. Grainne stood in the doorway. I turned my back to her and put the merrow down on the side table. I kicked off my shoes and slipped into bed, fully clothed. I closed my eyes and turned on my side facing the window. I said nothing. I heard Grainne moving about and then I felt her slip into the bed beside me. I moved over to the edge of the bed on my side and she did the same on the other side. No part of us touched the other. We both lay in silence. I could tell she was not asleep. I was determined not to fall asleep until she did. Eventually, her breathing became heavier and I knew she had drifted off. Only then did I allow myself to sink into a dreamless sleep.

ॐ

The next day was Sunday. I rose early and quietly pulled on my coat and a pair of boots and crept out of the sleeping house. I took my bicycle from the shed and pedaled down the road and out towards the Flagstaff. I was foundered with the cold but I didn't care. I enjoyed the slap of the wind on my face and the gnawing cold on my bare hands. It made me feel alive. I welcomed it after the suffocation of the Queensbrook house.

It was only eight o'clock in the morning, and the sun was not even up yet as I pushed my bicycle up the hill. Aunt Kate would be down the stairs by now, lighting the fire and fretting aloud about something. Soon Ma would come down and Aunt Kate would look at her to gauge her mood. The swings seemed to happen more often lately. One look at her face would warn you what was to come.

I smiled when I thought of Grainne. It wouldn't take long for her to realize Ma was a bit of a mental case. That would take the know-it-all look off her face in a hurry. Serve her right, I thought. What made her think she could just waltz into my house and take over the place? The jealousy reared up again inside me. I didn't under-stand at all where it came from, but it was clearly there. All I could do was keep my distance from the girl until I could get away. Some distance, I thought, when you were stuck in the same bed.

I settled down on the grass and leaned against a bench and watched the sun rise. I lit a cigarette and inhaled deeply and thought over the events of the day before. I thanked God I had not told anybody else my plans. I imagined the ridicule I would have suffered at the mill. From now on, I thought, I will tell nobody anything, not even Gavin O'Rourke. Gavin! What would he have thought if he'd found out I'd gone away to England with-out even telling him—without even saying good-bye? I shrugged. What business was it of his anyway? But I knew better. Gavin and I had shared everything since we were children. Not only would I have hurt him by going away without a word but, I realized, maybe for the first time, that it was important to me to share my plans with someone. If I had nobody to tell, what good was any of it? If you had nobody to witness your life, then it would be an empty thing indeed.

Thinking of Gavin made me miss his company. I had not seen him since we'd argued on the boat to Omeath the night of the air-raid warnings. I didn't know if he was out to sea or in port but

I decided I would go down to the harbor anyway on the off chance he was there. I stubbed out my cigarette and picked up my bicycle.

It was an hour later when I reached Newry I could have taken the tram but I welcomed the physical exertion of riding my bicycle. As I rode, my head cleared and my mood lifted. The dock was busy, especially for a Sunday. I reminded myself this was wartime. Cargo sat on the dock waiting for transport across the Irish Sea or through the North Channel. Merchant boats, like Gavin's, had become a lifeline for transporting goods, livestock, and munitions back and forth. Linen and cotton material for tents and uniforms sat alongside wheat, potatoes, corn, butter, eggs, milk, and tea. Many of the boats left full to the gills and came back empty. The biggest need was to supply the troops abroad. Sometimes the dock would be filled with cattle and other livestock bound for England. The only cargo that seemed to come back to Ireland on a regular basis was coal. Well, we'll keep our arses warm anyhow, I thought, no matter that everything else we grow and make is shipped elsewhere.

The *Ashgrove* was in port and I looked eagerly for some sign of Gavin. I wondered if maybe he was away to Mass with his ma. But then I saw him. He was bent over the side of the boat hammering a nail into a loose plank. His shirtsleeves were rolled up and the muscles of his arms stretched and relaxed as he swung a hammer to drive in the nail. I stood watching him, smiling at the familiarity of his movements. He had the sinewy strength of a sailor, vital and forceful. When he had finished hammering, he bent and picked up a cloth and poured some liquid from a bottle onto it. I guessed it was linseed oil. Gently he rubbed the damp cloth over the teakwood in a slow, steady motion. He appeared lost in thought. Maybe he was remembering his da. He had loved his da, and he loved this boat.

He must have felt me watching him. He looked up, the breeze ruffling his chestnut hair, and grinned. He raised a tanned arm in greeting.

"Hello, there. Come on down."

He was happy to see me—the previous argument on the boat

to Omeath already forgotten. I dropped my bicycle and ran forward. He leaned over and helped me aboard. I stood and looked
all around me. As always, I was reminded of my times with Da
down here when I was a little girl. The sounds of the water lapping against the hull, the slap of the fags as the wind whipped
them, and the cry of the seagulls were familiar and comforting.
Even the blare of horns, hum of engines, and thud and scraping of
cargo crates were pleasant to me. I inhaled the sharp, salty air and
smiled as I cradled old memories.

"What's the *craic*?" Gavin uttered his usual greeting. "Why
aren't you at Mass?"

"Why aren't you?"

"Ah, sure I'm doing God's work right here, taking care of my
da's boat."

"It's your boat too," I said.

"What brings you over here at this hour of the morning?"

I shrugged. "I was out for a ride, and I just took a notion," I said.

He looked at me, his eyes alight. "It's never that simple with
you, Sheila. Tell me what's going on."

"Give us a fag first."

He disappeared down into the belly of the boat. I sat down
on a wooden bench on the deck and inhaled the smells—fish,
salt, gasoline, oil. Most girls would have wrinkled their noses and
complained, but I drew energy from this place. Gavin came back
with two tumblers of lemonade and a packet of cigarettes. We sat
side by side in silence, sipping our drinks and smoking, and looking out at the horizon.

"Me ma and Kate took in an evacuee," I began, "a right wee git
from Belfast."

"And?"

"And I got so mad I packed my bags and ran out of the house. I
had my ticket for the train and everything."

It sounded stupid as I said it.

"You ran because of an evacuee? Because of a child?"

"I know I sound like an eejit," I admitted, "but I couldn't help
myself."

Gavin said nothing. He took a long pull on his cigarette, stretched out his legs, and stared out into the distance. Annoyance began to fill me. Why should I have to explain this to him? I ignored the voice that told me I needed to explain it to myself.

"Anyway, I found out now you have to have special permission to leave the country, and so I had to give up and come home. Bloody war. Bloody nuisance."

Gavin shook his head. "You don't give up, do you, Sheila? Haven't I told you a hundred times you're better off here."

"You could save your breath, Gavin. I'm still going one of these days. Maybe I'll have to wait for the war to be over—but I'll get away eventually."

Gavin turned and looked at me. He was smiling.

"You're a stubborn wee lass, aren't you?"

"No more stubborn than you," I said.

An odd feeling came over me. There was something in Gavin's voice and the way he looked at me that was unsettling, but pleasant. I was tempted to move closer to him, but I stopped myself. Instead, he moved closer to me, and put his arm around my shoulder. I could smell the faint scent of linseed oil. Slowly he reached over with his other arm and turned me towards him.

"I'm glad you didn't go, Sheila," he said. "I'd miss you something desperate if you left."

I wanted to make a smart remark, but I was at a loss for words. Something new and strange was happening. Gavin gazed at me in a way he had never done before. It was as if some invisible curtain that had always been between us had been ripped back and we were seeing each other for the first time. I held my breath. He leaned forward and put his lips on mine, softly at first, gently tasting them, and then more insistently. His breath came in ragged bursts and I felt his heart thudding against my chest. As he pressed closer into me, I reached up and wound my arms around his neck and returned his kiss. All restraint left me as I surrendered myself along with Gavin to this wild thing that gripped us. We stayed locked together until we went limp with exhaustion.

I pulled away first and sucked in air as if I'd been drowning. It took me a while to get my breath. I tried to calm the trembling that had taken hold of me. Slowly Gavin let his arms drop and he reached in his pocket for his cigarettes. I waited for him to say he was sorry, that he didn't know what had come over him, that it wouldn't happen again. But he said nothing. He simply lit two cigarettes and handed one to me. But he never took his eyes off me.

Thought and reason roared back into my brain. I jumped up.

"I have to be going," I said.

"Why?"

"I don't know why," I said. I was too flustered to explain anything. "I just have to."

He stood up then and took my arm and helped me down off the boat. As I stepped down he leaned over and whispered in my ear.

"I'm not sorry I did that, Sheila."

I didn't answer him. Without looking back I rushed across the dock and picked up my bicycle and threw my leg over it. I pedaled away, my back upright and stiff as if in defense against his stare that I knew followed me. I didn't let a thought enter my mind until I was well outside of Newry and on my way up to Queensbrook. Then I opened up my head and the thoughts swamped me, threatening to leave me dizzy. How could this have happened? It was not supposed to be this way between Gavin and me. This was not part of my plan.

Later that night as I lay awake listening to Grainne's ragged breathing, I admitted to myself that kissing Gavin had been like nothing I'd experienced before. For all the lads I'd kissed, I'd never had this feeling of . . . I couldn't even put my finger on it. All I knew was it had been intoxicating and frightening. I tried to put the memory out of my mind. I had no space for it. I was never going to marry Gavin. Why would I trap myself like that—sitting home waiting for him for weeks while he was away on a voyage? Look at what it had done to Ma. I would only be swapping one prison for another. I made up my mind. I would steer clear of Gavin O'Rourke from now on. I would keep to my plan of escape. I would let nothing stand in the way.

Chapter 7

❧

By the spring of 1942 I was beginning to learn that even unpleasant things can become comfortable. They can curl around you if you aren't watching and lull you into a state that paralyzes hope. In my case, the day I had let the Belfast train go without me I had voluntarily chosen to return to this limbo, knowing its dangers. And now I was becoming as comfortable with my life here as everyone else. I had come to believe that nothing much would change until the war was over. But I was wrong.

It was just after Easter, and the anniversary of the day Belfast was first bombed. I sat with Patsy and Kathleen and some of the other girls along the mill wall eating our midday sandwiches and enjoying the mild weather. A few mill lads lounged on the grass near us, nudging one another and making stupid jokes at our expense. They would do anything for attention. I was in the middle of a story about something that had happened over the weekend when we heard screams. We all turned and stared down the road past the tram depot. Mary McAteer and her friend Rose Boyle were flying up the road, bosoms and hips jiggling to beat the band. Rose was as stout as Mary and they palled around together.

"What's got into them two eejits?" said Patsy.

"Maybe a bull got out of the field and is chasing them." Kathleen laughed.

"Well, we know it's not fellas after them," Patsy said, grinning.

A distant rumbling sounded behind the girls. We stood up and shaded our eyes. "Maybe it's the Jerries," I said.

Kathleen's jaw dropped. "Och, don't be saying that, Sheila," she cried.

We waited. Then they came into sight. A convoy of lorries led by two uniformed men on motorcycles. We couldn't believe our eyes.

"Och, sweet Jesus," cried Patsy. "It's the Yanks."

We had heard rumors for weeks that American soldiers would soon be coming to the North and would be billeted here. Something had been said about Northern Ireland being a good place to assemble troops who would be flying sorties to Europe. And, since the Free State was neutral, people said, England was afraid the Jerries might sneak over the border from the South and bomb England from here. There were already soldiers stationed nearby, English and Welsh, but we didn't know whether to believe that the Yanks would actually come as well. Now, as we craned our necks we saw squadrons of men in khaki uniforms sitting in the open lorries. There was no mistaking them. They were indeed the Yanks. We dropped our sandwiches, scattering crumbs everywhere, and ran out into the middle of the road. I tore off my apron and threw it behind me on the ground and unwound my turban and shook out my hair. We jumped up and down waving and yelling like schoolgirls. I felt a rush of energy of a kind I had not felt in years. The sun was warm on my face and bare arms. I felt my hair fluttering around my shoulders and my heart began to race. As the lorries drew closer and the soldiers saw us they stood up and hung over the sides waving, shouting, and whistling at us. The convoy slowed down to a crawl. We squealed and waved back. The American soldiers were like no men we had ever seen. They were tall and suntanned and handsome. Their uniforms were immaculately clean and well pressed. Their hair was cut short under their jaunty caps and their teeth were shining white. It was as if they had stepped down off the screen right out of an American film and to a group of mill girls who had never seen anybody like them, they were gods.

Mary McAteer and Rose Boyle arrived beside us, sweating and out of breath. "Aren't they gorgeous?" crowed Mary, waving her fat arm in front of my face.

The first two lorries passed on down the road and we turned around to wave after them. Then we heard the rumble of another lorry and we turned back to look. There were more of them coming. But then we grew silent and our mouths fell open. The lorry was filled with soldiers also, but these boys were different.

"Och will you look at the wee darkie lads," screamed Patsy. "Aren't they beautiful? Did you ever see the likes of them?"

Indeed, none of us had ever seen the likes of them. They were as black as the pictures of the African babies the missionary priests always passed around.

"Are they from Africa?" asked Kathleen.

"Sure they're in American uniforms," I said. "They must be Yanks."

When we recovered from the shock, we began to wave and shout as madly as we had done before. The black soldiers were not as noisy as the white ones who had gone ahead. They smiled and nudged one another, and one or two waved at us. But they seemed shy. We waved and shouted anyway until they were out of sight.

After they had all gone, we stood in silence for a long while staring down the empty road. I think we might all have been wondering if it had been a dream. The screech of the mill whistle brought us back to reality. We slowly picked up the remains of our sandwiches and walked back up to the spinning factory. I wrapped my scarf back into a turban around my head, shoving my hair up under it, and I picked up the heavy black apron. I looked over at the mill lads. They were not grinning anymore. They hung their heads as they plodded back towards the mill. One of them picked up a stone and threw it in the river.

"Well, that's us done for now," he said. "They'll have eyes for nobody but the bloody Yanks."

Word of the arrival of the Yanks spread like wildfire. There was little work done at the mill the rest of that afternoon. The machine operators left the fax threads spinning in the air as they stopped to gossip. Patsy was in her element telling and retelling the story of the convoy of lorries that had passed up the mill road. Of course she exaggerated everything—how well the soldiers looked, what they said, how they greeted us. The girls who had not been there listened with mouths wide open. This was the biggest thing that had happened in Queensbrook in as long as any of us could remember.

As the closing whistle blared and we all rushed down the stairs from the spinning room and out into the cool, fresh air, our giddiness only grew. Where would the Yanks be staying? Would they be walking around town of an evening? Would they go to the pubs and the dances in Newry and Warrenpoint? Would they be allowed to go out with the local girls? The *craic* was ninety as we all talked and laughed at once. Ma came running out of the weaving shed and caught up with me.

"Sheila, love," she crowed, "wait for me. Did you hear the news? The Yanks have come and I hear they're lovely!"

I sighed. I should have known this would be right up Ma's alley. She might decide to go out on the hunt now along with girls half her age. It was bloody embarrassing, so it was. I would be scandalized.

"Och, they'll have money to spend," she went on, "and I hear they can get anything you want—nylons, cigarettes, even chocolate." She giggled. "As long as you're nice to them of course."

I rolled my eyes and made up my mind to avoid Ma as much as I could. If she wanted to go out and disgrace herself with her own cronies, let her, but I wouldn't be anywhere near her. For God's sake, would she ever realize that she was an oul' woman who should be well past such carry-on? It was the turn of the young ones like myself to have a bit of fun. I shrugged. Well, it didn't matter anyway—sure there'd be very few of the Yanks would even give her the time of day.

It was only a few days later, on a Friday, that I was called into

Mr. Carlson's office. I swore under my breath, but I was shaking with fear all the same. I'd never spoken to the mill owner since the night he put the Linen Queen crown on my head over a year before. What was wrong? There had been no competition held in 1942 on account of the war, and so I had remained Linen Queen. Was he going to take away my title? Had he heard a bad report about me? What would I do if he was going to sack me? I tried to control my shaking as I knocked on the door of his office. A woman's voice called for me to come in—his secretary, Miss Johnson, an elderly woman who never smiled. Mary McAteer's sly eyes followed me as I passed her desk.

"Mr. Carlson will be right with you, Miss McGee," Miss Johnson said, and went back to sorting through papers on her desk.

I sat down in a stiff chair and waited for what seemed like a dog's age. Eventually a buzzer sounded on Miss Johnson's desk and I jumped.

"He will see you now," she said, nodding towards a heavy oak door that led to an inner office.

My throat was dry as I pushed open the door and walked in. Mr. Carlson sat behind his desk. Again I was struck with the stacks of papers and boxes and ornaments of every sort that filled his office. It looked like a secondhand shop. And it was dusty too. I fought back a sneeze.

Mr. Carlson peered at me with pale eyes the color of dishwater.

"Sit down," he said. "You know by now of course that the American soldiers have arrived in Queensbrook."

My mouth fell open in surprise. This was the last thing I had expected him to say. I nodded and said nothing.

"We in Queensbrook want to do all we can to make them feel welcome. After all they are here for our protection." He paused but obviously was not looking for any comments from me. "To that end, I am hosting a dinner and reception—for the officers and other dignitaries—tomorrow evening at Temperance Hall."

I wondered briefly how the Yanks would enjoy a teetotaling dinner.

"And," Carlson continued, "it has been suggested to me that we should have the Linen Queen attend and make a presentation to them—some small token of our appreciation. I'm thinking of a set of our finest linen products for the commanding officer." He paused. "I have arranged for Mrs. McAteer to polish up the tiara and bring it over to the hall tomorrow evening and to assist you in looking your best for the occasion."

An image came into my mind of Hannah McAteer polishing away on the tiara, her teeth gritted, and I almost laughed aloud. Ah, that would be something to see all right.

Carlson stood up and signaled that I was dismissed. "Come at six o'clock sharp, Miss McGee, so that you can rehearse what you have to do. And remember, you will be representing not only Queensbrook, but all the linen mills in our province. It is an honor very few girls of your...er...very few mill workers would ever experience in their lifetimes. I hope you will take seriously its significance."

"Yes, sir," I said, and nodded. "Thank you, sir."

I made my way out of his office and past Miss Johnson and Mary McAteer and out into the corridor. I didn't realize until then that I had been holding my breath the whole time. I let it out now. I was so excited that my heart thudded to beat the band. Of course I had caught his remark about being a poor mill worker, but I let it go. I wouldn't be one for long. Maybe this was the chance I'd been waiting for. I was being asked to show myself off to the Yanks—to the top officers mind you, not the rank-and-file soldiers. A smile spread across my face and stayed there for the rest of the day.

ഇൻ

The next evening I marched through the front door of the Temperance Hall. The hall was empty and hushed. A long head table ran across the far end of the room, and a number of round tables had been arranged throughout the hall. The tables were covered with stiff white linen cloths, and fine china and crystal glinted in the evening light. I took a deep breath and felt myself swell with excitement.

"There you are!" Mrs. McAteer's sharp voice cut the silence. "You were supposed to come in the side door, you know." She sniffed loudly, and her lips drew into a thin line of disapproval. "Well, as long as you are here let me go through the procedure with you. You are to wait until the cue from Mr. Carlson, which will occur at the end of the speeches. Then you will walk, slowly and in a ladylike manner, from the door of the anteroom over there and pause in front of Mr. Carlson and the army commander."

"What's his name?" I interrupted.

"What? Who?"

"The commander."

"Turner," she said, "but that's none of your business, miss." Her face had flushed an odd purple color. "As I said, at Mr. Carlson's cue you are to walk towards the head table and pause. Then, when General Turner stands up you are to hand him the package of linens."

"Do I curtsy?" I asked just to annoy her, but she took me seriously.

"That will not be necessary, Miss McGee. You are to present the general with the package, smile, and turn and leave. You will not linger. And under no circumstances will you make eye contact with anyone at the head table or with any of the guests. Is that clear?"

I shrugged.

"Do I make myself clear, Miss McGee?"

Mrs. McAteer's face was so comical I almost burst out laughing. If she could only see herself—she looked like an angry turkey. She must have been livid that it was me who was getting this chance and not her daughter, Mary. I followed her into the small room off the hall where we had all got ourselves ready the night of the Linen Queen competition. It was hard to believe it had been over a year ago. I had brought the same blue frock that I had worn that night and at every Linen Queen event since. Mrs. McAteer sniffed as she eyed it up and down.

"I thought you might have worn something new. That dress appears to have seen better days."

"It's the only one I have," I said.

"Oh, and those shoes!" she exclaimed. "They're not suitable at all."

"What's wrong with them?" I said, looking down at my high-heeled, open-toed sandals. "Should I have worn my oul' boots?"

She ignored me, but I could tell by the way she dug the clips into my head to secure the tiara that she was very put out. When she was finished, she told me to sit down and wait. It was going to be a long night. I could hear voices as people began to fill the hall. I was dying to put my head round the door to see what was happening, but Mrs. McAteer stood like an army sergeant beside me and I dared not move. My chance came eventually when she was distracted with the arrival of a teacher from the local school along with a number of young boys and girls who were to sing and dance for the guests. I slid off my chair and opened up the connecting door just a crack. Mr. Carlson sat at the center of the long table at the head of the room. To his left sat the mayor of Newry with his big gold chain draped around his neck. To Mr. Carlson's right sat a good-looking, stiff-backed man in a uniform. I supposed this was General Turner.

"Miss McGee?" Mrs. McAteer's sharp voice startled me and I moved back to my chair.

In between the noise of the children in the back room, I overheard pieces of the goings-on in the main hall. Mr. Carlson made a long speech, welcoming his special guests, and then the chaplain said grace. Then came the clatter of dishes and the clink of silverware as the food was served. I realized I was starving, and the smell of roast beef made my mouth water. You'd think Carlson would have had the decency to feed us. In fact, I didn't understand why I, as Linen Queen, should not have been up there at the head table chatting with the general.

Eventually the dishes were cleared, and Mr. Carlson began to speak again. Something about thanking the troops and hoping they would enjoy Irish hospitality. Well, they wouldn't be enjoying much of it tonight, I thought, with not a drop of drink in sight.

"A hospitality committee has been formed," Mr. Carlson went

on, and I pricked up my ears. "My sister, Mrs. McAteer, will head the committee of worthy local women to arrange entertainments for your men—introduce them to suitable young ladies of good backgrounds." A cheer went up from the guests. I winced. I knew the word "suitable" would never be applied to me.

The youngsters fled out behind their teacher into the hall. The lilt of tin whistles filled the air as the wee boys played. I imagined their faces solemn in concentration and I smiled. When they stopped, accordion music sounded along with a fiddle, and I could hear the beat of the children's feet on the wooden floor as they performed some traditional dances. The performance was greeted by wild cheers and applause from the guests. I smiled. These Yanks were an outgoing lot, a far cry from stuffy old Mr. Carlson and his cronies.

"Get ready," Mrs. McAteer said from beside me. "Your cue is coming up."

I stood.

"Northern Irish linens are the best in the world and the pride of our province," I heard Carlson say. "Our very own Linen Queen, Miss Sheila McGee, will make the presentation."

Mrs. McAteer attempted to shove me out the door, but I turned and glared at her. Something strange had taken possession of me.

"I heard the cue!" I said.

Then I fixed a broad smile on my face and sailed into the main hall like the queen of Sheba. Ignoring everything Mrs. McAteer had told me, I turned and waved to all of the guests. The men cheered in response. When I reached the head table I looked General Turner straight in the eyes and gave him a flirtatious little curtsy. As I presented the package of linens to him, I spoke out as loudly as I could to make sure the entire hall could hear me.

"You are all very welcome here, sir. And you needn't worry about your soldiers. All of the girls here are just dying to entertain them."

I gave him a dazzling smile, and General Turner grinned back at me.

"Thank you, Miss McGee. I'm sure my men will appreciate it."

I gave him the package and turned towards the guests. Many of the men were on their feet whistling and cheering and applauding. I didn't even look at Mr. Carlson or the mayor as I made my way back, but I knew they were seething.

Mrs. McAteer reached out through the door and grabbed my wrist and pulled me into the anteroom. Furiously, she snatched the tiara from my head, tearing out strands of my hair as she did.

"You've cooked your goose now, my girl," she said.

I turned around and smiled at her. "Oh, I don't think so, Mrs. McAteer," I said sweetly. "I think General Turner was very pleased with me."

Chapter 8

❧

After my Saturday night at the Temperance Hall, I went back to the mill with a new spring in my step and a new bold attitude.

"I met General Turner," I said casually. "He's the boyo in charge of the whole lot of them, you know. Lovely man. There were only officers there, of course, no enlisted men." I said these things in order to rub it in. I loved making the other girls jealous. "I'm sure I'll be invited to more events, what with me being the Linen Queen and all."

"Me ma says you disgraced yourself," said Mary McAteer. "She says you carried on like a real tart, waving and smiling and offering to entertain the troops. Me ma says everybody there was scandalized."

I didn't care what Mary or her busybody of a ma thought. In fact, the hint of scandal pleased me. Anyway, she was just jealous. Who wanted the Linen Queen runner-up at their events when they could have the real McCoy?

❧

After the arrival of the American soldiers I was not the only one with a new spring in my step. It was as if everyone felt more important now that the Yanks had come to our wee part of the world. Some people threw themselves headlong into the war effort—joining the auxiliary, patrolling the streets to make sure windows were blacked out and headlamps were turned off at night, piling sandbags on rooftops in case of fires, and all the rest of it. Now that the Yanks were here, I swear these bloody volunteers puffed their chests out even more—they thought they were part and parcel of the army itself. They were comical to look at. But I didn't complain. It had put a smile on everybody where there had been only long oul' faces before.

Army camps were set up around the area. Big estates like Narrow Water Castle near Warrenpoint were taken over. Officers were accommodated in the main house, while enlisted men were given quarters in outlying buildings on the estate or were housed in small huts erected for that purpose. The troops were seen doing training exercises up on the Flagstaff or on nearby Slieve Gullion. The local streets were filled with soldiers, adding an air of festivity and adventure. Some went to Mass, and attendance by the local people went up accordingly. Others went to Protestant churches. Many of them seemed very religious—but they were hooligans when they drank. They were young—many of them the same age as myself and, like me, out for a good time. Two girls couldn't walk down the street without catcalls and whistles. We loved every minute of it.

The mill boys turned into sulky wee brats. They complained that they wouldn't stand a chance with the girls now that the Yanks had come to town. And they were right. Within a week, American soldiers started showing up at pubs around Newry. They threw money around like water, buying drinks for all and sundry. Of course the girls wouldn't give the locals the time of day. I was right there with them, making a beeline to wherever I heard the Yanks had been seen.

I had decided now that I was going to concentrate on getting to know officers. An ordinary enlisted soldier was hardly worth my time. The officers had more money and clout, and who knew, there might be a lovely single chap looking for an Irish bride to bring back home and set her up in style. There might be some fine pickings among the Yanks. For the first time I was glad I had not been able to run away to England.

I was very popular with the newcomers. I flirted to beat the band and soon I had half the regiment in love with me. At first, Ma was after me about being out every night in the week. She had fallen back into one of her down moods since the soldiers first arrived and now she sat home nights sulking and waiting for me to walk in the door. No matter her disapproval, she made a grab for anything I brought home—cigarettes and silk stockings. Then she asked could I not get butter or tea, sometime, or even chocolate. I shrugged and gave her what she wanted, hoping it would keep her quiet. There was always more where that came from.

ॐ

While I knew the local lads were wild with jealousy over my new admirers, they couldn't hold a candle to Gavin's rage. He found me one Sunday afternoon on the Flagstaff. I was sitting in my usual place, leaning against a big rock, when he appeared. Something in his face and the way he stood put me on alert. This was not going to be our usual relaxed meeting. I went on the offensive.

"What's got into you?" I asked. "You look like you lost a shilling and found a penny."

He took a long puff on his cigarette and said nothing.

"Well, I for one am having a grand time now the Yanks are here," I went on. "It took something to chase the fecking boredom out of this place—God love them."

Still Gavin said nothing.

"They go out every night of the week," I went on, ignoring him, "and they throw money around like men with no arms. Patsy and Kathleen and the rest are all in love with them. Not me, of course, I'm much more particular than they are. I wouldn't be throwing myself at just any Tom, Dick, or Harry."

"Aye, I hear you ignore the whole lot of them," he said. The sarcasm in his voice was heavy. "I suppose it's not your fault if they turn up just where you happen to be, minding your own business."

I felt a shot of anger. "I can't help it if they follow me around," I said, ignoring the fact that I'd been the one doing the following. "Anyway, what's it to you?"

He knocked the ash from his cigarette. "Nothing at all," he said, his voice defiant.

But it was clear it *was* something to him. I thought back to the way he had kissed me on the boat. I had not seen him since that afternoon, but he had entered my thoughts often enough at idle moments. I had found myself wondering what he was thinking, but then I would bat away the thought like an annoying fly. I needed to forget about the whole episode. I cursed myself for coming up here to the Flagstaff. I should have known I would run into him sooner or later. Just as he knew he would eventually find me here. No matter what else was happening in our lives, it drew us back like a magnet.

"I thought what we had that time on the boat was special," he said suddenly, turning his eyes directly on me. "I thought it might have changed things between us."

I bristled. "It was one bloody kiss," I said. "Sure I kiss a dozen chaps a week, if I kiss one!"

I said it to hurt him. And I said it to deflect my own feelings. I didn't want to be confused anymore. I had my plans made. I wasn't going to get sidetracked by Gavin or anyone else.

"Aye, including the whole American army," Gavin said, throwing down his cigarette and grinding it into the ground with his heel. "Bloody army of occupation," he said. "They've no right here on Irish soil."

"They have every right. They're here to protect us. And anyway it's my duty as Linen Queen to see they have a good time."

A dark scowl spread over Gavin's face as he bent and picked up his bicycle. "I can see there's no talking to you," he said. "I must have been astray in the head to think you might change your ways."

"You're leaving already?" I said. "You just got here."

"I've things to do," he said.

He strode off down the hill, wheeling his bicycle beside him.

I watched him go. Had that kiss really meant so much to him? Where had this sudden change come from? Gavin and I had been just like brother and sister. There'd never been anything romantic between us. I'd liked things that way. This new relationship frightened me. I leaned back and lit a cigarette. Men! You never knew where you stood with them. Bloody eejits would never come out and say what was annoying them. They'd just sulk, or throw a fit of temper, or get drunk. There was no point trying to understand what was going on in their minds. Not that I cared, anyway. Gavin O'Rourke was just like the others, I thought, lads to be used for a bit of fun when you needed them. But even as I thought it, I knew I was wrong.

ೲ

Gavin's disapproval didn't stop my gallivanting one bit. I was the most popular girl at the Castle ballroom in Warrenpoint and the toast of every soldier in Newry. But the only Yanks I was meeting were enlisted men. I needed to go where the officers went for entertainment. Of course, they had the officers' clubs on the bases, but you had to have a pass to get in. I needed to meet them on neutral ground.

I was glad for once that Mary McAteer had such a big mouth on her. One Friday afternoon she couldn't help boasting to anyone who would listen that her ma had organized a special dance for the officers at a private club on Canal Street in Newry. I stopped what I was doing and listened.

"Of course, the committee has only selected special girls to be invited," she said. "You know they don't want riffraff there. Just girls from good families. Only the likes of Doherty the draper's two daughters and the mayor's daughter are invited. Of course I'm going on account of Ma heading up the committee."

I could have slapped the self-satisfied smile off her face. Well, we'd see about that, I thought. After all I was the Linen Queen. If anyone should be invited it should be me.

Chapter 9

ை

The Canal Club was housed in a stately old building on Canal Street, which ran alongside Newry Canal. I had passed by the building often enough in the past but it may as well have been invisible. Places like that were never part of my life nor ever likely to be. Only the well-off went there, the toffs with money and connections. Nobody the likes of me would ever have call to set foot inside.

But on this Saturday night I walked towards the Canal Club with my head held high. I tried to ignore the fact that I was freezing in my flimsy dress and thin coat, my bare legs and peep-toe shoes. I passed by the dock at the Albert Basin and looked over out of habit to see if Gavin's boat was in port. There was no sign of it. Canal Street bustled with people—late-night shoppers, early revelers, sailors going home with their kit bags over their shoulders. It was an ordinary Saturday night, and then again it was not. I had made up my mind to go to the affair even though I had not been officially invited. They'd have to let me in, I thought. What else could they do?

I opened the front door that led into the hallway. The breeze from outside blew in with me, fluttering the edges of a white cloth on the reception table and causing the women sitting behind it to let out little shivery cries. I hesitated for a moment, taking in everything around me. The hallway was filled with young women in colorful silk and taffeta dresses and fashionable coats, older women in hats and stoles, and men in smart army uniforms. I didn't know a soul. A set of stairs with a brass hand-rail ascended from the hallway to an upper floor. From upstairs I could hear music—a piano and a horn, slow and restrained, along with the clink of glasses, and laughter. In the hallway, male American voices mixed with the lilt of female Irish brogues above the rustle of dresses as the women gave their coats over to the cloakroom attendant at a small window. The smell of roast beef cooking in a back kitchen blended with the fragrances of perfume and cologne. When the front door was opened I caught the occa-sional whiff of the brackish canal water across the road. The air was stifling, and I began to sweat. I removed my coat and took a deep breath and pushed my way over to the reception table.

"Name?" said a bony woman with a long jaw, eyeing me up and down.

"Sheila McGee," I said firmly. "I expect Mrs. McAteer has me on the list. I am the reigning Linen Queen."

I thought I heard some giggles behind me as I spoke, but I did not look around.

The bony woman frowned. "I don't see a badge for you."

Her long fingers crawled over the white printed badges to which pink ribbons were attached. "I shall have to find Mrs. McAteer. Wait here!"

I waited. Another woman at the table smiled at two newcom-ers—well-dressed girls with wee cloche hats and coats with fur collars.

"Well hello, Clara, hello, Evelyn, how well youse are looking."

I looked sideways at the two of them and they looked back at me. They were no oil paintings, I thought, neither one of them. Oh aye, the clothes cost a fortune but you can't make a silk purse out of a sow's ear. I shrugged. As they took off their coats and hung the badges on the pink ribbons around their necks I was aware of their eyes on me. Let them look, I thought, and tossed my hair back off my shoulders. Another pair of girls joined them, and soon I was aware again of giggles and hushed whispers. I knew they were talking about me. I looked down at my frock. I had bought it with the money I'd set aside in the mill savings club. I was tired of Kathleen's blue frock, which, as Mrs. McAteer had pointed out, had seen better days. This frock was made of a thin cream muslin material, and while it was a bit skimpy on me, I thought it showed off my figure well enough. I was a bit embarrassed about my bare legs, but Ma had stolen my last pair of nylons.

"Phew, and the perfume." One of them sniffed. "D'you think she filled up a bottle from the canal?"

Before I could do or say anything, Mrs. McAteer appeared beside me, her daughter, Mary, in tow. Her face was the color of an overripe beetroot.

"Well, of all the nerve!" she began.

"I told you this wasn't for the likes of you," Mary said.

A pair of soldiers walked past. One of them winked at me and doffed his hat. They exchanged grins. They must have recognized me from the presentation at the Temperance Hall. I smiled back and turned to the McAteers with renewed courage.

"I would have thought the Linen Queen would be automatically invited," I said as loudly as I could.

I was aware of a silence around me. Everyone had stopped to watch.

"You are not on the list and that's that!" Mrs. McAteer's voice was cold. "Leave now, and nothing more will be said about it."

My anger fared. "I won't leave," I shouted. "I have as much right here as any of these ones." I looked around the foyer. "I'm the Linen Queen. I represent all the mill workers in the North of Ireland."

Giggles and sighs ran through the watching crowd. An elderly usher in a ridiculous red and gold uniform pushed his way towards me and grabbed me by the arm.

"C'mon now, miss," he said. "No need to be making a scene in front of these fine people. Plenty of other places you can go. You don't want to stay where you're not welcome."

I tried to free myself from his grip, but he took me firmly by the elbow and turned me around and guided me towards the door. Just then a tall, dark-haired officer came towards us. I had not noticed him earlier, but he must have been watching the proceedings with the rest of the crowd.

"Let me handle this," he said firmly to the usher, and the old man dropped my arm as if it were on fire.

The stranger guided me back towards the reception table, where he bowed slightly and smiled around at the women. The two receptionists and the McAteers stared at him, but said nothing.

"This is Miss Sheila McGee, your Linen Queen," he began, turning his attention to the bony woman at the table. "She made a lovely presentation some weeks ago to General Turner at a dinner in Queensbrook. I am delighted to be her escort this evening. I doubt that she needs a name tag, but perhaps you should make one up anyway. I'm sure it was just an oversight."

His voice was soft and firm. The bony woman stared at him as if frozen, and then she grabbed a badge and quickly scrawled my name on it, her fingers shaking as she did so. She attached the badge to a pink ribbon and thrust it at me without a word.

"Thank you, ma'am," said the stranger. "Now, Sheila, let's check your coat and go upstairs."

I was in a trance as I allowed him to steer me towards the cloakroom window. The onlookers parted so that we could move through. Then, his hand still on my elbow, he led me to the staircase with the brass banister. As we climbed, the sound of the music grew louder. When I recovered myself I could not resist turning around and smiling down at the crowd as they stood gawking after us.

When the shock wore off I took a good look at the chap who now waltzed me around the dance floor. He was tall and slender with black hair and brown eyes darker than any I had ever seen. His skin was the color of polished teak—a color that reminded me of the wood on Gavin's boat. He was not as dark as the wee darkie soldiers we'd seen the day all the Yanks had arrived, but he was much darker than the local boys. I wondered if he might be Italian or Greek, maybe. He had a long thin face, a long nose and a wide mouth that stretched into a shy smile when he looked down at me. His smile was beautiful, I thought. It was the nicest thing about him.

"Thanks for the rescue," I said at last. "Not that I needed it. D'you think I would have let them throw me out on the street? I'm a match for them oul' biddies, so I am."

He smiled again and gave no hint that he saw through my false courage.

"I was glad to help."

"Aye, well thanks anyway."

He seemed not to notice the stares of the other dancers. I held my head up high as the same girls who had ridiculed me down in the hallway waltzed by. I wasn't going to let them see how their words had been like a knife through me. I was dancing with a good-looking officer—a captain, so his name tag said—so bad cess to all of them.

"How did you know my name?" I said.

"As I said, I remembered you from the officers' reception in Queensbrook." He smiled broadly and his brown eyes creased up in merriment. "You're not easy to forget, Miss McGee."

I flushed slightly. "Aye, I suppose not," I said, remembering how I'd turned and flirted with the soldiers after I'd made the presentation to General Turner.

The music stopped and we separated and stood looking at each other. A sudden panic rose in me. What now? Had he done his duty by me? Would he leave me now to fend for myself? Were there other girls who had taken his eye?

"Forgive me," he said as he took me by the elbow and led me towards the refreshment table. "I haven't even introduced myself. My name is Joel Solomon."

"Like the wise man?" I said without thinking. "You know, the king who threatened to cut the baby in two."

He sighed. "The same name, yes. But the wisdom? Well, that's another matter. Would you like a lemonade?"

I would have preferred a whiskey or a shandy just then, but I decided to be on my best behavior. I nodded and took the glass from him. He led the way to the far side of the room, where there was a leather sofa. I noticed he walked with a slight stoop but he was graceful all the same. I was careful to sit a respectable distance away from him on the sofa and arranged my skirt just so, trying to look as much like a lady as I could. We were silent as we watched the other dancers.

Slowly, I felt myself relax. I felt comfortable beside this man. I looked around the room. I had never set foot in a private club before. I took in as many details as I could so I could describe it later to Ma, provided she was in one of her good moods. The walls were paneled in dark wood and covered in gilt-framed mirrors and prints of red-coated men on fox hunts. The sofas were brown leather and the end tables a dark mahogany. Heavy table lamps cast a gold light on the room. A few green leather armchairs that had seen better days were placed here and there. All the furniture had been pushed back to allow for the dancing. The band was a quartet with a piano, bass, trumpet, and drums. They were all right, but no match for the bands that came to the Castle ballroom. So this was how the rich lived? To be honest, I wasn't impressed. It all looked a bit shabby and through-other to me. Give me the Castle anytime, in all its gaudiness.

"I suppose you must be used to these kinds of places," I said to Joel Solomon. "Is this what it's like in America?"

He threw his head back and laughed aloud. People turned to look at him.

"Well, some places in America are like this I suppose," he said, "but they're not places where the Solomons would be welcome."

"Why not?"

He stopped laughing and looked at me. "Because we're Jews."

I'd never met a Jew before. I wondered if he would think I was very ignorant if I told him that.

"What's that got to do with it?" I said.

"There are many places Jews aren't welcome," he said.

I shrugged and looked around. "You don't have to be a Jew not to be welcome in places," I said.

We settled into silence again. My earlier fears about his leaving me alone disappeared. He seemed perfectly content to sit with me just watching everything and not having to say much. And for the first time in as long as I could remember, I didn't feel any need to chatter away and try to impress him. I didn't even flirt with him. Not that he wasn't attractive—he was a very good-looking man. In an odd way it reminded me of the way things were with Gavin. Although even so Gavin and I seemed to spend a good deal of our time fighting with each other. I couldn't imagine fighting with this man. Odd, I thought, that I was so convinced I knew so much about him, when I hardly knew him at all.

We danced the next few dances, and at ten o'clock sharp, the lights dimmed and the band struck up with "God Save the King" to signal that the evening was over. I felt a brief stab of defiance. Why should I stand up for the king of England—what had he ever done for the likes of me? And I had a strong sense of not belonging with these women who stood proudly with their hands over their hearts. It was funny, I thought, because I stood up for the same anthem at the Castle without a second thought. It meant nothing to most of us there, but here was a different story—here it seemed like an alien thing to me. But Joel had stood up and so I stood along with him. I had caused enough scenes for one night. When the music finished Joel led me down the stairs and waited while I fetched my coat.

"It's still early," I said to him, as we strolled along Canal Street. "Mrs. McAteer and her cronies are devils for following the closing-time rules. There's plenty of places still open."

He shook his head. "Thanks for the invitation, but I think I'd rather take a walk before I head back to the barracks. You're welcome to join me."

For once, I was not the self-centered Sheila I usually was. I threw no tantrum to get my own way, nor did I attempt to flirt with promises of a good time if he took me where I wanted to go. I realized the man wanted to be alone. There was something in his face told me so. And after all, I thought, he had done more than enough for me tonight.

"No." I smiled. "Just dancing in these shoes is torture enough. I've no need for a long walk on top of it."

I put out my hand to shake his. He took it and held it briefly.

"Will you be safe going home alone?"

I laughed. "Aye," I said. "I'm an old hand at wandering the streets at night. Didn't you hear what the oul' biddies were saying about me?"

"I'm sure they didn't mean it."

"Oh yes, they did. And worse. Anyway, it was lovely meeting you. I hope to see you again."

He gave a slight bow, shyness spreading across his face.

"I hope so, Miss McGee."

"For God's sake, will you call me Sheila," I said, dropping my hand and shoving it in my pocket.

"Sheila, then. Good night."

"Good night."

I turned and walked away as if I had pressing business to attend to. The truth was I didn't know where I was going. Suddenly, the idea of the sweaty-palmed soldiers at the pubs held no appeal for me. There was still time to get the last train down to Warrenpoint and the Castle ballroom—it was Saturday night after all and the *craic* would be going strong. But I had no heart for it tonight either. I sighed. There was nothing for it but to take the tram home to Queensbrook and pray that Ma was already in bed. I didn't feel like putting up with her tonight, no matter what mood she was in. I understood now completely why Joel Solomon had wanted to go for a walk alone and in silence. I craved silence too.

Chapter 10

ర్యొ

B y Monday morning, Mary McAteer had filled the ears of the mill girls with details of the battle at the Canal Club and how they had tried to throw me out.

"Aye, but my Prince Charming came along just in time," I said, tossing my head, "and he was just gorgeous."

"And will you be seeing him again?" asked Patsy.

"Och aye. Any time I like. Sure he's mad for me."

But a week went by and there was no sign of Joel Solomon. I don't know where I had expected to meet him. Would he come up to the house in Queensbrook carrying a glass slipper? Not bloody likely. I was embarrassed of course and now I had opened my big mouth at the mill I had to keep coming up with excuses as to why I had not been out with him. Deep down I was also disappointed. There'd been something about him. Och well, easy come, easy go, I thought. And so I went back to my old habits of hanging around the pubs and dances with the enlisted men even though none of them interested me the way Joel Solomon had.

At home not much had changed. Ma still went in and out of her moods. Aunt Kate complained that she had heard very bad stories about me. Uncle Kevin tried to pin me in corners and paw me when he was drunk. And the girl, Grainne, was sullen as ever. We hardly spoke a word to each other. We had made our peace sharing the bed. She kept well over to her side and me to mine. But one evening I walked in on her when she was taking off her blouse in order to put on her nightdress.

"Jesus, Mary, and Joseph!"

I blurted the words out without thinking. On the girl's back was a mass of ugly red scars, some the width of her back, some running diagonally from her shoulder down to her waist.

"Mother of God," I said.

She swung around, clutching the nightdress in her hands. Her normally ruddy face was pale. She stared at me, her green eyes boring through me.

"What happened to you?" I began. "Who did that—"

"None of your bloody business," she said.

She pulled the nightdress over her head and turned off the lamp. She climbed into bed and pulled the bleached four sacks up over her head. I said nothing as I got myself ready and slipped into bed beside her. The mattress shook as her body trembled. What if she starts bawling, I thought, then what will I do? But she didn't cry. She was a stubborn wee thing. I felt a sudden rush of pity for her. Some bastard must have beaten her—or worse. Those scars could have been from burns. What bloody pervert would do that to a child?

I turned my back to her and tried to go to sleep. But instead, I lay tracing dim, moving shadows on the wall. Grainne's breathing became heavy and I knew she had fallen into a deep sleep. Best thing for her, I thought. I decided I would keep her secret. What was the point of telling anyone? The damage was done. But my resentment towards the girl eased and while I showed her no pity in the days that followed, at least I gave up glaring at her every time I saw her.

The following Sunday I went up to the Flagstaff. I had heard that the Yanks performed their drills up there and idly wondered if I might see Joel. But the place was empty and I sat down on my usual stone bench and gazed out over the river and down towards Carlingford Lough. I was glad there was no one around. I wanted to think. As I sat a late October wind came up and I shivered. I shoved my bare hands in my pockets. As usual, I was not dressed warmly enough for the weather.

After all the excitement of the arrival of the Yanks, my life was back to going nowhere. I was as bored now with the enlisted soldiers as I had been in the past with the local lads. The Yanks weren't that much different. They were all after just one thing— to find a girl who was easy, have their way, and move on to the next one without so much as a here's your hat what's your hurry. There'd been some awful stories of gangs of drunken soldiers cornering girls in alleyways and pushing themselves on them like a pack of louts. But it was never the soldier's fault. If a girl complained she was the one made out to be a tramp—she must have been asking for it, the police said. The authorities were bending over backwards to keep the Yanks happy and they weren't going to let some little nobody of a mill girl or farm girl cause a problem. It was a disgrace. And God help any girl who got in the family way. It was a rare soldier who would stand by her. I was determined it was not going to happen to me. Oh, I led them on all right, and I enjoyed a wee bit of slap and tickle as much as the next girl, but they were getting nothing else from me— condom or no condom. Aye, condoms. Sure we had never heard of the likes of them things before this. The priests would have been scandalized at the mere mention of the word. But the local authorities, nice as you like, provided the soldiers with condoms. Weren't they just encouraging them to prey on women?

I smiled to myself. I was beginning to sound like my aunt Kate.

I supposed in truth the officers would not be much better than the enlisted men if they could get away with it. But I hoped they were more respectable. They were better educated anyway. Some of the enlisted men, I learned, were just as ignorant as the local country lads. They were only just off the farms themselves and swaggered about as if they owned the world. But the officers had the education and seemed to be from a better class of people.

Mary McAteer had blathered on about the ones she had met through her mother's committee. Her mother had forbade her to mix with the enlisted men—only an officer would be acceptable,

she said. According to Mary many of them were very well off
and had joined the army to bring honor to their families, blah,
blah. I laughed—in Ireland you brought honor to the family by
becoming a priest; in America, it seemed, you went to war. Mary
had attached herself to one boyo—a short, stocky chap with a big
nose and a very loud voice. From Philadelphia, wherever in God's
name that was, and from a very good family, Mary said. I had
rolled my eyes as Mary was talking—but a wee wisp of jealousy
floated through me. I had not been back to any of their officer
receptions since the time at the Canal Club.

I straightened myself up on the bench as the wind whipped at
my hair. Out on the lough the small outline of a boat appeared.
I wondered if it was Gavin's. I hadn't seen him in a dog's age, not
since the time he had walked off disgusted with me. It worried
me to think that we might not get over this last argument as easily as before. But I shook the thought away. I wanted to believe
things could not have changed that much. Gavin was still my best
friend.

I thought back to the day I had tried to take the train to Belfast. I wondered if the two McTaggart sisters had joined up yet.
Would it have been a better choice for me than running back here
with my tail between my legs? I could still go, I supposed, but
surely there must be an easier way.

Well, if I was to find another way, I thought, it would have to
be with the help of an officer. I would have to make more of an
effort to find one. Joel Solomon would have been a fine choice
but he seemed to have disappeared off the face of the earth. I
shrugged. Sure one was as good as another. I just needed a fella
who could help me get papers to go to England—or even America. I didn't have to fall in love with the man.

☙

As the winter days grew short and the darkness drew in, my mood
darkened as well. I had just turned twenty and my life seemed to
be at a standstill. One night I pulled the Linen Queen sash out of

the drawer and rubbed my fingers along its length. How foolish I had been—thinking I was on my way to a grand adventure. Life, I had learned, had a way of crushing all your dreams and you were better off not getting too carried away with hopes. But still the sash gave me an odd comfort. Life had not denied me everything. I had been granted this one brief moment of success. Maybe God would grant me more in time.

"Is that all you got for winning the title?"

I swung around. I had not heard Grainne come into the bedroom. I stared at her. Those were the most words she had ever spoken to me.

"Well, this sash and two hundred pound that Ma's still dying to get her hands on."

Grainne sat down on the bed. She wore a jumper that I recognized as one of my castoffs and a long skirt and boots. The clothes hung on her like rags on a scarecrow. She would be a drab wee girl, I thought, if it wasn't for the bright crown of red curls and those piercing eyes. She ran a thin white finger gently up and down the sash.

"It must have been nice to win, all the same," she said. "I never won anything in my life."

I smiled. She made me feel old at twenty. "You've plenty of time yet," I said, although for the life of me I knew she'd never win a beauty competition.

She shrugged. "You're pretty," she said. "You must win a lot of things."

It was my turn to shrug. "Looks aren't everything, so I'm finding out, but you have to use what you can in this world."

Grainne grinned. I noticed how yellow and uneven her teeth were. "I bet you can get anything out of the fellas though. Me ma's the same way. She was very pretty once so I'm told—although she's getting on now."

"How old is she?" I asked, curious.

"She's almost thirty." Her wee face was solemn.

I smiled. "Aye, that's ancient all right."

I wondered what had made the girl suddenly so talkative.

Maybe I had earned her trust because I hadn't said anything more about her scars. Or maybe she was just lonely.

"Do you miss her?" I said suddenly.

She bowed her head. "Aye, sometimes."

"Have you no brothers or sisters?"

"No, just myself. And Ma says I was a mistake."

I shrugged. "I'm sure every mother thinks that at times. My own ma says it often enough to me."

I was surprised how easy it was to talk to the girl. Gone were the sour looks and the sharp tone that usually greeted me. An unfamiliar feeling had crept over me. I found myself wanting to cheer her up and make her feel safe. It was an odd turn of events, so it was. I must be going soft in my old age, I thought. Or maybe it was just curiosity. I was dying to know more about her life in Belfast.

"Does your ma work at one of the linen mills down in Belfast?"

It was an innocent enough question and I did not expect the response I got from Grainne. She threw back her head and laughed aloud. I had never heard her laugh before. But somehow, this laughter had no lightness in it at all.

"Work at the mill? Aye now, that's a good one!" she said between chuckles. "We live on Amelia Street. What d'you think she does for a living?"

I had no idea what she was talking about. "Amelia Street," she said again, "the bloody red-light district. Have you never heard of it?"

I shook my head. "You mean she's a..." I could hardly get the word out.

"A tart! A whore! On the game! Call it whatever you like."

My mouth fell open. I was not often left speechless. "But where's your da?" I finally said.

"Who's my da would be a better question. I doubt if Ma even knows. There's so many men come and go in that house. So far nobody's claimed me—probably afraid they'd have to fork over money for my keep."

Slowly a picture of Grainne's life in Belfast began to form in my mind. And I thought I'd had it bad. Now I understood the surly looks and that way she had of seeing through you. It was how she survived. And then I thought about the scars. I could hardly even bring myself to ask.

"Who beat you, love?" I said softly. "Was it your ma? Or one of the men?"

Grainne's anger rose. "If it was only one of them I'd count myself lucky. Ma wasn't bringing home any saints, I can tell you."

Another question occurred to me, but I could not bring myself to ask it. Had the men done more than beat her? I put the thought out of my mind.

"The worst time was when the fella burned me." Grainne was speaking so softly I could hardly hear her. I leaned closer, holding my breath. "His name was George. He was a big oul' fella from Liverpool. He came in on one of the boats. You'd have choked from the smell of fish on him." She paused and blinked as if blinking away a bad memory. "Anyway, when I wouldn't do what he wanted he came up from behind and threw scalding water over me. I had to be rushed to hospital. They grafted skin, but the scars will never go away."

As I looked at her I saw a frail, innocent child. Without thinking I reached out my arms and hugged her against me. She said nothing. We sat like that for a few minutes and then, as if suddenly coming to, she pulled away. The defiance was back on her face. She stood up. "It's nothing," she muttered. "It's over."

But how could it be over? The scars would be there for the rest of her life to remind her. I sat in silence for a long time after she went out of the room. I heard Ma talking to her, and Grainne answering with her usual one-word replies. As before, when I had first seen her scars, I understood that this new information was to remain a secret between us. Part of me wished she had never told me—that she had kept the horror to herself. I couldn't waste my time feeling pity for her, now could I? I had myself to be concerned about. But even as I thought this, I realized that the girl had caused something to shift deep down inside me. It was an alien feeling, and I didn't know what to make of it. I would have to shake it off as best I could.

Chapter 11

ॐ

Christmas Day 1942 was as grim as any of the previous ones at the house. Aunt Kate didn't believe in trees and festivity. She said only pagans carried on like that and good Christians should observe it as a holy day for prayer and contemplation. So after Mass we all came home, ate dinner, and sat around staring at one another. Kevin slept in the upstairs room, his snores the only sound breaking the silence.

I could stand it no more. I had to get out. The tram to Newry was not running, so I crept out of the house and jumped on my bicycle. I pedaled down to Newry and caught a train for Warrenpoint. I had a sudden overwhelming need to be near the sea.

I walked along the near-empty strand throwing pebbles into the water. There was hardly anybody about. Ahead of me an old man walked his dog. Up on the main road a bright red tinker caravan pulled by two sorry-looking horses stopped and a crowd of dark-haired children spilled out and ran onto the strand whooping and laughing. Their parents followed them, calling after them in Irish. White gulls wheeled overhead crying out and swooped down looking for crumbs. The sea was gray and restless. It reflected how I was feeling at that minute. I thrust my hands deep in the pockets of my coat, glad for once I had been smart enough to wear my old boots for warmth and comfort.

A tall, dark-haired figure walking towards me from way down the strand caught my eye. At first I thought it might be Joel Solomon. But what would he be doing out here on Christmas Day? You're seeing things, Sheila, I thought to myself, just the way Gavin sees ghosts. The tinker children ran towards the stranger. He bent down to greet them, and I saw him take coins out of his pocket and give some to them. The children ran on, and the stranger came closer, and my heart did a little dance. It was Joel after all. He smiled broadly when he saw me.

"Hello," I said, smiling back. "You shouldn't be giving them money, you know. Wee tinkers, they'll pester you every time they see you."

"They're only children," he said.

Sudden nervousness kept me talking. "So, are you walking off your Christmas dinner too? Seems like we both took the same notion. Did they have a big do at the base?"

He shook his head. "So I heard, but I wouldn't know."

"So you heard? Didn't you go?"

"No. I'm Jewish, remember. We don't celebrate Christmas." His tone was pleasant.

I stopped in my tracks and stared up at him. "You don't? Sure everybody celebrates Christmas, even the Protestants."

He smiled down at me. "We have our own holidays."

I waited.

"Around this time of year we celebrate Hanukkah, the festival of lights. At Easter we celebrate Passover, and our New Year is Rosh Hashanah."

I stood there fascinated. I loved the sounds of the words he was saying. They sounded foreign and exotic. I'd never met the likes of him.

"D'you mean you don't have a tree or anything like that?"

"Nope."

"Jesus. I wonder if Aunt Kate might be Jewish?" I said without thinking.

"Excuse me?"

"Oh nothing. Are there many Jews in your battalion?"

"Not many. We're few and far between."

"So you're a rare bird then," I said with a smile.

He smiled back. "I guess so."

He turned around the way he had come and walked with me farther down the strand. The evening was drawing in. Lights appeared in the terraced houses that lined the shore road. I wondered idly what was going on inside them. I imagined parents and children and grandparents all gathered round big warm fires, laughing and talking. I pulled my coat tighter around me.

"It's much cheerier here in the summer," I said to Joel. I didn't know why I thought it was important for him to know that. "The sea is blue and calm, and wee boats sail back and forth between here and Omeath, and people come from all around to swim and have picnics."

"Sounds nice."

We walked on.

"I haven't seen you around since that night," I said, trying to sound casual.

"I've been going back and forth to London. I'll be going again in the New Year, and then probably for a longer period."

"Oh, and here I thought you were away rescuing more damsels in distress," I said quickly, afraid that maybe he thought I was accusing him of ignoring me.

"No, I try to limit that to one a year," he said.

We both laughed, and I felt the tension go out of me.

"Well, it's grand to see you again just the same," I said.

"And it's grand to see you too." He laughed, imitating my accent.

I punched him on the arm. "Stop that!"

"I wrote to my mother about you," he said, after a while.

"Jesus! What did you tell her?"

"Oh, it was all good. My mom's very curious to know what the Irish are like. She's concerned they won't treat me well here after what they did to the Jews in Belfast." He stopped and looked at me and must have realized I had no idea what I was on about. "A boatload of Jewish refugees trying to escape Hitler were turned away from Belfast port and sent back into the middle of the war. And it seems many of the Jews that have been in Belfast for generations are being harassed." He sighed. "I wish people would understand how important this war is—how evil Hitler is and what he's doing to our people. We have to stop him."

I really didn't want to talk about the war. I'd had enough of that with Gavin. But something in Joel's voice stopped me from trying to change the subject.

"Is that why you joined up, then?"

He nodded.

"Your ma must be worried sick about you."

"I guess so."

"What about your da?"

I saw his face tighten. "My dad died some time ago," he said. It was obvious he was not going to say more.

I shrugged. "My own da left when I was ten. He died later, at sea."

"I'm sorry," murmured Joel.

Eventually we turned around and walked back up the deserted strand towards the town center. The Castle ballroom was closed, but soon other pubs would open up and people would emerge for an evening get-together. The young people, especially, would be anxious to escape their families. Sure enough, as we walked, the shore road began to fill up with cars and bicycles.

"Shall we go somewhere for a drink?" I said. "I'm freezing out here. It would be nice to get in somewhere and get warm."

He said nothing, but walked up with me to the sea wall and climbed over onto the pavement. We walked down to the square. The Prince of Mourne pub was open. It was one of my favorite haunts.

"Let's go in here," I said, anxious to lift the mood. "You'll see plenty of mad Irish that you can write to your ma about." Without waiting for an answer I took his sleeve and dragged him through the door with me.

The warmth of the blazing fire met us at the door. The old pub was strung with streamers, mistletoe, and holly wreaths. A big statue of Father Christmas stood at the entrance to the main bar. A ceiling-high tree stood beside the fireplace, covered with lights and glittering ornaments. In the corner an old man played Christmas carols on the piano. A few enlisted soldiers sat in clusters, drinking beer and laughing. They nudged one another when they saw Joel, and then saluted him when he walked by. He nodded in their direction. We found a table near the fire and ordered a beer each.

"Cheers," Joel said, as he lifted his glass.

"*Sláinte*," I said.

We relaxed into the evening and the company. Soon Joel was singing Christmas carols along with the crowd in a soft, mellow voice. I looked at him curiously. He grinned.

"What? I love carols."

Patsy and Kathleen and some other girls from the mill came in. They had come down with Tommy Markey. Tommy was seeing another girl now and his jealousy of me had passed. We greeted one another, and Patsy nodded towards Joel and winked at me behind his back. I was delighted to be seen with him. Now they knew I hadn't imagined him.

Eventually, Joel took out a silver watch from the inside pocket of his jacket and looked at it. It looked like an antique and had some engraving on it. I was about to ask him about it when he stood up. "I'm sorry; I have an early start in the morning. This has been fun, Sheila."

I stood up with him.

"Can I see you to the train?" he said, as he put on his coat.

I shook my head. "Last train is long gone. I'll get a lift with Tommy."

"Be careful. He doesn't look too steady on his feet. Maybe you should drive."

I burst out laughing and Joel looked bewildered. "Me, drive? You must think I'm Lady Muck!" But I was secretly pleased. He obviously had no idea of my station in life, but he'd shown respect.

"I'll walk out with you." I turned to Patsy. "Save my place."

Outside, we stood on the pavement looking out over the dark sea lit up by a bright moon.

"It's so beautiful here," Joel said. Then he turned to me. "I understand tomorrow is another holiday. Box Day?"

"Boxing Day." I laughed.

He hesitated. "I was wondering—er, I'll be done around noon. If you're free could I pick you up? I have a car at my disposal. I would love to drive up into the mountains around here. You could be my guide."

He waited. He could not have known that my heart did a somersault at that minute.

"Aye," I said, trying not to sound too keen.

I gave him my address and directions to my house. He leaned over and gave me a hug. Then his soft fingers caressed my cheek and I held my breath. His brief kiss was like a whisper—soft and warm.

"Good night, Sheila."

I sailed back into the Prince of Mourne on a cushion of air.

∽

As I climbed into bed that night I couldn't wipe the smile off my face. Joel Solomon was interested in me and he was a fine catch. I put aside in my mind all the palaver about his being Jewish and his mother not liking the Irish and all the rest of it. He was single, good-looking, and he was an officer. That meant he must have some money behind him—enough to pay my fare to America anyway. I intended to find out more about his family. I hoped he was very wealthy. America! I was giddy at the thought. I'd have been well satisfied with England, but America? Now that was a different kettle of fish altogether. I could go far on my looks there—plenty of the enlisted boys had said so. All I needed was to get Joel to take me there and I'd be set. California, maybe? Or New York? I'd drop him as gently as I could and be on my way. But even as I thought these things I felt like a stranger to myself. Yes, it was me, Sheila McGee, following my plan. But deep down somewhere inside me there was another voice whispering. I turned over and pulled the four sacks up over my head. Whatever that other voice was trying to say, I did not want to hear it.

The next morning, Boxing Day, a knock came at the door at exactly twelve o'clock. I raced out of the scullery, but Ma beat me to it. She was in one of her high moods. She had dolled herself up even though it was still early in the day. Maybe she had a date, I thought, and I rolled my eyes. Joel Solomon carried a bunch of flowers and before he could get a word out Ma had snatched them out of his hand.

"Aren't these lovely!" she said, her voice tinny and a bit hysterical.

"They're not for you, Ma," I muttered from behind her, but Joel smiled at her and winked at me.

"I'm glad you like them, Mrs. McGee." He put out his hand to shake hers. "I'm Joel Solomon. It's a pleasure to meet you."

She looked him up and down. He was wearing his civvies—black trousers, a polo-necked white jumper, and a lovely brown suede jacket. He looked more handsome than I remembered.

"He's a captain in the army," I said. "I'm going to show him the sights."

Ma's hands fluttered over her dress, smoothing it out, and she smiled up at him. "You're very welcome, Captain Solomon. My daughter has many friends actually, but she's not mentioned you. Keeping you to herself I suppose."

Ma had put on the strange accent she used when she wanted to sound posh. She never used the word "actually" in everyday conversation. My cheeks grew hot. I hoped she wasn't going to disgrace me before I could even get my plan off the ground. But Joel seemed not to notice anything. He followed Ma to the best armchair beside the fire and sat down. He looked around the house and made polite comments about how cozy and quaint everything was. I excused myself to go to the granny room and get my coat.

"Who's yer man?" said Grainne as I came into the bedroom.

"A Yank!" I said. "An officer. And we're going to be very thick together if Ma doesn't manage to ruin things."

Grainne chuckled. "I think she has a notion for him, Sheila. You'd better watch out."

I clucked my tongue. "Will you whisht, Grainne. Just the same, I'd better get him out of here before she gets her hooks into him. Have you seen my scarf and gloves?"

"Jesus, they're staring you in the face over there, Sheila," Grainne said, pointing to a pile of clothes in the corner. "If I didn't know better I'd say you have a mighty notion on him your-self. You seem awful distracted all of a sudden."

I buttoned up my coat, wound my scarf around my neck, and pulled on my gloves. "You've a quare imagination, my girl," I said.

When we went outside we found the neighbors crowded around the motorcar. A car was a rare sight in our village. If it wasn't for Tommy Markey's da's car, I would never have set foot in one myself. I shooed them away and waited for Joel to open the car door for me. I climbed in carefully, copying the way the women did this in the American films, and I waved at them through the window as we pulled away. You would have thought I was royalty.

We drove down to Newry and out the Warrenpoint road that ran along the Clanrye River. It was a bright, dry afternoon, and perfect for sightseeing. I relaxed back in the seat, enjoying myself. We passed Narrow Water Castle on our left, which was no longer a castle but some rich chap's estate. It was a beautiful sight stand-ing where it did on the hill above the riverbank overlooking the Cooley Mountains across the water.

"That's my new home," said Joel as we drove by.

"You're joking me," I said. "Most of the fellas told me they're staying in them brick huts up on the Burren road."

He looked pleased with himself. "Rank has its privileges," he said.

"It must be lovely in there, is it?" I asked, curiosity getting the better of me.

"Well, it's a beautiful estate, that's for sure. Of course the army has made a few changes. We don't exactly get a room with a view all to ourselves. But the grounds are lovely and we do get to relax in the library of an evening. I'll have to bring you over sometime."

"That would be grand," I said.

We drove on in silence. We passed through Warrenpoint. The square was quiet, and the funfair was shut down. The tide was still out, but waves lapped towards the strand. Joel pointed to our right.

"Is it true that's part of the Republic over there?"

I followed his gaze. "Aye, that's Omeath and Carlingford. They're both in the Free State. Well, we still call it the Free State. A few years ago they changed the constitution to call it Ireland, or Eire. But, like I say, we still call it the Free State. After all, the whole island is Ireland as far as I'm concerned, not just the twenty-six counties."

I realized with surprise that I was sounding just like Gavin.

"Gavin lives in Omeath," I said, without thinking.

"Gavin?"

I could have kicked myself. I forgot I'd never mentioned Gavin to him.

"Gavin O'Rourke. He's just a friend of mine. He captains a cargo boat called the *Ashgrove*. His da and mine were great friends."

He nodded. "Merchant marine? Risky business these days. The Germans have been using them for target practice."

"Aye," I said. "We're coming into Rostrevor, now," I continued, anxious to turn the subject away from Gavin. I didn't want Joel to think he had any competition. Of course he didn't as far as I was concerned, but I knew how men thought. "It's a lovely wee village. Lot of history. Named after some oul' fella by the name of General Ross. I think he fought in America. Some say he was among a crowd of boyos tried to burn down the White House."

"Really?" said Joel. "I'll have to read up on him. I'm fond of history."

"Well you'll find plenty of it in these parts."

We drove on through the village and out the Kilkeel road, still hugging the coast.

"Turn left here," I said. "We'll drive up Kilbroney Mountain. There's a grand view from the top. Then we can come back down and drive on up the coast road to Newcastle. There's a lovely hotel there where we can have a meal."

"Sounds like a plan," said Joel. "I put myself in your hands."

I liked the feeling of being in charge of things. I surprised myself with how much I knew about the area. I had spent so much time planning to get away from this place that I hadn't realized how much a part of me it was. I had to admit it really was beautiful. Parts of it would take your breath away. I could hear Gavin's words in my head—"There's no place more beautiful than this, Sheila." I took a deep breath. No matter, there was nothing beautiful about slaving at that oul' mill every day.

"Penny for your thoughts?" Joel's voice startled me.

"Oh nothing," I said sweetly. "Just admiring the scenery."

"It's stunning," he said.

When we got to the top of Kilbroney we climbed out of the car and walked to the edge of the land and looked down over Warrenpoint and Rostrevor and Carlingford Lough.

"Wow," Joel said. "This is beautiful. I can't imagine anyone born here would ever want to leave it."

I almost slipped and said I would go at the first chance. How could I tell him that my dearest wish since I was fourteen had been to leave this place? He would be onto my plan in no time. Everyone knew that the local girls were dying to find a soldier to marry them and take them away from their drudgery.

"Aye, there's many that feel that way." I nodded. "I have a favorite place like this closer to home. It's called the Flagstaff and you can see three counties from the top of it. I've been going there since I was young."

"You'll have to show me sometime."

"I usually go alone." I didn't mean to sound abrupt, and I startled myself when I said that. "But I'll take you if you'd like," I added hurriedly to take the sting out of it.

"That's all right, Sheila," he said. "We all have our favorite solitary places. There's a country road near my house in Ohio where I love to go for quiet walks—just me and the birds."

"You live out in the country then?" I said, trying to sound off-hand.

"What? Oh, no. I live in what we call a suburb outside a big city—Cleveland. My father ran a bakery there."

"Oh?" A bakery? A bank would have been better, but I passed no remarks. I remembered that he had said his da died. "Does your ma run it now, since your da passed away?"

His jaw tightened, hardly as much as you'd notice, but something had bothered him just the same. I cursed myself for bringing up his da.

"No, we had to sell it." His gaze was far off now. He was looking down at the scenery spread out below us, but I could tell he was seeing something else.

I shrugged. "Pity," I said. Then, "Shall we go?"

We walked to the car in silence and Joel drove back down the mountain.

"Turn left here," I said, "and we'll go on down towards Newcastle."

"Aye, aye, skipper." His mood had lightened again.

I pointed out more sights along the way as we drove down into the fishing village of Kilkeel and then out on the road towards Newcastle, which was one of the bigger towns in the area, filled with tourists in the summer. It was late afternoon but there were still not very many people about. All sleeping it off, I supposed. Some families strolled along the beach. Children threw colored balls and laughed and ran. It was a very peaceful sight. Who would ever think there was a war on? We stopped to eat at a lovely old hotel on the water named the Railway Hotel. They gave us a window table with a view of the water. Joel ordered a beer and I had a shandy. He wasn't much of a drinker; I could tell that. But that was all right with me.

The beer seemed to relax him. He told me amusing stories from his childhood, about his family, his crazy aunts as he called them, and his extremely bright and ambitious younger brother. We did not speak of his da again.

We drove home in easy relaxed silence through the mountains on an inland route through Hilltown and back down into Newry. When he stopped the car outside the house he turned to me. His eyes were warm and they creased up as he smiled.

"Sorry I have to get back on duty. Maybe next time we can go to those places you pointed out across the lough. Carlingford and Omeath?"

I nodded. "Surely," I said.

So we were to have another date. I tried to tone down the smile on my face—I didn't want to look too eager. He reached out and took my hand and caressed it for a moment. Then he brought my face close to his and kissed me gently on the lips.

When he had gone, I stood outside the house for a while touching my lips where he had kissed me. What was happening? I should have been delighted that my plan was working and that he was obviously taken with me. But it was not his feelings I was anxious about—it was my own. When he kissed me it had caused a reaction in me I could not explain. It was not the same as when Gavin had kissed me and left me trembling in fear of a wild thing unleashed. Joel's kiss had been soft and without urgency, like a silken sheet enfolding me and making me safe. I shook myself and took a couple of deep breaths and promised myself I would not let my feelings run away with me. I was determined not to get involved with Joel Solomon.

Chapter 12

❧

Nineteen forty-three dawned and the war went on with no end in sight. By now the community had settled into the way of wartime life: blackouts, sirens, rationing, soldiers everywhere.

"You're tripping over the bastards going up to Mass of a Sunday morning," said Ma when she was in one of her bad moods.

I didn't bother reminding her that she liked the soldiers well enough when she got her cigarettes and nylons and all the rest of it from them. I had tried to stay clear of her when she went out with her cronies in search of soldiers, her skirts so tight her arse looked like an apple in a handkerchief. She never brought one home as far as I knew—Kate would never have stood for it. But sometimes she crept in late at night giggling to herself and tripping up the stairs.

Other people welcomed the soldiers with open arms. Some of them even became like one of the family. They enjoyed home-cooked meals at a family's table—particularly if there was a pretty daughter in the house. I would not have subjected any of the poor chaps to a dinner at our house, though. I think they would have preferred dinner at the barracks any day of the week. Between Ma's odd behavior, Uncle Kevin's drunkenness, and Aunt Kate's piety they would have got a quare idea of the Irish.

Since Joel was away on some mission, I went back to my

rounds of the dances and pubs and the company of the enlisted men. I reasoned it was better than staying home nights and listening to Ma. Patsy and Kathleen had both pulled in their horns. Kathleen was seeing a wee Welsh soldier named Ollie—a lovely quiet chap. Kathleen was quiet herself, so he suited her much better than the loud Yanks. They'd been walking out since before Christmas, and even though he was Protestant, her family loved him. They would probably get married when the war was over. Patsy, on the other hand, had taken up with a soldier from New Jersey in America. His name was Sylvie, short for Sylvester, and he was great *craic* altogether. His family was Italian, he said, and he loved to sing opera and drink wine, which was, he said, what Italians did. Between himself and Patsy there was never a dull moment. I could see that he was just out for a good time and I didn't blame him, but Patsy was out for something more. I knew it in the way she looked at him. I hoped she knew how to take care of herself, because this boyo would no more marry her than the man in the moon. But I said nothing, because it was none of my business. I didn't envy either of the girls. I had my sights set on better things.

Young Grainne had begun mitching from school.

"I'm fourteen," she said after the schoolmaster came to the house to look for her. "I'm too old to be going to school."

By all accounts she was bright enough, but she had a bad attitude and so her marks were low. I suspected there was more to it than just that, but it was hard to get any talk out of her.

"You want to end up in the mill all your life?" I said to her one night. "Ma forced me out of school when I was your age and put me up there to work. It's no picnic I can tell you. I'd stay in school as long as I could if I were in your shoes."

"Well you're not!" Her old surly tone was back.

"Suit yourself."

It was her life, I thought. She'd probably end up on the game like her ma. She must have read my mind.

"I know what you're thinking," she said more quietly, "that I'll be just like my ma. Well, it's what I'm used to. I've had a good teacher over the years. And I can make more money than at the bloody oul' mill youse are all slaving at. Anyway, what other choice would a girl like me have? I'm plain, and I have no education, and I'm poor. Could you see me working in a shop or an office?"

"You could join the convent," I said with a laugh.

She grinned back, her mood lighter. "Or the bloody army."

"Aye, I met two sisters from Mullaghbawn last year who were off to join the WAAFs. I often wondered what happened to them."

"Probably bombed to smithereens by now," said Grainne.

We were silent for a while. I supposed Grainne was right. A girl like her didn't have many choices. It made sense that she would fall back on something she knew, no matter how terrible it was. I thanked God again that at least I had been born with good looks. Without that I could well have been in the same boat as Grainne. Still, something inside me hurt when I thought of the girl going back to Amelia Street. For her sake I hoped the war would go on for a while so she could stay here.

"By the time this bloody war's over we could both be old women," I said with a laugh, "too far gone to be worrying about our futures."

❧

Joel came back in February. He appeared at the house on Valentine's Day, which fell on a Sunday. When I opened the door, I was delighted to see him. He carried a bunch of red roses. I snatched them off him before Ma could grab them.

"Come in," I said.

He grinned as he looked around the parlor. "Where's your mom?"

"She's up the stairs, still sleeping I hope. Sit down. Let me get these flowers in water before she gets her mitts on them."

He looked a bit disappointed. He pulled a red box out of a paper bag he was carrying and set it on a table. It was heart shaped and I knew it was chocolates.

"Oh, Joel," I began, but he waved his hand.

"Sorry, these are for your mom. I think all mothers deserve something nice on Valentine's Day."

I opened my mouth and closed it again. I bit back the words I was going to say. I didn't want him to see how jealous I was.

"That was nice of you," I said.

"My pleasure."

"What happened to your civvies?" I said, looking at his uniform.

"I'm due back on duty this afternoon. But I thought we'd have time to go for a ride and have lunch before I report back."

I got my coat and he stood aside and let me out the door. I was pleased that he'd been so keen to come and see me. I didn't quite know what to make of the flowers, but I put it down to his being a Yank. Maybe everybody gave everybody roses over there for Valentine's Day. Maybe it didn't mean the same as it would here. Anyway, if he was taking a notion for me, so much the better; I would worry about letting him down easy later when I was landed in America.

I thought about taking him up to the Flagstaff but it was Sunday and I was worried that Gavin might be there. I didn't want the two of them meeting up. So we followed the coast on down towards Omeath and on into the little town of Carlingford, which stood between the lough to the east and Slieve Foy to the west. We parked the car and got out to walk. It was freezing cold, and a strong wind blew, but I didn't mind it. I was enjoying being with him and telling him all about the history of the place. I was surprised again by how much I knew. Carlingford was a lovely old medieval town, built in the thirteenth century and dominated by King John's Castle and lovely stone walls. A big iron gate called the Tholsel led into the heart of the town. Joel was captivated. He had to stop and examine every plaque on the walls. His questions tumbled over one another. What I didn't know I made up rather than disappoint him.

When we had walked in a circle around the town we were almost numb with the cold.

"C'mon," I said. "Let's go in here and warm up. I'm foundered."

I led him in to P. J. O'Hare's pub, which claimed to be one of the oldest pubs in Ireland. There was a wee sweet and tobacco shop at the entrance, as was the custom in many of the old rural pubs, and a door led into a long, narrow room with dark wood and a roaring fire. We settled ourselves at a small corner table. It was only after I noticed the stares of the customers and the glare of the barman that I remembered Joel was in his uniform. I leaned over and whispered to him.

"I'm sorry, I forgot. We're in the South. You might not be too popular here. So we shouldn't be staying too long."

Joel gave me a confused look. Then the penny dropped.

"I'll try to be as discreet as I can be in this getup," he whispered back.

The barman served us drinks and sandwiches without a word. The other customers went back to their own conversations.

"I suppose I'd be more welcome in a German uniform," Joel said after a while.

"Maybe."

His face turned darker. He reminded me of Gavin when he went into one of his bad moods.

"If they only knew what those bastards are really like they'd not be harboring them."

"Oh, I don't think they harbor them," I said, trying to deflect his anger.

"Sure they do. When they capture them they don't turn them over to the British, do they? They set them up in holiday camps for the remainder of the war." His tone was bitter.

He was right of course. Sometimes German planes crashed on Irish soil, and more times their boats wrecked on the coast. The authorities in the South never turned them over but put them in prisoner of war camps. I'd heard from many that the camp rules were very slack and the prisoners could come and go as they liked as long as they signed in and out—and no doubt paid off the guards. I'd never paid much attention to the stories. I couldn't understand why Joel was so upset about it.

"Why do you hate the Germans so much?" I said as we walked back to the car.

All the good seemed to have gone out of the day. Joel's earlier enthusiasm for Carlingford had faded.

He turned on me. "Don't you read?" he said sharply. "Don't you know anything about what those people are doing to us?"

"To who?" I said. I didn't much like his tone.

"To the Jews, for God's sake."

"No," I said, "I don't. So why don't you tell me."

"Hitler and his soldiers are rounding up men, women, and children all across Europe and stuffing them into big rooms and turning on the gas and suffocating them to death."

I was stunned. I could hardly take in his words. His breathing was ragged and his eyes were blazing.

"I'm sorry," I said, "but I never heard a word about it."

"That's because very few people want to admit it's happening," he went on more evenly. "The American and British governments have yet to acknowledge the severity of the situation. It's the Jewish communities around the world that are getting the word out."

He stopped outside the car. "If more people knew, they'd understand why we have to beat the bastards. They have to be stopped. Who knows what they'd do to other people they took a dislike to? What if they won the war and decided to annihilate all the Catholics?"

We drove in silence back towards Omeath. The sky had clouded over and rain began to spit on the windshield. Whitecaps rolled over one another on the gray waters of the lough.

"I'm sorry I shouted at you, Sheila," he said at length. "It's just that it makes me so sick to think about it. And it wasn't fair to accuse you of not reading—heaven knows there's been very little in the newspapers. The *New York Times* published an article back in December, and that was the first one anyone paid attention to."

He reached over and squeezed my hand. "Anyway, I'm sorry."

I nodded. There was nothing I could think of to say. I wasn't happy about the turn of the conversation. I had gone out with him expecting a good time, and until we got to O'Hare's pub things had been grand. But then he had forced me to think about things I didn't want to think about. I didn't want to think about people being poisoned in gas chambers. I no more wanted to talk about things like that with Joel than I did when Gavin brought up politics and the Uprising and his da being shot and all the rest of it.

Eventually we pulled up outside my house. As Joel helped me out of the car he leaned over and kissed me on the cheek. His lips were warm against my frozen face. Something in his eyes looked so sad my heart sank a little in my chest. I had never met the likes of him. While his moods changed as quickly as Ma's often did, it was not the same thing at all. There was a sweetness and a sadness that always lay underneath whatever other mood Joel was showing the world. The sadness seemed to come from somewhere far away. I wondered again about his life, and his da's death, and all the rest of it. Did something happen to him as a child? Was there some hurt he had never got over? I fought back my feelings of sympathy and curiosity. This was more than I had bargained for. I'd have to think long and hard as to whether this boyo was the right one for me to be spending my time on or not.

Later that night as I lay in bed listening to Grainne's soft breathing, I couldn't get Joel's face out of my mind. There was something about him that seemed to have crept inside me and taken up residence. And despite what I had told myself earlier, I knew I would see him again.

Chapter 13

ⁿⁿ

I stayed close to home after my date with Joel. I was in a strange mood that I couldn't seem to shake. Normally my reaction to sadness or confusion was to run out and find some distraction, but I couldn't seem to bring myself to do it this time. March came in like a lion and went out like a lion as well. I bundled up and waited for spring. It took Kathleen, with her innocent wee face, to finally coax me out.

"It's Ollie's birthday next week," she said one day in early April. "We're going out with some of his friends to the Ceili House. Won't you come, Sheila? Everybody will be there. We've missed you something awful."

The Ceili House was the oldest pub in Newry. It had been famous during the Uprising. The Irish Republican Army members and some of the musicians used to meet in a secret room above the pub to plan their missions. The older people still told stories about those days. Glorious days, they said. I had no interest in it myself. I was just an infant when those things happened. But Gavin always talked about it as if he, and not his da, had been the one in the thick of it.

The warm, stale smells of turf and stout assaulted me as I opened the front door. The big room was dark, with a heavily carved wood bar and an old wooden floor full of splinters. How many feet, I wondered, had thudded on this floor in time to the traditional music that was played over the years? The walls were covered with photos of men in uniform and newspaper clippings about events in Newry during the Uprising.

The place was already packed when I arrived. Patsy waved and called to me the minute I came through the door. I pushed my way through the crowd at the bar—local lads, soldiers, seamen just off the boats, and mill girls—and squeezed in beside Patsy and Sylvie and Kathleen. Ollie sat beside Kathleen looking shy as some of his Welsh soldier friends hoisted drinks in honor of his birthday.

Soon a céilí band began to play and part of the floor was cleared for dancing. Patsy and Kathleen and I got up to dance the Walls of Limerick. We hadn't danced together in years—ever since we'd been in dancing school together when we were young. I smiled at the old memories and was glad that I had come. The crowd clapped as we danced, but none more than the Yanks who were there in force tonight. They were great ones for the drink. They could match any Irishman. And when they drank they grew loud. Between Ollie's friends singing in Welsh and the Yanks shouting the noise was deafening.

When the dance ended, we came back to the table and ordered another round of drinks. But something had changed. The earlier good humor had ebbed, and something dark was taking its place. I glanced around. The Yanks had become even louder. They had spotted Ollie and his friends.

"Will you look, it's the goat lovers," yelled one. The mascot of the Welsh regiment was a goat, which led all their parades.

"Can't get a gal, a goat will do!" crowed another Yank to loud laughter.

Ollie and his friends stiffened. Ollie took Kathleen by the arm.

"We should leave," he murmured. "I don't want trouble."

Patsy, who had been drinking all night, pushed Kathleen back down in her chair. "It's Ollie's birthday, for God's sake!" she yelled. "Don't let them chancers drive you out."

She looked at Sylvie, who was glancing anxiously from one

group to the other. "Sorry, love, I know they're your mates, but they've awful bad manners."

The Yanks kept up their taunts. One of Ollie's friends could take it no longer.

"Shut up, you big-mouthed louts," he yelled. "If it wasn't for Pearl Harbor you lot would still be sitting on the sidelines watching us get our arses shot!"

Boos went around the crowd. "You had no hope of winning the war without us," shot back one of the Yanks. "Old Churchill came begging for us to come and save you."

"Youse have no right here," said a drunken voice from the crowd. "Youse are an occupying army, all of youse. Get out of Ireland and leave us alone. We want nothing to do with England's war."

We held our breaths as the insults few. Long-held resentments were erupting on all sides. A couple of the Welsh soldiers threw their fists at the loudest Yanks, and a free-for-all started in earnest. Tables were shoved back and chairs began to fly. Local lads cheered on the Welsh soldiers—their jealousy of the Yanks showing through. A beer bottle spiraled through the air and hit Ollie on the side of the head. Kathleen screamed. Both Patsy and I turned on Sylvie at the same time.

"Do something!" we both cried.

Sylvie looked around. I could see he was torn as to what to do. Ollie was bleeding from the head, Kathleen trying to stem the blood with her handkerchief. Sylvie jumped up. Good, I thought, he's going to show what he's made of. But he ran over to his mates and started throwing punches along with them at the Welsh soldiers. Patsy stared at him with her mouth open. Kathleen began to cry. I looked down at my hand and saw blood. Splinters of flying glass had lodged there. I got up and ran to the bathroom. As I ran I bumped straight into Gavin, who stood in the hallway watching the fight. My heart leaped at the sight of him.

"Oh, thank God, Gavin," I cried. "Can you do something to stop it? They're killing one another, and Ollie's hurt and..."

He looked down at my bleeding hand. I expected him to grab it and wrap his handkerchief around it. Instead he merely shrugged and nodded towards the soldiers.

"They deserve each other," he said. "None of them have any right to be on Irish soil."

"I never took you for a coward, Gavin O'Rourke!"

"What do you want me to do? It's none of my business. It's not my bloody war."

"Well, it should be your war. It's disgusting the way you and your southern countrymen are refusing to lift a finger to help. You don't care if the Germans win even though they're doing awful things to the Jews."

Gavin raised an eyebrow. "Ah, I see Joel the Jew has been filling your head with nonsense."

I stiffened. "How do you know about Joel?"

"You forget it's a small world here, Sheila. You were seen in O'Hare's pub with him and him in a Yankee uniform. And I heard he's different from the rest. Keeps to himself. Word got around that he's Jewish."

My temper rose. "For a boyo you've never met," I said, "you're taking a quare interest in him."

Just then the bathroom door opened and a tall, fair-haired girl came out. She smiled at Gavin and took his arm as if she owned him. I stared at her, forgetting about the blood that was beginning to drip from my hand to the floor.

"Did you miss me?" she said to him.

I glared at her. Gavin patted her arm. "I did indeed," he said. "Let's get a drink."

He took her elbow and steered her towards the main bar. As he walked he looked back at me. "You'd better take care of that hand," he said.

Later the military police arrived and escorted the Yankee soldiers out of the pub. The Welsh soldiers cheered and started singing hymns. The band came back up onstage and began to play as if nothing had happened.

☙❧

The fight at the Ceili House was all the talk at the mill on Monday morning. As to be expected, the local boys who'd been there made heroes out of themselves—you'd have thought they'd taken on the entire American regiment by themselves—and beat them.

"How's Ollie?" I said to Kathleen as I cranked up my machine.

"Och, he's grand now," she said. "Not much of a birthday, though."

"No," I said.

"It's Patsy I'm feeling sorry for at the minute," said Kathleen quietly. "She's in an awful state and she won't tell me what's wrong."

"Well, I suppose there were ructions between her and Sylvie after he joined up with the Yanks against Ollie and his friends. Maybe they fell out."

Kathleen nodded. "Aye, they did. But I think there's more to it than that. Maybe you can get it out of her, Sheila."

I really didn't want to know about Patsy's problems. I had enough of my own. Anyway, she'd tell me eventually. Patsy could never keep any news to herself—good or bad. I threaded the bobbins on my machine and went on about my work trying to put the events of that night out of my mind—particularly the way Gavin had acted. At first I'd been ft to be tied. How dare he walk off with some floozy and leave me standing there helpless? I tried to tell myself I was angry with his attitude about the war, but deep down I knew that was not the real cause. It was that I no longer held the special place in his heart that I had occupied since we were children. I had lost him. Granted I was the one who had pushed him away. And granted I was the one who was seeing another man. But I had always counted on Gavin to be there when I needed him. I realized now how selfish that had been of me. Well, there was nothing I could do about it. I would just have to get along without him.

At the beginning of May, Patsy came to my house after work with a face on her as long as a drink of water. I pulled her into the granny room away from Ma's prying ears. Grainne sat on the bed reading a book. She had gone back to school, even though she still wasn't over the moon about it. Patsy eyed her and then looked back at me.

"I've something to tell you," she said. "In private."

If you're looking for privacy in this house, you'll be searching a long time, I thought. There were eyes and ears everywhere.

"She's all right," I said, nodding towards Grainne. "She's good at keeping secrets."

Grainne looked up and rolled her eyes and went back to her book. "Pay me no mind," she muttered. "I've heard it all before."

Patsy opened her mouth to say something but hesitated. That's when I knew something was up. Patsy never missed a chance for a smart remark.

"Sit down," I said to her, pointing to a rickety old chair in the corner. I went over and closed the door while Patsy cleared some dirty clothes off the chair. I sat at the bottom of the bed with my back to Grainne.

"Well?"

Patsy took a deep breath. "I'm in trouble," she said.

I heard Grainne shift suddenly behind me. The girl had understood.

"Och, Jesus, Patsy," I said. "Didn't I warn you?"

Patsy nodded. She looked miserable. "Aye, you did, Sheila. But it just—it just happened. I didn't mean for it to."

"Are you sure you didn't do it on purpose?"

Her face reddened. "Jesus, Sheila, and why would I do such a thing?"

I shrugged. "So he'd marry you and take you away from all of this," I said, my voice full of sarcasm. The truth was I had no pity for Patsy at the minute. She had cooked her own goose.

"What am I going to do?"

"Have you told him?"

"Aye," Patsy said. "I told him the other night when we were celebrating Ollie's birthday. I wasn't even sure—I was only a fortnight late—but you know me, I can never keep me mouth shut."

"And?"

"And, nothing. He said nothing. Just ordered more drinks. And then the fight started, and I was so annoyed with him for not helping Ollie that I was raging at him." She paused to stifle a hic-cup. "And all he did was rage back at me and said that the only thing that mattered to him was being a Yank and the rest of us could go to hell."

We were silent for a while. Grainne slid over closer to the only lamp in the room. It was pitch black outside and a ferocious wind blew. In the parlor I could hear Ma laughing and carrying on even though she was only getting one-word answers from Aunt Kate and grunts from Uncle Kevin in reply. I suddenly wondered if Ma had had a friend to talk to when she found out she was pregnant with me? Such a thing was bad enough now, but in her time it must have been an awful disgrace. I felt a rush of sympathy for her.

I turned back to Patsy.

"Was that all was said between the two of you?"

She shook her head from side to side. "No. I met him at the Savoy on the Sunday evening after our night at the Ceili House. We had arranged to go to see the new film and then go for fish and chips at Morocco's. To tell you the truth I was shaking in my boots afraid he wouldn't come. So I can't tell you how relieved I was when I saw him waiting." Patsy looked up, smiling briefly. Then she bowed her head again. "But he said he wanted to go for a walk instead of seeing the film. He had something to say to me."

I waited. Something told me Grainne was not reading a word of her book.

"We walked up across Sugar Island Bridge and down by the docks and sat on one of the benches there. It was friggin' cold, I can tell you. Anyway, he looks at me and he says, 'Patsy, if it's true and you are pregnant, you can keep the child or get rid of it, but I won't marry you. I can't, you see, because I'm already engaged to a nice Italian girl back home.' I didn't even hear the rest of what he said."

I sucked in a breath. I wasn't shocked that he had a girl at home. But to tell Patsy to get rid of the child! "But I thought he was Catholic?" I burst out.

Patsy shrugged. "I suppose Italian Catholics must be different than the Irish Catholics. Jesus, Sheila, what am I going to do? Me ma will be disgraced, and me da will take the strap to me and then he'll throw me out of the house."

"Are you sure you're not just late?" I said.

Patsy bowed her head. "I prayed that was the case. But deep down I knew. I've never missed once since I was eleven years old. And now I've missed twice in a row. I've never had any luck, Sheila, and that's the truth." She looked up then and laughed. "If I wasn't the age I am, they'd probably put me with the nuns beyond at the Convent of the Holy Mother."

I winced at the mention of the convent. It was housed in a stern gray building on a hill overlooking Newry. No matter where you walked in the town it seemed to be watching you, its eyes following you. Mothers used the threat of the place to put the fear of God into their daughters. While the nuns who taught me at my convent school were for the most part kind, the word was that the Convent of the Holy Mother nuns were devils dressed up in habits. Many's the story I heard about girls up there being beaten and half-starved and their heads shaved. The poor unfortunate girls left there by their family because they were pregnant, or maybe just too hard to control, were seldom seen again. Their babies were taken from them, as well as their own names and all their belongings. Many of them went mad.

After Patsy left, I sat up on the bed beside Grainne.

"Ma used to threaten me with that place—that convent."

"Mine too," Grainne said. She leaned against the pillow, having given up any pretense of reading her book. "I suppose there's one of them places in every town."

"And the girls hardly ever get out," I said, "unless they're thrown out on the street because they're too old or too insane to work. Like poor oul' Mad Biddy—you know your one who goes up and down Hill Street dressed in black and cackling like a goose?"

Grainne shivered. "I'd kill myself before I'd go into a place like that."

We sat in silence for a while.

"So you heard all?" I said.

"Aye."

"And what d'you think?"

"Patsy should have taken care of herself better. All the Yanks have condoms."

I looked at Grainne with a new respect. For all Patsy's loud mouth and confidence, this fourteen-year-old girl could take care of herself better than Patsy any day of the week.

"Aye. Sure I warned her that if something happened he'd never marry her. Men are all the same. I'd never let myself be caught in a pickle like that."

"She's not the only one," said Grainne. "At school they're always talking about this one or that one's sister who's up the pole. Ever since the soldiers came it seems as if half the girls in the town are in the family way."

I almost laughed out loud at the face of her—she was like an oul' woman. You could almost forget she was still just a child.

"I suppose we should be a wee bit sorry for them, just the same," I said. "Poor things, they're just looking for a way out of this place like the rest of us. Some of them will be lucky enough to get the boy to marry them. I'm sure Ollie would not see Kathleen stranded. But the Yanks..."

"Ursula Fearon at school says there was a Yank wanted to marry her sister, Brea, but the army brass found out she was pregnant and told the priest to refuse to marry them."

"What?"

"It's true. She says anytime a soldier wants to marry a girl the first thing they do is examine her to see if she's in the family way. And even if she's not, they look into her background to see if she's from a decent family and not just using the soldier to get away from poverty. And most of the time they decide she won't do."

"Who looks into them?" I said, astonished.

"The likes of your friend Mary McAteer's ma and her cronies. And the local magistrate, and the army brass, and the priests. They're all in on it. It's a rare girl gets accepted. Unless she's from money the odds are against her." Grainne paused for breath. "You'd think every girl in the North was a bloody whore."

I was astounded not only about what Grainne was telling me, but the fact that she knew more about the way things were than even I did.

"So if a Yank wanted to marry Mary McAteer I suppose she'd pass with flying colors," I said.

Grainne laughed aloud. "Aye. But who'd be after asking her?"

Chapter 14

❧

Joel came back at the end of May, He'd been away again, he said, on assignment. I didn't ask what he'd been doing—I didn't much care—but I was delighted he was back. I invited him to go with me the next Sunday evening to the Flagstaff. Starting in early May and on through the summer months it was tradition for people from Queensbrook, Newry, and elsewhere to bicycle to the Flagstaff of a Sunday evening to hear music and dance. Some even walked, strolling with their children, carrying picnic baskets. It was an innocent ritual, a celebration of summer and music and life itself.

We drove down in Joel's car and parked on the Lower Fathom Road near the river. Joel opened the boot and took out a leather case. I was stunned.

"Is that a fiddle?" I said.

He nodded. "Yes, I play it once in a while. Thought I might try it out here."

I was delighted. "You're a man full of surprises," I said.

We walked on up the hill towards the summit. Everyone was in good form, shouting and talking and laughing. On the top of the hill there was a broad flat stone where the musicians set up and where people danced. Others had brought blankets and spread them out on the grass. Everywhere the whin bushes bloomed with glorious golden flowers. Boat horns sounded once in a while from the lough in the distance and evening church bells rang out. It was still light, and would be for a while. I looked around to see if Gavin was about. I was certain he would be there—I knew the *Ashgrove* was in port. I had decided to give up worrying about what would happen if he and Joel met up. And anyway, Gavin had his own fish to fry what with a new girlfriend and all the rest of it. Things were no longer the same between us and it was time for me to accept it.

I pulled Joel down to sit on my favorite stone bench and we opened a couple of bottles of beer we had brought. I stretched out my legs and looked around. The place was filling up. Children ran past us, laughing and screaming. Some of my neighbors from Queensbrook nodded in our direction. Suddenly I felt sorry for Ma sitting home in a bad mood—she would have loved being here. A few soldiers appeared, both Yanks and Welsh, and I prayed there'd be no repeat of the shenanigans at the Ceili House. But the atmosphere here was different, more relaxed and civilized.

A Belgian military band set up and played a few lively tunes. I had seen them before down at the Castle ballroom. They were brilliant musicians and very popular with the locals. While they were playing Joel got up and walked over to the edge of the grass to look down at the view. I watched him, imagining his pleasure.

The Belgian band finished their set and the Irish musicians climbed up on the stone and slapped the Belgians on the back. Eileen O'Neill, a famous fiddle player from South Armagh, was among them, and I knew we were in for a treat.

"She's the best there is," I whispered to Joel, who had returned to sit with me. "Just wait until you hear her."

Eileen was a tall, imposing woman. She wore her hair in a long braid that fell down her back. Word was she had glorious red hair when she was young. Now it was flecked with gray, but she was still a handsome woman. As her music danced through the air, Joel let out a low whistle.

"Amazing," he said. "Now I'm not sure I want to follow that."

He stroked his fiddle case, which lay across his knees. "I'm a bit rusty," he murmured to himself.

"I'm sure you're fine," I said. "Where did you learn to play?"

"What? Oh, my dad was very accomplished. Played with the Cleveland Orchestra when he was young. He gave it up when he had a family. Couldn't live on what a violinist was paid. But he loved the instrument. He taught my brother and me to play when we were quite young."

He stared off into the distance as he spoke. I patted him on the arm.

"You'll be grand," I whispered. "I'll just go and ask them to give you a chance later."

I got up and made my way towards the makeshift stage on the big stone and gave one of the musicians Joel's name. As I turned I found myself looking at Gavin. Even though I was expecting to see him, it was still a shock. I was at a sudden loss for words. I nodded to him and kept walking.

When Gavin took the stage I nudged Joel. "That's my friend, Gavin, I was telling you about," I whispered.

Gavin did not play an instrument, but he had a fine tenor voice. The crowd grew silent in anticipation. I held my breath as he began to sing. His voice always made me tremble. He began with a song called "Isle of Innisfree," the words of which had been written by his favorite poet, William Butler Yeats. You could have heard a pin drop. Even the children stopped playing and listened. When he was finished the crowd clapped loudly and called for more. He bowed and then whispered something to the musicians. I recognized the strains of the next song immediately. It was called "My Lovely Rose of Clare," and Gavin had sung it to me often, because my middle name was Rose. During the first song he had been looking out towards the lough, but now he looked directly at me. I smiled back until I realized he was not looking at me at all. He was looking at someone behind me. I swung around and there sat the fair-haired girl I had seen with him at the Ceili House. She smiled at me.

"He's singing for me," she said. "My name is Rosaleen. Isn't he grand?"

I turned back to Joel without answering her.

Gavin finished singing and when the applause died down the bandleader introduced Joel.

"And now will you give a hand of applause to Joel Solomon here who's going to give us a couple of tunes on the fiddle."

There was polite applause and I nudged Joel to get up.

"Go on!" I said.

He and Gavin nodded at each other as Joel climbed up on the rock and Gavin stepped down. Gavin strode past me and sat down with Rosaleen. Joel nodded shyly towards the crowd. He took out his fiddle and tuned it for what felt like an eternity. The crowd was beginning to lose interest. I wished he would hurry up. I was suddenly nervous. God, I thought, I hope he can play.

At last he tucked the fiddle under his chin and the first few notes danced out into the evening air. He played a lively tune that sounded like gypsy music. As he gathered steam, people began to clap and cheer. Children jumped up and started dancing like wild things. I clapped along, aware of Gavin behind me. Joel played faster and faster and the children spun around until they were dizzy. Soon everyone on the hill was clapping or tapping to the music. It was infectious. The music reached a crescendo, Joel's bow flying over the strings and his long fingers dancing on the neck of the fiddle. He played so fast and hard I thought the strings would break. Sweat covered his forehead and his eyes were closed. When he stopped the music seemed to carry on. It was a second or two before we realized it was over. People jumped to their feet and called for more. Joel bowed and gave them a shy smile.

I couldn't resist a look at Gavin. His jaw was rigid as he stared at Joel.

Joel said nothing but picked up the fiddle again and this time played a slow air I had never heard before. It sounded like a lullaby you would sing for a child. The sweet, plaintive notes sent shivers through me. My God, he was amazing. There wasn't a sound out of the crowd. They watched mesmerized, some hugging their children to them. When the music faded and stopped they stood and cheered even louder than before. Joel bowed deeply and stepped down off the stone without saying a word.

I jumped up and gave Joel a hug. "You were brilliant!" I cried.

Joel smiled and sat down. At that minute Eileen O'Neill came over, and Joel jumped back up. She was as tall as he was and she smiled as she shook his hand warmly.

"You're a fine fiddle player, young man," she said. "One of the best I've heard."

"Thank you, ma'am," said Joel.

"You know, anytime you want to play with us down at the Ceili House just come in. You'd be very welcome."

Joel smiled. "Thank you, ma'am," he said again. "It would be a great honor."

She left and I stood up. It was now or never. I turned around.

"Gavin, this is Joel Solomon," I said. "Joel, this is Gavin O'Rourke."

Both men stood and shook hands stiffly. "I enjoyed your singing," said Joel softly.

"You're not bad yourself on the fiddle," said Gavin.

I breathed a sigh of relief. Well, that was that over with. But I should have known it would not be that easy.

Joel looked around. "This is a lovely gathering," he said, "everybody getting along. Not a hint of anger or evil. It's the way it should be—and will be when we get rid of Hitler."

I winced. I knew Joel had gone too far. Gavin's face grew dark. He moved closer to Joel.

"Look, we're not interested in your opinion here. And your man Hitler is no threat to us. Go and fight your bloody war somewhere else. We don't want the likes of you here." Gavin dropped the cigarette he'd been smoking and ground it angrily into the grass.

"C'mon, Rosaleen," he said to the girl, and strode away.

I wanted to yell after him to come back and apologize but Joel put his hand on my arm.

"Come on, Sheila," he said quietly. "Let's go."

As we made our way through the crowd and down the hill the strains of bagpipes, slow and melancholy, followed us, but I was raging. How could Gavin have done this to me, to Joel? He had ruined a beautiful evening.

We drove in silence down to Warrenpoint. Dusk had fallen and I could only see the faint, somber outlines of buildings along the Sea Road. Blackout blinds had been drawn and the street lights were dimmed. To my right, the lough was a black sheet stretching across to Omeath. Not even a moon shone on the water's surface. On the distant shore lights twinkled like fireflies in windows along the beach and up through the hills. It looked like a magical, fairy world.

Joel parked the car and we got out. There was no one about. It was late on a Sunday night. People were either in bed or still up on the Flagstaff. I gazed in that direction but could see nothing. Joel took my hand and we climbed over the sea wall. The tide was in and the water lapped over the small rocks not too far from where we sat. I lit a cigarette and offered one to him, but he refused.

"I'm sorry for what happened up on the Flagstaff," I said after a few silent moments.

"No need to be, it wasn't your fault."

"But Gavin was ignorant to do that all the same," I said, my anger returning. "He knew you were my friend. He could have kept his opinions to himself."

"It's a popular opinion in some parts," said Joel. "Nothing I haven't heard before. Let's forget about it." He paused. "So what's *your* talent, Miss McGee?" he said, obviously anxious to change the subject.

I shrugged. "None at all," I said.

"Ah now, you must have some. Can you sing? Dance? Recite poetry? All the Irish seem to be able to do at least one of those things."

"Well, I'm the exception then," I said. "I used to do some Irish dancing, but I was nothing to write home about."

"You must at least know some poetry."

"Not a bit of it. Gavin's the one for poetry; he could recite anything."

I could have bit my tongue off for bringing up Gavin's name. I scrambled to change the subject. "Well, I do know one wee poem my da taught me," I said. "It's about a mermaid. We call them merrows. That was his nickname for me."

"Go on then, let's hear it."

"Och, no," I whispered, suddenly shy.

"Please?"

I took a deep breath, and on that dark night in late spring I gazed out across the black water and began to recite aloud my father's poem.

> *She sits upon a rock by night*
> *and gently sheds her smooth, seal skin.*
> *Merrow, maiden of the sea, singing*
> *to the earth-bound man.*
> *Wanting what he cannot possess*
> *he swiftly steals her abandoned skin*
> *and hides the precious contraband, cooing*
> *awkward words of love.*
> *She sits upon a beach by night*
> *shivering for her warm, lost skin.*
> *Merrow, prisoner of the earth, yearning*
> *for the womb-black sea.*
> *Possessing what he cannot own*
> *he knows a loss as grave as she.*
> *Man and Merrow, hand in hand, mourning*
> *both their severed souls.*
> *She sits upon a rock by night*
> *cradled in her smooth, seal skin.*
> *Merrow, creature of the sea, weeping*
> *for the earth-bound man.*

When I was finished I could not move for the emotion that filled me. I hadn't thought of that poem for a long time. Now I realized how much it was meant for me. I was indeed a prisoner of the earth. With her refusal to love me Ma had stolen my soul, and when my da left he had taken my skin with him. Would anyone ever bring them back?

We sat in silence looking out towards the dark waves.

"I love the sea," I murmured at last. "My da taught me to love it, just like yours taught you to love music. I miss him. D'you miss yours?"

I couldn't see Joel's face in the dark, but I felt him stiffen beside me.

"Yes, all the time," he whispered.

I put my hand on his arm. "What happened to him?"

"Killed himself."

I bent over as if from a punch in the stomach. "God Almighty," I said. "How?"

"Shot himself. Put a revolver in his mouth and pulled the trigger."

Joel's voice was harsh. I could hear the anger in it. "Jesus, Mary, and Joseph," I said, and without thinking I made the sign of the cross.

I didn't know what to say or do. I wished I could see his face. I heard a noise that at first I thought was the sea lapping on the rocks, but I realized that it was coming from Joel. He was crying.

"Ah Jesus, don't," I said, and I reached over to him. He grabbed me then and pinned me in a tight embrace. He kissed me on the lips and face and then buried his head in my neck and sobbed. The dampness of his tears soaked my skin. We rocked against each other for a long time.

At last he let go and moved away from me.

"I'm sorry," he said. "I don't know where that came from. Can I have that cigarette now?"

I lit one for him and another one for me. We sat in silence, each lost in our own thoughts. What was there to say after that? I took a deep breath and waited for all the feelings to pass.

∞

After the doings on the weekend, I could hardly think straight. I tried to put it all out of my mind—Gavin, Joel, the war, my feelings—the whole lot of it. But none of it would leave me alone. God spare me from men, I thought. When I arrived at the mill on Monday morning and saw Patsy's long face, I decided I'd throw myself into her business so as to distract myself from my own.

"Any word?" I said.

She shook her head. "Not hide nor hair of him, the feckin' bastard."

I smiled. Patsy's anger was a good thing, I thought. I wouldn't have known what to do if she'd started whimpering.

"Have you told them at home?"

"God, no. I'll wait until I'm showing before I do that. There'll be ructions, I can tell you." Patsy was beating the living daylights out of a hank of flax. "To think he had one over in New Jersey all this time, and not a word of it to me!"

For once I didn't mention that I had warned her. "Aye. Sure they're all the same."

Patsy looked at me. "Your chap might have a Jewish one hidden away over there too."

I shrugged. "He might."

I tried to sound offhand, but up until she said that the possibility had never even crossed my mind. Joel was not the type. I didn't want to think that I could be wrong about him, but now I supposed I'd better watch myself all the same. I had come close to breaking my own rules with him the other night. I had shared more than was wise with him and he with me. Not only that, thank God I had not said anything about wanting to escape across the sea and away from this place. The way we were sharing everything so openly, I could easily have slipped. I promised myself I would be very careful not to fall into an emotional trap.

"Should you go to his sergeant? Or I could go to Joel; he's in charge of Sylvie's squad," I said, bringing the conversation back to Patsy. "It's not right that he should get off scot-free. You should at least get some money out of him for the child—even if the bugger won't marry you."

"Much good that would do. They stick together like glue. But I was thinking of going to see the priest—the old one, Father Toner, not that jumped-up young whippersnapper Father Flynn. There's still time to make an honest woman out of me. After all, Sylvie is a Catholic. Father Toner could scare the shite out of him—tell him his mortal soul's in danger."

"Aye, maybe," I said. I didn't tell Patsy what Grainne had said about the clergy all being in league with the army brass. She'd find out soon enough.

"Will you go with me, Sheila? I'd be awful nervous going by myself."

"What?" I'd hardly heard what Patsy said.

"To see Father Toner. You'll go with me, won't you?"

God, what was I going to say? My first thought was that Patsy should be fighting her own battles and not dragging me into it at all. I cursed myself for having started the conversation with her in the first place. But, I supposed it would take my mind off my own troubles. And there might be some *craic* in it to see the priest's face when he heard Patsy's story.

"Aye. I'll go."

Patsy looked relieved and I went on about my work. But her relief didn't last very long. At dinnertime when she and I and Kathleen were sitting on the wall outside the mill, Mary McAteer came sauntering up to us with Rose Boyle sniggering behind her. I rolled my eyes. What the feck did these two want?

"Hello, everybody," said Mary in a sweet voice that reminded me of Aunt Kate's. "How're youse?"

"We're just grand, Mary," I said. "We're enjoying our life of luxury at the minute."

She laughed. "Oh, you're always so funny, Sheila. Isn't she, Rose?"

Mary turned to Rose and put her plump hand up to her cheek, waving it about like a bloody canary in a cage. I wondered what she was up to, and then I saw it. Something glittered on her finger. Jesus, it was a friggin' ring—as big and shiny as the chandelier above the ballroom in the Castle Hotel. But I wasn't going to give her the satisfaction of mentioning it first. Poor, innocent Kathleen fell for it right away.

"Och, Mary," she said, "is that an engagement ring?"

Rose sniggered again and Mary looked at her finger as if shocked to see the ring there. "This?" she said. "Oh yes, George gave it to me at the weekend. It was my birthday and he wanted to surprise me. I almost forgot."

Forgot, my arse, I thought. Then I looked over at Patsy and all the life had gone out of her face. This time the sympathy I felt for her was genuine. I could have strangled Mary around her fat neck.

"Well, good for you, Mary," I said. "When's the baby due?"

Mary's eyes grew wide. Her face flushed. "What?" she cried. "There's no baby; what are you talking about?"

I shrugged. "Oh, pardon my mistake. I thought surely that was the only way you'd ever get any man to marry you, Mary."

Rose Boyle giggled and Mary gave her a black look. "Come on, Rose," she commanded. "These ones are only jealous."

She linked her arm in Rose's and the two of them walked away, arses waddling from side to side. But Mary had not had enough. "I'd invite youse all to the wedding," she said over her shoulder, "but it's going to be at George's family estate in Philadelphia. I'll send photos back, though."

"Feck off," Patsy muttered under her breath.

"That's an awful thing you said to her, Sheila," said Kathleen.

"She deserved it."

Chapter 15

ℯℵ

I f I'd thought I was mad in the head to be worrying about Patsy and her troubles, it was nothing to the mess I was going to get myself into with young Grainne. While I cared about what happened to Patsy, it was not going to change my life. I still had my eyes set on my goal of getting away from this place the first chance I got, and right now I still thought Joel was my best bet. If he had another girl, like Patsy said, well so much the better. When I turned him loose after he brought me to America, he'd have somebody to run back to and my conscience would be clear. But the episode with Grainne was a different kettle of fish altogether.

It started on a Sunday night not long after the concert at the Flagstaff. I had gone back up there after Mass, as I often did, to try to clear my head. Joel and Gavin were both away so I had no fear of running into either of them. My plan had been to go on to the Ceili House later, but something made me change my mind and go home instead. God knows, I wish I had just gone there and the rest of it never would have happened.

It was still light as I pushed open the front door of the house. Ma and Kate were away doing visiting rounds of Kate's charity cases and I assumed Kevin was upstairs sleeping as usual. Grainne was probably in our room. Poor child didn't seem to have any friends.

In the parlor the fire was almost out, but a suffocating fog enveloped me. Something was wrong; I could sense it. I walked back through the scullery towards the granny room. As I approached I heard voices. Maybe Grainne had a friend visiting after all. But as I reached the door what I heard was not two wee girls talking and laughing, but a rough male voice and a girl's cries. My heart rose to my throat. I knew what I was going to find. I took a deep breath and thrust the door open. There on the bed was Grainne, her arms pinned against the pillow and her dress up around her neck. On top of her was Kevin, his trousers down around his ankles and his white arse bouncing up and down. Grainne thrashed from side to side, crying and whimpering.

A madness came over me. I took my handbag and swung it at Kevin, savagely beating his bare bottom and legs.

"You dirty oul' bastard," I roared, "get up out of that! Leave the child alone! Get off her now!"

The metal clasp of my handbag raised red welts on his skin. He rolled off Grainne with a grunt. His eyes were burning. When he stood up I saw his hairy belly and his bulging organ, a dreadful purple color, and I wanted to vomit. Grainne rolled on her side, pulled her knees up to her chin, and began sobbing. Kevin pulled up his pants and fastened his belt. His face was red and his breathing heavy. Without warning he drew out and walloped me across the face with the back of his hand. I reeled backwards from the blow, staggering against the wall.

"What in the name of God...?"

Kevin and I swung around, and there stood Aunt Kate and Ma in the open doorway. Ma's eyes were the size of buckets and Kate's face was like chalk as she blessed herself.

"Come out of there, the two of you," she commanded, then turned and went back into the parlor along with Ma.

I steadied myself and Kevin pushed me ahead of him. "Say a word and you're done for," he snarled in my ear.

I could smell the drink on his breath.

When we reached the parlor Ma stood by the fireplace literally wringing her hands while Kate stood stiff as a statue.

"That bloody wee whore in there tried to make out I was interfering with her, and this one took her word for it and started beating me black and blue!" said Kevin.

"You were more than interfering with her," I yelled. "You were bloody raping her so you were!"

Ma put her hands to her mouth.

"Did you see him in the act?" said Kate sharply.

"He was on top of her with his trousers down round his ankles," I said. "What would you say he was doing?"

"She's a liar," roared Kevin, "a vicious liar. It was the girl called me in to help her with something and when I got there she was lying on the bed with her dress up and her legs spread out just asking for it. I was bending over her to tell her to make herself decent when this one came in and started screaming at me like a banshee."

"He's the one lying," I yelled. "He's been after me for the same thing these years but he never got the chance. Now he's forcing himself on the child—"

"She's no child," interrupted Kevin. "She's a whore just like her ma."

Ma let out a whimper. "Oh please, Sheila, stop it. We don't want any trouble."

I swung around to face her. "I'm telling the truth, Ma."

We fell silent, as Kate looked around from one to the other. Then her eyes fixed on me. "I'll not have you telling these lies about my husband, miss. From everything I hear about you, you have that kind of thing on the brain. Sex crazy, that's what the women at church say about you. It's a wonder you haven't tried to seduce my husband before now, but the other one beat you to it." She stopped and laughed—an ugly snorting sound. "Maybe you were jealous when you saw…when you saw what you thought you saw. Go on now, leave us alone. We have some decisions to make about this matter. Go on now."

I was dismissed. Why did I even think it would be any different? Of course Kate wouldn't believe my side of the story. And even though I knew Ma believed me, she wasn't going to back me up. She was afraid we'd get thrown out. I turned around and strode back into the granny room, shaking with anger and resentment.

"I'm sorry," whispered Grainne.

"What are *you* sorry for? It's himself out there should be sorry."

"I didn't mean to cause you trouble. Anyway, maybe I deserved it."

"Shut up, Grainne. Nobody deserves that."

"Maybe I led him on without realizing it," said Grainne, sitting up and leaning against the pillow. "More than one man told Ma that back on Amelia Street. Maybe I'm a bad seed. That's what Ma always said."

"Jesus, will you listen to yourself? The man's a brute. He's been trying to interfere with me ever since I came to live in this house—but he never got the chance beyond putting his dirty paws all over me and slobbering in my face in the dark."

Grainne put her head down and whispered almost to herself. "It's not the first time he's done it."

"Och, Jesus."

"Aye, always on Sundays when everybody else is gone. I try to sneak out but he's always waiting for me. So I stopped trying—I was afraid he'd send me back. I don't want to go back."

Grainne began to sob. I reached over and hugged her. "It's all right, love. Nobody's making you go back."

"They will. They will now. Nobody will believe me... except you."

❧

There was an uneasy silence in the house for the next week. Hardly anyone spoke a word. It was as if nothing had ever happened, and yet at the same time as if everything had changed. Ma and I went back up to the mill every day, Grainne went to school, Kevin went to work, and Kate went about her business with a face on her as stony as the granite in the nearby quarry. We ate our meals in silence. Once in a while Ma would mention something about the mill, or inquire after some old woman whom they visited on Kate's charity rounds. Kate always made some short but polite answer. Nobody looked at anyone else. Grainne was as sullen as I'd ever seen her. Her eyes were ringed in red from crying. My heart went out to her before I could stop it. Kevin made himself scarce every night, away down to the pub as soon as he had his tea finished. What he and Kate had to say to each other in the privacy of their upstairs bedroom, I didn't want to know. It was a quiet house, as I waited for the other shoe to drop.

Kate put us out of our suspense the next Saturday afternoon. Ma and I had come home from our usual overtime shift. I was working all the hours I could get and then I was going off out—anything but stay in that house for any longer than I had to. I was about to go into my room to get changed when Kate stopped me.

"Sheila, I need to talk to you and your mother."

Kate's voice was firm. I swung around and stood rooted to the floor. I saw Ma out of the corner of my eye. She had just sat down, and she jumped up again. She was shaking. I knew she was afraid we would be thrown out of the house. I thought she was probably right. I had told Ma I didn't think it would be so awful. We could always get a wee house down in Newry—something cheap enough that we could manage on both our wages. I hadn't stopped to think what would happen to her when I eventually left. She was quick to remind me, of course, so I stopped talking about it. Now, I waited for Kate's decision.

"Kevin and I have talked over the situation," she said.

Kevin was nowhere to be seen. He had obviously left Kate to do the dirty work. And Grainne was on a rare school outing for the afternoon. I thought she should have been present to hear the verdict. But, as it was, it was just the three of us.

"We've talked it over," Kate said again, "and the decision has not been an easy one."

I heard Ma suck in her breath. Kate stood tall and straight. Her face was drawn, and her lips pale. I wondered how much of Kevin's story she believed. Surely she must have seen him for the blackguard that he was. But he was her husband, and she could see by my ma and other women like her that Northern Ireland was a cold place for an older woman on her own. She wouldn't be the first woman to turn a blind eye to the doings of the bastard she was married to.

"Our first thought was that it would be better if you all left this house."

Ma let out a little whimper.

"But, I am a Christian woman, and I would not see your mother out on the street. She has no one to depend on really besides Kevin and me."

She looked pointedly at me when she said this. I bit my tongue.

"So we have agreed that if you will make an apology to my husband for your terrible accusation against him, and of course go to confession and tell the priest how you have lied, then we are prepared to have you and your mother stay on." She paused and pursed her lips. "The girl will have to go, of course."

There was silence. Ma blessed herself and then she looked over at me. Her eyes were huge. I knew she wanted me to agree there and then, but I could get no words out. I couldn't even think. Kate's words buzzed around me like summer wasps. I tried to take in what she was saying. Ma could stay; well, that was a relief. But apologize? I'd burn in hell before I'd do that. And Grainne? My God, they would send the child back to the hell she had only just come out of? It was all too much for me to take in at once. Part of me wanted to scream at Kate and part of me wanted to shrug and walk away.

"I see you want to take your time. Kevin was right. He said you're a stubborn girl. And while any good daughter would not upset her mother by refusing to do the right thing immediately, I will give you until Sunday night to make your decision."

"Sheila, love?" Ma looked at me with wide eyes.

I ignored her. "I'm going to change my clothes now," I said. "Then I'll be going out again. I'll be away again tomorrow while youse are at Mass. But I will be back tomorrow night."

They said nothing as I went to my room and quickly changed

my clothes. I was shaking as I did so. My stomach tumbled over and over. I thought I might vomit. But I put on a bright smile as I walked back through the parlor and opened the front door.

"Cheerio, then," I said.

Neither of them answered me.

ⓧ

I ran down the hill to the tram station, my mind in turmoil. I didn't know what to think about first. I could make things all right for Ma and myself by apologizing to the dirty bastard, Kevin, and having done with it. And what I told Father Flynn in confession was none of their fecking business. Things would go on as before. It wouldn't be that hard. Kevin knew I despised him, and words were not going to change that. And Kate knew he was lying, and my words were not going to change that either. No, it was not just the apology that was eating at me. It was Grainne. Whether I apologized or not, Grainne would not be let stay. Where would she go? I doubted that anyone else in the village would take her in—she had a reputation as trouble at school, and her bad attitude had pushed people away from her. At fourteen, she hardly even qualified as an evacuee anymore. She was no longer a child to be protected. She would be sent back to Belfast and that would be the end of it. And the end of her.

I was deep in thought as I pushed in through the door of the Ceili House pub. It was still early on Saturday evening, and there were few people in the place. I was glad. I was in no mood to be talking to anybody. I ordered a shandy and sat down at a table in a dark corner.

"I was hoping to find you here."

My head shot up at the sound of the familiar voice. Joel's smiling face hovered above me. I broke into a smile.

"You're back?"

"In the flesh. I haven't even been to the base yet. I almost went up to your house but I thought I'd stop here first just in case." He grinned. "You see, I'm getting to know all your habits, young lady."

"Not all of them, I hope," I said.

He kissed me lightly on the cheek and sat down opposite me, stretching his long legs out towards the fireplace. He looked well, but tired. He called the barman over and ordered a beer.

"How was England?"

His grin faded. "All right, I suppose."

"What are youse doing over there? Planning an invasion?"

I didn't know what made me say it. I suppose I must have heard some talk somewhere about how the Allies would have to plan something big soon to get a grip on the war.

Joel's face turned pale. "It's top secret, Sheila. You know I can't tell you anything. And you shouldn't be listening to rumors. People don't know what they're talking about."

The barman served his drink and he took a long gulp. "I'm sorry," he said more quietly. "It's just that … well I'm … we all are under a lot of strain. The war is not going as well as we'd hoped. And at this point, I don't even know if there is any good solution. But we have to do something. We can't let that bastard win."

I nodded. Normally I would have changed the direction of the conversation, but tonight I was glad of anything that distracted me from my own thoughts.

"You must be a very important chap if they keep calling you over there to consult," I said, hoping to cheer him up.

"I'd rather they left me be," he said. "That way I wouldn't have to shoulder the responsibility if things go wrong." He drained his glass and then leaned over towards me. "But there may be a silver lining to it all. I have something I want to talk to you about."

I sat up straight. "What? Tell me?"

"No, not here. Let's go."

He stood up and I stood up with him. I was filled with curiosity. I linked his arm as we made for the door. My earlier bad mood disappeared like a wisp of smoke.

We drove down the Warrenpoint road and through the town. As usual for a Saturday night the place was hectic. People crowded the main square and the funfair and strolled along the strand. It was early summer and the weather was unusually warm.

"Are we going to the Castle Hotel?"

He shook his head. "No, I think somewhere quieter might be the ticket. I've discovered a lovely little place just out the road. I went there a few weeks ago with some of the other officers. It will be perfect for what I have in mind."

I knew he wanted me to ask him just what he had in mind, but I said nothing. I liked the feeling of someone else in charge. It occurred to me that most of my life I was the one who had to make decisions, had to be in charge of things. This was a welcome change. I sat back and looked out at the sea and smiled.

Joel pulled the car up in front of a small hotel and restaurant called the Balmoral. It was a three-story terraced building overlooking the water. It was a Protestant place, and I had never set foot in it before. There were a number of well-dressed people sitting at white-clothed tables in the dining room. Some of the men nodded at Joel. He was still wearing his uniform. I was glad I had taken the time to change out of my work clothes into a blue cotton summer dress before I left the house. I straightened my shoulders and tossed back my hair. I was as good as any of them, I told myself, and tried to put the scene at the Canal Club and the sniggering well-bred girls out of my head.

After the waitress had cleared away the dinner plates, Joel leaned forward and took my hand in his and gazed into my eyes. I couldn't read the expression on his face. I waited.

"Sheila," he said, "I have something to ask you."

"Ask away," I said, trying to break the seriousness of the moment.

He cleared his throat. "Well, I know you may think this is very forward of me, but, well, I—what I want to say is, well I've been thinking, and—"

"For God's sake, Joel, just say whatever you have to say." The suspense was killing me.

"I want you to come away with me to England."

The words hung in the air. It was as if the room itself had gone silent; no cup chimed against a saucer, no glass clinked against another, no whisper was exchanged.

Joel rushed on. "Sheila, we have something special—something I've never felt with another girl before. I can talk to you—about anything."

I nodded. Panic and excitement rose up in me.

"The whole time I was away I couldn't get you out of my mind. I want you to be with me."

"I am with you," I said. "I'm sitting right here."

He shook his head. "No, that's not what I mean." He leaned back and sighed. "You see, I'm going to be spending a lot of time in England in the next few months and I don't want to be separated from you. Life is short, Sheila. We need to grab what pleasure we can from it. None of us knows what the future holds."

He paused, and I waited, my heart thumping.

"And before you say anything, I know it's asking a lot," he went on. "I know how much you love your home here in Ireland. But it would only be for a while, Sheila. After the war's over, if God spares us, we could come back here if you like." He put me in mind of an eager young boy.

I stared at him, trying to take in what he was saying. I'd often heard the saying about looking a gift horse in the mouth. Well, I was looking straight at the horse now. I should have been over the moon. Christ, I should have been dancing on the table. Instead I could only sit like an eejit with my mouth wide open. I was stunned.

"I realize it's sudden, Sheila," Joel was saying. "But promise me you'll think about it."

I nodded and put my hand out and touched his wrist. We sat in silence. Joel filled my wineglass and I took a sip without even tasting it. My mind was whizzing around faster than the roundabout at the Warrenpoint fair. I could go. After all this time and trouble, here was my escape sitting right in front of my eyes. I had taken up with Joel in the hope he would be my ticket out of here, and now he was. Granted, it wasn't to America yet, but that would come. At least England was a start. Half a loaf was better than none. I dismissed what he'd said about more permanent plans after the war. I'd worry about that when the time came. If he was thinking of marriage, I was sure I could play him along for a while, at least long enough to get to America. It was all falling into place. Thank God. Thank God.

It was late when we stood up to go. The restaurant had long ago closed and we were the only ones left.

"Fancy a dance at the Castle?" I said, knowing the ballroom would still be open. "I can tell my friends the good news."

Joel looked serious. "Does that mean you'll come away with me?"

"Of course," I said. "Of course I will."

A grin spread over his face. He stood and took my hand to help me up. He put his arm around my waist. "We could go to the Castle," he said, "but I think we have some celebrating to do. And I think we should do it alone."

I waited while Joel picked up a key from the receptionist in the hall and paid for the room. The clerk gave me a sour look that left me in no doubt what she was thinking, but I just grinned back at her. "Lovely evening," I said.

ര‌ൊ

I had never set foot in a hotel room before. I looked around me in awe. I took in the big mahogany bed with the blue and white floral bedspread, the polished dresser, and blue wing chair with a wee table beside it piled with magazines. The room was at the front of the hotel and overlooked Carlingford Lough. My feet sank into the blue carpet as I rushed to the window. I pulled back the white curtains and raised the sash so I could smell the sea. I turned back to Joel all smiles.

"This is grand," I said, excited as a child.

I turned back to the window and looked over towards Omeath. Dusk was falling and small lights glittered from the dark houses on the hills. I wondered was Gavin home and then chased the thought out of my mind.

"Come and sit down," Joel said. "Have some champagne."

He had removed his uniform jacket and sat down on the bed.

He patted a spot beside him. A fancy looking bottle and two crystal glasses sat on the bedside table. I wondered had he planned all this ahead of time. Was he so sure he would be able to get me to go to the room with him? So what, I thought. I owed him that much. I was never a great one for champagne—it turned my stomach—but I took a glass from him and watched him pour the golden liquid into it.

"Just a wee drop," I said. "I want to keep my wits about me."

"Afraid I'll get you drunk and have my way with you?"

"Och no." I laughed. "I want to remember every bit of it."

When we had drained our glasses, Joel took off his shoes and lay down on the top of the bed and I did the same. My heart was beating fast and I was suddenly self-conscious. Did I still smell of oil from the flax? I had not taken time to wash before I left the house. Were my knickers clean? Why hadn't I put on my best pair? But how could I have known? In my nervousness I pulled down a corner of the bedspread and began stroking the smooth, white sheets.

"Och, these are lovely, aren't they, Joel?" I said, thinking of the rough four sacks on my own bed.

"Shhh."

Joel sat up and removed his shirt and tie. I watched the muscles move in his smooth back and I wanted to put out my hand and touch them. He lay down again and rolled over to face me. He kissed me on the brow and cheek and began to open the buttons on the front of my dress.

"Is this OK?" he murmured, his voice huskier than usual.

I nodded.

Moments later we slid together in between the fresh, cotton sheets. I loved the feel of them against my bare skin. Joel pulled me close, rubbing his hands up and down my body in a gentle caress. He lowered his lips to my breast and I let out a small whimper. I raised my arms around his neck and pulled him close. How different this man was from the boys I knew—the ones who grabbed and tugged at me with sweaty, dirty hands. Joel treated my body with reverence. I turned my head away from him so he would not see my unexpected tears.

He raised his head and put his fingers to his lips. Then he sat up with his back turned to me and reached for something on the bedside table. It was a condom. I was relieved I had not had to ask him. I thought of Patsy and shuddered. He lay back down and rolled over on top of me. I rubbed my hands up and down the smooth skin of his back and the sinewy muscles of his buttocks. This was good, I thought. This was wonderful. But as he entered me I let out a scream. A sharp pain pierced the center of me and my body tensed. I clutched Joe's thighs. Alarmed, he pulled away from me.

"Sheila, are you all right? What did I do?"

I shook my head from side to side. "Nothing. I'm sorry."

Joel sat straight up. "My God, Sheila. You're a virgin. You never told me. I never thought . . . Oh, God."

"It's OK," I said. "I want to do this."

But Joel was already standing up and had removed the condom and thrown it in the wastebasket. "If I'd known, Sheila, I never would have . . ."

I raised myself up on my elbows. "I have to get past it sometime," I said. "And who better than with you? Honestly, Joel. It's OK."

He sat down beside me on the bed. "Why didn't you tell me, Sheila?"

I attempted a laugh. "It's not the kind of thing you bring up in polite conversation, Joel."

I put my arms around his neck and attempted to bring him close to me again. But he would have none of it.

"No, Sheila. This is your most precious gift and I will not take it from you like this."

My anger rose unexpectedly. I felt rejected. "But you thought it would be fine and dandy to jump into bed with Sheila the whore?"

He looked at me openmouthed. "I never took you for that!"

"Oh yes you did. And I can't blame you. With my reputation around here, everybody thinks the worst. And you're no exception. I'll be going home now. Maybe it's not too late for you to run out and find a more suitable girl."

I made to jump out of bed, but Joel took my shoulders and held me still.

"You're right, Sheila," he said. "I didn't think you were a virgin, but it made no difference to me. I still meant what I said. I still wanted you to come away with me. But now that I've found out that you are, it makes you even more precious to me. I realize now how much I was asking of you. I had no right to do it."

My God, was he going to change his mind? I couldn't let that happen. I swallowed the anger and frustration that had risen in me and took a deep breath.

"I still want to go with you, Joel."

He lay down and pulled me down beside him. He held me close and smoothed my hair with his hand.

"You are so beautiful, Sheila," he said. "I love you."

Chapter 16

❧

I stayed at the hotel until late the next morning. Joel had left to report into the barracks at first light. I had watched him get dressed in the dawn shadows. His movements were graceful and slow. He took out the silver pocket watch I had seen before and glanced at it. I smiled and snuggled down into the warm sheets. I must have drifted off. The knock of the housekeeper on the room door woke me. I panicked and shot up out of bed, grabbing my dress as I rushed to the door. I opened it and peered outside. A big, burly woman stared back at me, grunted, and went on about her business. Relieved, I walked over to the window and raised the blinds. The sun glinted on the lough as gulls called. As I turned back I noticed a tray sitting on the wee table beside the wing chair. On it was a silver coffeepot, a cup and saucer, and a plate with two scones and wee bowls of clotted cream and jam. Real cream! Jam! I hadn't seen the likes of it since before the war. I let out a little scream of delight. Joel must have ordered it before he left. I felt like a queen as I sat in the wing chair enjoying my breakfast. Then I giggled. Well, I *was* a queen. I was the Linen Queen.

When I finally left the room, I was giddy with the new possibilities for my future. I almost sang aloud as I made my way home. Home! It would not be home for long now, and good riddance to it. I expected the house to be quiet. They would all be away at Mass. But I was wrong. As I came closer I saw a crowd standing outside our house. There was a police wagon there as well. I began to run. Jesus, had something happened to Ma? Was she sick, or had she gone wild and lost her mind altogether? I elbowed my way through the crowd and pushed in through the front door. Ma sat in her usual armchair beside the fire. I let out a sigh of relief.

"Are you all right, Ma? What in the name of God's going on?"

She didn't answer me. Instead she looked over her shoulder towards the scullery and the granny room. It was then I heard the noises—shouts and cries and thumping. What in the hell was happening? I rushed towards the scullery and bumped into Kate. She put out her arms to restrain me.

"Don't go near there. The police will take care of it. That girl has barricaded herself in the room and she has a knife. She's screaming that she'll kill us all!"

I shoved her aside. "Grainne!" I shouted. "Grainne, love. It's Sheila. For God's sake come on out of there."

Two policemen, along with Kevin, were charging at the door with their shoulders.

"Stay out," she cried. "Leave me alone!"

I didn't know what to think. I knew she'd be unhappy when she was told to leave, but I never expected her to react like this. I realized now I'd had a bad feeling about it all, and I had put it out of my mind while I was with Joel. God forgive me, I'd been so excited about getting away to England, I'd almost forgotten about the whole situation.

"We've sent for Father Flynn," Kate said from behind. "He'll put the fear of God in the little pagan, mark my words."

"If you don't come out now you wee bastard, you'll be locked up for the rest of your life," cried one of the policemen. He was red in the face from the effort of trying to break down the door.

"Feck off!" cried Grainne.

If the situation wasn't so serious I might have laughed. The girl was afraid of nobody. I supposed when you'd lived your life on the streets of Belfast it would take a lot to put the fear of

God in you. The second policeman had gone out and come back with a hatchet. He swung it at the door. Long streaks of wood peeled down like banana skins. Aunt Kate let out a scream. Then he swung the hatchet at the hinges and they fell apart. The three men put their shoulders to the door again and this time it gave way. As they shoved, the furniture Grainne had piled behind the door grunted and slid backwards into the room. One final push and a gaping hole appeared where the door had been. I tried to see over their shoulders. Grainne stood beside the bed, the knife clutched in her hands. The police grabbed her and pulled her forward. She cried out and dropped the knife.

"Let me in!" I shouted.

The police were as surprised as I was at the strength of my roar. They dropped their hold on Grainne and she ran into my arms. She was sobbing. The brave soldier in her had melted away and she was a frightened child again.

"Don't let them take me, Sheila," she cried. "Please."

I stroked her hair. "It's all right, wee Grainne," I whispered.

I wasn't sure what I was thinking at that moment. In fact, the truth was that I wasn't thinking at all. I was acting out of some compulsion to protect the girl. It was an urge so strong I could do nothing to stop myself.

"Ah, Father, thank God you're here." Kate's voice reached over my shoulder. "She's possessed by the devil, so she is. Look at the damage she's done to my house. And she nearly killed us all!"

Father Flynn's face was dark with anger. He took in the situation in one glance. Then he nodded to the older policeman.

"Can I have a word with you outside, Sergeant?"

The two of them turned and walked through the parlor and out the door onto the street. I smoothed Grainne's hair. She clung to me, her entire body shaking. "Don't worry, love," I whispered. "It will be all right."

When Father Flynn returned he wore the same smug look he always wore when chastising the drunks down at the tram station on Saturday nights. He was the boy who waited for the lads coming off the last tram, nearly kissing them as he smelled their breaths, and then ridiculing them at Mass the next morning. I shivered. Something bad was about to happen. I could feel it.

"Sergeant Riley and I have agreed. The girl will be given into my care." He paused and looked around at all of us. Ma had left her chair and hovered in the scullery beside Kate. "This girl has been a bad article from the moment she arrived here," Father Flynn continued. "The reports I have about her from her teachers and schoolmates and others in the parish are that she is beyond help. Her behavior has been abominable. She shows no respect for authority, her language is worse than any sailor, and as far as I know she has never set foot in confession—even though she marches up to communion every Sunday with decent people."

Kate let out a faint scream and put her hands to her mouth.

"She is in mortal sin," Father Flynn shouted, and he thumped his fist on a nearby table. "There is no alternative but to send her to the nuns, and I pray that the good sisters will in time be able to save her soul."

"You can't do that!" I shouted. "Kate? Kevin? Please. Surely there's another way. What about her ma? Even that would be better than the convent."

Kate shrugged. "The women who arranged for her to be billeted here in the first place have been in touch with the mother. Apparently she wants nothing to do with her daughter. And if you ask me, the girl will be much better off with the nuns than that tramp."

"Me ma's not a tramp!" Grainne blurted out. She had pulled away from me and was glaring at Kate and the others. "And I don't believe that she doesn't want me back."

Kate pursed her lips. "Believe what you like," she said. "And to think I was prepared to pay your fare home to Belfast. If your mother had been willing to take you we would have got rid of you a week ago."

Sergeant Riley and his partner put on their caps. "We'll be leaving you in the good father's hands," said the sergeant. He turned to Grainne. "You're lucky Father Flynn here took pity on you, my girl, or we'd have had you locked up—mark my words."

"Lucky my arse," I said under my breath, but Kevin heard me. "Watch your mouth," he said, "or you're next."

I watched helplessly as Kate threw the few belongings the child owned into the old battered suitcase Grainne had brought with her when she first arrived and thrust it at Father Flynn. Ma clung to my elbow and I hadn't the strength to shove her away. Grainne's face was drained of all color. She stood quietly like a prisoner awaiting arrest and then walked outside with the priest without protest. Ma and Kate and I went to the door. Out on the street Grainne turned and looked directly to me. There was a strange look on her face. It was not anger, as I might have expected, but accusation. Mortified, I watched her thin figure disappear down the street with the priest in his black suit.

∞

I didn't even remember how I got to the Flagstaff. I must have pedaled furiously away from the house and out the road and up to the summit. I was out of breath with the effort of it. I dropped my bicycle on the grass and slumped down on the nearest stone bench. I couldn't get Grainne's face out of my mind.

I sat without moving. Some gulls circled overhead making a mournful noise. A mist had fallen over the lough. I could see no boats, even though there were usually plenty of them on a Sunday. I had the odd feeling the world was in mourning. Sighing, I pulled out a packet of cigarettes and lit one. I inhaled deeply and sent curling wisps of smoke into the air. How things had changed in a few hours, I thought. One minute I'd been over the moon. My dream had come true at last. Joel had offered me my pass to freedom. I was finally on my way. The mill, the house in Queens-brook, the poverty—all of it would be left behind. But now the light had gone out of everything. I couldn't even bring myself to be angry. All I felt was exhaustion.

That evening I crawled into the empty bed in the granny room. It was still light outside and I pulled the covers up over my head to shut it out. I could still smell Grainne's scent on her pillow. I wondered how she was at this moment. I hoped at least she was safe and warm, even if she was up at that awful place on the hill. The poor girl must be scared out of her wits, I thought. I remembered the nightmares I'd had as a child every time Ma threatened to take me to the convent. The big gray building turned into a monster in my dreams and opened its huge mouth and swallowed me up. I turned the events of the day over and over in my head. How could life have turned so upside down in less than twenty-four hours? This time last night I had been sipping champagne with Joel, toasting our new adventure in England, and now? Well, now I felt as if the bottom had dropped out of my life leaving me suspended in midair, not knowing which way to go.

I twisted and turned in the bed and thumped the pillow. I was looking for anger. I had every right to be raging. Why now? Why did all this have to come to a head the very day I had held my freedom in my two hands? It wasn't fair. None of it was fair. I'd done nothing wrong. All I had done was to try to help the girl, when I should have stayed out of it and minded my own business. I turned from side to side, twisting the sheets into a ball, and the sweat poured off me. At last I sat up. There was going to be no sleep for me this night, I realized. I got out of bed and dressed. I had to get away from here.

"Where are you going at this hour?"

Ma's voice startled me. She sat in the armchair beside the dying fire.

"Why aren't you in bed minding your own business?"

"Sure who could sleep after what happened? That poor wee mite." Ma sighed. "Och, sure maybe it's the best place for her. Better than back with that ma of hers. Anyway, it's God's will."

I rolled my eyes. "What kind of God would wish that place on a child?"

I tugged the front door open and stepped out, pulling it closed behind me. The cool air revived me. Darkness had finally fallen. I hadn't even looked at the clock. It must be past midnight, I thought. I shrugged and lifted my bicycle, which leaned against the wall of the house. I wheeled it down the hill. I had no idea where I was going. As I walked, I breathed deeply and tried to clear my head. It was a Sunday night, and all decent people were in their beds asleep and waiting for the mill horn to blow on Monday morning. There was not a light to be seen in any window. The road ahead of me was black as pitch. Not a soul passed me on the road. Even the birds were asleep. I had the strange feeling I was the only person alive in the world.

∞

An hour later I was cycling up to the guard station outside Narrow Water Castle where Joel was billeted. I got off my bicycle, my legs so weak they almost buckled under me. I leaned against the wall for support. I didn't even remember making the decision to go there. All I knew was I got on my bicycle and started pedaling into Newry and then out the Warrenpoint road and along the water in the direction of the base. I felt Joel pulling me towards him. I knew I had to see him. It made no sense of course, showing up there in the middle of the night. I'd likely get arrested. But I didn't care.

The door of the hut opened and a young soldier charged out carrying a rifle. He aimed it right at me.

"Halt!" he shouted. "What's your business?"

The look on his face was almost comical. I must have shocked him out of a doze. He probably thought I was a German. And when he saw me, he blinked his eyes open and shut, as if he thought he was dreaming.

"What's your business, miss," he said again when he had recovered himself.

"I need to see Captain Solomon," I said. My voice was calm.

"At this hour of the night?"

I nodded. "It's urgent," I said. "Very urgent."

"The camp's closed. You'll have to come back in the morning."

I slid down on to the ground and began to laugh. I suppose it was nerves. "How can the camp be closed? What if I'd been a German?"

The young soldier moved closer. He prodded me with his rifle. "Have you been drinking?"

I shook my head and laughed louder. "No," I said. "But it's a good idea."

He grabbed one of my shoulders and hoisted me to my feet.

"You can't stay here, miss. Or I'll have to arrest you."

"Then do that," I said. I was suddenly so tired I didn't care what happened.

The soldier cursed under his breath. I felt sorry for him.

"Look," I said, "call Joel—Captain Solomon. You won't get into trouble. I'll make sure. I'll tell him I badgered you until you had no choice."

He hesitated for a minute. Then he said, "Stay here!"

He went into the hut and I heard him on the telephone. I couldn't make out what he was saying. I slumped down on the ground again and closed my eyes.

"Sheila? Sheila? What on earth is going on? What's wrong?"

I opened my eyes and Joel was leaning over me, shaking me. I must have fallen asleep. I looked up at him and shook my head.

"Nothing's wrong," I said. "I just needed to see you, that's all."

Any other man might have roared at me for getting him out of bed in the middle of the night and embarrassing him in front of a subordinate, but not Joel. His voice was calm as he helped me to my feet and took me firmly by the elbow.

"Let's go inside," he said, "where we can talk."

He turned around and nodded at the soldier. "I'll take care of things from here, Private Watson."

The soldier saluted and went back into his hut.

Joel picked up my bicycle and wheeled it with one hand while he took my arm with the other. He said nothing as he led me towards the main building on the estate. He left my bicycle at the front steps and steered me up towards the big wooden front door.

"Let's go into the library," he said. "It will be private in there."

We walked down a wide, dark hallway and into a cavernous room. A small lamp burned near the empty fireplace, casting a copper glow over everything. Joel pointed to an armchair and turned on some more lamps.

"I'll get you some brandy," he said. "You look like you could use it."

While he stood at a giant sideboard pouring brandy from a crystal decanter I looked around. Shelves climbed from floor to ceiling crammed with books. I had never seen so many in one place in my life. Had anybody read them all, I wondered? Gilt-framed oil paintings filled the other walls, arranged carefully on red flock wallpaper. A huge globe sat on a table near me, and carved sailing ships perched on shelves around the room. In one corner stood the bust of a woman that must have been the prow of an ancient boat. I smiled absently at the sight of it. I imagined old men sitting in the worn leather chairs, reading newspapers and drinking brandy. The room gave off the scent of old money and people who were sheltered from the chaos of the outside world. I envied the people who had lived here, and yet the room frightened me just a little. If I believed in ghosts, I was sure they would have haunted this room.

"Here. Drink this," said Joel, handing me a glass of golden liquid.

The glass was heavy in my hand. I lifted it and swallowed. The brandy burned my throat and I spluttered.

Joel sat down in an armchair across from me. He had not poured himself a drink. He waited silently while I settled down. I couldn't tell what he was thinking. I put the glass down on a side table and nervously pulled out a pack of cigarettes. I rummaged in my handbag for matches but could find none, and Joel didn't offer any. I shoved the pack into my pocket.

"Now," said Joel at last, "what brings you here in the middle of the night?"

I tried to joke. "I couldn't get enough of you," I said.

His face was solemn. "No jokes, Sheila. What's going on?"

What was I to say? I didn't even know myself what had driven me to come down here. It was as if I'd had no choice in it at all. Joel waited for my answer. Somewhere in the house a door creaked and I jumped.

"They sent Grainne to the nuns," I burst out suddenly.

"To the nuns?" He looked confused.

"Aye. Father Flynn came and took her away. He said it was the only way to save her soul from mortal sin."

I took a deep breath and told him the story beginning with what I had found after I returned to the house that morning and finishing up with the look on Grainne's face as Father Flynn took her away. I began to cry.

"There wasn't a thing I could do to help her, Joel. I just stood there and watched her go."

"Doesn't sound like there's much you could have done."

"At least I could have gone with her. Maybe we could have given Father Flynn the slip."

"It wouldn't have been a permanent solution, Sheila," said Joel gently. "They would have found you eventually and would have taken her away again."

"You're right; I know you are. But I just can't get rid of the guilt."

Joel stood up and came and sat on the arm of my chair. He put his hand on my shoulder. "It will be all right, Sheila. Just go on home. From what you tell me of Grainne, she has the grit to look after herself."

"You don't know what it's like with the nuns. Once you're in there everybody forgets about you and you never get out again. Or you go astray in the head and they throw you out just like oul' Mad Biddy on Hill Street."

"Where's her mother?" said Joel.

"Och, don't ask. The mother is a whore in Belfast. She wants nothing to do with Grainne."

Joel stood up. "It's a sad state of affairs. But it's not your business, Sheila. You're not related to her."

A sudden anger rose in me and I lashed out at him. "Aren't you the hypocrite? You're the one always saying about how we have to save the Jews from terrible things beyond in Europe, particularly the children. Shouldn't we care just as much about the likes of Grainne?"

Joel was annoyed. "It's not the same thing at all."

We said nothing for a while. The big clock I had passed in the hallway chimed the hour. I looked up at Joel.

"I want to go away with you, Joel, really I do. You're the best thing that's ever happened to me. But can I just go now and leave Grainne behind? Would that be a right thing to do at all?"

Joel's face tightened. "I can't tell you what to do, Sheila. I want you to come with me to England, but I cannot force you against your will."

I could feel my frustration building. I needed him to reassure me that it was all right to go, but he was refusing to do so.

"I'll have it on my conscience the whole time."

A flash of anger shot across Joel's face. "I must say you have hidden your conscience very well up until now. You haven't shown much concern for others."

His words cut like a knife. What was he talking about? I stood up.

"Is that what you think of me? Is that so? Well you're right. I have no conscience. Otherwise I would not have been using you to get me out of this place. Any Yank would have done, but you just happened to come along..."

Oh Jesus, what was I saying? I put my hands out towards him but he backed away. "I didn't mean that...," I began.

"I'm afraid you did, Sheila." I couldn't read what was in his voice. "Deep down I realized you were using me but I was hoping that...in time...you would come to love me for myself. And after last night, well, I was more hopeful. But I was wrong, wasn't I?"

I was frightened now. "Och, Joel. It might have been that way at first, but things were changing; they really were..."

He sighed and walked over to the sideboard and poured himself a brandy. He turned back to me.

"Well, it's just as well the truth has come out now and not later when you're stuck with me in England. Go home, Sheila. Go home and decide what it is you really want. Are you using Grainne's situation as an excuse not to go with me, or do you really care what happens to the girl? I'd like to think the latter is true, but as they say, a leopard doesn't change its spots. It's not like you to let a little matter like that stand in your way. Perhaps it's your friend Gavin you don't want to leave. Whatever it is, just promise me something. Be honest with yourself, and with all of us. We'll all be the better off for it."

I was stunned. Was it over? What had I done? Joel walked over and took my arm and helped me out of the chair. Without a word he led me back down the hall and out the door. He picked up my bicycle and wheeled it across the courtyard as he had done before. He saluted the young private in the hut and handed me my bicycle.

"It's best if we don't see each other before I leave for England," he said. "I hope I'll be back in Ireland before I have to see action. But if that is not the case…who knows…I always want you to remember me kindly, Sheila, as I'll remember you."

I couldn't see his face in the dark, but I suspected there were tears in his eyes. I was fighting back my own. I felt the same sadness as the day my da left me at the pier. I could find no words. I nodded towards him and climbed on my bicycle and rode away down the driveway and out onto the main road. I did not look back.

Instead of going back to Queensbrook, I went to the place I always went to when I was in need of refuge. Dawn broke over the Flagstaff, painting the sky and water red. Birds awoke and began to sing. I sat down on a bench and looked out over the lough. Somewhere in the distance a ship's horn sounded. I buried my face in my hands. I heard Joel's voice. "Remember me."

"Och, Joel, I never meant to hurt you."

Something I didn't understand had cracked open inside me, like an egg, and spilled out. I knew I would never be the same.

Chapter 17

ᏬᎯᏬ

Habit is often the only thing that saves us from going mad. That morning my body took over from my mind and led me to the mill. I made no conscious decision to go there. I was not capable of such a thing as a decision. My mind was empty and numb. I thought nothing, felt nothing. And so habit came to my rescue. It steered me firmly towards the mill along with my fellow workers, all of us heeding the horn that summoned us as if to religious service.

Patsy stared at me with her mouth open. I looked down at my crumpled dress and muddy boots. I'd had no time to change my clothes that morning. I'd arrived back in Queensbrook just as the mill horn was blasting. There was only enough time to splash some cold water on my face and drag myself out of the house and up the road to the mill.

"Are you all right, love?" murmured Kathleen. "Did something happen to you?"

"Ah, now," I said wearily, "I wouldn't know where to start to tell you."

Just then Mary McAteer came strolling by, her fat face stretched in a false smile. "Good morning, girls. Beautiful day, isn't it?" She stopped and looked me up and down. "Why, Sheila." She pursed her lips. "I do hope no one of importance sees our Linen Queen looking like a gypsy. Wouldn't do, would it?"

She sailed off and Patsy stuck out her tongue behind her.

"Bitch!" she said.

I took a deep breath and began to tell Patsy and Kathleen the story. I needed to speak it out loud to be sure it was real. I told them about Sunday afternoon and the ructions I found with Grainne and the police and Father Flynn. I deliberately left out the night with Joel and his offer to take me with him to England and my visit last night when like an eejit I had told him I'd only been using him. I hadn't even let the reality of it sink into my own head yet. And what would they think of me for losing the offer of a lifetime because I was worried about some whore's daughter? They might not have believed me. I hardly believed it myself.

"And I could hardly sleep after all that. So in the middle of the night I got up and rode my bicycle up to the Flagstaff. I dozed off up there, and when I woke up the sun was coming up and I was freezing my arse off."

Kathleen clasped her hands in front of her as she listened.

"Ah, the poor wee child," she said, "sent to that awful place. You wouldn't wish it on your worst enemy."

Patsy just shrugged her shoulders. "There's worse things," she said. "At least the girl has a roof over her head, which is more than I'll have when my da finds out about this." She looked down at her stomach, which was still fat under her apron. Kathleen followed her gaze and then threw her hand to her mouth in understanding.

"Och, Patsy, no," she said.

In the midst of all my own troubles, I'd completely forgotten about Patsy and the baby. It made me twice as glad I hadn't said anything about turning down Joel's offer of escape. In the same situation, Patsy would have jumped at the chance even if the pope himself had ordered her to stay.

"Any word from Sylvie?" I asked.

She shook her head. "No. And not likely to be." She looked up at me, her brown eyes intense. "You'll still go with me to see Father Toner, won't you? He's the only one can help me. You said you'd go."

A ripple of annoyance filled my head. Why was I expected to

save everyone but myself? This wasn't the way it was supposed to be. I, Sheila McGee, owed nothing to anybody. I'd had a hard life, and I deserved every bit of happiness I could get. I had no obligation to other people in trouble. They were old enough to look after themselves. I wouldn't have lifted a hand to help Patsy if it had meant giving up my dream of escape. But now, Grainne's face floated in front of me. Why? Why in God's name had I run to Joel worried sick about leaving her? I silently cursed her. I knew she was trouble the day I saw her. But little did I know how much her presence would cost me. A splitting pain seared through my head and I closed my eyes.

"I can go with you, Patsy, if you'd like," said Kathleen in a soft voice.

I opened my eyes and sighed.

"It's OK, Kathleen. I said I'd go and I'll go."

๛

The presbytery where Father Toner and Father Flynn lived was a huge gray stone house set between the church and the graveyard. I wondered what it would be like to look out at graves in the middle of the night. The thought gave me the willies. As we stood on the doorstep preparing to ring the bell beside the big oak door, Patsy shivered. She gripped her handbag between her fingers as if afraid it would take flight any minute. I wondered how I would feel in her shoes. Well, luckily I wouldn't have to find out.

An old woman with gray hair and a black apron opened the door.

"We've an appointment with Father Toner," I said.

She looked us up and down and opened the door wider.

"Come in. He's finishing his tea. Youse can wait in here."

She led us into a big parlor with high carved ceilings and dusty furniture. It smelled of mothballs. The room was so big it made you feel very small. I wondered if that was the point of it. For centuries people had been coming to see the priest in the biggest house in the village. They were supposed to bow and scrape and beg the good father for whatever small indulgence they needed. And for centuries, the local priest sat in judgment—judge, jury, and executioner. There was no going against the priest.

"Fecking freezing in here," Patsy grumbled. "D'you think they let you smoke?"

I shrugged. "Dunno."

She took out a cigarette and lit it and passed the pack to me. Her hands were shaking.

"He's nicer than the other one," she murmured. "Father Toner, I mean."

I nodded and lit my own cigarette.

We heard a man cough in the doorway and we looked up. It was Father Flynn. He glared at the both of us.

"Put them things out," he shouted, nodding towards our cigarettes. "Have youse no respect at all?"

I looked around and didn't see an ashtray. Where was I supposed to stub the thing out? I could feel the heat of his stare. In desperation I rubbed the lit tip of the cigarette between my thumb and forefinger, sending sparks into the air. Jesus, it hurt. I had nearly burned the fingers off myself. Patsy spat on her butt and shoved it into her handbag. I waited for the bag to catch fire.

"What do youse want?"

Father Flynn moved into the room. He was tall and boyish with close-cropped blond hair. He was the kind of man that older women wished their sons looked like. I thought he was nothing but an arrogant, ignorant lout, full of himself with his training in Rome and all the rest of it. If this was the new crop of priests coming up, I thought, we were all in trouble. He was also the man who had taken Grainne away. My heart began to thud in my chest and I clenched my fists.

"We're here to see Father Toner." Patsy sounded like a wee mouse—not like herself at all. "We have an appointment with him."

"He's finishing his tea at the minute. And then he has to go out on a sick call. You can talk to me."

He pulled out a faded armchair and sat down in front of us. I looked at Patsy. Her face had turned white.

"It's a private matter," I said.

A crimson flush rode up his cheeks. "There can be no secrets between a sinner and her priest." He glared at us. "Since it's not something you wanted to tell in confession, then I have to assume it's a more serious matter." He pointed a long white finger at me. "What've you done now, miss? Out with it!"

I nearly jumped out of my chair. "Nothing!" I yelled back at him. "And if I had, you're the last person I'd be telling."

"Watch your mouth, young woman, or I'll be dragging you up to the convent like the other one. You are two of a kind."

"I'm a grown woman," I said. "You can't do anything to me."

"I can excommunicate you. And don't think I wouldn't."

I suppose he thought that would shut me up, but I was so angry I didn't even take in the seriousness of his words. I jumped up and turned to Patsy.

"C'mon, Patsy. We'll come back another time when Father Toner is free."

Patsy looked from me to Father Flynn and back. Her face was chalk white. She looked as if she might vomit. Father Flynn fixed his eyes on her.

"Is there something you have to say to me, Patsy Mallon? Oh, don't look so surprised. I know well who you are. I know your father and mother." He looked at us with a smirk on his face. "I make it my business to visit all the people in the parish. Your parents are good people. But I hear you've given them a lot of bother over the years. I hope you've done nothing to disgrace them."

"Ah, there you are. I'm sorry I have been called out on an emergency." Father Toner poked his head around the doorway. "I'll leave you to young Father Flynn here. I'm sure he can help you out."

I didn't know if I imagined it, but I saw a dark look pass over Father Flynn's face. Before I could get a word out, Father Toner was gone.

"So, Father Toner has left me to the dirty work here," Father Flynn said.

I grabbed Patsy's arm to leave, but the priest put up his hand.

"Stay!"

It was a command, not a request. I dropped Patsy's arm as if it were on fire and sat back down.

"You are pregnant, Miss Mallon." A sneer spread across his face. "Don't look so surprised. I see weak, stupid, sinful girls like you every day. Admit it!"

Patsy bowed her head. "Yes, Father," she murmured.

"And the father is a soldier."

There were no flies on this boyo.

Patsy nodded, biting her lip to fight back tears.

"And you want him to marry you?"

Patsy looked up at him, wide eyes hopeful. "Yes, Father, I do. I was hoping you could persuade him—"

Father Flynn raised his hand to interrupt her. "Go no further, Miss Mallon. I will tell you what I have told the others—I will not force a marriage on a young man who has been tricked by a tramp like you. And how dare you even think you have any right to enter into the sacrament of holy matrimony in your sinful state?"

My temper boiled over. I jumped up from my chair. "How dare you treat her like that?" I yelled. "He's the one got her in trouble, and him a Catholic."

Father Flynn stood up to face me. "And how dare *you* question my authority, Miss McGee? Are you sure you're not in the same predicament yourself? From what I hear..."

"You bloody...," I began. But before I could get out the insults that crowded my tongue, Patsy pulled me back down into the chair.

"It's all right, Sheila," she said. "I expected as much."

I had never seen or heard Patsy this defeated. It was as if somebody had let all the air out of her. I was raging, but the ferocious look on the priest's face silenced me. I had said too much already.

"What about the baby?" Patsy murmured.

Father Flynn sniffed. "It will be born illegitimate of course, a terrible burden on a child. But when the time comes we will arrange for it to be put in the care of an orphanage, and hopefully adopted into a good Catholic home."

He walked to the door. "Now if you will excuse me, I have other parish work to attend to."

Patsy and I linked arms as we walked back down towards the village. For a while neither of us spoke. I sucked on my thumb and finger trying to calm the burn from the cigarette. I didn't know what had got into me. I had lost control altogether, talking back to a priest like that. Aunt Kate and Ma would not be long hearing about it—and Mrs. McAteer, and maybe even oul' Carlson himself. What was I thinking? I'd already lost Joel; now maybe I'd lose my job at the mill. Father Flynn only had to say the word to Carlson and he'd sack me.

"He'll tell my da!" Patsy said.

"Jesus, Patsy. Don't be saying that."

"He will, he'll tell him. God, what am I going to do?"

She walked on ahead of me sobbing. So much for the comfort of the church, I thought.

☙

The following Sunday I stood at the bottom of Convent Hill in Newry, staring up at the huge gray building that housed the Convent of the Holy Mother. I had made two earlier tries to go there that afternoon, but each time I had turned on my heel and hurried away. This time I willed myself to stand in place. I have to do this for Grainne's sake, I told myself. "You're a grown woman now, Sheila," I said aloud. "They can't touch you." But inside I was the frightened wee girl who put her hands over her eyes every time her ma pointed up to the building and told her to behave herself. Swallowing hard, I forced myself to put one foot in front of the other and walk up the hill. My dread deepened as I drew close to the heavy oak door and put out my hand to push the bell. Everything in me wanted to turn and run. And I might have done, except the door opened quickly and an old, bent woman waved me in. She never looked me in the eye as she led me into a big drawing room. I supposed she was old and a bit simple. I wondered how long she had been in this place, and my thoughts moved to Grainne. Abruptly I turned away from her. The sight of her made me shiver. The place smelled of polish and candle wax and was quiet as a funeral home.

"May I help you?"

A tall, thin nun wearing a black habit and white wimple swept into the room. Her long, white fingers caressed the crucifix hanging from her belt. She smiled at me as she spoke, but her eyes were sharp as a fox. "I am Sister Thaddeus. Won't you sit down, please?"

It was clear she had no idea why I was there or she would hardly have been so polite. I sat down on a flower-patterned sofa. I expected the cushions to be soft, but they were as hard as boards. She sat in a wing chair opposite me and waited. My earlier resolve began to melt under her gaze and the speech I had practiced went completely out of my head. Coming here had seemed logical at the time. I had let Joel go on account of Grainne. Now I had to get Grainne out of this place or my sacrifice would have been for nothing. I squared my shoulders—it was now or never.

"Good afternoon, Sister," I began, as politely as I could, trying to keep my voice steady. "It's good of you to see me without an appointment. My name is Sheila McGee."

I was used to being around nuns from my school days. The more polite you were the better. I pretended to myself that this nun was no different.

"I'd like to speak with you about a young girl who was recently brought into your care."

"Of course. What would be her name?"

"Grainne Malloy."

That did it. Sister Thaddeus's spine straightened like a stick and her eyes pierced my face. The smile, however, remained.

"Yes, I know the girl." She shook her head from side to side. "Unfortunate. Very unfortunate." She sighed. "She may be too far gone even for us to help her. But God has sent her to us as a challenge and we must do our best to measure up to it."

Her grip on her crucifix tightened, and she paused as if inviting agreement from me.

"Ah, yes, Sister," I said. "The girl has had a very difficult life. And evidently she has had very little spiritual direction."

That was a nice touch, I thought. My courage was growing. Sheila McGee could do this.

"But," I went on, "you'd agree wouldn't you that maybe some other alternatives could have been found? Bringing her straight here to the convent was an awful big step. I know Father Flynn must have thought it best at the time, but now I've had time to think about this, I'm prepared to take her off your hands, so I am."

I thought the good Sister was about to burst. Her face grew exceedingly red as I was speaking and I could see she had a hard time not leaping out of the chair and grabbing me by the throat.

"And just why, young lady, do you think that you are in a better position to offer her the guidance she needs than we ourselves are? After all, we here at the convent are called by God to protect the purity of our young women. Our work here has gone on for more than a century, and please God it will continue for another."

"I didn't mean to offend you, Sister," I said, swallowing my temper, which was boiling inside me. "It's just that I believe the girl deserves a second chance, and I'm prepared to look after her... and protect her."

The ructions began in earnest then. Sister Thaddeus rose from her chair and stood over me. "How dare you, Miss McGee! How dare you put yourself on a level with the sisters of the Holy Mother Convent! It's been many a year since I have witnessed such false pride. Shameful, Miss McGee. Shameful. And a mortal sin, I might add." She paused briefly for breath. "And wait until I tell Father Flynn about this. He will know how best to deal with such arrogance. All I can do is pray for you."

She stared at me and I shivered. I was suddenly as cold as a corpse. But, strangely, my fear of her had gone. An image of Grainne's frightened face as she was dragged out of the house by Father Flynn rose up before me. How dare they have done this to her? And I thought of Patsy's tears as she begged Father Flynn for help. How dare they treat girls like them, and me, like the scum of the earth? Had we no rights at all? All the years of ridicule and judgment at the hands of my supposed betters came rushing back to me in a blaze of hot anger. I jumped up and put my face so close to Sister Thaddeus's that I almost gagged on the carbolic soap she used to scrub her skin. All my earlier pretense of politeness was gone.

"You haven't heard the last of this," I shouted. "You won't make a prisoner of that girl the way you've been doing to others for years! Mark my words, I'll get her out of this place—"

"Father Flynn will stop you. He'll—" cried Sister Thaddeus.

"The entire Church won't stop me!" I yelled.

As I raced out into the hallway the housekeeper blocked my way.

"That's right, love," she said. "Steal wee Grainne. Steal her now!"

She straightened up and peered at me with a peculiar light in her eyes, and I saw that she was not old at all. Her mouth contorted and she let out a lewd laugh then clapped her hand over her face. She was astray in the head. There was no doubt about it.

"Marian! See that tramp out. Now!" Sister Thaddeus's voice was shrill behind me.

I pushed past the housekeeper and out the door and down the steps. I felt like I was running from hell itself. I didn't dare look back. Part of me felt like a schoolgirl who had been severely scolded by the nuns. But that was the old Sheila. As I ran another more powerful feeling took hold of me. What fueled it was the need to right a wrong and it was unlike anything I had ever experienced.

"I'll get you out of there, Grainne," I muttered. "No matter what I have to do."

Chapter 18

ॐ

Later that day I sat in P. J. O'Hare's pub in Carlingford with Gavin. I had sent word with a young lad up to his house telling him to meet me. I didn't know if he would come, but I hoped he would sense I was in trouble and needed his help.

"So, what's the *craic*?" He set two glasses of lager on the table and sat down opposite me.

I relaxed a little. Maybe this would be easier than I thought. I studied his face. There was no anger in it but no pleasure either. He sipped his drink and said nothing.

"Thanks for coming," I began. "I need your help, Gavin."

He raised an eyebrow and waited.

"It's about wee Grainne. Father Flynn brought her to the convent and who knows what will happen to her in that place. They do awful things to girls in there. I need you to help me get her out."

"But what about Joel the Jew?" he said, his voice full of sarcasm. "A man in his position ought to be—"

"Stop calling him that," I interrupted. "And anyway he's not here. He's gone to England."

"So you came running to me." Gavin shrugged his shoulders. "Sorry, Sheila, it's not my business to get involved."

My frustration threatened to choke me. "Jesus, Gavin," I said, "d'you want me to get down on my knees and beg you? This isn't for me; it's for the girl."

Gavin had a decent side. I'd always known that. I prayed that it would get the better of his anger and jealousy. "Please hear me out, Gavin."

"Talk away. It'll make no difference."

I took a deep breath. As the story tumbled out, Gavin's jaw tightened, but he didn't say a word until I had finished. Then he stood up and began pacing back and forth. He turned and glared at me.

"And you let the priest take her?" he shouted. "Jesus, Sheila, how could you stand by and let her go?"

His sudden accusation caught me by surprise. "And what was I supposed to do?" I said. "Stand up to the police and the priest and the rest of them? How was I supposed to do that, tell me?"

"Don't be giving me excuses, Sheila. You're a selfish wee bitch. I'm surprised you're even still worrying about her."

His words stung. A selfish bitch was what my mother often called me and it triggered something wild in me now. I stood up to face him.

"For your information I just came from the convent and the head nun threw me out. You have no notion what it took for me to go near that place. And on top of that I refused Joel's offer to go with him to England on account of Grainne, so you've no right calling me a selfish bitch."

I hadn't meant to mention anything about Joel, but Gavin's accusation had goaded me into it. I slumped back down in my chair, my breath ragged from the effort of shouting. Gavin looked me up and down with a disgust I had never seen from him.

"Well, well," he began, "so your scheme worked, did it? You got the man to fall for it." He shook his head. "I didn't like him, but I thought he was smarter than that."

"You don't know what you're talking about. Joel loves me and he wanted me to go away with him. And when the war's over he plans to marry me."

"And so now you want a medal for refusing his offer so as you could protect the girl?" He chuckled. "You're so used to fooling others, Sheila, you've finally fooled yourself. You didn't refuse him because you were worried about Grainne. There's more to it than that."

"What? D'you think maybe it was because I'm in love with you?" I laughed out loud. "Now who's fooling himself?"

I wanted to hurt him. He had made me angry, accusing me of being selfish and questioning me when he had no right to. His face turned red and then pale again. He sat down and became very still. I looked around the pub. Our fight had drawn the attention of the few patrons who were there. Nosy bastards, I thought. I stood up.

"I thought our friendship counted for something, but I can see I was wrong. I won't be bothering you again."

I turned and walked to the door, ignoring the stares of the men at the bar. I opened it slowly, giving Gavin time to come after me. But he didn't move.

ॐ

During the days that followed I waited for something to happen. I knew it was only a matter of time until everything blew up around me. I was still living in the house at Queensbrook, but you could have cut the tension with a knife. I had spat out an apology to Kevin in front of Aunt Kate. They both knew I had not meant a word of it. Ma tried to hug me after I did it, but I shook her off. I would not have said anything at all, but as it was I had no place else to go. I had burned my bridges with Joel and with Gavin.

I was also waiting to see what would happen with Grainne. I went over and over in my mind my conversation with Gavin. If I had never brought up Joel and all the rest of it maybe I could have persuaded him to help. But I could hardly blame him for not lifting a finger after all I had said to him. I couldn't settle to anything, so anxious was I to see Grainne released. Anxious? I told myself it was because I cared so much about the girl. But what if Gavin had been right and I needed to know my sacrifice had been worth it? If nothing happened and she stayed up in the convent, how would I live with myself knowing I had sacrificed my one chance at freedom for nothing? It was a selfish attitude, I knew. But I had never thought of myself as anything other than selfish. Gavin was right. I was a selfish wee bitch. That's why the truth of his words had stung me so much. But being selfish was how I had protected myself all these years. The thoughts tumbled around in my head until I thought I would go mad.

Then one night a knock came to the door. I opened it, and there stood Gavin, a look of triumph on his face, and beside him, Grainne, her head bowed and looking thinner than ever.

"Jesus!" I cried. "How . . . ?"

Gavin put up his hand. "Better you don't know," he said. "Let's just say I called in one or two favors."

Instinctively I looked over their heads, expecting to see Father Flynn glowing like the devil in the darkness. But there was no sign of anyone else.

"Is that Gavin? Don't keep him standing on the doorstep, love." Ma's voice brought me back to reality.

I opened the door wide. "Come in," I said, reaching out to take Grainne's small case from her. "You look famished. Come in and get something to eat."

The odd protective feelings were back again as I looked at the girl. She was pale and silent. God love her, I thought, she must be frightened to death. God knows what they did and said to her up at that place. I turned back to Gavin.

"So what happened? Who got her out?"

Gavin turned up the collar of his coat. "I've to be going now to get ready to sail," he said, ignoring my question. "There's an early tide in the morning. They won't be coming after her. I made sure of that." He turned and walked away.

"Who is it, Sheila?" Aunt Kate's voice drifted down the stairs from above. She and Kevin were already in bed.

"Oh, just Gavin," I called back. "He had a message for me. He's away home now."

I put my finger over my lips to warn Ma to keep quiet. I hurried Grainne to the granny room at the back of the house.

"Get into bed now, there's a good girl. And keep quiet."

I closed the door and came back out into the parlor.

Ma waited for me. She was trembling. "She can't stay, you know. She'll get us all thrown out and then what will become of us? Sweet Jesus, I can't live like this, Sheila, and me not a well woman. I can't. You have to get rid of her before they see her."

I nodded. "Good night, Ma," was all I said.

I brought a slice of bread and some cheese and set it down on the table beside Grainne, but she ignored it. I sighed and turned out the light. In the darkness I could hear her breathing. She was not asleep, I knew, but I was in no mood to ask her questions, and I supposed she'd be in no mood to answer them. There'd be plenty of time for that later. For now, I had to find a way to keep her presence a secret, but I knew that was not going to work for very long. And when Kevin and Kate spied her, all hell would break loose.

∞

The deception lasted exactly eight hours. At six o'clock the next morning, Aunt Kate threw open the door of the granny room and began to scream. You would have thought she'd seen a ghost. Her banshee wails could have wakened the dead. Ma flew down the stairs, her nightdress flapping at her ankles. She was followed by Kevin, a day's growth of beard on his big, ruddy face.

"What in God's name...?" he began.

"I knew it," cried Aunt Kate. "I knew she was back in the house. I could feel the evil presence of her." She ran over and tore the bedclothes off Grainne and myself. "Get out!" she cried. "Get out of that bed and out of my house! How dare you come sneaking back in here like a thief in the night?"

Kate was screeching now. I stared at her in astonishment. She had lost her head altogether. I knew she'd be upset when she saw Grainne, but I never expected this kind of carry-on. Instinctively I reached over and pulled Grainne to me to try to protect her from Aunt Kate's fists. Even Kevin tried to restrain her.

"Now, now, love," he said, coming up behind her and grabbing her arms, "we'll have her back up to the convent in no time. Calm yourself, now."

Grainne sprang from my grip. "I'll not go back to that place!" she shouted. "Never! You may kill me first." Her eyes blazed as she looked from one to the other. "I didn't ask to come here. And it's the last place I want to stay."

She leaped out of bed in one movement and I saw she had not even undressed. She reached down and grabbed her suitcase and then elbowed her way past everybody and out the door.

"Wait!" I shouted. "Grainne, wait!"

I couldn't let the child leave alone. Where would she go?

"Wait. I'll go with you."

I scrambled into some clothes and raced after Grainne. Ma was sobbing but I ignored her. I had no time for her self-pity. When I reached the street Grainne stood there as if deciding which way to go. Without thinking, I ran over to a neighbor's house and took the bicycle that leaned against the wall.

"Here!" I called to her. "Ride this."

Then I picked up my own bicycle and threw my leg over the bar. "C'mon!" I yelled to Grainne. "Just follow me."

I gave no thought to where I was going, save to get us both away from the house. Kevin and Kate and Ma stood outside the front door watching us with their mouths open. They looked comical, as if they belonged in a play. But there was nothing funny about the situation. I really feared at that moment for Grainne's life. Kate had lost her mind altogether. Who knows what she might have done to the girl?

At first I automatically pedaled towards the Flagstaff, but as I calmed down I realized that I needed to take Grainne to a place where, for the moment, she would be safe. I turned off the Fathom Road and rode towards Omeath and Gavin's house. He was out at sea, I knew, but he never locked the door of his cottage. Grainne could stay there until I could find a place for her. And for me too, I thought. There'd be no going back to Queensbrook now for me either.

◌◌

After I had settled Grainne into Gavin's house and made her promise to stay there, I turned around and pedaled back to Queensbrook and the mill. When I arrived I looked down at myself. I had thrown on an old, torn dress and stuffed my feet into a pair of Ma's old boots that lay on the floor. At least I had thought to pull on a coat. But my hair was uncombed, my face unwashed, and I wore no makeup. I would have given the ghosts on Halloween a fright.

I waited outside the mill for Ma. She was white as a ghost herself.

"Ma?" I said as I came up to her.

She jumped and clutched her breast. "Sheila? You frightened the life out of me. What are you doing here?"

"Going to bloody work the same as you are."

She clutched my arm. "You can't come back to the house," she said. "Or we'll both be thrown out."

"Don't worry. I've no intention of it. But I need you to bring my clothes up to me tomorrow morning. I've only got what's on my back at the minute. Will you do that?"

She looked as wary as a rabbit. "I . . ." She hesitated.

"For Christ's sake, Ma, I'm not asking you to blow up a bank. Just bring me my bloody clothes."

She began to wail. "Oh, what's going to happen to me? What in God's name will become of me now? What have I done to deserve this?"

For once I was glad when the mill horn blew. It drowned her out. Whether she would bring me the clothes I would have to wait and see. I thought about the bit of money I had saved that was hidden in a drawer in the granny room along with my prize money. I'd have to find a way to get it later.

And to think I could have been in England by now away from all this madness, I thought. Not for the first time.

Chapter 19

ख७

When Gavin returned from sea he did not seem surprised to find Grainne and me in his house. Nothing was said about our meeting at O'Hare's. I recounted what had happened when Kate discovered Grainne in the Queensbrook house and he listened without expression. Grainne watched us as I told Gavin the story. She had hardly said a word since we had arrived at the cottage. But as promised, she had not tried to leave either. Poor mite, I thought, where would she go? I was on tenterhooks up at the mill, waiting for Father Flynn to sweep in and drag me out of there in front of everybody.

"You have a great imagination so you have, Sheila," Gavin said.

"It's not so far-fetched. I'm surprised it hasn't happened before now."

Gavin shook his head. "He'll not be coming for you, or for Grainne. I told you, I've seen to that."

"But how? You can't tell the priest what to do."

"Maybe I can't. But there's others can."

"Who?"

Gavin shrugged and got up to make tea. "Best you don't know."

He had said that before—the night he brought Grainne home from the convent. And again I was riddled with curiosity. But it was no good asking. He'd never tell me.

"We can't stay here with you forever, Gavin," I said. I hated the thought of asking him for help again, but I had nobody else to turn to.

"You could. There's nobody hurrying you out."

"Live here with a man, and us not married? What would that do to my reputation? I'd be destroyed altogether." I smiled as I spoke, trying to lighten the mood.

"Oh, aye, I suppose you're right there. You do have a high standard to uphold. After all, you're still the Linen Queen!" I detected the sarcasm in his voice but I ignored it.

"Not for long, I suppose," I said. "They'll find a way to take it away from me. God knows they've been trying hard enough. Mary McAteer runs to her ma with every bit of gossip about me. Imagine if they found out I was staying at your house?"

"Well, then, I suppose the sooner we find you a place the better."

The place turned out to be a row house in a part of Newry called the Valley. From the sound of the name you would imagine the Valley lay at the foot of sloping green hills, surrounded by trees, and maybe a stream. Far from it. The Valley in Newry was an area of old gray terraced houses, huddled together like war-weary soldiers. Mrs. Gloria Hollywood, seventy years old and spry as a fairy, lived at number 6 Walker's Row, a dead-end street of small houses that backed up to a stone wall behind which ran the railway lines. She was the stepmother of Alphonse Holly-wood, a ruddy-faced sailor who had worked for Gavin's da for years and now sailed with Gavin. He was a lifelong bachelor who until recently had lived with his ma. But now, according to Mrs. Hollywood, he had taken up with a fancy woman and was living in sin with her when he was in port. So Mrs. Hollywood had an empty room and was glad of the company.

The first evening that Gavin brought Grainne and me round to her, she opened the door wide and cackled like an old goose.

"Well, there you are, Gavin. As handsome as ever, aren't you? And two pretty girls alongside you. Come in my dears, come in!"

I was surprised at her English accent. She threw open the

front door and ran ahead of us into a small parlor, turning on the lamps as she went. I stopped dead when I saw the room. It was pink. All pink! The sofa, the chairs, the cushions, the curtains, the fringed lampshades, all pink! I couldn't help but giggle. Grainne looked around with her mouth open, and Gavin shrugged and grinned.

"I suppose I should have warned you," he said.

"It's gorgeous!" I said.

Mrs. Hollywood laughed aloud. "It's a happy little room, isn't it? My Alphonse hated it, so I hardly ever let him set his arse down in it. He had no appreciation for it at all." She clapped her small hands together. "Come on now, girls, let me show you where you'll be sleeping. Mind the stairs now."

She led the way up a crooked wooden staircase into the attic. I held my breath. A pink parlor was one thing, a pink bedroom, however...But the room was dark and plain. It was tiny, but immaculate—cleaner even than Aunt Kate's—even though she had prided herself on the state of her house. "Cleanliness is next to godliness," as she'd say.

"Will this suit you?" There was a double bed and a small single bed, a chest of drawers, and a good-sized wardrobe all crammed into the room. A skylight was cut into the slanted ceiling, and the floor was covered in worn linoleum.

"The lavatory is out in the yard," Mrs. Hollywood continued. "Two houses to one lav. I share it with the Cowans next door. Lovely, clean people, they is."

I swallowed hard. Well, beggars can't be choosers, I thought.

"It's grand," I said. And then I hesitated. "How much do you want for it?"

Mrs. Hollywood clutched her small hands to her pink cardigan. Her skin was white as parchment, and her round cheeks rosy pink with rouge. She looked like a Christmas doll.

"Oh, lovey, I'm just glad of the company. Gavin here told me the whole story about you girls."

For a moment I thought she was going to say we could stay there for nothing. But she was not as soft as she looked. "Would two pound a week for the two of you suit? That will include your meals and a packed lunch."

I nodded. Two pound a week out of my wages was far less than I gave to Ma. I thought of the ten shillings and sixpence a week Kate had been collecting for Grainne from the evacuation committee. I could do with that money now. But she was too old to qualify anymore.

Grainne must have been reading my mind. "I can get a job," she said, jutting out her chin. "There has to be someplace will take me on."

"No," I said, looking over at Gavin. "It's too soon. We don't want anybody to know you're here for a while."

"So I'll be as much a prisoner as I was in that oul' convent," she said. "Well, you may as well have saved yourselves the trouble and left me there!"

Ungrateful wee bitch, I thought to myself. Gavin stepped forward and put a hand on Grainne's shoulder.

"Sheila's right," he said. "It'll be better if you keep out of sight for a while until things die down. I don't think they'll come looking for you—I was told they'd been warned there'd be consequences if they did—but all the same, better not to tempt fate."

Grainne turned a sullen face to the wall. I followed Gavin and Mrs. Hollywood down the stairs.

"Poor little mite," whispered Mrs. Hollywood.

"She'll get over it," I said.

I followed Gavin to the door.

"Sorry, it was the best I could do," he said.

"The best you could do—lodging me with an Englishwoman?"

"Mrs. Hollywood is different," he said. "She was married to my da's first engineer, Sam. He signed on to the *Belfast Star* after my da died, and after it sank she took care of Alphie. Stayed on here, when she could have legged it back to England." Gavin grinned. "She's a wee bit mad—all that pink and everything; even flies the Union Jack on St. George's Day—but she's harmless."

I didn't know what made me do it, but suddenly I put my arms around him, pulled him tight to me, and kissed him on the lips.

He kissed me back hard. As we stood locked together the wild thing I had felt the time on the boat stirred in me. We pushed each other away. Without a word he climbed on his bicycle and was gone.

"Thanks, Gavin—for everything. Safe home," I called after him.

Gratitude, I thought to myself as I went back into the house at number 6. Gratitude. That's all it was.

ಞ

At the end of the week, Patsy was sacked from the mill. Father Flynn had not been long in letting it be known that she was pregnant. Mr. Carlson might not have worried about it too much, but Mary let slip that Mrs. McAteer poisoned his ear with stories about Patsy and her wild behavior, and how she set a very bad example in front of the other girls. And what would the army think of one of his workers acting like that? And when Patsy's da found out, he beat her and told her to pack her bags while her ma stood by and bawled. Patsy came to number 6 Walker's Row because she had nowhere else to go. And there was nothing I could do but ask Mrs. Hollywood to take her in.

I fell into a routine of leaving early in the morning and catching the tram up to Queensbrook and the mill. I saw Ma once in a while but it was obvious we were doing our best to avoid each other. She had brought me the clothes I had asked for, but after that I had not spoken a word to her. I supposed she was frightened out of her wits to be seen talking to me, in case she'd be thrown out on the street as well. I didn't want to cause her any more trouble, so I steered clear of her.

The summer turned into autumn. There was no word from Joel. Of course I had no reason to expect any. I assumed he was still in England. At nights in bed beside Patsy I imagined what my life would be like now if I'd gone with him. By all accounts the war was not going well, even with the Americans in the fight. The soldiers around the town seemed less lively than they had been at the beginning. I supposed they, like us, were getting sick and tired of the whole thing. The German bombers still flew overhead occasionally, and the blackout rules stayed in place. Sirens blared at all times of the day and night.

I hardly went out anymore. Instead I stayed at number 6 enjoying the *craic* with Mrs. Hollywood and Patsy. The two had become very thick. They shared the same sense of humor and love of gossip. Patsy was more relaxed than I had seen her in months. She looked in the best of health despite the circumstances. Mrs. Hollywood's son, Alphie, took pity on her and brought her out for ice cream at Morocco's Café. They made an odd couple. Alphie was a big bruiser of a chap who talked so slow you would have thought the words were coming all the way up from his big toe. I thought Patsy would have been better off if she'd fallen for the likes of Alphie than for Sylvie Sartori.

Once in a while I still made appearances as the Linen Queen. There had been no competition held in 1943 either. I was the longest reigning Linen Queen in history. It was a small triumph that I held on to with both hands. When I put on the sash and the tiara, my old confidence and defiance returned. I was somebody special. People looked up to me. I could still achieve my dreams. The only sour note was the constant presence of Mary McAteer and her ma, who stalked me like a criminal. Even when there was no invitation for the runner-up, they came anyway, Mary flashing her huge diamond engagement ring and trying to elbow me out of the way.

One evening at an event for local business leaders, Mary sidled up to me and whispered in my ear. The smell of her perfume nearly knocked me over.

"I know I have no business telling you this, Sheila, but I just wanted to warn you."

I stiffened. What was coming now?

"You see, Mr. Carlson's secretary has been asked to bring you in tomorrow morning for a meeting with Mr. Carlson. I'm sorry to be the one to tell you, but I do think it's better if you hear it from me first."

She paused and looked at me, a tight smile on her face. "You're going to be sacked. You see the rumor was going around that you had moved in with an unmarried man." She paused and covered her mouth as if scandalized by the thought. "I didn't believe a word of it of course, and neither did my mother. But she owed it to Mr. Carlson to find out. And apparently it was true. You had been living with Gavin O'Rourke."

"But I was only there a week," I burst out.

Mary put a plump hand on my arm. "I believe you, Sheila. I'm sure there was no harm in it. But you have to admit it doesn't look good—and what with your reputation and all..."

I shook her off. I wanted to reach out and smack the smug look off her face, but at that minute the band struck up my cue to go in to the dinner. A sweat erupted over me and it was all I could do to walk a straight line into the room and make the presentation of linens to the businessman of the year. My hands shook as I handed him the smooth tablecloths and serviettes all tied up in a blue ribbon. Then I turned and fled, ripping off the tiara and sash as I went.

എഠ

I thought about not even going near the mill the next day. Why should I give them the satisfaction, when I knew what they were going to do to me? But I had wages coming, and if I didn't show up, I probably would never see them. I said nothing to anybody as I trudged down the road and boarded the tram for what was likely to be the last time.

Mr. Carlson handed me a letter and told me to sit down and read it. The print blurred in front of me, but the words "unacceptable behavior" jumped out. It was all I needed to read. The rest of it was just blather. I looked up at him.

"I'm truly sorry, Miss McGee," he began, his voice stern. "It always pains me to have to discipline an employee, especially when they are a good worker, as you have been, with a good attendance record. In your case, it especially pains me because you have reigned as our Linen Queen now for three years—a role

that represents the highest standards of employees in our industry. I am very disappointed to think that you should have treated
that honor with such evident disregard. However, it was the fact
of your good record and service as Linen Queen that led me to
make my own inquiries."

He broke off and cleared his throat. I waited. Just sack me and
get it over with, I thought.

"It's not that I don't respect the opinion of Mrs. McAteer but I
believe she can sometimes be a little overzealous when it comes
to protecting me and the mill."

I thought I detected a slight smile on his craggy face.

"So I wanted to verify their reports for myself. As it turns out,
yes you did indeed move into Mr. O'Rourke's house but he was
out to sea during that time. And you left after a week and are
now living with a respectable lady down in Newry. It was these
clarifications that led me to my decision to put you on probation,
and to place that letter of reprimand in your file. I hope you will
reflect well, Miss McGee, on the disgrace you could have brought
to yourself and this mill, and I hope it will cause you to mend
your ways in the future. That is all. You may go now."

I was stunned. I could do nothing but murmur thanks and
flee from his office clutching the reprimand letter in my fist. I
could hardly believe it. I was not sacked after all. I still had a job.
I ran to the toilet and splashed cold water on my face. Then I
took a deep breath and walked back into the spinning room. I put
my apron back on, ready to go to work. But as I walked towards
my machine I realized the place had turned deathly quiet. The
workers stared at me with their mouths open. Then I realized
what had happened. Mary McAteer had been spreading the
news that I was sacked faster than you could spread margarine
on brown bread. I looked around and laughed for the first time
that day.

"What's wrong, girls?" I said lightly.

I took the letter out of my pocket and waved it around. "Mr.
Carlson was just congratulating me on what a great job I'm doing
as the Linen Queen. He even put a letter of praise in my file.

Wasn't that good of him? It's nice to be appreciated once in a while."

I shoved the letter back in my pocket and went to work, a contented smile on my face.

"But Mary said...," began Kathleen.

"Och, that Mary," I said loudly. "Thinks she knows everything."

One by one the girls nodded and went back to their work. There was going to be no gossip to be had at my expense this day at least.

Chapter 20

ର୍ଦ୍ତ

On the following Sunday afternoon I came home from Mass and went straight upstairs to lie down. I was tired. I had been working all the overtime I could get at the mill. I needed to make money while I could. After all, I had people depending on me now. I heard a knock on the front door and Mrs. Hollywood speaking to someone. I felt sure it was a man because her voice went up a pitch or two the way it always did when she was flirting with a man. Silly oul' bat, I thought, and paid no further attention.

"Sheila, oh Sheila love. You have a visitor. And a lovely one at that. Ever so 'andsome and well-spoken."

Without leave, she pushed open the bedroom door and bustled into the room.

"Come on now, get up and don't keep 'im waiting. I'm going down to make him some tea."

Sighing, I pulled myself out of bed, finished dressing, and went downstairs. When I opened the door to the parlor, I froze. There, sitting on the pink sofa, surrounded by pink lamps and bric-a-brac, was Joel. My immediate instinct was to turn tail and run. How could I face him after admitting I'd been using him? But it was too late. I saw the pleasure in his eyes as he smiled at me. He stood up and came towards me with his hand extended. I did not move.

"Sheila," he said softly, "it's good to see you. It's been a while."

I looked at his outstretched hand but made no effort to take it. The truth was I was ashamed to do so after the things I had said to him.

"I'm back for a few weeks. I wanted to see how you were doing. I went up to Queensbrook but your mom said you had moved out. She gave me your address here. I have to say, I had a hell of a job finding the place."

He turned briefly to Mrs. Hollywood, who was watching us with sharp eyes.

"Please excuse my language, ma'am."

Mrs. Hollywood waved a hand at him. "Oh, I've heard a lot worse, young man. I was married to a sailor. Mr. Hollywood, now, he 'ad a colorful way of speaking you might say. Would even make other sailors blush."

Joel smiled at her and turned back towards me.

"I'm glad you've found a place with such a charming lady," he said, as Mrs. Hollywood preened. "Cozy," he continued, looking around the pink room. If I hadn't been in shock, I'd have been giggling my arse off at the cut of him bent over from the low ceiling trying to look comfortable in this doll's room. As it was, I took pity on him.

"Would you like to go somewhere?" I said. "I can be ready in a few minutes."

Relief flooded his face and he nodded. "Actually, I have just the place in mind," he said.

Minutes later we were driving north out of Newry towards Belfast. Joel drove with confidence. It was clear he had made this journey before. I had never been as far as Belfast, so I sat back and let him take charge.

"You're still at the mill?" It was an innocent question. He couldn't have known I was on probation. I nodded.

"And I understand from Mrs. Hollywood that Grainne is living with you."

I nodded again. I didn't know where to begin to tell him all the things that had happened. So I chose to say nothing.

We drove on in silence, up through the towns of Banbridge and Hillsborough.

Eventually Joel spoke again.

"Is everything all right, Sheila?"

"Why wouldn't it be?"

He hesitated. "Something about you has changed. I can't put my finger on it exactly. But you seem more serious than you used to be. You were always as light and carefree as a bird. It's one of the things I liked so much about you."

"We can't all go around like happy eejits all the time," I said. "Times are supposed to be hard. There's a war on."

He sighed. "Yes, there is indeed. And it's not going so well for the Allies."

Grateful to get the subject away from me, I quickly peppered him with questions as to the state of the fighting. The truth was I couldn't have cared less, other than wanting it to be over. But it kept him talking and it broke the tension between us. Joel was serious as he talked about the challenges the Allies were up against. It seemed like they were losing ground to the Germans everywhere.

"If we don't score a major victory soon, we could lose the whole war," he said at last. He paused. "And even if we manage to pull it out, I'm not sure I'll be around to see it."

There was something in his tone that sent chills through me.

"What d'you mean?" I said.

He shrugged. "It's just that I have a premonition. I don't think I'm going to make it to the end of the war."

"Well that's an awful thing to be saying," I said. I was frightened by the way he was talking.

"It's true. Ever since my dad died, I've always had this feeling I was not going to live a full life either. I don't mean to be morbid. It's OK. I've made my peace with it."

"So you have a feckin' death wish, is that it? What kind of bloody nonsense is that?" I was angry with him now. For all of my own troubles I had never for one minute thought I'd be better off dead.

"I know it's hard to understand, Sheila," Joel said softly. "I'm going to be involved in a major campaign in a few months. I can't go into details, but it will be dangerous, and a lot of lives will be lost. If it works, it will be worth the sacrifce. If not...well, I'm not sure I'd want to go on living in a world dominated by Hitler." He sighed. "Let's not talk about it anymore. Forget I said anything."

Forget he said anything? How could I ever do that? I cast a sideways look at him. He was troubled; there was no question. I wondered what part I had played in it. My rejection of him could not have helped matters. But surely there was more to it. I recalled his story about his da's suicide. Did that run in families, I wondered. Again, I found myself pitying someone other than myself, and again it shocked me.

We turned east and then drove north again along the shore of Strangford Lough. I smiled at the sight of it. I had never been this far up on the coast.

"It's beautiful," I said.

"Yes. D'you remember that night after I played the fiddle at the Flagstaff when we sat looking out at the lough and you recited that beautiful poem—the one about the merrow?"

I nodded, remembering. What sweetness there had been in that night, and what sadness too. He reached over and touched my shoulder.

"You look like a mermaid, Sheila, with your blue eyes and your black hair and your white skin. You look just like the mermaids I used to read about when I was small. I've always had a fascination with the sea too. There's a theory we all evolved from fish—and maybe the sea will claim us again. Maybe one day we'll all return to the sea."

"The sea claims many a one around here," I said. "Many's the boat has been sunk, particularly lately."

He'd sounded sad and far away. There was no hint of the anger he'd shown when I'd last seen him, but the sadness was still there—a deep melancholy that hurt me.

"So how far is it now to Belfast?" I said to break the mood. "I've never been there before."

"Oh, we're not going to Belfast, Sheila. There's somewhere much more important I want you to see."

∞

We drove through Newtownards, which stood at the northern tip of Strangford Lough, and across the Ards Peninsula into the small coastal town of Millisle. I'd never heard of the place before. My curiosity was choking me but I said nothing. We turned away from the sea and climbed a steep hill. Two twin-gabled buildings dominated the horizon. I had never seen anything quite like them. A farm appeared to our right, the fields dotted with haystacks. To our left were dense woods. Joel turned the car in through the farm gate.

As we drove along the gravel road towards one of the buildings I had seen, I noticed people working in the fields. It was late harvest season and they were gathering crops and baling hay. As we drew closer I saw that they were young, some mere boys. I peered at them. Just like the buildings, they looked different from boys I had seen before but I couldn't put my finger on how. I twisted around and looked to my left. A few little girls were on their knees digging in a kitchen garden. They turned and waved as we drove by. I could stand it no longer.

"Where are we? What is this place? Why are all these children here?"

Joel laughed. "In good time, Sheila. First, help me with these bags."

He stopped the car and got out and walked around to the boot. As I followed him the wee girls who had been digging in the garden came running up to us. They grabbed Joel by the hands, jumping up and down and squealing.

"Herr Solomon," they cried, "what have you brought us?"

An older girl came up behind the children clapping her hands.

"Leave Captain Solomon alone, children," she said. "It is not polite to ask such things."

I realized that they all spoke with a foreign accent.

"It's all right, Sonya," Joel said. "I have brought enough for everyone." He turned to me. "Here, help me bring these into the kitchen."

He handed me two bulging paper bags and took the rest himself. Together we followed Sonya in a side door of the building and dropped the bags on a table. The children went back to their work, but their eyes followed us. Inside the building was light and airy. The kitchen was small but spotless. Just as I was about to ask Joel what was going on, a small, gray-haired man came rushing into the room.

"Captain Solomon," he said, showing dimples as he smiled, "I heard the car. Welcome, welcome."

He pumped Joel's hand up and down in greeting. "So good to see you. We missed you at Havdalah last night."

Joel nodded his head. "Army business, I'm afraid, Rabbi." He took my arm. "Rabbi, this is my friend Sheila McGee. Sheila, this is Rabbi Hurwitz."

I didn't know what to do. I stood there like an eejit with my mouth open.

Rabbi Hurwitz smiled at me. "Welcome, *fraylin*."

I stared at him. I had never met a rabbi before. I wasn't sure I knew exactly what the word meant, but Joel had used it a few times. I thought it must be a priest or something. If he was a priest, he was nothing like the priests I knew. Certainly not like Father Flynn with all his arrogance. This man could have been anybody's granda. His accent puzzled me. It was foreign, slightly different from that of the children, and with a hint of a Northern Irish lilt. I relaxed and smiled at him.

"I wanted Sheila to see the farm, Rabbi," Joel was saying. "Would you be kind enough to show her around? I want to talk to some of the children."

With that he picked up a couple of the bags and walked out of the room, leaving me with Rabbi Hurwitz.

"Come with me, *fraylin*; it will be my honor to show you around Magill Kinderfarm."

As we walked, the rabbi explained to me that the farm was

originally owned by a Mr. Magill, who used it as a place to bleach linen. But just before the war started a group of Jewish business-men from Belfast had bought it and set it up as a place for refugee Jewish children, mostly from Germany. The children had been evacuated under a program called Kindertransport. I thought of Grainne. She was no different than these wee ones. But as I lis-tened to Rabbi Hurwitz, I realized there was one big difference. Many of their parents had been killed by the Nazis. These chil-dren had fled for their lives.

We walked around the fields where the boys were stacking hay into tall towers. I noticed that they all wore wee skullcaps. I wished Joel were there so I could ask what they were called. I was too embarrassed to show my ignorance by asking the rabbi.

"All the children work on the farm," he said smiling, "starting from as young as six years old. They learn all aspects of agricul-ture, taking care of the soil, planting, and harvesting. We grow wheat and barley and, of course, potatoes." His eyes squeezed shut as he laughed at his own wee joke. "We grow other vegeta-bles in the kitchen farm over there, and we have our own cows and chickens. We are very self-suffcient."

I thought of the young half-timers at the mill. "But don't they go to school?" I said, shocked at the thought that these children worked all the time.

"Oh, they do, *fraylin*," said Rabbi Hurwitz, throwing his hands up and wide. "Education is our highest priority. As a mat-ter of fact our children attend the local schools." He paused and touched his hand to his heart. "And your people have made them most welcome. We are very grateful."

I supposed he hadn't heard of the famous Irish hospitality. Why wouldn't we make them welcome? I looked at the rabbi's face. Pain was stamped on it. I thought I saw tears. I wanted to put my arms out and hug this lovely wee man. After we had finished touring the fields, we walked back towards the building where we had left Joel. A small sound made me swing around. There, sitting on the ground with her hands around her knees was a young girl about ten years of age. Her head was bowed and she was weeping. Without thinking I seized Rabbi Hurwitz's arm.

"What's wrong with her?" I said.

"Homesickness. She only came to us last week. Poor child."

He bent down beside the child and put his hand on her head and said a few words to her that I did not understand. I supposed he was speaking German. She looked sadly up at him. He stood and put his fingers to his lips.

"It will take time," he said.

We came on through the door and he turned to me and smiled.

"Before we join Captain Solomon, I'd like to show you something else," he whispered. "Something we are very proud of."

He led me down a hallway and opened a door. We stepped through and I found myself in a wee chapel. Well, it wasn't a chapel exactly. It looked different. Yes, there was an altar and rows of chairs and one beautiful tiny stained glass window. But in the middle of the altar was a large wooden cabinet with two doors.

"What is that?" I said, pointing to it.

The rabbi went up the two steps and opened the cabinet doors. Behind them hung a pair of curtains, which he pulled open. He gently touched a rolled-up scroll that lay behind the curtains and smiled at me.

"This is the Torah," he said, "our most precious possession. It contains all our teachings."

But before I could move closer he drew the curtains back together and quickly shut the cabinet doors.

"I'm sorry but I'm not able to show it to you, *fraylin*," he said. "It is not allowed."

I nodded.

He waved his arms around. "So what do you think of our wee synagogue?"

I smiled at the "wee" that had crept into his question. "It's beautiful," I said.

We found Joel sitting in a large playroom at the other end of the hallway, surrounded by a group of young boys. They were munching on sweets he had brought them, some laughing, others asking him questions with serious young faces.

"Captain Solomon comes often," Rabbi Hurwitz whispered. "The children love him. They ask him questions about America, and about the war, and all sorts of things. He is a good man."

It was dark when we left the farm. My head was filled with thoughts and images. I wanted to batter Joel with questions but something stopped me. Instead I stared into the black night as we drove down towards Newry. I thought of the day Joel had given money to the tinker children on Warrenpoint Beach. He'd had that same look then as he'd had today with the children at the farm—full of peace and contentment. The sadness that was so often his companion had disappeared. I stole a look at him in the dim shadows, his strong jaw and straight nose, and the smile that played around his soft mouth. I wanted to move closer to him, to touch him, but somehow I felt it would be wrong. It was as if I had no right to touch him; as if he didn't belong to me, or to anyone else, as if he moved through the world alone maintaining a space around him that no one could enter.

Who was this man? I wondered. How could I ever have thought I could use him and then discard him? He was like nobody I'd ever met. I couldn't act around him the way I did other men. Being near him changed who I was. As I watched the dark fields speed by, I thought of the way I had changed since I met him and somehow I knew this experience at Magill Kinderfarm would change me even more. I was moving further and further away from the old self-centered Sheila. I didn't know whether to be grateful to God or angry with Him for shaking up my life like this. First Grainne, and now Joel. What was God playing at? I'd been happy enough with my simple dream of escape and concerning myself only with my own needs. I'd had no time for other people and their problems. And now look at me—playing nursemaid to Grainne and Patsy, and my dreams of escape lying in an envelope at the bottom of a drawer. I looked over at Joel again. Honest to God, I thought to myself, if I didn't love you, Joel Solomon, I would curse the day I met you.

Newry was deserted when we arrived back in the town. The pubs were closed, and the street lights were out and the window blinds down. It was like a ghost town. I shivered a little. Joel coughed as he pulled the car into Walker's Row and stopped in front of number 6. He turned towards me and touched my arm. "It's those kids we're fighting for, Sheila," he said.

"I know," I whispered as I got out of the car and waved goodbye. "Safe home."

∞

After my visit to Millisle something began eating away at me. I tried to ignore it but it persisted. I could not get the faces of those children out of my mind, particularly the wee girl crying beside the wall. I tried to imagine them all going back to Germany only to find their homes gone and their parents dead. I finally understood Joel's passion about the war. At first I thought it was enough to say a prayer for them at Mass on Sundays. What else was I going to do? Join the bloody army? Well, I wasn't about to join up before, and I wasn't now. But maybe I didn't have to go that far.

Before I could talk myself out of it I marched into the local police barracks and asked about volunteering for the Air Raid Precautions service. It was the role of the ARP wardens to enforce the blackout restrictions and to put out fires and help with first aid when called for. I thought how often I had joined in with my friends down at the Castle ballroom in jeering the wardens when they came in to stop the dances. We all thought they were silly eejits, impressed with their newfound authority. I never thought I'd see the day when I'd be asking to join their forces. But then, I never thought I'd see a lot of things that had happened to me.

I took a deep breath and walked up to the sergeant at the counter. Fortunately I didn't know him, nor did he know me. If he had he may not have thought I was a fit one to join. Even though I had stopped my running around months before, my old reputation still haunted me. He was kindly enough, though, and thanked me for my patriotism. The sign-up was quick. In the beginning women volunteers had been confined to working in the offices or canteens, or assigned to cleaning duty. I wanted more than that and I told him so. I wanted out on active duty. I wanted to feel like I was doing something important. I was willing to take a risk.

On Monday morning of the following week I went down to the center for the training program. I was issued a helmet and uniform, rubber boots, a gas mask, a torch, and a notebook and pencil. The notebook and pencil were the only items that spoiled the notion that I was really going into a war zone.

I was told that for the first fortnight I would be assigned to another volunteer. I was nervous. What if I was paired up with some grumpy oul' fella who wouldn't take me seriously? But to my surprise it turned out to be a woman. And more of a surprise, it turned out to be a woman I knew.

"Aren't you the girl from the train station?" Mary McTaggart said with a raise of her eyebrow. "I thought you'd be well away to England by now."

I hadn't recognized her immediately. I had been too busy staring at the stump of her right arm trussed up in a sling. It was her voice that brought the memory back to me. She had been one of the sisters from Mullaghbawn who'd been off to join the Women's Auxiliary Air Force when I met them at Edward Street train station. That was the day Grainne had arrived and I decided to run away to England. What a lifetime ago that seemed now.

I started to reply that I'd changed my mind, but I shrugged and told the truth instead. "You were right about needing papers," I said.

She smiled. "And your pretty face didn't see you through? Can't say we didn't warn you."

"Did youse go? To the WAAFs, I mean?"

"Aye. We went."

There was a silence. I was dying to ask more, but I waited.

"Anne—well, Anne didn't come back," Mary said. She looked down at the stump of her arm. "And after this I wasn't much good to them. So they discharged me."

"And the farm?"

"Well, I wasn't much use on the farm either." She laughed. "Could you see the cut of me trying to milk a cow?"

I realized as I looked at her that even after all her hardship her face was serene, and quite beautiful. I admired her courage.

"So I came to the big city and decided to make my mark with the ARP."

Her good humor was infectious. I began to laugh.

"Aye, well life makes strange bedfellows of all of us, I suppose."

Chapter 21

ᘓᕲ

Just one week after I had joined the ARP I found myself marching through the streets of Newry as part of the Step Together Parade, which had taken place every year since the war started. Home Guard, auxiliaries, and volunteers all marched under one banner to show off our unity in protecting civilians from the ravages of war. I was embarrassed not so much by the political implications of the parade but by the way I looked. I wore my uniform and helmet and boots and I had never in my life felt like a bigger eejit. I had tried to hem the trousers but they were still too long. I was swimming in the jacket, it was that big, and the helmet fell down over my eyes. I had to keep pushing it up. But as I marched, I realized I didn't care as much anymore what people thought of me. The realization was another sign to me that the old Sheila was fast disappearing. Part of me still mourned her loss, and part of me was uncertain and afraid. I took a deep breath and put my shoulders back and my head up and marched along with Mary McTaggart by my side.

"Bad cess to them all," I muttered aloud.

When the parade was over we scattered in all directions. I went into the Ceili House with Mary. I sat down beside her and ordered lemonade. I was in my uniform after all and I didn't want to be seen drinking. The crowd was loud and filled with good humor. I smiled as I looked around at the other volunteers. It felt good to be part of something. I smiled at Mary.

"There's a chap at the bar staring in this direction, Sheila," she whispered, smiling back at me. "I'd say he has a notion for you the way his eyes are boring through you."

"Och, Mary," I began. But when I looked over at the bar all talk went out of me. There sat Gavin. And his eyes were, as Mary had said, boring through me. But it was not because he was pleased to see me. I knew that look of Gavin's too well. He was angry. I looked down at my uniform and braced myself as he walked towards me.

"Well, well. I never thought I'd live to see the day you'd be wearing a British uniform!" His tone was filled with sarcasm.

"It's not British," I said. "And besides, it's no business of yours."

He shrugged. "You're a teetotaler now as well, I see," he said nodding towards my lemonade. "Next thing you'll be joining the convent."

I began to protest, but I stopped. Why did I need to defend myself to the likes of him?

"What's got into you?" I said.

"What in God's name do you think you're doing? Have you gone mad altogether?"

Anger boiled up in me. Who the hell did he think he was telling me what to do? He must have sensed my anger. Roughly he pulled me up by the arm.

"Let's go for a walk," he said.

I shook his hand off. But the heat and the crowds in the pub were beginning to close in on me. I felt faint; I needed fresh air. So I walked ahead of him to the door and out onto the street. I walked fast towards the bridge, trying to get away from him. But he caught up with me.

"Your IRA friends wouldn't approve of the company you're keeping," I said.

"No they wouldn't," he said stubbornly. "Nor would any self-respecting Irishman."

"Nobody's keeping you," I said.

"I need to talk to you. After that you can be on your way."

He took my arm again and steered me down along the water to where the *Ashgrove* was anchored. He pushed me in front of him so that I had no choice but to jump onto the boat or fall in the water.

"Give us a bloody fag," I said as I collapsed on a bench on deck.

Gavin always had cigarettes despite the rationing. One of the benefits of being a seaman, I supposed. He took out his pack and thrust a cigarette at me and a box of matches. Normally he would have lit it for me. I lit it myself and took a long pull, feeling the smoke burn my lungs.

"What is it you want?" I said. "Shouldn't you be out with your fancy woman instead of annoying me?"

"Who?"

"You're one Rose, or whatever her name is."

He lit his own cigarette and looked out towards the water. It was already dark. A pale moon reflected on the black water as the boat rocked gently underneath us.

"I'm just back in port and I needed to talk to you," he said again, ignoring my question.

The docks were still busy, even at that hour of the night. Gavin nodded towards the men loading cargo on a nearby boat.

"Will you look at all that going to help the bloody English."

"Youse are getting well paid for it."

"Not near enough money to risk our lives. The bloody RAF is nowhere to be seen. Another two boats were torpedoed last month, and there'll be more. And d'you think we get any compensation? Not a penny, not even a bloody word of thanks to all the merchant marines who've drowned supporting the English and their sorry war."

Gavin's complaints echoed those of many of the seamen around Newry. Too many boats were being torpedoed by the Germans, they said. They believed the Royal Air Force should be giving cover to the merchant boats the same way it did for troop ships but, as Gavin had said, often it was nowhere to be seen and the merchant boats were left to fend for themselves.

Gavin took another pull on his cigarette. "My da would turn

over in his grave if he could see what I'm doing. That man died for a united Ireland. He hated the English, and here I am using his boat to run food and supplies to support their army."

"Is that all you have to tell me? Sure I've heard it all before."

"No. I wanted to warn you."

I looked at him puzzled. I had no idea what he was on about.

"You see, it was the IRA boys took Grainne out of the convent and put the fear of God into that Father Flynn. And now they want the favor returned."

A bad feeling gathered inside me. "What do they want?"

"They want to use the *Ashgrove* to smuggle guns for them." He paused and looked at me. "They want me to pick up guns from the Germans and bring them back here. The guns will be disguised as cargo waiting in France. The Germans want to arm the IRA so they can go after the English here in the North. Anything that distracts the English helps the Germans."

"Jesus," I said. "You're not going to do it, are you? It's too dangerous. No British boats are going across to France—it's occupied by the Germans for God's sake."

"Exactly. But the *Ashgrove* will be flying the Irish flag. The Free State's neutral."

"But what about your reputation? You've built up a fine business; why would you throw it away for a crowd of stupid blackguards? And besides, once they get you involved they won't stop at this. They'll want more."

Gavin's eyes glinted in the dark. "What choice do I have? If I don't they'll take it out on Grainne, and maybe on you. So in case something goes wrong, I want you to make sure the girl stays inside the house for the time being. And you'd better watch yourself—particularly after this!" He glared down at my uniform. "Go home and burn that getup."

"I'll do no such thing," I said. "I joined up for good reason."

"Doing the Joel feller's bidding, I suppose. I hear he's back."

"I have a mind of my own. It has nothing to do with him. It was my own decision. He doesn't even know about it yet. And I'm not giving it up."

Gavin shrugged and ground out his cigarette with his foot. "Suit yourself. I warned you."

"Aye, thanks a million."

I got up to go, but Gavin grabbed my arm and pulled me around.

"Be as sarcastic as you like, you selfish wee bitch, but don't come crawling to me next time you want something. It's over, Sheila. I wouldn't lift a finger to help you if the pope himself asked me."

As I walked away from the dock I heard shouts and singing in the distance as people drifted out of the pubs. Somewhere someone sang the Irish national anthem, the alcohol obviously oiling his patriotism. Patriotism? I looked down at my uniform and quickened my step.

ल्⊙

I walked along Monaghan Street towards Walker's Row, turning over in my mind the cost of saving young Grainne. I had lost my home, almost lost my job at the mill, and I had lost my one big chance for escape. And now on top of that it had put Gavin in the debt of the IRA. Part of me realized it wasn't the girl's fault, but part of me wanted somebody to blame. I was angry when I arrived at the front door, but when I entered my temper spilled over. Patsy, Mrs. Hollywood, and her son, Alphie, all sat around the kitchen table drinking tea and talking and laughing to beat the band. Grainne sat in her usual chair by the fire, her legs up under her, stroking Mrs. Hollywood's cat, Pirate, a big gray thing with a patch of black fur over its left eye. I glared at her and it. How dare they all be sitting here nice as you like as if they hadn't a care in the world?

"Hello, love," said Mrs. Hollywood. "Sit down and I'll make you a cup of the lovely tea Alphie's just brought me. He brought butter, too. Nice to have a sailor son, ain't it? He can get around the rationing a treat."

I would rather have sat down with the devil just then. If I spoke I would create a scene. Instead I walked towards the stairs.

Patsy and Grainne exchanged looks and Patsy began laughing.

"Jesus, Sheila, you're the cut of Charlie Chaplin in that getup. Isn't she, Alphie?"

"A far cry from the Linen Queen right enough," said Alphie in his slow, stupid voice.

I hadn't kept the fact that I'd joined the ARP a secret, but I hadn't let them see me in my uniform. Usually I carried it with me and changed at the barracks.

"You're one to be talking," I said to Patsy. "Just look at the cut of yourself."

Patsy was almost eight months pregnant and big enough you'd have thought she was ready to deliver any minute. She didn't take the remark in good humor, and I hadn't meant it as such.

"Bitch," she said. "You're as bad as the rest of them. I can't walk down the street in Newry without oul' biddies gawking at me. Some even step off the pavement. You'd think I was bloody contagious, so you would. And then there's the young ones in the shops refuse to serve me. And them no better than I am."

"It's true, so it is," said Alphie. "I've seen it."

Patsy put her hand on Alphie's arm. "Aye, if it wasn't for the likes of Alphie I don't know what I'd do. He and Kathleen are my only real friends these days."

Her words stung. And who was I if not her friend? Who'd taken her in? Who was paying her keep? She read what was going through my mind.

"And don't be looking at me like that, Sheila. You think you're better than me what with your parading around as Linen Queen and joining up with the auxiliaries. Well, you're not."

"I'm nothing like you, you ungrateful bitch."

"Once a tramp, always a tramp."

Mrs. Hollywood slammed the kettle down on the stove and swung around.

"Now that will do, girls."

Alphie stood up. "Time to go, Ma," he said. "Cheerio, all."

Mrs. Hollywood went to her room and Patsy walked outside with Alphie. I heard them whispering. Probably complaining about me, I thought. I slumped down in a chair and sipped the tea Mrs. Hollywood had poured for me. What had got into Patsy? And what had got into me? I sighed. It had been a long day. Grainne eyed me from her chair by the fire. We were alone now in the kitchen. I wanted to round on her too, but I had no energy left for it. I tried to ignore her.

"I suppose you think I'm ungrateful too," she said.

"Och, don't start. I'm tired."

She set the cat down and stood. "I can tell by the way you look at me. You expect me to go down on my knees and thank you. Well, I won't."

I stood too. It was all I could do to stop myself from slapping her.

"It wasn't you saved me from the convent," she said. "It was Gavin. If it was up to you I'd still be rotting in that oul' place."

So that's what she thought. Gavin was the hero.

I sighed. "Well, you'd better be getting down on your knees to thank him, then. He's after getting himself in deep with the IRA over the head of you. It could get him killed."

I dragged myself up the stairs to bed. A heavy, dark feeling filled my head and heart. I realized it was loneliness.

Chapter 22

I saw Joel often after our visit to the farm in Millisle. He was delighted I had joined the ARP. I let him think it was on account of him. Well, I suppose in part it was. But I wouldn't have done it just on his say-so. The image of those children's faces had never left me, particularly the little girl crying for her home. More than once I dreamed about her. She was sitting not at the farm but on the dock beside my da's boat.

Joel hadn't brought up the topic of his premonitions again, and I was glad of it. Maybe he had just been depressed after coming back from England and seeing the way things were going for the Allies. I had no doubt the "major campaign" he had talked about was real. There'd been rumors flying all over the North about some big doings that were planned. Once in a while a drunken soldier would blurt out something about a plan that was going to use them as "cannon fodder." I didn't even know what the term meant, but it was clearly something that scared them. The officers denied the whole lot of it. But it was obvious to everybody that, as Joel had said, the Allies were going to have to pull off something big to destroy Hitler. The details were top secret he had said—but that didn't stop the rumors. Anyway, Joel knew far more than he was telling. It was no wonder it was making him a wee bit crazy.

One afternoon as we hiked up through Kilbroney Park in

Rostrevor, I tried to explain to him what was really going on the night I went to see him at the barracks. At first he didn't want to talk about it.

"It's all water under the bridge, Sheila," he said. "We're still friends, and that's what's important."

What he didn't understand was that by trying to explain it to him, I was really trying to explain it to myself. I pressed on.

"I was angry with you because you wouldn't tell me what to do."

Joel raised an eyebrow. "Why would I do that? It was your decision. If you came with me it should have been of your own free will and not because I convinced you to come." He looked me in the eyes. "It wasn't fair of you to lay that burden on me."

I bowed my head. "I know. It's just that—well, I didn't understand it myself." I looked at him. "God, Joel, asking me to go away with you was the best thing that had ever happened to me. For the life of me, I couldn't understand what was holding me back."

"Conscience, maybe?" Joel's gaze was direct.

"You said that night you didn't think I had a conscience."

"I was angry. And hurt. We all have one, Sheila. Even you."

We reached the Big Stone at the crest of Kilbroney Mountain and sat down. We had come here on Boxing Day almost two years before. I had not been back since. The weather was mild for November. The wind brushed the fallen leaves along the ground and lifted them up into a swirl. An amber leaf landed in my lap and I picked it up and held it in my palm. Joel glanced down at it.

"I love this time of year," he said. "Back in Ohio nature puts on a beautiful show—oranges and cinnamons and deep yellows. I used to love walking on the trails. The only sounds would be the birds and the crunch of the leaves under my boots. It was where I found peace." He looked at me. "Of course the season has passed already in Ohio. It holds on here a bit longer."

There was such sadness in his face and voice that I wanted to reach out and hug him. Instead, I said, "Sounds beautiful."

We sat for a while in silence, looking out over the hills towards the sea.

"Besides, you weren't in love with me."

I swung around. What was I to say to that? But Joel went on talking.

"I knew you weren't, so it wasn't fair of me to ask you to come away. I just thought if we could spend more time together—away from everything and everybody here—you might, in time, fall in love with me." He leaned back and stretched out his legs. "So you could say we were using each other. All's fair in love and war."

He attempted a smile, but it was empty.

"I wasn't using you…," I began. But what was the point of lying. "Och, you're right. It's just what I was doing. If it hadn't been you it would have been somebody else. But I was fond of you, Joel. I really was. And in time—who knows?"

"Well, we'll never know now, will we?"

Was it really over? An unbearable sadness filtered through me.

"For the life of me I don't understand why you would want to leave, Sheila," said Joel, waving towards the horizon. "This is the most beautiful place I've ever seen."

"You don't have to live here. All I've wanted since I was a child was to escape. It's a prison to me. And when the war's over I still mean to go."

Joel looked thoughtful. "It's not Ireland you want to leave, Sheila. It's your situation. You have the power to change that."

"No I don't," I said. "I'm a mill girl with no money and a bad reputation. How'm I supposed to change that, I'd like to know?"

"Change comes from the inside," he said quietly.

I wanted to tell him he was full of shite, but I held back. It occurred to me that if I'd been talking to Gavin I would have said it without a second thought. I was always more careful around Joel.

Joel looked at his pocket watch and stood. "C'mon, it's getting chilly."

A sharp ache stirred in my heart. I wanted to put my arms around him and pull him close. I wanted to tell him that I *did* love him and had been too blind or too preoccupied with my own ambition to see it. I wanted to tell him that if I had it to do over I would go with him in a second. But it was too late.

As if reading my thoughts, he pulled me up and folded me in his arms. He held my head to his chest and stroked my hair. The gentleness of his touch almost made me weep.

"Oh, Sheila," he whispered, so low I could hardly hear him above the wind. "I'm not the one for you. I never was. I had no right even to harbor a hope of it. You have your whole life ahead of you. And I can offer you no future. All the time I was seeing you, I knew in my heart it was wrong. Please forgive me."

My tears erupted, this time more from anger than sadness. I backed away and looked up at him. "Feck you!" I cried. "Is it that bloody death wish you're on about again?"

"It's not a death wish. It's just something I know, Sheila. Call it what you will. But it's very real."

"You're mad, so you are," I cried. "How can any sane person talk like that? Just because your da killed himself doesn't mean you have to."

I was out of control now. I didn't care what I said.

"I'm not talking about suicide," he said evenly. "It's something deeper and more profound…"

"Profound my arse," I said. "Just because you're depressed you think you're going to die. No, not even thinking it. You're fecking willing yourself to die."

My shoulders sagged and I began to sob. He grabbed me again and held me close to him. As we stood entwined together, two lonely souls on top of the mountain ankle deep in the dying leaves, the words of the merrow poem my da had taught me drifted into my head.

☙

Joel agreed to spend Christmas night with me. I had told him I wanted to bring Ma, which at the time had seemed like a good idea. I hadn't seen her in a dog's age and I knew she would be lonely up in Queensbrook with Kate and Kevin and no *craic* at all. I had persuaded Joel to take us to O'Hare's even though he would rather have gone to the Prince of Mourne pub in Warrenpoint. But O'Hare's was where my da used to take my ma every Christmas in the good days, and I knew she'd be delighted.

"OK, it's a date," he'd said. "I would hate to miss an evening with the lovely Mrs. McGee."

He'd grinned and dimples punched his sallow cheeks, lighting up his face. My heart leaped a little as I looked at him. He was what Mrs. Hollywood would call "a charmer" when he smiled. I wished he would do it more often.

Christmas Day at Walker's Row was pleasant enough—certainly better than the days spent at Queensbrook with Aunt Kate preaching about God's grace and Uncle Kevin drinking himself into a stupor. Mrs. Hollywood had insisted we all help decorate the tree. She pulled out a box of ornaments. They were all pink, of course. Patsy and I looked at each other and burst into giggles. Our harsh words to each other the night of the Step Together Parade were long forgotten, and even though she had fits of temper more often now, I overlooked it because she was already more than two weeks past her due date. That morning we opened gifts that were under the tree. Patsy, who had taken up knitting, made matching scarves, hats, and gloves for all of us.

"I made two pairs of gloves for you," she said with a laugh, "because you lose them as fast as you get them."

Grainne had no money of her own, but Mrs. Hollywood had slipped her a few pound so that she could buy herself something. Instead she spent the money on the rest of us—a box of sweets each for Patsy and me, and a lovely wee pink angel for Mrs. Hollywood to hang on the tree.

Mrs. Hollywood bought each of us a lace blouse. She had surprisingly good taste. And she made her famous plum pudding with brandy, which she served aflame and to great applause. I bought Patsy a nightdress to wear in hospital, a new jumper for Grainne—one that fit her instead of the old hand-me-downs she usually wore. And for Mrs. Hollywood I bought a delicate gold necklace. She was delighted with it. Joel had helped me get it. There was not much jewelry to be had under the rationing. I got another one just like it for Ma.

We lazed around the kitchen table for a couple of hours, stuffed from Mrs. Hollywood's Christmas dinner. Mrs. Hollywood got a bit tipsy on port wine and started telling us stories from her childhood growing up around the carnival in Brighton where her da had worked.

"Oh, my dad now, 'e was a caution, 'e really was!" she said. "He was a barker and his job was to get the people to pay their shilling and come into the carnival. Oh, the stories 'e made up about the acts—the two-headed woman, and the 'alf man, 'alf ape. Honest, it would make the hair stand up on your head."

Eventually I looked up at the clock. I could put it off no longer. I knew the Christmas dinner up at Queensbrook would be over by now. Aunt Kate would be out on her charity rounds and Uncle Kevin would be sleeping it off. If I was lucky I could get in and out without having to confront either one of them.

I put on the new blouse from Mrs. Hollywood, a colorful skirt, and my best coat. I wrapped Patsy's scarf around my neck, shoved the hat in my pocket—I didn't want to ruin my hair, which I had painstakingly curled earlier that morning. I put on the gloves, picked up the gift for Ma, and waved good-bye, looking cheerier than I felt.

"I'm away," I called from the hallway.

As soon as I stepped out into the late, gray afternoon, I missed the brightness and warmth inside number 6 Walker's Row. I was grateful to Gavin for finding us this place. I thought back to our last meeting when he had been so angry. I wondered had he done what the IRA had asked? If he had, I prayed he had not been caught. Silently I wished him well—I could never stay angry at Gavin for long.

I knocked on the door of the Queensbrook house, shivering as old memories rose up.

"Happy Christmas," I said when Ma opened the door. "Are you going to let me in or do I have to stand here foundered with the cold?"

The words rushed out. I was an anxious child again home from school and wondering which Ma I would find. This evening I found the happy one. A smile spread across Ma's face and she let out a wee cry of surprise.

"Sheila, och, Sheila love. Come in. Come in. You missed Kate. She's gone out, and Kevin's sleeping. Och, you look well."

She bustled into the kitchen. "Sit down, sit down. I was just making a wee cup of tea. We've no milk or sugar, but sure aren't we used to that by now? At least we have tea."

Compared with the brightness of Mrs. Hollywood's, the Queensbrook house was dreary. A few embers burned in the fireplace, and there was a lingering smell of onions and cabbage, but of course there was no tree. I realized how grateful I was for my new home.

"I brought you a present, Ma. Here, try it on. And Joel and I want you to come with us to O'Hare's for a Christmas drink."

Ma tore open the package like a child. She held the necklace in her hand and her eyes glowed.

"Och, Sheila, it's beautiful. I'm sure there's no other one like it in the world."

I felt a pang of guilt as I thought of the identical one I had given Mrs. Hollywood. But the chances of their meeting up while wearing it were small.

"Go on and get ready," I said. "Wear something nice, and wear the necklace."

I sipped the tea as Ma went into the granny room.

"Kate finally made me move back in here yesterday," Ma called out to me. "I liked it better upstairs."

I sat bolt upright. It hadn't occurred to me that Aunt Kate would make Ma move back to the granny room. But now that I thought about it I supposed she didn't think Ma was good enough to go on sleeping in the sainted Donal's room—particularly now there was no money coming in for Grainne.

I thought of my prize money still buried in one of the drawers and swore under my breath. I prayed Ma hadn't had time to find it. I would have to get it back tonight. Old resentments began to build in me, but I beat them back down. I would not let them ruin my Christmas. Instead I fixed a smile on my face, prepared to compliment Ma on whatever she was wearing.

"You look gran—" The words stuck in my throat.

Ma wore a bright red dress that I recognized as one of mine. I knew that she had not given me all my clothes after I moved out, but I'd let it go. Now, when I saw her spinning around for me to admire her, a strange, sick feeling came over me.

"Och, I know it was yours, love, but I always thought it would look better on me. It does, doesn't it? I mean, you never had the bust for it. It needs to be filled out. D'you think Joel will like it? Who do you think will be there tonight? Oh, I hope the *craic* is good. Is that what you're wearing? Well, I suppose it will do."

I blocked out the rest of her words. This woman would never be a mother to me. She was too self-centered. And I had learned my own self-centeredness from her. I wondered would I be this ridiculous when I was her age. The thought made me flinch.

"I have to use the loo," Ma said.

Now was my chance. I waited until she was gone and dashed into the granny room. I rummaged frantically through the dresser drawer and pulled out the envelope containing the prize money and tore it open. Thank God, the money was still there. I shoved the envelope in my pocket and taking a deep breath strolled back out into the living room.

"Come on, get your coat," I said. "Joel is going to collect us at the tram station in Newry."

ᴏᴚᴏ

Ma sidled into the front seat of Joel's car, leaving me to climb into the back. Joel smiled at me but said nothing. He looked handsome in dark brown slacks, a tan shirt, and brown tweed jacket. I looked down at my modest blouse and skirt and shrugged. Anybody would think I'd come out of the convent. I regretted not wearing my best Linen Queen frock. Ma talked nonstop until we arrived at O'Hare's. The place was warm and festive. Holly wreaths and red ribbons lined the walls while colorful streamers crisscrossed the low ceiling. Sprigs of mistletoe hung down

from the streamers. A huge fire blazed in one corner and candles
burned in old glass ships' lanterns.

Ma led the way in, sashaying across the room looking for the
best seat she could find. She did not mean to miss anything. She
had left her coat in the car, and even though she must have been
freezing, she wiggled across the floor in my red dress, making
sure everyone saw her. Joel smiled and took my arm. He seemed
well amused by Ma, even though I was mortified. We followed
her to a table near the fire, where she sat down with her back
against the wall.

"This is grand," she said, smiling at us. "I can see everything
from here."

Joel went to the bar to get us drinks. I was grateful to him for
agreeing to come here. If he was uncomfortable in the place, he
didn't show it. I was the one on edge. I hoped Ma would behave
herself, and that nobody would pick on Joel. But the pub was
filled with good cheer this evening. The radio had been set to
a station playing Christmas carols, and everyone sang along.
I relaxed and sipped the shandy Joel had brought, while Ma
downed her whiskey in two gulps.

Eventually a fiddler and an accordion player came in, to the
delight of the crowd. The radio and the carols were nice, but it
was not a great night in any country pub without a bit of traditional music. I had seen the fiddler before. He had come once in a
while into the Ceili House, always wearing a long black coat and
carrying his fiddle under his arm. Some nights he played; other
nights he took a drink and left as quickly as he had come. Tonight
he was in the mood to play. He tuned up and then launched into
a couple of jigs with the wee old man on the accordion. People
clapped and stamped their feet—Joel along with them.

I looked around the pub. There were no soldiers to be
seen—probably all at the Prince of Mourne in Warrenpoint, I
thought, remembering our night there last Christmas. I recognized some of the locals—married couples out for an evening drink, and old bachelors with stubbled chins and calloused
hands. In a corner of the bar were some rough-looking customers,

huddled together, with fierce looks on them. I shifted in my chair.
I didn't know them but by the cut of them I guessed they were
IRA fellas.

The musicians began to play an old-time waltz and one of the
men in the corner came over to our table.

"How about a dance," he said, as he put his hand out towards
me. He was the biggest one of the crowd, with the meanest look.

I shook my head. "No thanks," was all I said.

He glared back at me, muttered something, and walked away.

Another boyo came up behind him and put his hand out to Ma.
She smiled and got up. As she moved past me she leaned over.

"You shouldn't refuse them, love. Joel won't mind."

She tottered unsteadily out onto the dance floor and was soon
twirling around, as if she were dancing by herself, throwing up
her skirt to show off her legs. A sick feeling came over me as I
watched. Was that how I used to look when I was drunk and carrying on?

When the tune finished, Ma stood in the middle of the floor
as if waiting for someone to claim her. A short man with a round
belly came up and began to dance her around the floor with more
enthusiasm than skill. The big boyo came up to me again, his
hand out, and again I refused him.

"Me ma's looking for a partner," I said. "And she's not
particular."

Joel eyed me sharply. I knew I shouldn't have said what I did,
but something about that big lout set me boiling. As the music
flowed, so did the alcohol, and so did the conversation. In time
people became louder, more insistent. Soon the arguments would
start. The door opened, creating a sudden draft. I looked up and
glimpsed Gavin and the girl, Rosaleen, making their way to the
bar. I began to think it might be time to go. But Ma was dancing
away and Joel seemed to be enjoying himself, so I tried to relax.
I convinced myself that even if Gavin saw us he would probably
keep to himself. I watched him as he stood with his back to me.
He chatted easily with the other men, laughing at someone's joke
and patting another chap on the back. Gavin was the type of man

everybody liked. He looked like a man easy with himself and his surroundings.

As the talk grew louder, the word "war" began to dominate and most of it was coming from the direction of the IRA boyos in the corner. One of them raised his glass.

"To Hitler," he shouted. "Just the man to put England in her place."

There was a mild gasp around the room, but the crowd at the bar cheered.

"To the führer," yelled the one that I had refused. "Go ya boy ya!"

I looked directly at Joel. His face had turned tight and pale. We had no need to speak. I turned to reach for my coat. "I'll get Ma," I said.

But by the time I fought my way through the crowd, Ma was dancing with the big IRA fella. "No, not yet, love," she slurred. "Can't you see this handsome bloke I'm dancing with?"

Her partner glared at me. "Leave your ma be," he snarled. "Just feck off!"

I didn't realize Joel was standing behind me.

"That's no way to talk to a lady," he said, pulling me behind him and reaching for Ma's arm. "Come on now, Mrs. McGee. Time to go home."

Sensing the possibility of a fight, the dancers moved away, leaving us alone in the middle of the floor. The IRA man glared at Joel, and then his big face broke into a grin. He let Ma's arms drop.

"Well, well. A Yank! I should have smelled you a mile away. Brit lover!"

Joel stiffened. "On the contrary, I'm a Hitler hater."

Ma broke in. "He's Jewish, love," she said. "They don't like Hitler much."

My stomach sank and my knees buckled. A feeling of dread filled me. I grabbed Joel's arm. "C'mon, we'll wait for Ma outside."

But as Joel turned the IRA boyo swung around with a speed that shocked me and grabbed Joel from behind.

"Not so fast, Jew!" he said. Then he turned to his comrades.

"Hey, lads, we've got us a Jew. Let's give Hitler one less to worry about!"

At that the others piled on to the dance floor and lit into Joel. Ma stumbled backwards and screamed. The crowd sat still and gaped. Suddenly Gavin leaped from his stool and grabbed the leader roughly, tearing him away from Joel.

"Leave him alone, Sean," Gavin said.

"Jesus, Gavin," Sean cried. "Don't tell me you're a Jew lover."

Gavin moved in front of Joel. "It's hardly a fair fight, Sean."

The barmen moved in to interfere. The owner turned on the lights and the musicians stopped playing.

"Switched sides have you, boyo?" Sean was yelling. "Need to be taught a lesson in loyalty?"

Sean freed himself from Gavin's grip and before the barmen could stop him, threw a punch that landed Gavin on the floor. As the barmen herded everybody out, Joel and I both sank to our knees over Gavin. Ma and Rosaleen stood behind us crying, while the other IRA boys closed in. Gavin was unconscious.

"Mother of God," I cried. "Please, Joel. Help him."

Joel looked up towards the bar and signaled a young man over, whom I recognized as the guard from the base at Narrow Water Castle. He was in his civvies with a couple of other lads. I hadn't noticed them earlier.

"Here," Joel said, taking his car keys out of his pocket and handing them to the soldier. "Take him to my quarters at the base and get the doctor. Then bring the car back here." He turned to me. "Go on, take your mother and start walking. Get somebody to give you a lift home."

"But what about you?" I said.

"I have a score to settle, Sheila. Don't worry, you forget I'm a soldier."

I hesitated. The IRA boyos stood watching us. The pub owner was on the phone to the Gardaí. Most of the patrons had cleared out.

Suddenly Ma seized my wrist. "Take me home, Sheila. I'm afraid."

She was on the edge of hysterics. I took a last look at Joel and then I led Ma out of the pub and into the blackness of the night.

ༀ

I didn't sleep that night. I lay in bed waiting for the morning so I could go to the barracks at Narrow Water Castle and find out what happened. Were Joel and Gavin dead or alive? But in the middle of the night a storm swept in, bringing snow and ice that paralyzed the country. Well, it wasn't going to stop me. I would get there by hook or by crook.

"You can't go out in this weather, love," Mrs. Hollywood said. "You wouldn't get more than a few yards on your bicycle."

"I'll walk then," I said.

"Oh, be sensible, Sheila. You'd freeze to death before you even reached the top of the street. Let it be, for now. There's a good girl. There's nothing you can do for either of them. Tell me again what happened."

I repeated the whole story. This time Patsy and Grainne were there to hear it. Patsy was fascinated.

"Sounds like great *craic* altogether, Sheila," she said. "I wish I'd been there to see it."

Grainne, on the other hand, stared at me with an odd expression.

"Is Gavin dead?" she whispered.

I was shocked. "No, of course he's not. He was knocked out that's all. But if it wasn't for Joel interfering he might well have been killed."

Mrs. Hollywood gasped.

Grainne's face turned crimson. "So the Joel fella is the hero? Is that it? It was his fault that Gavin had to get into it in the first place. His fault and yours. If something happens to Gavin, I'll never forgive you."

She jumped up, tears streaming down her thin face. We watched her run up the stairs.

"What in the name of God's got into her?" I said.

Mrs. Hollywood and Patsy looked at each other but said nothing. "I'm going to give it a try," I said suddenly. "I have to find out what's happened to Joel."

I was worried for Gavin too, but I was more worried for Joel. Gavin at least had been taken out of the pub before any more harm could come to him. But Joel had deliberately stayed to face the IRA men, and nobody there was going to lift a finger to help him. Oh, God, what had they done to him? Had they killed him and thrown him in a ditch? Was he lying freezing on the side of the road?

Despite Mrs. Hollywood's protests, I put on my coat and boots. I pulled on the hat and scarf Patsy had knitted, opened the front door, and stepped out. The wind cut my face like a knife and I put my head down. I lifted my bicycle from against the wall, but it was covered with ice. I'd have to walk. Maybe some good soul out there would come along and give me a lift. But Mrs. Hollywood had been right. By the time I slipped and slid up to the top of Walker's Row, bent over in half against the wind, I was out of breath and frozen. I fought back tears of frustration and returned to number 6.

The following morning the mill opened again after the holiday. Normally it would have been closed until the New Year, but this was wartime and production needed to continue. The weather had not improved much, but the wind had died down. I made my way slowly, along with some of the neighbors, down to the tram station. We shivered as we rode, huddled together, up to Queensbrook. The spinning floor was freezing, and so we kept our coats and boots on for a while until the place warmed up. The girls began to sing, as much to keep themselves warm as anything else, but I hadn't the heart for it.

None of the girls had been at O'Hare's on Christmas night, so the subject of the fight never came up. I was glad of it. Kathleen came over to talk to me at the dinner break. She inquired about how Patsy was keeping and whether Christmas had been good. But I told her nothing about Joel and Gavin. What was the point?

Later that evening I was on duty with the ARP. Part of me was glad of the distraction, and part of me wished I was free instead to go and find Joel. I would have to wait another day. I sat in the small back room of the converted house beside the police barracks where our headquarters had been set up. It hardly looked like a headquarters, more like somebody's kitchen. A fire blazed in the grate and the kettle whistled on the stove. Mary McTaggart was on duty, as well as a couple of older men. The head warden was in his "office" in the parlor.

"Bloody cold to be parading up and down Hill Street," grumbled one of the men, whose name was Hugh.

He was a lazy oul' sod. Always complaining. I wondered why he had joined up in the first place. The other one, a wee chap called Eugene, agreed with him.

"You're right there, Hugh. A night not fit for man nor beast."

Hugh looked at Mary and me. "Youse girls are a lot younger than us. I think you should take the outside duty tonight. Eugene and I will stay here and practice our first aid. After all, there won't be much doing on a night like this."

Mary began to protest, but I was glad of the chance to go and do something. Still, I wasn't letting them off so easy.

"Youse are lazy oul' bastards, the pair of you," I said, "sending us out while you sit here on your arses. Mary and I will go, but only providing you finish rolling that pile of bandages over there in the corner, and youse clean and sweep the place, including the lav. Otherwise I'll report you to the regional inspector."

They glared at me, while Mary grinned.

"You'd better watch yourself, you wee bitch," Hugh said.

I shrugged my shoulders as I pulled on my overcoat and lifted my helmet from its peg. They knew they had no choice but to do what I said. They knew I wasn't shy. And besides, they knew the regional inspector had a big notion for me.

Mary and I shivered as we walked along Hill Street. A few pubs were open but not a sliver of light showed through the heavy black blinds on the windows. All the street lamps had wee hoods on them that dimmed the light enough so it couldn't be seen from above. But tonight all the precautions in the world would have made no difference because the snow that covered the streets was so bright the ground may as well have been lit by chandeliers. We should be finished with our rounds in no time, I thought.

As we came up Water Street, a pub door opened and a crowd of soldiers spilled out onto the pavement. Yanks. I exchanged glances with Mary. I knew we both hoped they wouldn't give us any trouble. We usually ignored them as best we could. I squared my shoulders and prepared to walk through the small knot of soldiers. As expected the catcalls began. I swung around when I heard one voice. There was no mistaking it. It belonged to Sylvie Sartori.

"Well, well, boys. If it isn't the Linen Queen herself. Hey, Sheila, that's a hulluva tiara you're wearing."

Mary clutched my arm. "C'mon, Sheila. Just ignore them."

But Sylvie blocked my path. His face was so close to mine I could smell the beer on his breath.

"Get out of my way, Sylvie," I said.

"So how's that slut of a friend of yours, Sheila?" he slurred. "Still trying to pass that bastard off as mine?"

"You know fine well it's yours," I said, trying to hold my temper. "You're just not man enough to admit it and marry her. You're a bloody coward, Sylvie, and worse. You should at least be paying for her keep. As it is, I'm the one supporting her, when it should be you."

Sylvie hiccupped in my face. I stepped back in disgust. He turned to his comrades.

"Almost sweet, ain't it, boys, how whores look after each other in their time of need."

His friends laughed and my temper broke. I reached out and slapped Sylvie hard across the face before Mary could stop me. He flinched.

"You bitch," he said. "I'll report you for this."

"Report away," I said. "Your captain knows all about you. One word from me and—"

"Oh, that's right. I forgot you're Captain Solomon's whore." He chuckled. "Well, you won't be seeing much action from him for a while. You'd better find yourself another officer."

I froze. "What are you talking about?"

"Seems he got himself in the middle of a donnybrook—with the IRA of all people. I'd swear that man has a death wish going up against those guys without any backup."

"What's happened to him?" I said, trying to control the tremble in my voice.

"Oh, he'll live," said Sylvie. "Banged up a lot, though. Broke a few ribs, sprained a few muscles, face cut up like a jigsaw puzzle. Like I said he won't be much good in bed for a while."

"That's enough, soldier!" Mary roared at him. "Go home now before I call the police." Mary reached with her one hand for her two-way radio.

"Settle down, stumpy," said Sylvie. "We've got better things to do. C'mon, boys. Let's go to the Ceili House for a nightcap. Coming, Sheila?"

He was a brazen lout. I swallowed the insults that crowded my tongue and stepped off the pavement into the road along with Mary. We walked away from them, the insults and catcalls still echoing in our ears. As I walked, my anger subsided and relief took its place. Thank God, Joel was alive. Thank God.

Chapter 23

ᘓᗢᘓ

The scream of a banshee awoke me. It pierced my ears like a siren. I sat up. The German bombers were coming. The alerts were slicing the silence of the night. But then I realized the noise was coming from Patsy.

"The baby's coming, Sheila. Jesus the baby's coming. I think I'm dying."

The lights in the attic room blazed as Mrs. Hollywood burst in the door.

"Oh, lordy. Calm down now, Patsy. Take deep breaths, love. That's right. Now just hold on."

I jumped out of bed. "Grainne," I said, "go next door and fetch Mrs. Cowan."

Grainne glared at me.

"Now!" I said.

Grainne pulled on her clothes and ran out of the room. Mrs. Cowan was the local midwife. She had agreed to come the minute Patsy was ready to deliver. We'd been on edge waiting—Patsy was over three weeks late. I went downstairs and put water on to boil and pulled out the clean towels Mrs. Hollywood had set aside. Upstairs I could hear her trying to soothe Patsy but she kept screaming. Could the pain be that bad? I wondered. Patsy was always one for dramatics. Maybe she was just being hysterical. Mrs.

Cowan came flying in the door, Grainne behind her. I handed the towels to Grainne.

"Here, bring these up. Then come back down. You have no business up there."

I expected back talk from her, but she came running down the stairs again in seconds. It was then I realized she was scared. I tried to smile at her.

"Patsy'll be all right," I said. "Women give birth every day of the week."

When the water had boiled I carried it in a pan back up to the bedroom and set it on a table beside the bed. Mrs. Cowan was bending over Patsy, examining her, feeling her stomach, while Patsy screamed at her to leave her alone. I ran down to the kitchen and got a jug of cold water and a facecloth. I brought them up and began to bathe Patsy's forehead. Mrs. Cowan nodded to Mrs. Hollywood to come away from the bed out of Patsy's hearing.

"Something's not right," Mrs. Cowan said. "The baby's turned the wrong way. I'll try to turn it but in the state she's in she might not let me touch her again."

I took Patsy's hand and tried to calm her down. A bad feeling took a hold of me.

"Help me turn her on her side, Sheila," Mrs. Cowan was saying.

We tried moving Patsy, but she fought us so ferociously we gave up.

Mrs. Cowan sighed. "We need to get her to the ambulance in a hurry. The cord might be choking that baby."

I jumped up, ran downstairs, and grabbed my coat off its peg.

"I'm going to ring the ambulance," I said to Grainne. "You wait here."

I ran as fast as I could up Walker's Row and down Cecil Street to the phone box that stood on the corner. All I could think of was that I had to get to the phone. Patsy needed help. Her screams still echoed in my ears. I slid on a patch of ice and fell. Swearing, I pulled myself up and ran on. It was hard to see where I was going and I cursed the blackout. I fell again and hauled myself up, holding on to the wall of a house, and limped towards the corner.

"Took you long enough," Grainne snapped at me when I got back to the house. Jesus, could I do nothing right in that girl's eyes?

Instead of waiting at the house I limped back up to the top of the street to wait for the ambulance so that I could direct them. God forbid they should go to the wrong address. Grainne would blame me. Eventually the ambulance appeared at the bottom of Cecil Street, its siren squealing. Doors and windows on the street opened one by one and people came out of their houses. They probably thought it was an air raid. I waved it down and directed it to Walker's Row. When I got back to the house, the attendants were already loading Patsy into the ambulance. I climbed in beside her. She had stopped screaming. Instead she let out small groans. I held her hand as we rode to the hospital.

"Name, please?" a big stone-faced nurse with a southern accent demanded as Patsy was wheeled in.

"Mallon," I said, "Patsy."

"Address?"

"Six Walker's Row."

The nurse eyed me. "And who are you?"

"A friend."

"Where's the husband?"

"There isn't one. Can't you hurry up?"

The nurse's eyes were an odd yellow color. They put me in mind of an old diseased cat that used to roam the Fathom Road. Those eyes looked me up and down now in disgust.

"Don't be telling me my job, miss."

She motioned the ambulance attendants. "Leave her there in the corridor, lads. We're very busy tonight. She'll have to wait her turn."

I grabbed her by the wrist. "What do you mean, wait her turn? The baby's turned the wrong way. It could be choking. She needs a doctor now!"

She shook me off. Her face had turned scarlet.

"There's plenty of decent women here deserve to be seen to before that one! Now I'll have to ask you to leave."

I wanted to grab her again and shake her until her teeth fell out. But it would have done no good. Instead I ran out after the ambulance attendants. I knew them slightly through my ARP work.

"For God's sake," I said, "can you do something? That nurse in there's refusing to get her seen to—and the baby might be dying. Please!"

"Wait here, Sheila," said the older one, and he ran back through the hospital doors.

A few minutes later he came back with a big grin on his face.

"I found the doctor in charge and they're getting your friend ready now for surgery. I'd say they'll have to do a caesarean."

He looked pleased with himself that he knew the medical term.

"That's grand, Eamonn," I said. "Thank you."

"No bother, Sheila. You can buy me a drink sometime."

ᘒᕲ

Mrs. Hollywood and Mrs. Cowan sat drinking tea in the kitchen when I came back to Walker's Row. I told them all that had happened and they sighed and shook their heads. Wearily, I went upstairs. Mrs. Hollywood had changed the sheets on the bed and I lay down without even taking my clothes off. Grainne lay awake in the other bed. She muttered something in my direction, but I was too tired to listen. I turned my back to her and put out the light.

ᘒᕲ

Patsy was let home on Sunday of the following week. There was an old superstition that it was bad luck for patients to be released from the hospital on a Saturday. The doctors kept the baby for observation. Apparently Patsy and the child had both been in a worse state than even we thought when they arrived at hospital. The doctors had feared for both their lives. And if it had been left up to that bitch of a nurse, I thought, they wouldn't have stood a chance. As it was, the baby had eventually been delivered, blue faced and silent. If not for the persistent efforts of the staff she would probably not have lived. But live she did—although no one knew what damage had been caused to her oxygen-starved brain.

Mrs. Hollywood gave up her own bed to Patsy so she wouldn't have to climb the stairs. I was delighted to have a bed to myself for the first time since I was a child. It was still hard to sleep, though. When the baby eventually came home she wailed like a banshee every night. She was a lovely looking child. Her hair was blond and she had big brown eyes. Patsy called her Sylvia. The old Sheila would have made a smart remark about saddling the child with that blackguard's name. But I said nothing. Patsy and I had never mentioned Father Flynn's assumption that she would give the baby up for adoption. And when I saw Patsy holding Sylvia I knew wild horses would never drag the child away from her.

I was still very worried about Joel. I realized he couldn't come to see me because he wouldn't be fit to drive. It was all I could do to stop myself from running down to Narrow Water Castle to see him. But first I had to find Gavin and thank him. I pounced on Alphie the minute he walked in the door on his next visit.

"Have you seen Gavin? Is he all right?"

"He's grand. Why wouldn't he be?"

"He was knocked out Christmas night."

"Och, aye, that wee scrap. That's all forgotten. We're sailing out on the morning tide, so we are."

The next morning before dawn I rode down to the docks. I didn't know what drove me, but I was determined to see Gavin before he sailed. When I arrived, men were loading cargo onto the *Ashgrove*, and Gavin stood on the dock shouting orders.

He nodded when he saw me. "Been up all night, have you?"

"No. I heard you were sailing this morning. I wanted to talk to you before you left."

"I'm busy."

"It won't take long." I moved closer to him. "I wanted to thank you."

"For what? For being stupid enough to get my teeth knocked out?"

"You know what I mean. For standing up for Joel."

"I would have done the same for anybody."

"Well, thanks anyway. And I know he'd thank you too."

"He already did."

"You talked to him?"

"I was lying in the man's bed when he came back that night. I had to be polite."

I was getting nowhere. I shrugged. I had done what I had come to do. I turned to go.

"How is he getting on?" Gavin said over his shoulder. "He was in a bad way that night."

"I haven't seen him. But I hear he's OK."

Gavin nodded his head and turned back to the men loading the cargo.

☙

If there is ever anything good about being imprisoned by harsh weather, it is the joy that comes from entering the world again. On the morning when I rode my bicycle down to Narrow Water Castle to see Joel, I felt like a child newly emerged from the womb. Colors were deeper, smells were sweeter, sounds were clearer than ever before. All of my senses were on alert and life coursed through me like an electric current.

As I rode I inhaled deeply, filling up my lungs as if they'd been starved for air. My hands and even my lips were nearly frozen—but I felt alive. I smiled at everything around me, giddy as a child. I rode on through the gates of the big estate and stopped at the gatehouse. The last time I had been here was in the middle of the night. Now I saw the beauty of the place for the first time. A narrow road wound up past green slopes of grass, shaded with trees. As I looked up, the gray stone castle looked back at me like something from a child's fairy tale, with its narrow windows and turrets outlined against the sky.

I was so lost in thought I didn't even notice the jeep that had pulled up beside me and stopped. In it sat General Turner. He doffed his cap.

"Well, if it isn't our very own Linen Queen," he boomed. "Here to see our Captain Solomon, I presume," he said with a wink.

I blushed and nodded. I had not expected such a welcome.

He signaled to the young guard at the gatehouse to let me in. "You'll find him in the library," he said. "Seems to be where he spends most of his time. Thinks too much, that young man."

He saluted me and sped off again, gravel hopping beneath the wheels of his jeep. I wondered how he knew about me and Joel. It seemed everyone, neighbors and strangers alike, knew the details of my life. I leaned my bicycle against the front wall of the main house and walked up the steps to the big wooden door. I pushed it open and entered the hallway. I vaguely remembered that the library was on the right-hand side, but I had no need to wonder for long. The strains of a violin met me and I knew at once the sound came from Joel. He was playing the same melancholy tune he had played on the Flagstaff.

I tiptoed to the half-open door of the library and stood watching him. He stood near a window with his back to me, looking out as he played. My emotions tumbled one after another as I watched him—joy, love, pride. As if sensing someone watching him, Joel stopped playing and swung around.

I sucked in my breath as I looked at him. He had lost weight, and his skin was more sallow than I remembered. A cast wrapped his left leg, and fading bruises still covered his face and lips. His eyes carried no light and he looked weary. He was not in his uniform. Instead he wore dark slacks and an open-necked shirt. I repressed an impulse to run over and hug him.

"Sheila?" It was a question, as if he could not quite believe it was me.

"Aye, in the flesh. Hello, Joel."

He laid down his fiddle and lifted a walking stick from the top of the piano. He limped forward and took my arm. "Come in. Sit down. How're you doing?"

"Just grand," I said, as I sat down on a sofa.

"Can I fetch you something? Tea? Soft drink?"

I shook my head no. I fumbled in my handbag for my cigarettes and took one out and lit it. My fingers shook. Joel went slowly around the room and raised the blinds on all the covered windows. When he came back to stand in front of me his face betrayed his earlier calm.

"How is Gavin?" he said.

I was surprised at the question. "He's grand. I saw him before he sailed out."

"He was a brave man to do what he did."

"Aye. You don't go up against those boyos." And then another thought slipped out. "Oh, Joel, I'm afraid for him."

Joel sat down and I told him what Gavin had told me about the IRA's request that he smuggle guns for them.

"I don't know how far in he is with them, but he didn't help himself one bit defending you," I said.

Joel looked at me for a moment as if making up his mind whether or not to say something. "You know why he did it, don't you?" he said eventually.

I shook my head.

Joel smiled. "He believes that you're in love with me. I tried to tell him it wasn't true, that you admitted yourself you had just been using me. But he didn't buy it. Said he knew you better than I did. And while he didn't mince words about what he thought of me and the other soldiers, he said he didn't want to see you hurt."

I sat up straight on the sofa. "He said that?"

"Yes. But if you ask me, I think he's in love with you himself. We may disagree on many things, but he's a fine man, Sheila. We did a lot of talking the night after the fight, and I came to understand a little about his point of view. He told me about his father. And I believe he came to understand more about my hatred for Hitler. Anyway, I urged him to distance himself from those IRA guys, but I didn't know about the smuggling. It will be difficult for him to turn against them now. They may ask him to do more things to prove himself. They're already suspicious of his loyalties."

"God, I hope not," I said.

I could see the conversation was tiring Joel. I stood up to go. Part of me wanted to stay and comfort him, but part of me needed to get away and think. The fact that Joel and Gavin had talked about me was unsettling.

He insisted on seeing me to the door. "I'll have to go to England in the next few days," he said.

"But you're hardly fit to travel."

He smiled. "Duty calls. I'll come and see you when I get back. It may be a couple of months."

I nodded. There was no point asking questions. I kissed him gently on his bruised lips and lifted my bicycle and rode away.

Chapter 24

ꙮ

Winter faded into spring, and by early May the world began to look brighter. Sun shone, flowers appeared on the roadside, and the birds sang more loudly. The only thing that was apparently not looking brighter was the war. I was now fully part of something larger than myself—I was part of the war effort. In that way, I was like most of my neighbors in the North of Ireland. Before the war we had been like orphaned children, unsure of our place in the world and without a strong purpose to hold us together and give us an identity. It had just taken me longer than most to realize how this war could change my outlook on the world and, more importantly, on myself. I had found a purpose, and I wasn't sure I wanted the war to end too soon, selfish as that was. I wanted the Allies to win eventually of course, but in the meantime I yearned for a chance to try on this new life and adapt to the changes it was bringing.

I kept up my volunteer work with the ARP. Mary McTaggart turned out to be a good friend. Over time, she told me more about what had happened to her and her sister in England. Neither of them had seen any war action. Anne had been killed when a plane she was flying from the factory to the airfield malfunctioned. Mary had lost her arm in a horrible accident when she was trapped beneath a jeep at the same airfield.

"Some fighters we turned out to be," Mary joked. "We never even got near the battle." There was a dark edge to her laughter.

"We should have gone into nursing like our ma and da wanted us to," Mary said. "That way we might still have been doing some good."

"You're doing good here," I said. "You could have sat on your arse at home feeling sorry for yourself, but instead you marched right back out again into the world." I put my hand out to touch her arm. "And I'm glad you did."

I wanted to tell Mary she was an inspiration to me. She was living proof that what Joel had told me was right.

I hadn't seen Joel since he'd gone to England. I knew there was no point going to look for him. He'd said he'd see me when he returned. I would have to wait. One Sunday morning a knock came to the door and I rushed downstairs. I pulled open the door, a big smile on my face, but instead of Joel, there stood Ma. My smile faded.

"What do you want?" I said, more harshly than I intended.

"Lovely way to treat your mother," Ma said as she pushed past me into the hall.

I shut the door and followed her in. Mrs. Hollywood poked her head out of the parlor and then shut the door again. Ma marched into the kitchen and sat down at the table.

"Don't stand there like a statue, you lazy bitch," she said. "Make me a cup of tea."

I'd hardly ever seen Ma in such a bad temper. I braced myself for the worst.

"Kate wants me out of the house," she said. "It's your fault. Ever since that Grainne business she's just been looking for an excuse to get rid of me."

Her breathing was ragged and her eyes bright. I set a cup of tea down in front of her. "We've no milk," I said.

She sniffed and blew on the tea to cool it. I sat down opposite her. "What happened?"

Ma rolled her eyes. "That oul' hypocrite. Just because I brought a friend home a couple of times she—"

"You did what, Ma? You brought men to the house?"

Ma shrugged. "I need a wee bit of company the same as the next woman," she said. "I'm not dead yet."

I stared at her. I didn't know what to say. I knew she had been seeing soldiers but I hadn't asked questions. I didn't want to know the details. But I never thought she would dare to bring them home. Part of me wanted to smile at the thought of Kate's face when she caught them, but it was no laughing matter and the thought passed.

"In the name of God, Ma, did you not think she'd throw you out?"

"She wouldn't have if you hadn't poisoned her against me. She would have given me a second chance. I blame you, miss."

What else was new, I thought. People were always blaming me for everything. "Well, you can't stay here," I blurted out. "There's no room."

"It's your duty to look after me," she said. "Where am I going to get the money for rent?"

"You have a job," I said.

"I'm not a well woman," she said. "I don't know how long I can last at that oul' mill."

Anger and guilt fought inside me. "Get one of your soldier boys to pay for it then."

Ma reached across the table and slapped me on the face.

"You ungrateful girl," she said.

The pitch of her voice rose. She was on the edge of hysteria.

"Oh how I rue the day I married your father. He should have taken you with him when he left. It would have been good riddance to both of you. What have either of you ever brought me but trouble? I should have poisoned you years ago along with that old dog. God help me, what's to become of me?"

I sat up and looked at Ma. I couldn't believe what I was hearing, and yet I believed it totally. She had always resented me. She had resented my relationship with Da. And when he left she resented the little crippled dog that I had come to love. She'd always had to be the center of attention. She was a selfish, hateful woman. And I had been well on my way to becoming just like her. I jumped up and ran up the stairs and rummaged in a drawer. I pulled out a fistful of pound notes and ran back down to the kitchen. I thrust the money at her.

"Here. And get out. I never want to see you again. You're nothing to me. You never were. You're a selfish, mean old woman. And don't come back looking for more money, because that's the last you're ever getting from me."

She snatched the money and stood, calm as you please, counting it.

"Is this all?" she said. "This won't last me very long."

"That's all I have."

"What about that prize money you stole from me?" she shrieked. "You owe me that too."

I stared at her fighting with myself as to what to answer. Then the stubborn Sheila rose up.

"I told you, I never got the prize money," I lied. "After Belfast was bombed all the records were lost. Who knows if I'll ever get it."

"You're lying," she said. "I came right out and asked that McAteer girl, and she said you got the prize money the night of the competition! You stole it from me."

"I did not! It was mine. I won it."

I was trembling now, fighting back the tears that pricked my eyes. All the memories of fighting with Ma flooded back. Was I to find no peace at all? Och, why hadn't I gone with Joel when he'd offered me a way out? I beat down the self-pity that threatened to drown me. I would not give in to her. I would hold on to my dream with everything I had.

Rage blinded me. I pulled her up from the chair. "Get out!" I yelled. "And don't ever come back."

She stuffed the money I had given her in her handbag and left the room. Out in the hall I heard her greet Mrs. Hollywood in a sweet voice, as if nothing had happened. I sat down at the table and began to sob. Mrs. Hollywood came running in.

"Sheila, love, what's wrong? What did that horrible woman say to you?"

I looked up. "Am I that bad a person, Mrs. Hollywood? Am I that bad that everybody turns against me? Haven't I done any good in the world at all?"

⚬⚬⚬

Joel came on a beautiful late spring night in the middle of May carrying flowers for me and a big box of chocolates for Patsy, Grainne, and Mrs. Hollywood. He brought a present for the baby too—a wee gold cross on a delicate gold chain. Patsy was delighted.

"Get your coat. I want to take you out to dinner," Joel said.

He looked well and fit.

"How do you know I'm not on duty?" I said, smiling.

"I checked your schedule." He smiled. "Don't look so surprised, Sheila. I've learned that this is a very small town and news is easy to obtain. One of your comrades, Hugh I think his name was, told me you were off tonight."

I shrugged. "I'll get my coat," I said.

As I went upstairs, I couldn't help smiling, imagining the face of Hugh when an American army captain came looking for me. We drove to the Balmoral Hotel in Warrenpoint. Had it really been a year since we had last been there? Since we had spent the night together? Since I had come home filled with excitement at the prospect of escaping? It all seemed so distant now. It was as if it had never happened at all.

We enjoyed a quiet dinner in the hotel's dining room at a table overlooking the water. The days had begun to stretch out, and it was still light enough to see across the lough to Omeath and Carlingford. I wondered why I had never appreciated the beauty of the place before. The Cooley Mountains, already lush with bracken, rose gently behind Omeath, and gulls played above the lough, gray and white and graceful. A boat came through, blowing its horn. A group of children on the seashore jumped up and down and waved.

"It's beautiful, isn't it?" said Joel, looking out the window.

I nodded.

"I'm going to miss it." He turned back towards me. "And I'm going to miss you."

I swallowed my tea. Whatever it was he was trying to tell me I didn't want to know. So I said nothing. Joel called for the bill, paid it, and stood up. He reached out his hand to me.

"Come upstairs with me, Sheila. I just want to talk somewhere private. We haven't been alone in a long, long time."

Silently I stood and took his arm. This time I didn't even pay attention to the stern-faced clerk as Joel picked up the room key. I felt neither embarrassed nor defiant.

We sat down in two armchairs beside the window of the third-floor room. It was the same room we had stayed in before, and the memories felt good. I took the glass of champagne that Joel offered, and we sat in silence watching the sun set over Carlingford Lough.

"I'll be shipping out at the end of the week," Joel said.

I nodded. It was what I had expected.

"I wanted to see you before I left."

"I'm glad."

"I was wrong, Sheila, and you were right."

I looked up at him, trying to read his face in the dim light.

"I was doling out advice to you when I had no right to. I was telling you to buck up and pull up your bootstraps while I myself was ready to give up on life. I was a hypocrite, and you were right to point it out."

I waved my hand. "Och, that was a long time ago."

Oddly, as I listened to him I had no sense of satisfaction. The old Sheila would have been delighted and would have made the most of the situation, insisting he repeat his words and drawing out the apology. But all I felt was his sadness.

"I shouldn't have said those things just the same," I said.

"I'm glad you did, Sheila. And I've been thinking about them ever since."

He sighed and turned away from me and stared out the window as he spoke.

"Ever since my father died, I've had this strange feeling that I have no right to be living when he's dead. You see, I worshipped my father, and I couldn't understand why he should be gone and I was still here."

"But he took his own life," I said. "He had a choice."

Joel went on as if he hadn't heard me. "At the time I went through a lot of emotions. I was angry with him for leaving us, and ashamed that he had not been brave enough to face his troubles. Afterwards, I was guilty for being angry, and I buried the anger. What took its place was fear—fear that I might do the same thing. And over the years, my fear took the shape of a premonition about my own death. I was convinced I would not live very long. And, as I think about it now, that's maybe why I joined up. If I put myself in harm's way, then my fear could be realized." He shook his head. "Doesn't make much sense, does it?"

"Aye, it does actually," I murmured. "I've felt anger and shame at my mother. I recognize now that my own fear of being stuck here was that I might turn out just like her. But instead of wanting to end my life, I suppose I just wanted to end *this* particular life here. I wanted to start a new life, as somebody else entirely." I shrugged. "Anyway, in the middle of it all, I lost who I was. I'm only now finding out who I really am."

I reached in my bag for a cigarette and lit one. I inhaled deeply and blew the smoke up towards the ceiling. We did not speak for a while. A noise came from downstairs, like somebody moving furniture about. Footsteps sounded on the landing outside the room, and the voices of a man and a woman drifted through the door. Their key sounded in the lock and the room door across the hall banged shut. Then all was silent again.

"I'll make a deal with you, Sheila." Joel's sudden voice startled me.

"I've decided to take my own advice and get out there and do something useful besides wallowing in my own self-pity. If nothing else I owe it to my men to have a positive attitude about our mission. But more than that, I owe it to myself, and..." He hesitated. "And to us."

"Leave me out of it," I said, a sudden panic rising in me.

Joel chuckled. "I didn't mean it that way, Sheila. I need to do this regardless of whether or not you are in my life. I just meant that, well, if we are ever going to have a chance at a future, I need to embrace life, not run away from it."

He got up from the chair and came over to me. Taking me by the arms he pulled me up to face him. He brushed the hair away from my face and stroked my cheek. I felt myself tremble. "The next few months are not going to be easy for either of us, Sheila," he whispered. "If I know that you are waiting for me along with my future it will keep me brave. And, maybe, knowing that I am coming back to you after the war's over will keep you brave as well. We were meant to help each other, Sheila."

I listened to his brave words, but I was not convinced he really believed what he was saying. I prayed that I was wrong.

His lips closed on mine. We stood in that embrace for a long, long time.

"Say you'll wait for me, Sheila."

"Aye." I nodded. "I will."

We slept together that night, although we did not make love. I did not expect to. We would save that moment for when he returned. I clung to him as he rose to leave the next morning, the sun not even up yet. He leaned over and kissed me.

"Remember me, Sheila. Always remember me."

ഇഊ

Joel's battalion shipped out along, it seemed, with most of the troops who had been stationed in the area. Newry was like a ghost town, as was Queensbrook and Warrenpoint and everywhere else. It was as if a cloud had fallen over the place and we were all in mourning for departed friends. Young girls sulked, pining for departed lovers, or at least pining for the fun that was now over. Older people talked as fondly about the "lads" as if they were their own sons. All around there was a heavy sense of dread. Everyone knew something major was about to happen—something that could change the outcome of the war. But optimism was a rare commodity. The war had been rough sledding for the Allies, occasional victories always matched by new German assaults into more countries. Hitler showed no signs of backing down. Everyone sensed an impending crisis.

For myself, though, after my night with Joel, a calm I had never known before settled over me. There was nothing I could do now except wait and hope that Joel would keep his promise. The gravity of the situation made all the other problems in my life seem trivial.

We went about our daily routines, while keeping a watchful eye and ear for news of the soldiers.

"That Joel seems like a nice chap," Patsy said one evening as she and Kathleen sat in the pink parlor. "That was a lovely cross he brought for Sylvia." She looked at me and hesitated. Then almost shyly she asked, "Did he ever say anything about Sylvie? After all, Sylvie's in his battalion."

I shook my head. "I'm sorry, Patsy."

She shrugged. "No bother. I didn't really expect ever to hear from him again. It's just, well, I thought he might have heard about Sylvia, you know?"

Mrs. Hollywood rushed in to change the subject. "More tea?"

"No thanks."

A knock on the door interrupted us. Mrs. Hollywood opened it and in came Alphie, and behind him, Gavin. I stared at him as if I'd seen a ghost. I'd been so preoccupied with Joel that I hadn't stopped to think about him.

"What's wrong?" I said, without even knowing why I said it.

"Why would anything be wrong?" he said. "Alphie and I have come to visit the lovely Mrs. Hollywood. We're sailing out in the morning."

There was something more to it, I knew. Gavin had not come to the house since the night Grainne and I had moved in. Mrs. Hollywood waved us all into the kitchen and rushed about like a little bird making the men comfortable and making them tea and slicing brown bread. Gavin picked up Sylvia in his arms and cooed at her.

"Lovely child," he said, and Patsy glowed.

Alphie gave Patsy a fond look, a silly oul' smile on his face. I was convinced he had taken a notion for Patsy, even though she didn't seem to notice. Better him than that blackguard Sylvie, I thought. Mrs. Hollywood would have approved as well—she had no time for Alphie's "fancy woman" as she called her.

Alphie scoffed at the tea Mrs. Hollywood offered.

"I think something a little stronger is called for, Ma. I don't know what you're saving the good whiskey for."

I got up to fetch the whiskey and some glasses. I felt Gavin's eyes on me as I moved around the kitchen. The talk had turned to war. Some sort of invasion, Alphie said. Gavin said little, but I suspected he knew more than he was letting on. Grainne took up her seat by the fire. She stroked Pirate the cat, but she never took her eyes off Gavin. Every time he looked her way, she blushed. I smiled to myself. So, she had a notion for him? That was why she'd been defending him so hard. I wondered if Gavin noticed it too.

It was midnight when they stood up to leave. Alphie had drunk more than his share of whiskey and was crooning away to the baby. He had a surprisingly sweet singing voice. I was standing at the sink washing the glasses and smiling at Alphie when Gavin tapped me on the shoulder.

"Can we go outside?" he said.

I dried my hands on the dishtowel and walked behind him towards the door, aware of Grainne's eyes following us.

"What's the *craic*?" I said, imitating Gavin's usual greeting.

Gavin lit two cigarettes and handed me one. "Let's walk a bit," he said.

We walked up to the top of Walker's Row and around the corner.

"We're sailing tomorrow," he began.

"Sure I know that."

"This voyage is going to be dangerous," he said.

My heart clenched. "What d'you mean? Are you smuggling the guns?"

"Shhh," said Gavin. "I've been doing that all along. No, this is different."

"What?"

"I can't tell you."

I was annoyed. "Then why bring it up?"

Gavin took a long pull on his cigarette. In the distance we could hear Alphie laughing with Patsy. "It's just that—well, you might hear some things in the future. Rumors and the like. Well, it's going to be up to you what you want to believe."

Jesus, what in God's name was he on about?

"I want you to know I'm not a bad man, Sheila."

"Sure I know that."

"And I don't hate Joel. In fact I respect him. And...I don't hate *you*, either."

"I should hope not."

He ground out his cigarette with his shoe and moved closer to me. His body was trembling ever so slightly. Instinctively I put my hand on his arm.

"What is it, Gavin?"

"Och, Sheila."

Were there tears in his eyes?

Suddenly he threw his arms around me and buried his head in my shoulder.

"Don't think the worst of me, Sheila," he said, his voice muffed. "Whatever you hear, please try to understand."

He raised his head, and taking my face in his two hands pressed his lips against mine with a passion that left me light-headed. The wild thing inside I had known the first time we kissed roused itself again. But before it could take hold of me, Gavin pulled away, his breathing ragged.

"So long, Sheila," he said.

I stood watching him walk down the street. He never looked back.

Chapter 25

ରୁ

On June 6, 1944, the singing stopped. At eight o'clock in the morning we streamed in through the mill gate, the conversation bright and noisy as always. We climbed the stairs to the spinning room and, as always, went to the corner to take off our shoes and put on our aprons. We started up our machines just like on any other day. But by ten o'clock something in the air around us changed—something so dense you could almost put out your hands and touch it. Miss Galway, the doffing mistress, and Billy Taylor, the mill manager, walked to the front of the room and stood at attention, their hands folded in front of them, their faces grave. We looked at one another as we waited for them to speak.

"For God's sake, who died?" Dora Rafferty yelled from the back of the room. "Tell us and put us all out of our misery."

A few chuckles circled through the workers, but nobody else spoke.

Then Billy Taylor cleared his throat and banged a hammer on a table for attention. He hardly needed to do that. All eyes were already fixed on him.

"For those of you who have not been tuned in to the wireless," he began, "there is news coming out that the Allies have staged a ferocious attack on the Germans along the beaches of France."

A cheer went up throughout the room. Billy Taylor raised his hand for silence.

"Before you celebrate, you should know that it's been hard going. Word is coming in that hundreds, maybe thousands, of our boys have been killed or drowned."

"No! God save us!"

The cheers turned to cries of surprise and protest.

"They are still pushing forward, though. And word is they will take the Germans, despite the terrible loss of life." Billy bowed his head. "God rest the souls of each and every one of them poor chaps."

He looked back up at the workers who stood stunned in front of him.

Kathleen gripped my arm. "Och, Jesus, Sheila. What about Ollie? What about Joel?"

I said nothing.

The office door opened and Mr. Carlson strode out, along with Hannah McAteer, to join Miss Galway and Billy Taylor. As I watched I saw an ashen-faced Mary standing at the door. For once she is no different, I thought. She is as worried as the rest of us.

"We can all be very proud here in Queensbrook," Mr. Carlson said. "Through our efforts in making material for tents and uniforms and parachutes we have in our own small way provided support and comfort to our troops. Let's say a prayer now for the safety of the brave chaps still fighting their way into France. And let's say a prayer also for the repose of the souls of those poor men who won't be coming back to us."

We bowed our heads and prayed, some of us aloud, others to ourselves. I stood frozen as if I were watching a pantomime. Maybe I was still asleep down in Walker's Row. Maybe I was dreaming. I closed my eyes, willing myself back into bed, willing the hands of the clock to turn backwards. But when I opened them again, I still stood in the middle of the spinning floor surrounded by women, some weeping, some praying, all of them talking hysterically about the turn of events.

As the day wore on, news bulletins came in one after the other.

Rumors took over from facts. France had been taken back from the Germans. No, the Germans had routed the Allies and they had fled back to their ships. The entire Allied fleet had been sunk. Not at all; sure Hitler had already surrendered. On and on it went throughout the morning and afternoon. Hardly any work was done. Half-timer boys strutted around, chests out, as if they had fought the battle themselves and won victory. Older women who had become close to some of the young soldiers wept as if they had lost one of their own sons. Girls cried and prayed over the fate of some chap they had been seeing. Others cried and swore that now all the fun would be over and done with. None of the soldiers would be back and they'd be stuck in the same old rut as before.

As I trailed out of the gate that evening, I couldn't even bring myself to form Joel's name in my mind. If I didn't think about him, maybe he'd be spared. If I didn't pray for his safety, maybe God would not be tempted to kill him. If I pretended I didn't care, then maybe he'd be all right. I rode home on the tram, my head swimming in confusion. When I arrived at Walker's Row, I found everybody huddled around the kitchen table. Patsy cried for Sylvie. Mrs. Hollywood cried for all those "poor boys." Only Grainne was dry-eyed. She gave me a curious look.

"What's wrong with you?" she said. "I thought you'd be crying for the Joel feller."

I ignored her. If I cried I would be giving in to the possibility that Joel could be gone. And I would not do that. Instead I walked silently to the stove and poured a cup of tea. Only Mrs. Hollywood guessed what was happening.

"Leave her alone, now," she said to Grainne. "Can't you see as how the poor girl's in shock?"

We crowded around the wireless that night. After a while the announcer's words began to run together and my ears closed up as if they'd been stuffed with cotton. Quietly I rose and went up the stairs to bed. I crawled in and turned out the lamp. I had no expectation of sleep—no hope that dreams would come and blot out the horror that filled me. The best I could hope for was to be left alone for a while.

∞

All of us kept vigil waiting for news. Candles were lit, rosaries said, novenas made. I went into the cathedral at night when it was empty. I lit candles and prayed to the Virgin Mary for Joel's safe return. I didn't know if she would listen to a sinner like me, but she was a woman after all, and she had a woman's heart, and she knew a woman's love.

I thought of all the other women like me here and abroad who waited for news of loved ones. We were the women who were not mothers and wives to whom official information would be delivered by telegram or by uniformed officer. We were the women hidden in the corners and crevices, behind doors and curtains, the women who must wait for scraps of information, for hearsay and rumor. And yet for us, the waiting was just as painful, if not more so. For we knew that often we had been the last to hold the fallen warriors in our arms and that those men had loved us keenly and passionately. And yet our sorrow must be hidden away from respectable society, unacknowledged and unvalued.

Details of the D-Day battles began to filter in. The landing craft had run into seas that were rougher and tides that were higher than expected. Underwater obstacles had hampered the landing craft and made them sitting ducks for German gunners. People talked of beaches with names like Omaha, Utah, Juno, and Sword as if they'd known those names their whole lives. Normandy was now a place as familiar to us as our own backyards. In time it was clear this operation marked the turning point in the war that everyone had been hoping for. The cost of that hope in lives lost was likely to number in the thousands.

I listened to all of these discussions with a strange detachment. I went to work each day, numb as the day before. It was as if everything moved around me in slow motion. I made one-word answers when spoken to, but I started no conversations on my own. I did not allow myself to think about anything but the task in front of me at that minute. Silence hung over Walker's Row like a shroud as each of us grieved in our own private way. Kathleen came every evening and held hands with Patsy. Mrs. Hollywood lit pink candles in her parlor. Only Grainne showed no emotion at all.

ை

On the Monday after D-Day, Miss Galway announced that there would be no spinning. Instead we were to clean the machines and the passages that ran between them as well as the corridor outside and the stairs. Most of the girls groaned. We were used to "wipe-down" days once a month when you were expected to clean your spinning frame, emptying and rinsing the trough and wiping down the rollers and the creel and the bobbins. We all took pride in our machines and did our best to keep them clean. Cleaner frames meant cleaner yarn, as Miss Galway was fond of saying, and she inspected each of our work areas, sniffing like a fox hunting a rabbit. But today was to be a thorough cleaning of the whole place. The half-timers brought out buckets of water, black soap, and big brushes, and we were told to set to work.

I welcomed the task. I worked ferociously, wiping and brushing and scrubbing until my fingers were numb. The harder I worked, the more I hoped to drive away the torment that roiled inside me. And for a short time I succeeded. I even found myself laughing when Miss Galway called out her usual command of "Clean your back passages well, girls." This remark had always brought out giggles from the spinners.

I volunteered to help scrub the stairs.

"Work," I whispered to myself, "work away the pain."

A cockroach ran over my foot. I ignored it, but a girl's scream made me look up. Mary McAteer stood frozen on the stairs.

"I hate those things," she said.

I shrugged. "You should be well used to them by now. They've been here longer than any of us."

She pressed herself against the wall. "It's the smell of the soap that's bringing them out. Can you stop? I have to get back up to the office."

I glared at her. "You'll have to wait 'til I've finished."

She turned and went down to the foot of the stairs, where she waited for me. I was surprised she hadn't ordered me to stop and let her pass. But then nothing seemed normal these days. I went on with my work, and eventually I reached the bottom of the stairs and stood up.

"You can go on up now," I said.

"Thanks, Sheila," she said, and began to climb. But she hesitated and turned around.

"Have you heard any word on Joel?"

I stared at her, looking for traces of her usual smugness. But I saw none. If anything, her eyes reflected sympathy. I must be dreaming, I told myself.

"There's a list of the dead and the missing up in the office," she said quietly. "You know, the local lads, and the soldiers from Narrow Water. Come on up and I'll show it to you."

The shock must have registered on my face.

"Don't worry," she said. "Ma and my uncle are away out. There's nobody there but me."

Stunned, I followed her back up the stairs and into the office. I was aware of my filthy apron and soiled, bare feet. I tried to tidy myself up a bit, but it was no use. I stood just inside the doorway. Mary went into Mr. Carlson's office and returned with a large brown envelope. She pulled a pile of papers out of it and laid them on the desk. Her face had turned ashen.

"I thought maybe we could look at it together," she whispered. "I was afraid to do it by myself. It's been there all morning and I've been dying to look and see if George's name is on it—but God, Sheila, I wouldn't be able to bear it if it is."

Her hands shook as she began to run her fingers down each page. There must have been a hundred names, every one of them somebody's son or brother or lover.

"It's by alphabet," she said. "George's last name is Russell."

She flipped quickly through the sheets until she found the one she was looking for. She bit her lip as her finger crawled up and down the names on it. Then she took a deep breath and let it out.

"Oh, thank God, George's name isn't here." She glanced up at me and then back down at the paper. "Now, let's see. What was Joel's last name?"

"Solomon," I whispered.

"Solomon. Solomon."

Her finger paused at a name on the list, and I knew.

"It's there, isn't it?"

She nodded. "I'm sorry." She looked up at me. "But he's on the missing list, Sheila. He's not been confirmed dead."

She came over to me and put her hand on my arm. I was too frozen to shake it off. "That means there's still hope, Sheila."

She led me to a chair and sat me down. Then she poured a glass of water from a jug and handed it to me.

"Well, Ma won't be pleased," she said suddenly. "I think she was hoping George was dead. She never wanted me marrying a soldier—even an officer. She had me tortured about it. My father was a soldier, you see, and he ran off to the war and got killed. She always said she didn't want the same thing for me." She paused and sighed. "I think the truth was she didn't want me to be happy."

I realized Mary had said something important—something that would change the way I looked at her in the future. But I couldn't recall her words. My whole being was filled with Joel. His face and voice swirled around me and his presence choked me from the inside out. Suddenly I couldn't breathe. I began gasping.

Miss Galway came bustling into the office.

"And what do you think you're doing here, miss? Get back to work."

"It's all right, Miss Galway. She fainted on the stairs, and I brought her in here for water."

"That was kind of you, Mary, but we don't want the likes of this girl getting above her station."

"You forget she's the Linen Queen," said Mary.

৩৩

I could stand it no longer. I had to find out what happened to Joel. Short of sending a letter to his mother in America, which was out of the question, I had no choice but to go to his base at Narrow Water Castle and see what they would tell me. What did "missing in action" mean? Had there been any further news? The thought of what I might find out sickened my stomach, but I had to know. Part of me wanted to believe that Mary McAteer had played a cruel joke on me. She had made it up to torture me. But the sane part of me knew that even Mary would never do a thing like that.

It was a Saturday morning late in June when I cycled down the road along the river towards Warrenpoint. My heart thudded in my chest and my palms were wet as I clutched the handlebars. I prayed over and over that the news would be good. I pedaled faster, anxious to get there. There was probably a new guard on duty and he would not be likely to let me through, so I got off my bicycle and laid it down at the side of the road beside the gate. I walked on down the road a few yards and climbed over the fence. Keeping low among the trees I made my way up to the edge of the estate buildings. I lingered for a while under the cover of a big oak tree and looked first at the main building where the library was housed, and then over to the side buildings where Joel had been billeted. There was no one about. No troops practiced formations in the courtyard. No jeeps sped over the loose gravel. A few doors banged open and shut in the wind. The place looked haunted. I shivered. How many of the young chaps that had laughed and marched here were dead? I could hardly stand the thought.

Slowly I crept over to the main door and pushed it open. It creaked against my touch and I pulled my hand away quickly. I slid into the darkened hallway. The place smelled musty. No warm fire or clatter of dishes or smell of cooking greeted me as it had done in the past. Today there was only silence, save for the ticking of the huge clock in the hallway. I turned towards the library, half expecting to see Joel standing playing the fiddle. But the room was empty. The blinds were down and the only light was from the sun that shone dimly through the cracks where the blinds did not reach the sills. I crept over to an armchair and sat down. I fought back tears and took deep breaths to calm myself down. I knew it

was useless to sit there on my own, but I felt rooted to the chair
and the room and the memories.

I tried to hold Joel's image steady in my mind. I tried to picture
his face, his smile, his sadness, his laughter. But it was like trying
to hold on to the wind. Alarm filled me. What if his image began
to slip away from me? What if in time it disappeared altogether?
I concentrated harder. I saw him sitting with the children at the
Magill Kinderfarm in Millisle. I saw him standing on the Flagstaff playing his fiddle. I imagined the feel of his lips on mine.
I recalled our conversations over and over again, trying to keep
him beside me, trying to keep him safe.

I sat for a long time lost in thought. Voices outside the window
startled me and I stiffened. But the voices drifted away. At least
there were people alive in the bloody place, I thought, or maybe
they were ghosts. God, I was getting jumpy. I got up at last and
went to the front door. I peered around it, but nobody was in
sight so I stepped out. There was no point staying here. There
was nobody about who could tell me anything. With an odd sense
of relief I raced across the courtyard towards the trees.

"Sheila? Sheila, is that you?" A familiar voice behind me
stopped me in my tracks. I swung around. There stood Sylvie.
I hadn't seen him in a dog's age—not since the night he had
accosted me and Mary McTaggart in Newry. Now he leaned on
a crutch in front of me. I looked quickly down at his right leg.
There was nothing below the knee.

"Hello, Sylvie," I said.

I had a thousand questions. Had he been involved in the landing? What was he doing back here? Had he news of Joel? If he was
back, why wasn't Joel back? But I could not bring myself to utter
a word.

"Got shot," he said. "Gangrene set in. They had to take it."
Then he grinned. "Didn't really need two anyway."

He held out his crutch and pointed to a stone bench. "Want to
sit down? Ain't too comfortable standing for long."

I nodded and followed him over to the bench. I was trembling
inside.

"Anyway, I'm lucky to be here. Lot of my buddies, well, they weren't so lucky." His eyes filled up with tears and he brushed them away with the back of his hand. "Drowned, most of 'em."

I nodded again. "So I heard," I managed to say.

I stiffened. I bit my lip so hard I could taste the blood. Then madness overtook me. I reached over and grabbed Sylvie by his two arms and shook him. "What happened to Joel?" I yelled. "Where is he?"

I knew I sounded like a madwoman but I didn't care. Sylvie stared at me in fright. He let me shake him until I had no energy left to do it, and no breath left to shout.

"I'm sorry, Sheila," he whispered. "I don't know. He was there at the landing, but I blacked out after I was shot."

"You're lying! You're saying this just to get even with me. You never liked me. Now you're trying to make me suffer."

"I'm not, Sheila," Sylvie said. "If I knew, I'd tell you. All I know is that he's on the missing list."

I rode back to Newry in a daze. My brain and body were numb. When I reached Walker's Row I went straight to the lavatory in the backyard and vomited until there was nothing left inside me.

Chapter 26

ॐ

The next Sunday I went up to the Flagstaff. My first instinct after D-Day had been to rush there, as I always had when I craved refuge. But I had been afraid to go. Flagstaff was the place where ghosts appeared. I thought about the time I had seen my da there, just before his letters had stopped coming. I had always protested to Gavin that it was my girl's imagination. But now I wasn't so sure. What if I saw Joel's ghost?

I finally plucked up the courage to go. I wheeled my bicycle up to the big, flat stone and sat down on the grass. I looked out over the summit, tracing the flow of the Clanrye River down into Carlingford Lough. The water sparkled under the midday sunshine. My eyes landed on Narrow Water Castle, but I turned away quickly. Even at this distance, I could not bear to look at it. Instead I stared at the point where the three counties of Louth, Down, and Armagh all met. I smiled remembering how Gavin and I used to argue over the exact point where this happened. I found myself wishing Gavin were with me now. I desperately needed him to talk to. I missed him.

I lit a cigarette and leaned back against the stone. A loud rustle sounded behind me and I swung around expecting to see Gavin walking towards me. But it was only a squirrel. And anyway, Gavin was away on a voyage. I inhaled deeply on the cigarette.

Images of the night Joel and I had sat up here on the big stone drifted into my head. I heard the beautiful, mournful music of his fiddle and saw his kind, solemn face as he lost himself in the tune. I saw Gavin's face too, dark and smoky, filled with jealousy towards Joel. How full of myself I had been then, enjoying playing one man off against the other. How foolish. How young.

I closed my eyes and lifted my face to the caress of the soft breeze. I felt Joel's fingertips on my cheek wiping away tears that had begun to flow. I put up my hand to touch them, but I felt only my own wet cheeks. I saw Gavin standing at a distance, watching me, his face filled with sorrow. My eyes shot open. There was no one there.

I stayed until the sun slid low in the sky. There was no need to stay longer. I had come to see if there were any ghosts and I had found none. A voice whispered in my head that ghosts only come out at night. Everybody knew that. I shivered. Well, I wasn't staying here all night. Only an eejit would do that. I got up and lifted my bicycle from where it lay. I took one last look out over the lough and turned away. As I walked down the slope, wheeling my bicycle beside me, a white, wispy form blew across the path in front of me. At first I thought it was a stray piece of paper or cloth, but as I stopped and watched it, the form turned into that of a woman in a cloak. I shuddered.

"Get a hold on yourself, Sheila," I muttered out loud.

ᘒᘓ

"That was the White Lady you saw," said Patsy, her eyes wide. "I heard tell of her appearing many a time when there was death coming. Me da said he saw her once not long before the *Connemara* sank in 1916."

"It was my imagination," I said. "I don't know why I mentioned it."

I had mentioned it because I was frightened. All the way home I could not put the sight out of my mind. I must have been the color of chalk when I arrived because right away they all knew something was wrong. Patsy had finally coaxed it out of me. Now I was sorry I had said anything.

"Well, if it *was* the White Lady, it means somebody's dead," whispered Patsy, making the sign of the cross.

I had told Patsy that Sylvie was alive and was back at the base. She had reacted with anger. How dare he come back to Newry? Hadn't he caused her enough pain? Why hadn't he just gone back to America where he belonged? I had let her talk. She never once said she was relieved he was alive.

Grainne cut into my thoughts. "Will youse all shut up!" she shouted. "All you people around these parts are astray in the head with your ghosts and superstitions. Youse are full of shite."

None of us knew what had got into Grainne. She had been acting angrier than usual these past days. Something was scaring her, but she would never tell us. She was too stubborn.

"Believe what you want," retorted Patsy. "But it's true. Sheila saw a sign."

But a sign of what, nobody could be sure. Maybe it had been my imagination. I had gone to the Flagstaff half expecting to see something, and maybe I had conjured the vision up in my own head. I was too weary to say any more.

"I'm going to bed," I said.

Later that night I was awoken from a deep, dark, dreamless sleep. Someone was pounding on the front door. I sat straight up in bed. Grainne reached over and switched on the lamp. She looked terrifed. I held my breath as Mrs. Hollywood opened the door. I heard a male voice, slow and deep and full of agitation. Then a loud cry pierced the air. I leapt out of bed and ran downstairs, Grainne behind me. We collided with Patsy as we all made for the front door. Mrs. Hollywood stood holding on to the latch, her face ashen in the dim light.

"He's gone," she wailed.

My heart lurched.

"Our Alphonse, the *Ashgrove*, all disappeared."

A loud buzzing filled my ears and drowned out the cries of the women. Sweat poured off my head and neck. My heart squeezed tight. My mouth opened and a cry came out of me that would have wakened the dead.

"No! Not Gavin. Ah, Jesus, no!"

I sank to my knees. The sobs I had been holding in for weeks erupted.

"Not Gavin," I whispered. "Please God, not Gavin too."

∞

I didn't even remember how I got to the mill the next morning. The day passed in a blur. Everyone talked about the *Ashgrove*. But how was I to join in? I hadn't the room inside me to think about Gavin. I put the news out of my head as if it had just been a dream. That evening as I dragged myself home from the tram I saw Sylvie Sartori in front of me turning the corner into Walker's Row.

I arrived at the house just as Patsy came into the kitchen and saw him. She stared at him, and then down at the stump of his leg, and burst into tears.

Sylvie was at a loss for words.

"I went to your house to find you," he began. "And your father took a shovel to me. Believe me I got out of there as fast as I could go with this." He waved his crutch. "But your ma caught up with me and told me where you were living." He paused. "She said to tell you she's been praying for you."

Patsy shrugged.

Sylvie eased himself into a chair Mrs. Hollywood pulled out for him.

He looked at Patsy. "How are you?" he whispered.

"What's it to you?" Patsy said. "You didn't give a tinker's curse before; why would you care now?"

Sylvie looked helplessly at me and Mrs. Hollywood. "I suppose I deserved that," he murmured.

"I'd say you did, young chap," said Mrs. Hollywood. "But it looks like you've paid your price for whatever wrong you've done."

Sylvie looked down at his stump and shrugged. He fixed his eyes again on Patsy. "Can we go somewhere to talk—in private, I mean?"

Patsy shrugged. "Whatever you have to say to me you can say it in front of these ones. These are my friends."

Sylvie drew a deep breath. "I'm sorry, Patsy. I was scared and confused. And I had a girl back stateside that my family expected me to marry. Can you understand at least?"

"All I understand is that you ran away with your tail between your legs and you didn't fecking care what happened to me, or the baby. You've some neck on you coming here now and expecting understanding." She sneered as she said the last word.

She stood and towered over Sylvie, her hands on her hips. "Where were you when my da threw me out on the street? Or when I was sacked from the mill? If it wasn't for Sheila here I'd be lying dead in a ditch somewhere."

Sylvie swallowed. "You're being a bit dramatic..."

"Dramatic my arse!" roared Patsy. "Go on, get out. I never want to set eyes on you again."

Patsy's shouts wakened wee Sylvia and she began to wail. Patsy rushed into the back bedroom to get her. Sylvie looked from Mrs. Hollywood to me helplessly.

"I came to tell her I want to marry her," he said. "She won't even give me the chance."

"Give her time, love," said Mrs. Hollywood.

Sylvie slumped in his chair. "I learned a lot in that bloody battle," he said.

I sat down at the table. A strange feeling was gathering inside me as I looked at him. Patsy returned carrying the child. Sylvie couldn't take his eyes off them.

"My memory's beginning to come back. After I was shot I sank down under the water more than once. I knew I was drowning. And—well you know how they say your whole life passes in front of you at a time like that—well, it's true. And the face I saw was yours, Patsy. And I saw the baby too, even though I'd never actually seen her. And I said a prayer for forgiveness."

Sylvie's eyes misted over as he spoke.

"And, then," he continued, his voice choking, "then somebody put out his hands and lifted me up out of the water. And I thought it was God. I thought I was dead." He paused and we waited. "I found out later it was Joel. He must have heard me screaming and he came back for me. He loaded me up onto his back and ran with me—well, stumbled more like—to safety. He threw me down behind a temporary barricade of sandbags and went back into the water." Sylvie inhaled a deep breath. "I don't know how many guys he saved that day. It could have been dozens."

Mrs. Hollywood reached over and touched my knee as Sylvie was talking, but I was rigid, my eyes riveted on his face. I saw everything he was describing as if a film reel were playing in my head. I saw Joel's face, dark and intense, as he stumbled towards the water. I saw his arms reach out to drowning men. I heard his soft voice reassuring them that they were safe. I saw the exhaustion that set in on him after a while, and the burning in his eyes.

"He saved my life, Sheila," Sylvie was saying to me. "Mine and God knows how many more. They'll give him the Silver Star."

It was then the strange feeling erupted into anger. I stood up.

"They can give him a thousand Silver Stars and it won't matter to me. He broke his promise to me. He had said he would let go of that awful death wish and would fight to stay alive so that we could be together. But he lied to me. If he cared about me, then how could he have put himself in danger—not once, but over and over again? How could he have done that to me? How?"

I realized I was shouting. Mrs. Hollywood and Patsy took me by the shoulders and tried to settle me. But I shook them off. I wasn't finished.

"He used the war as an excuse to get away from me. He's probably gone home to Ohio and abandoned me just like my da."

Sylvie shook his head. "Now, you know that's not true, Sheila. I don't think—" he began.

I rounded on him. "And who cares what you think! You have no right to be here when Joel could be lying wounded somewhere on a battlefield. Where's God's justice?"

I realized I was out of control but I didn't care. My anger at Joel for having risked his life to save Sylvie was raw. And my anger at God for allowing it to happen was even greater. Eventually, Patsy walked outside with Sylvie. He carried their daughter in his arms. As I watched them, I thought my heart would burst from the pain. A loud noise made me swing around. Grainne stood banging the kettle as hard as she could on the stove and muttering to herself.

"What's wrong with you?" I said.

She turned. The look on her face was so dark it scared me.

"All you can think about is Joel!" she said. "What about Gavin? Does anybody care that he's missing too?"

She began to sob. "I spent all day down at the docks looking for news of him. I tried to talk to the sailors. But nobody would answer me." She swallowed hard. "I had a feeling something bad was going to happen to him. I just knew it. And now it has, and nobody cares but me."

"Now that's not true, love. We all care," said Mrs. Hollywood. "But there's not much we can do except wait and pray. You forget my Alphonse is with him."

Grainne pointed at me. "She's the one who should care, and she doesn't give a tinker's curse what happened to him. The only one she cares about is that soldier. She never cared about Gavin."

I wanted to tell the girl that I had no room for any more sorrow. I was almost paralyzed with grief as it was. But it would have done no good. I wanted to put my arms around her and comfort her. But she would have pushed me away. Up until that moment I thought I wasn't capable of bearing any more pain, but as I watched Grainne's anguish my heart opened as a new weight lodged itself within.

∽

The death of sailors is seen as a death in each and every family in a community that makes much of its living from boats. My community was in double mourning: sorrow for the soldiers who had lived among us and who had perished on D-Day, and sorrow for the sailors on the *Ashgrove*.

Gavin's boat had disappeared in the English Channel, close to the French coast. Reports came in that a boat the size of the *Ashgrove* had been seen in flames in the general area where it had disappeared. It must have been torpedoed, they said, by a German U-boat. Gavin had often warned about such dangers. Royal Air Force cover, which should have been available to the merchant ships, had been diverted, it was said, to cover the Allies on D-Day, and thus the merchant ships had been left vulnerable and unprotected. People shrugged and accepted this as truth. What else could it be? The boat had disappeared—lock, stock, and barrel. Boats didn't just disappear without a reason. But I refused to accept what they said. I would not accept that Gavin was dead until his body washed up on some foreign shore and was brought home to be waked. To accept the alternative was more than I could bear.

I stopped every sailor who disembarked from other boats, but they shook their heads and passed by silently, just as they had done with Grainne. It was bad luck to talk about such things. Rumors few about ghosts of *Ashgrove* sailors that had been seen up on the Flagstaff. Many of them had lived on the Upper Fathom Road near the Flagstaff where Gavin and I had lived as children. I thought again of the time I had seen Da's ghost the night his ship sank.

I decided to go to O'Hare's pub. If there was anybody at all who knew something more about the *Ashgrove* they would be at O'Hare's. It was a favorite haunt of seamen from both North and South. The place was crowded as it always was on Friday nights. I wondered how things were across the lough at the Castle ballroom. I'd had some good times over there along with Patsy. I thought about her now. I'd hoped that she would hold out to see if Alphonse came home, but she seized the chance in front of her. She and Sylvie planned to marry after his discharge from the army. She never told Sylvie about the problems with the baby when she was born, afraid he would change his mind. The wedding would be in a registry office since the church would refuse to marry them. Afterwards, they would move to America. I tried not to let jealousy poison me as I thought about how it was Patsy who was going to escape this place. It was supposed to have been me.

I sat up at the bar and ordered a shandy. The bartender was pleasant enough, but the glares of the male customers brought back memories of the old Sheila. And just as the old Sheila would have done, I smiled sweetly and nodded, and they turned away, cheeks blazing. I tried to listen to their conversations. They talked about the *Ashgrove*, but there was nothing said that I had not heard before. I had resigned myself to the fact that there was nothing new to learn. I finished my drink and was getting ready to leave when the pub door opened and in came the group of IRA boyos I remembered from Christmas night. The big, burly one named Sean was in front. He was the one I had refused to dance with. The one that had charged at Joel, threatening to kill him. I froze, remembering Gavin's words to me last time I had seen him.

"Don't think the worst of me, Sheila."

He had told me I would hear bad things about him. What kinds of things, I wondered? Deep down I knew that it had something to do with the men who had just walked into O'Hare's. I ordered another drink and braced myself.

"Well, if it isn't wee Miss Stuck-up," came a rough voice beside me. "Little Miss Yank Lover."

Sean beckoned to his mates. "It didn't take long for her to come back out on the prowl. Maybe now her Yank has gone she might stoop to one of us."

My head shot straight up at him. What on earth was he saying?

"News travels fast. Your lover boy got himself shot on D-Day, so I heard. Good riddance, I say."

His friends roared in agreement, "You're right there, Sean."

I choked on my drink. "He's not dead," I said. "He's missing in action."

"Go on, tell yourself that," said Sean. "Convince yourself he's coming back to you." He spat on the floor. "You and all the other stuck-up northern tarts with your crying and whining and lighting candles, you make me sick. Even if they survived, there's none of them coming back here to youse and that's the truth. They used you and you used them. It's over."

I wanted to cry out that he was wrong. But I held my tongue. Instead I shoved my half-empty glass towards the barman and stood up.

"I'm sorry about Gavin," the barman said as I passed.

I stiffened, almost as if I had forgotten what he was talking about.

"Aye. At least he died a patriot," roared Sean.

"What d'you mean?"

"He went out on a job for us and sacrificed his life doing it. He died a patriot."

My knees weakened and I had to clutch the bar to stand up. I don't know where I found the strength but I steadied myself and pulled Sean by the arm out into the hallway.

"What are you talking about?" I whispered. "Gavin wanted nothing to do with the likes of youse."

He grinned. "That's where you're wrong."

He leaned over me and I could smell his stale breath. He looked around to make sure no one was listening.

"Ah, it was a bold plan all right," he began. "We had made a deal with the Germans. Arms for prisoners. Gavin had a few passengers with him on this trip."

He paused and ran his tongue around his lips. He leaned closer to me.

"German prisoners. All he had to do was bring them to France, to a place where their mates were waiting for them, and in exchange we were to get more guns and ammunition for our war here at home."

Sean's narrow eyes shone with excitement in the lamplight.

"Even though he was flying the Irish tricolor, he was to paint "Eire" in big letters on both sides of the *Ashgrove* the way many of the Irish boats did—just to remind them he was from a neutral country so as the Jerries wouldn't fire on him. But it seems a

German U-boat got to them anyway." Sean shook his head and sighed. "I suppose when all hell broke loose on account of the invasion the Jerries were shooting at anything that moved. It was a brave effort just the same. God bless Gavin."

"You're making it up," I said. "You're away with the fairies. Who in their right mind would believe a thing like that? How would you even have got German prisoners of war out? And why would you be telling me any of it?"

Sean leaned in closer to me, his face inches from mine.

"Believe it, girl. You know yourself the German camps in the South are more like holiday camps than prisons. And it wasn't the first time Gavin did jobs for us. He hated the soldiers as much as we did. He was proud to do this for his country."

"He wouldn't have done that!" I protested. "He would never have taken German soldiers back to the battlefield. He would never have gone that far to help Hitler."

My body and spirit were sick as I pedaled home. I had gone to O'Hare's to find out if Gavin was alive or dead. But now I had a new question. Had he betrayed the Allies? Had he gone against everything Joel stood for? Gone against everything I now stood for? I wanted to set my thoughts alight and burn them to cinders.

"Don't think the worst of me, Sheila." Gavin's words echoed around me.

"Och, Gavin, I won't," I whispered aloud.

Chapter 27

ॐ

By late July it began to rain, and it rained every day after. People complained, but I was glad of it. The wet, miserable weather matched my mood. I would have gone mad if the sun shone every day demanding joy. As it was, I could hide myself by day under the cover of the clouds, and at night I could weep along with the rain.

In time my anger exhausted me and a physical pain took over. Every morning when I awoke the pain assaulted me. When I tried to get up, every movement hurt, every step was labored, and every gesture such an effort that all I wanted to do was lie back down and never get up again. I walked among others like a ghost. I listened to others talk but I did not hear what they said. There was no comfort anywhere. The pain never left me—not for a moment.

I was no wiser about what happened to either Gavin or Joel than I had been a month ago. I still didn't believe a word that IRA boyo had told me. I had asked Mary McAteer to look at the list again for Joel, but she shrugged and said Mr. Carlson had it locked up. I didn't know whether to believe her or not. She was all smiles now that her George was safe. I suppose she wanted to forget all about the day she'd been so scared she'd wanted me to look at the list with her. Kathleen had heard from Ollie's family that he was safe, and I was glad for her. But even so, a pinprick of jealousy seized me when I heard the news. So God had sent Sylvie, Ollie, and George home from the battle. But he had not sent Joel. Nor had he sent Gavin home from the sea.

I could think of only one other place I could go to find out more about Joel. The following Sunday I boarded a bus from Newry to Newtownards. I had to see Rabbi Hurwitz. I rubbed my sleeve against the bus window, making a small clear patch on the glass, which was misted from the rain. I looked out. There wasn't much to see. Rain drenched the streets and grass and houses, wrapping them all in a gray web. I waited an hour at the depot for the local bus to Millisle. The other passengers eyed me as they would any stranger. I had made an effort to look my best. I was dressed in the blue frock I often wore to Linen Queen ceremonies, along with my best shoes and a bright white handbag. I looked out of place among the local people in their drab overalls and long skirts. At one time I would have been delighted to stand out in a crowd. Now it meant nothing.

The bus dropped me at the bottom of the hill that led up to Magill Kinderfarm. Across the street the Irish Sea was gray and wild, the waves charging the shore like roaring warriors. I thought back to the year before when Joel and I had looked out across that same sea, calm and blue and welcoming. I turned and walked up the hill. I should have dressed more warmly, I realized, as I huddled against the wind. I opened the gate to the farm and stood for a moment. The fields were empty. No children were about on account of the rain. I had a fleeting feeling that the place was in mourning, but I shook it off. I walked towards the building where Joel and I had gone before, my heels sinking into the mud as I went. Suddenly a little girl came running up to me. She looked up at me with a solemn face and took my arm. It was the wee girl I had seen last year crying by the wall. She had haunted my dreams so often—I would have known her anywhere.

We walked through the garden and into the kitchen. I put the bag of sweets I had brought up on the counter. I had traded ration coupons with Mrs. Hollywood and Patsy in order to buy them.

The girl murmured a thank-you and disappeared. I was standing alone wondering where I would find Rabbi Hurwitz when I heard his voice behind me.

"*Fraylin!*"

I turned around as he approached me with open arms and the familiar, kind smile on his face. He hugged me, looking me up and down.

"Welcome, *fraylin*. It is good to see you. Come."

He led me down the corridor and into a small office crammed with books and papers and photographs. He pulled out a chair from the corner and quickly dusted it off. I sat down and he pulled up a chair opposite me. He bent forward, his hands on his knees.

"You have come to hear about Joel," he said. It was not a question.

I swallowed hard and nodded.

Rabbi Hurwitz sighed. "I think you already know what has happened. Yes?"

I swallowed again, fighting back tears.

He leaned over and patted me on the arm. "I'm sorry, *liebchen*. But he died a brave man."

There it was! The truth that I had known deep down but had fought with everything I had to deny. I let the tears flow.

"We are all so sad here," Rabbi Hurwitz went on. "We miss him. But we are grateful that we knew him."

"How...," I began. But I could get no more words out.

The rabbi sighed. "He went back into the water one time too many and a German gunner shot him and the man he was trying to save. They both drowned. I pray he did not suffer long."

So Joel had returned to the sea. He once said the sea might claim us all.

"I was angry with him, Rabbi," I said, feeling like a small girl in confession. "For leaving me. For putting others' lives above our happiness."

"It was never his choice. God had a plan for him. Besides, did he ever promise he would come back?"

Rabbi Hurwitz looked at me with clear, gray eyes.

...ook my head. "No," I whispered. "He said he would do his ...st."

The old man nodded. " *Fraylin* Sheila, Joel brought you gifts. He talked to me often about you—how he wanted you to know yourself, to see yourself as special. He said you were stronger than you thought. He tried to teach you that. He was a messenger, Sheila, that is all. He was never meant to stay in your world."

We sat in silence for a while. Outside I heard the cattle lowing as the rain eased its patter on the windowpanes. Children's shouts and footsteps echoed up and down the hallway outside the door.

"There is a part of Joel's soul in you now, Sheila," Rabbi Hurwitz spoke again. "I have always believed that when a person dies his soul melts into tiny pieces and lodges in the hearts of those he loved. He loved you, Sheila, and now he is a part of you. He will give you the strength to go on and find happiness."

He stood up and I stood with him.

"Wait a moment, *fraylin*."

He walked over to his desk, opened a drawer, and took out a package. He came back towards me, opening the package as he walked. Then he pulled out a silver watch and handed it to me. I recognized it immediately. It was Joel's father's watch—the one I had seen him take out so often when we were together.

"Joel's mother sent it to me for safekeeping. She said Joel had written to her some time ago that he wanted you to have it should something happen to him."

I held the watch in my left palm, tracing my fingers over the initials engraved on it. Joel, I thought, always conscious of time. He was always aware he didn't have that much of it.

Rabbi Hurwitz smiled and his eyes crinkled. "You see, Joel knew you would come here."

I bit my lip and tried to smile back. "Thank you, Rabbi," I said.

The little man hugged me again. "Go now, Sheila. Go back to your own world. You are stronger than you know. Cherish the time you had with Joel, and respect his memory."

"I will," I whispered.

I walked back down the corridor and into the kitchen. The

small girl who had greeted me smiled but said nothing. I nodded at her and went on out the door. The rain had stopped and my senses were filled with the smell of wet grass and crops. Shouts in the distance made me turn. A group of boys from the farm were playing Gaelic football in a field. They had settled into Ireland well, I thought. I smiled in spite of myself and I felt Joel smiling beside me.

ೞ

Over the next weeks, Joel's image haunted me. When I woke in the morning he greeted me, smiling. When I arrived at my spinning frame he was already there. When I climbed into bed at night, he was waiting for me, whispering. At first I sank into my sadness, as if sinking deep into sand. I memorized our conversations, our kisses, our tears. All of the memories were shrouded, as if wrapped in gauze. I floated towards them, seeking comfort, ignoring the world around me. I forgot to eat or speak—in Joel's world I had no need of either.

Eventually, I had to let him go. I recalled Rabbi Hurwitz's words.

"He was a messenger, Sheila, that is all. He was never meant to stay in your world."

My journey out of the hole in which I had buried myself was slow and painful, but in time I was able to crawl up to the rim and peer over the edge. The outside world had not changed, but my view of it had changed utterly. My sadness was replaced with pride—pride in the man I had known. I knew I could never rise to his level of strength and sacrifice, but I would do my best to honor it. Joel had come to me as an angel to help me find my own strength and purpose. He came to teach me to recognize my own value. He had seen something in me that I was not able to. And now I had to let him go. But his memory would be with me forever.

One evening I sat in my bedroom at Walker's Row. Beside me on the bed I had laid out Joel's watch, the wee carved mermaid

Da had given me, and my Linen Queen sash. I ran my fingers over
each article in turn, allowing the associated memories to food
through me. The sea had taken Joel and Da. Had it taken Gavin
as well? Two months had passed and no further news had come
of the *Ashgrove*. Rumors of sailors' ghosts seen up on the Flagstaff
still persisted. A memorial service was planned at Newry Cathedral for the following Sunday. I had yet to accept that Gavin was
dead, but hope was fading.

I turned to my Linen Queen sash. I smiled, remembering the
night I won the crown. How triumphant I had been. How excited
and innocent and full of hope. I smoothed out the sash, lifted it,
and put it on. I went over to the mirror. Where had that young
Sheila gone? The person who looked back was not a pretty, naïve
girl, but a woman—a woman who had known pain and sadness
and loss. And yet as I turned back and forth in front of the mirror, a familiar comfort and pride took hold of me. God may have
taken away everything else, but he couldn't take away the special feeling I had every time I wore it. Slowly I removed the sash,
folded it, and put it to my lips and kissed it. As I did so, I ignored
Joel's voice telling me I no longer needed it.

As I lay in bed that night listening to Grainne's soft breathing,
I dared for the first time in months to think about my future.
What was left for me here? Everyone I loved was gone. No mat-
ter how much good I had tried to do, God had still punished me.
A wave of self-pity overcame me and I wept quietly, my knees
curled up to my chest like a child.

Chapter 28

ை

The memorial Mass for the sailors of the *Ashgrove* was said at noon on the first Sunday in September. The cathedral had not been so full since the night of the blitz, when the missionary priest came to speak. This time was different, though. Gone were the excitement and anticipation that greeted the missionary that night. Today a weary sadness hung over the congregants, even the children. Sailors with sunburned faces and watchful eyes filled the pews at the back of the church. Their calloused hands, more suited to pulling on thick ropes, threaded worn rosary beads as they murmured prayers.

I sat near the front, Mrs. Hollywood and Patsy on one side of me and Grainne on the other. Mrs. Hollywood wept quietly. She had not said much since Alphonse had disappeared, but a shadow had fallen across her lovely, bright spirit. Sylvie had stayed home minding the baby so that Patsy could come with us. She let her tears flow freely for Alphonse now that she no longer had to guard them in front of Sylvie. Grainne stared straight ahead. If I hadn't known the girl better, I would have said she was a cold wee bitch who didn't care about anyone but herself. But I knew that was not true. She was suffering like the rest of us. She loved Gavin, we all knew that. And he had been taken away from her. My heart went out to her. I knew how it felt to be abandoned.

As for myself, I cried no tears. Maybe I had none left after Joel. I'd had no anger towards Gavin for leaving me. I'd exhausted my anger on Joel. And there'd been no point in begging God to return him. God had already shown me he didn't care how much I prayed. More and more I had become willing to accept Gavin's death. How could it be otherwise? It had been over two months since the *Ashgrove* had been torpedoed. Surely if there'd been survivors, they'd be home by now. The one thing I would not accept was Gavin's treachery. The newspapers had reported that several German prisoners of war had escaped and crossed the border into the North. There had been no further details. In spite of the fact that the reports seemed to confirm some of what Sean had told me, I refused to believe Gavin was capable of such a thing. But even if it turned out to be true, I would forgive him. I had learned through Joel's death that men have their own reasons for the decisions they make—reasons that are bigger than *my* happiness. If Gavin had helped the German soldiers escape, he would have had his reasons for doing so.

Father Flynn strode to the altar, tall and splendid in his vestments. Patsy muttered something under her breath. I knew she was remembering the cruel way he had treated her when she went to him for help. I felt Grainne stiffen beside me. I put my hand on her arm, but she shook it off. I had expected the older, kinder Father Toner to be the one saying Mass. I looked up at the ornate ceiling. Another one of God's cruel tricks, I thought.

Prayers were said to St. Brendan, patron saint of sailors, and St. Christopher, the patron saint of travelers, and I said prayers for Gavin and Joel and my da. Father Flynn gave a sermon about the benefits of sacrifice and how suffering cleanses our souls. Well, our souls would be scrubbed clean all right with this boyo around—he had caused more suffering than anybody I knew. Before the Mass ended, a young acolyte, the son of one of the sailors, read out the name of every sailor who had been aboard the *Ashgrove*, while a bell tolled at each name. Gavin's name was called last. The sorrow I had been cradling deep down in my heart escaped in one cry of anguish. As the echoes of the bell faded so did my last hopes of ever seeing Gavin again. Mrs. Hollywood took my arm and pulled me close to her. Grainne turned her back to me, but not before I saw the tears flooding her cheeks.

When the service was over we filed out while the choir sang the hymn to the Virgin Mary, "Ave Maris Stella," or "Hail, Star of the Sea." In ancient times Our Lady was seen as the protector of those who earned their livelihoods from the sea.

As I reached the cathedral steps somebody tugged at my sleeve from behind. "Och, Sheila love, there you are. I thought it was you."

I turned around. There stood Ma, her hand linked into the arm of an older man I didn't recognize. There were tears in Ma's eyes.

"Wasn't it a beautiful service, Sheila?"

She let go of the man and linked her arm in mine as we walked on down the steps. "I prayed for Gavin, Sheila. And I heard about poor Joel. Lovely boys, both drowned." She sighed. "But I prayed most for your da."

I wanted to get away from her. I tried to shrug her off, but she gripped my arm even harder. I was reminded of the night of the blitz when she had my arm in a vise. She looked around at her companion as she shoved me away out of his hearing.

"I know you don't believe me, Sheila, but I loved your da. It nearly destroyed me when he left."

She was right; I didn't believe her. "I always loved him. It's just that, well, I couldn't help the way I was. When my good moods took me over, I didn't realize what I was doing. And I was young, and lonely. I only had you for company. We were happy in the beginning though, love. We really were."

I tried to turn away but she held on to my arm. "Wait, I have something for you."

I sighed. "What?"

She rummaged in her bag and pulled out a small box and thrust it at me. "Here. By rights this should be yours. Your da often said we should give it to you on your wedding day. But since there's no hope of that now, I thought I'd give it to you today. I knew I'd see you here."

I opened the box. Inside, on a silk cushion, lay the blue and silver necklace Da had given Ma the day I was born, the one she had lent me the night of the Linen Queen competition.

"But I can't take this, Ma," I said. "Da gave it to you."

Ma put her hand over mine and squeezed it. "Take it."

I didn't know what to do. Would Ma come running back next week accusing me of stealing the necklace? But as I looked at her face smiling back at me, happier than I'd seen her in a long time, a faint hope crept through me that maybe at last she'd changed. I shoved the box in my pocket.

I should have known better. Ma giggled like a young girl and nodded towards her companion. "I have new fish to fry now you see, and I don't want to be cluttered up with memories of your da."

All energy went out of me. "Who is he?" I said wearily.

She giggled. "Och don't you recognize him? That's Shane Kearney. You remember he ran a pub in Glenlea. I took you there a few times when you were small. He and your da were great friends." She looked over at the man and smiled. "He was always in love with me, but I wouldn't give him the time of day. I only had eyes for your da. Shane married another girl and raised a family. But he's widowed now."

I listened, but said nothing.

"He came and found me," announced Ma with pride. "And he says he'll take care of me."

"He must be a saint," I said.

"Och he is, love, he is. Come on over and say hello."

Reluctantly I shook hands with Shane Kearney. I wondered if he knew what he was getting himself into. Well, better him than me. I made my excuses and ran to catch up with Mrs. Hollywood and Patsy and Grainne. Later I was sorry I had not wished Ma luck. But at that moment I'd had nothing generous left inside me. I hoped that she would find some happiness with Shane. She deserved it. She'd had a hard life. Maybe if she had someone beside her who loved her she would get better. I supposed it was all any of us wanted.

☙

The next evening when I returned from work at the mill, I found Grainne in our room. She stood with her back to me forcing shut the rusty clasps on her battered old suitcase. The yellow light from the attic lamp beside the bed cast a glow on the girl's bent head, turning her red curls to fire. She swung around.

"You can't stop me," she said. "My mind's made up." Her eyes were defiant as she glared at me.

"And just where in God's name do you think you're going?" I said, trying to control my sudden anger. "Is this how you repay us for all we've done for you?"

God, I thought, I sounded just like Ma. But I couldn't help myself.

Grainne scowled. "I knew you were going to say that. It's all you've ever said since I came here. I told you before, I never asked you to save me, and I've no intention of going down on my two knees to thank you."

"I know," I said. "You think Gavin was the only one ever helped you."

Grainne's face turned red. "Leave him out of it," she said. "He's gone, and a lot you care."

She turned back to closing her suitcase, but I went up behind her and spun her around to face me. I wanted to slap her.

"How dare you say that? You've no notion how I feel about Gavin. You're just a jealous wee bitch. Don't think I didn't see the way your eyes followed him around like a bloody wee puppy dog. D'you think he would ever have given the time of day to the likes of you?"

My breathing was ragged, and the sweat poured down my neck. I was out of control. Why was I saying these things to her? Why was I hurting her like this? I wanted to stop but I couldn't make myself do it.

"You've been nothing but a dose of salts ever since you arrived on that train. So go on now. Get out and good riddance to you."

I sank down on my bed, exhausted. Grainne's face crumpled

up and she began to cry. Och, Sheila, I said to myself, what have you done now?

"There's nothing left for me here," Grainne said quietly. "I'm sick of being a prisoner in this house—afraid to go out in case the IRA men come after me. And Gavin's no longer here to watch out for me." She bit her lip. "He's gone, and I have nobody left. I may as well go."

She looked up at me, her green eyes softer than I'd ever seen them.

"I was stupid to have such a notion for him," she went on. "It's you he loved, and I was jealous. That's why I was so angry with you. And angry that you picked the Joel fella over Gavin." She swallowed hard. "I'm sorry for all I did. I *am* grateful, Sheila."

I thought of the talk we'd had back in Queensbrook the night I saw her scars. I could have cut my tongue out now for what I'd just said. But it was too late. Once the words are out you can never take them back.

"I'll never have the chances you have," she said. "I'm not pretty like you, and I'm not clever. But I'll make my way somehow."

"But you're only fifteen!"

"Almost sixteen, now," she said defiantly. "Old enough."

A horrible thought came over me. "You're not going back to Amelia Street, are you?"

Grainne shrugged. "I'm not that stupid. I'd never go back to that life. I saw what it did to my ma."

"Then where will you go?"

"Belfast. I know the streets there like the back of my hand. And I know some people who might give me a place to stay..." Her words trailed off.

An anxious feeling came over me. "What about money?"

Grainne smiled and shrugged her thin shoulders. "I'm good at stealing. One of the benefits of being reared on Amelia Street."

I threw my hand to my mouth. "God, no, Grainne!" I shouted.

Without thought I got up and went over to the drawer beside my bed and pulled out the envelope containing my Linen Queen prize money. I held it in my hands for a moment and then I held it out to Grainne. "Take it, love," I said. "I can't stop you going, but at least this will help until you get on your feet. You'll not go far without it."

She shrank back as if I were offering her poison. "I can't," she said. "It's yours. It's for your dream. It's for all you've ever wanted in this life."

"Take it. Take it as my gift to you. I can save more for when the time comes for me to go." Even as I said the last words, they sounded hollow.

I helped Grainne carry her things downstairs. There was no point trying to talk her out of it, just as I would not have been talked out of it back at the time. All I could do was give her the best advice I could and wish her well.

Mrs. Hollywood met us at the bottom of the stairs. Her eyes were ringed in red.

"Good-bye, Mrs. H., and thanks," said Grainne.

Mrs. Hollywood pulled Grainne to her and hugged her.

"Take care of yourself, love. And remember, you'll always have a home here."

Sadness welled up in me as I stood at the door of number 6 watching the girl walk up the street for the last time, carrying her suitcase with her. She was escaping into her future just as I had hoped to do three years before. But what I saw was not a girl skipping excitedly towards new adventures, but a vulnerable and frightened waif trudging bravely into the unknown. Pirate, the cat, nuzzled against me, as Grainne disappeared around the corner.

"Let her be safe," I whispered aloud. "Let her be safe."

Chapter 29

ɘⱷ

Life at the mill was more punishing than before. The girls hardly ever sang. A collective depression hung over us all. If we'd never known the excitement and hope of the war we would never have missed it. But we had known it, and now it had been taken away from us. How could we ever go back to the innocent way we had lived our lives before we knew there was something better?

One morning I was waiting for a doffer to change the bobbins on my spinning frame when Mr. Carlson's secretary, Miss Johnson, came up to me.

"You're to come with me, Miss McGee."

"We're in the middle of changing the bobbins—" I began.

"Now, Miss McGee."

She turned without another word and marched towards the office. I followed her, dread sinking into me. I remembered the time when I had been summoned to the office and put on probation. I'd not had a bit of trouble since that. I had no idea what he wanted. I shrugged; maybe it was a new Linen Queen assignment. Mary McAteer looked up at me as I entered the outer office. She said nothing.

Mr. Carlson did not invite me to sit down. Instead he leaned back in his chair and stared at me, a frown on his craggy face.

As before, I was aware of my naked feet, and I moved behind a chair.

"Do you remember the last time you were here, Miss McGee, when you were placed on probation?"

I nodded.

"At the time, I recall, the problem had to do with your involvement with a Mr. Gavin O'Rourke."

The mention of Gavin's name sent chills through me.

He tapped a newspaper on his desk. "Have you been reading the papers?"

I froze. There had been more stories in the newspapers about the German prisoners of war. New details had emerged. The theory now was that the prisoners had been smuggled aboard a boat in Newry Harbor. Neither Gavin nor the *Ashgrove* had been named, but I became more and more nervous every time I picked up a paper.

"I don't know, sir," I said.

"Surely you've heard of the German prisoners who escaped?"

The big grandfather clock behind him ticked louder than a bomb. I nodded.

"And you will know, then, it appears the prisoners were taken on board a boat in Newry Harbor. My own investigators tell me it was the boat owned by your friend Gavin O'Rourke."

He paused, waiting for my reaction. What was I to say? My knees threatened to buckle under me and all the blood ran out of my legs. I held on to the back of the chair for support.

"Tell me what you know about this, Miss McGee."

"Nothing, sir," I blurted out, almost too quickly. "I haven't seen Gavin in months," I went on. "And now he's dead."

The words cut through me.

"Be that as it may, Miss McGee, you were seen talking to some IRA men in O'Hare's pub just recently. They are known cohorts of Mr. O'Rourke."

A flush rose up my face and there was nothing I could do to stop it. There was no point denying it. "I went to O'Hare's because that's where the sailors in these parts go. I thought I might find out something about the *Ashgrove*. I didn't go to meet the IRA men. They were the ones came up and annoyed me."

"Aiding and abetting the enemy is treason, Miss McGee. If you are withholding any information you are guilty of such a charge. I hope this is not the case. But if there is anything you know you must tell me now."

"I don't know anything other than Gavin's dead!" I couldn't stop myself from talking. "And even if he did something, you could never prove it. And besides, he's a citizen of the Free State, and so even if he was still alive youse couldn't put a finger on him."

"But *you* are a citizen of the United Kingdom, Miss McGee. And that is a very different matter."

"I've told you. I don't know anything!"

I was exhausted. I felt my shoulders droop as I waited for Carlson to speak.

"You are right, Miss McGee; we have no proof as yet. But we will get it. And if it turns out Mr. O'Rourke had involvement, then I would advise you to think carefully about what I have said. You are on very thin ice. Now go back to work."

I could hardly walk straight as I trailed out of his office. Mary McAteer looked up but again she said nothing. I went back to the spinning floor, ignoring the looks of the other girls. I tried not to let anything show on my face. I didn't even look at Kathleen, who studied me with concern. There was nothing to talk about. Gavin was dead. Why couldn't they let him rest in peace?

ᐒᐒ

The night after the meeting with Mr. Carlson, I sat in the kitchen with Mrs. Hollywood. We said little to each other these days, but we took comfort in each other's presence. Sylvie had received his discharge and Patsy had become Mrs. Sylvie Sartori. She and the baby had moved into a hotel with Sylvie until they could book their passage to America. Only Mrs. Hollywood and I were left in the Walker's Row house. The emptiness hung heavily over us. I told her nothing about what had happened at the mill. What was the point? There was no proof of anything, and there was nothing Carlson could do to me. But deep down I was frightened. Treason? The word overwhelmed me. It must be a bad dream.

I was draining the last of my tea before going up to bed when a thump came at the front door. Mrs. Hollywood and I looked at each other. Who could that be at this hour of the night? Grumbling, Mrs. Hollywood got up from her chair and went out into the hallway. Maybe Patsy had forgotten something, I thought. But a queer foreboding came over me just the same.

Mrs. Hollywood screamed and I rushed to the front door. She had sunk to her knees and raised her arms up to heaven. Towering over her was Alphie. My hand few to my mouth and I stood rooted to the spot. Was I seeing ghosts? Mother of God, it couldn't be true. Alphie bent over and raised Mrs. Hollywood to her feet and then wrapped his big arms around her. She sobbed into his chest, saying his name over and over. I made the sign of the cross. Alphie looked at me and grinned.

"Come on over here, love, and give me a kiss."

I could tell he was drunk, but I didn't care. I rushed to him and he pulled me into him alongside his mother, holding us so tight we were nearly smothered. Mrs. Hollywood recovered first. She backed off and looked him up and down.

"Alphie, son. Come in. I'll make some tea."

I let out a nervous laugh. Only Mrs. Hollywood, the lovely, sweet Englishwoman, would offer tea at a time like this. Alphie followed his ma into the kitchen and I turned to shut the front door. As I did, I noticed a shadow outside. I peered out into the darkness. The shadow moved again and I held my breath. Had a ghost followed Alphie home? Was it waiting to reclaim him the minute he left the house? Was the Alphie I'd just seen alive at all? Hurriedly I stepped backwards into the hall and tried to push the door closed. But a force pushed back against it and I dropped the latch in terror.

"Sheila. Sheila, it's me."

The door opened wide and there under the hall light stood

Gavin. A scream caught in my throat. My head went light and the world spun around me.

"Sheila, it's me," he said again. "I'm not a ghost."

Trembling, I put my hand out and touched his sleeve. His arm felt solid beneath the rough material. He stood very still.

"I'm sorry. I didn't mean to frighten you," he whispered.

Slowly I focused my eyes on his face. It was as gaunt as a scarecrow and black shadows hung beneath his eyes. Tiny wisps of hair, light as feathers, covered his scalp. Och, what had happened to his lovely, thick waves? I looked down at the rest of him. He had lost a stone weight and his clothes hung loosely on him. My heart burned in my chest. I threw my arms around him, crushing him against me.

"Thank God," I whispered. "Thank God."

I stepped back and looked at him again. "What were you waiting out there for?" I said. "You put my heart crossways with the fright."

"I thought his ma should see Alphie first," he said. His voice was hoarse. "And, well, I didn't know if you'd even be here. I thought maybe you'd be gone to America by now."

I turned to face him. "Och, Gavin, Joel's dead. He drowned on D-Day."

Gavin's face turned paler than it already was. "I'm sorry, Sheila," he whispered. "He was a good man."

A good man. That's what Joel had called Gavin.

In the kitchen, Mrs. Hollywood was firing questions at Alphie like bullets from a rife. When she turned and saw Gavin walk in behind me, I thought she might faint. I grabbed the teapot from her before she dropped it. She threw up her hands and let out a wail.

"My two boys," she cried. "My two boys have come home."

I sat her down and pulled out a chair for Gavin. In the bright light of the kitchen he looked even worse than I had first thought. He was thin and frail as a ghost. His hands shook as he clutched the mug of tea I gave him. I wanted to burst into tears, but I held them back.

"Shelled. Caught in the crossfire," Alphie was saying, his words thick from the drink. "The blast lifted her clear out of the water. Flames from stem to stern. The fire hissed like the devil when it met the water. We lowered the jolly boats and rowed away from her. All the lads had made it into the boats, but one of 'em was caught by a shell and set on fire. The others in our boat either died from injuries or drowned. All I know is, Gavin here and me were the only ones who lived through it."

He took a gulp of his tea, while Mrs. Hollywood repeated, "Holy Mother, save us" over and over again.

I looked at Gavin. He had yet to say a word.

"When did you get in?"

I spoke quietly, as if to a spirit. If I spoke too loudly, I was afraid the dream might dissolve. I realized my words sounded like matter-of-fact conversation, as if I were asking a casual question in a normal world.

"Just a couple of hours ago," Gavin said. "The lads on the *Cedar Star* that picked us up in Plymouth insisted we go to the pub with them. I'd say the news is all over the country by now that Alphie and I are home."

Mr. Carlson's face drifted into my mind and I flinched. The minute he heard Gavin was home he'd be after him.

"I'm glad you came here," I said.

Gavin shrugged and looked at the clock. "I can't stay long. I have to go and see Ma."

I nodded.

Alphie spoke up suddenly. "Where's Patsy? I have presents for wee Sylvia."

Mrs. Hollywood and I exchanged looks. She took a deep breath.

"She's gone, love. Her soldier came back and married her. She's gone to America."

Alphie's big face crumpled. I thought he was going to cry. My heart went out to him. I knew he'd grown fond of Patsy. I had long suspected he might have been in love with her. Looking at his face now, I knew I'd been right.

Gavin looked around then. "And where's wee Grainne?"

"She's gone as well, love," said Mrs. Hollywood. "Back to Belfast. We miss her something awful."

Alphie moved his chair back and stood up.

"Where are you going?" his mother said. "Aren't you staying the night?"

"No, Ma. I'll be away down to Moira's. She'll be delighted to know I'm safe."

Moira was the "fancy woman" Mrs. Hollywood complained about. Alphie stayed with her when he was in port. Poor Mrs. Hollywood. She had hoped as much as I had that Alphie and Patsy would get together. Gavin stood up.

"I need to be going as well. Thanks for the tea, Mrs. H."

"But you're not cycling all the way to Omeath at this time of night, surely?" Mrs. Hollywood protested.

Gavin managed a smile. "You wouldn't want me to keep my ma waiting, would you, Mrs. H.?"

"No, of course not, love. Safe home."

I followed Gavin out into the street and closed the door behind me.

"I need to talk to you, Gavin," I began.

"Och, it's late, Sheila. Can't it wait?"

"No."

I took a deep breath and explained everything to him, beginning with what Sean had told me at O'Hare's, the articles in the newspapers about the escape of the German prisoners, and finally my conversation with Mr. Carlson.

"I don't know what you did on this voyage, Gavin, but I will believe whatever you tell me. I know you wouldn't lie to me. All I want you to know is that you could be in danger."

Gavin made a noise that sounded like a laugh deep down in his throat.

"I'm a citizen of the Free State. They can't touch me."

"But they can touch me," I whispered.

Gavin drew closer. "And what do *you* believe, Sheila? What do you think I did?"

"Jesus, Gavin, how in God's name would I know? I told you it doesn't matter."

"Aye, but it matters to me what you believe about me."

I took a deep breath and faced him. "I believe in my heart that you could never have done what they said."

He put down his kit bag and pulled me close to him. His breathing was ragged as he kissed my hair and face. His frail body shook so much I feared it would shatter into pieces.

"I'm back because of you, Sheila," he whispered. "It was your face that kept me going in the freezing water that night. It's what kept me going for the weeks we were hiding out in Guernsey. And it's what led me all the way across the Channel, and then across the Irish Sea." He stopped and kissed me hard on the mouth. "I prayed you would still be here."

He pulled away at last and lifted his bicycle from against the wall. As I watched him disappear into the darkness I wondered if it had all been a dream.

"Safe home, Gavin," I whispered.

Chapter 30

☙

The next day news of the return of Gavin and Alphie commanded banner headlines in all the newspapers. The return of the two men who'd been given up for dead was a miracle, people said, and they thanked God. With their homecoming, Gavin and Alphie had brought a slender thread of hope to everyone. Good news was possible, even in the midst of such sorrow and death. God did listen to prayers. The girls at the mill talked of nothing else. They harped at me to introduce them to Alphie. Any one of them would have been delighted to marry such a lucky man as himself. But poor Alphie's heart was broken.

"I suppose you'll be marrying Gavin now," they said.

I didn't answer.

Within days of their return new headlines shouted out from the newspapers.

"Local men heroes!" they proclaimed. "Jerry prisoners turned over to Allies!"

I couldn't believe what I was seeing. I bought every newspaper I could find and read the accounts line by line. The story was the same in all of them. The escaped German prisoners had stowed away aboard the *Ashgrove* and tried to force Gavin and his men to bring them to the French coast where they could rejoin the battle. Instead, Gavin and his men had subdued the prisoners and had deliberately sailed into the middle of the D-Day chaos to turn them over to an Allied ship in the English Channel. In doing so they had put their lives in danger. They had been caught in the crossfire between an American warship and a German surface battleship and the *Ashgrove* had been set on fire and sunk along with one of its escaping lifeboats. The other lifeboat had headed for the Channel Islands, but only Gavin and Alphie had made it safely to shore. They had been hidden by an old friend whose brave son had eventually brought them in his boat to the safety of Portsmouth on the English coast. The story had been confirmed by the English captain who had taken the prisoners aboard his ship.

I didn't know what to think. Was it true? All I was sure of was that Gavin would not have given them the story—it was not his way to draw such attention to himself. It was Alphie. I could picture him, his chest swelled with pride, telling the story and adding details here and there to make it more dramatic. Still, the Allied captain had confirmed it. There must be some truth in it.

That evening Gavin came to the door of number 6 and asked me to go for a walk. We strolled down to the docks and sat looking out over the water. It felt odd to be here without the *Ashgrove* tied up in her usual berth. I wondered if Gavin were thinking the same thing. He lit two cigarettes and gave one to me.

"It's only half true," he said.

Sudden anxiety rose in me. "What?" I said.

"It's true I turned the prisoners over to the Allies. But they didn't stow away. I took them on board because Sean and his mates threatened to harm you and Grainne if I didn't."

I nodded. What he said made more sense to me than the newspaper stories. "Did Alphie know that?"

Gavin clucked his tongue. "I love Alphie like a brother, but he's got a big mouth on him, so he has. I wish he'd never gone to the papers. All this praise makes me feel like a bloody fraud."

Gavin paused and took a long pull on his cigarette. "As far as Alphie and the other boys knew, they were stowaways. Sean and his mates and I had taken them on board the night before and hid them in a cabin. They agreed they would act as if they'd stowed away." He looked directly at me. "The truth is, Sheila, when I started out I wasn't sure what I was going to do with them. We dropped off our regular cargo at Liverpool, and I told the lads we were going on down to Cherbourg to pick up some French cargo. We'd done it before, so they weren't suspicious."

"What made you change your mind?" I whispered.

He sighed. "One night I was up on deck and I looked out in the water and I saw Joel's face. I swear to God, Sheila, it's true. And he was smiling at me. And I knew there and then what I had to do."

This time I didn't laugh at Gavin and his ghosts. This time I believed him. We sat in silence for a while and then another thought struck me.

"Jesus, Gavin. What will Sean and his boys do to you now the word is out?"

Gavin shook his head. "Don't worry. Turns out he wasn't acting under orders. He'd taken on this business without permission, and the IRA head men don't like that. And the British police are going to be looking for them too. I'd say Sean and his boys are going to be lying low for a while."

"And what if you're asked to smuggle guns again?"

Gavin laughed hoarsely. "Hard to do it without a bloody boat!"

"Still, you put your men in danger by taking the Germans on board the *Ashgrove* in the first place, no matter why you did it." I couldn't disguise the accusation in my voice.

Gavin looked at me. "And that's something I'll have to live with for the rest of my life, Sheila. God bless them, they all agreed we should get the prisoners to the Allied ship even though we knew the invasion had started and the Channel was crawling with warships. But it was me put them in the situation to begin with. And that's something I'll never forgive myself for."

He turned his back to me, brushing away tears. I reached out and put my hand on his arm. As we sat looking out at the moonlit water I felt something warm surround us, and I knew it was Joel's spirit.

☙

Almost immediately word went out that Fisher and Sons, the biggest owner of coal boats in Newry, was throwing a celebration for the returning heroes at the harbor. The whole town was invited, and of course Alphie and Gavin were to be the guests of honor. And on top of that, Fisher's had requested that the Linen Queen be there to make a special presentation. Miss Johnson, Carlson's secretary, brought the word; I would be expected to be there.

It was a mild Saturday evening in late September when I joined the crowd at the docks. The boats in port were lit up and the place looked like a fairyland. Townspeople, strangers, sailors, children, mill workers, and farmers mingled together like old friends. Everyone from three counties must be here, I thought. I had never seen the likes of it. It reminded me of the carnival down at Warrenpoint Beach. Stalls of food and ice cream had been set up, and there was lemonade for the children and beer for the adults. I smiled to myself. Sober oul' Carlson wouldn't approve of the alcohol. A stage had been set up near the water. When I arrived a band was playing traditional music. I saw Eileen O'Neill with her fiddle, along with her two daughters, Aoife on the tin whistle and Saoirse on the mandolin. An image flashed into my head of Joel playing his fiddle on the big rock at the Flagstaff, and I pushed away the sadness that threatened to well up in me.

As I made my way through the crowd to the stage, people called and nodded to me. I wore the same blue frock I had worn the night of the Linen Queen competition. That frock had seen some times over the years. I waved to Kathleen and Ollie, who were standing nearby. Sweet Kathleen, who had given up her place so that I could enter. I wore Ma's blue and silver necklace again and I wore my sash over the dress: "Linen Queen, 1941." I had arranged my hair carefully so that it fell in waves to my shoulders, and I wore a new, bright red lipstick that Alphie had brought home for Patsy. I carried my coat and the bag containing the linens I was to present to Gavin and Alphie. I climbed onto the stage. Gavin and Alphie were already there. Alphie was dressed in a suit and tie his ma had made him wear. His face was bright red, and he looked as if he were choking on the collar. Beside him, Moira, his fancy woman, wearing a bright red dress, clung to him like a leech. She reminded me vaguely of Ma. Gavin, on the other hand, looked relaxed in dark trousers and a fisherman's pullover. I knew he was embarrassed by all the show, but he hid it well. He had put on weight already. His ma must be feeding him, I thought, and smiled.

Besides the Fisher family, the mayor, the local bishop, and other dignitaries I recognized from my other outings as Linen Queen sat on chairs arranged across the stage behind the musicians. Mr. Carlson sat with them. I avoided his eyes. As usual Hannah McAteer was there glaring at me as she prepared to place the tiara on my head. Mary stood beside her. Mrs. McAteer shoved the tiara roughly down on my hair and secured it with clips. It's a wonder she hadn't taken the scalp off me all these years. I climbed up onto the stage and took a chair at the end of the row.

A mild breeze blew in off the water, and I inhaled the mingled smells of salt and fish and oil. An image of my da flashed in my mind. In the distance I saw Ma on the arm of Shane Kearney. Mary McTaggart, in her ARP uniform, walked by and waved. I hoped there'd be no sirens tonight. I wanted nothing to spoil this. Eileen O'Neill and the band stopped playing and stepped down off the stage to loud applause. The elder Mr. Fisher got up to greet the crowd. He gave a short speech about how much we should admire and respect all the seamen in our community and honor the sacrifice of those who had died. People clapped politely, but I could tell they hoped he didn't blather on too long. They had come to celebrate and dance, not to listen to long speeches.

Mr. Fisher's speech was followed by short speeches from several of the others on the platform. The bishop called for a prayer and then took out his holy water and shook it three times in the direction of the boats, blessing them. Mr. Carlson was not called upon to speak. It was not his night, I thought. This night belonged to the sailors.

At length Mr. Fisher stood up again and called on Alphie and Gavin to join him at the front of the stage. The cheer that went up from the crowd could have been heard in Belfast. I clapped until my hands were sore. When the noise died down, Mr. Fisher handed an envelope to Gavin.

"A token of our appreciation," he said. "And maybe enough to buy a new boat." He turned to the crowd and chuckled. "I can give the lad a good price," he said, referring to the fact that he sold more boats than anybody else in the country.

Gavin held the envelope and stepped forward. Again a cheer went up. I watched him from behind. He stood erect, and his voice carried over the crowd like a soft breeze.

"Alphie and I have discussed it," Gavin was saying. "And we'd like to donate this money to the families of our comrades who went down with the *Ashgrove*. They were brave men all. And we will miss them."

The crowd murmured its approval.

It was time for me to make my presentation, and Mr. Fisher introduced me. There were cheers as I picked up the linens, stood up, and walked to the front of the stage. The old feeling of pride washed over me as camera bulbs flashed and men whistled and the mill girls cheered. I smiled and waved at the crowd just as I had done the night of the competition. Never had I felt so special, or so confident. I was in my element. I presented the linens to Alphie and Gavin, who in turn handed them to their mothers. When I turned back to the crowd, the words that had been building inside me roared to the surface. I walked up to the microphone.

"Ladies and Gentlemen," I began. "Tonight is my last night as your Linen Queen."

A few in the crowd booed, but the rest stood in silence, waiting.

"I have enjoyed representing Queensbrook Mill all these years. I know no other Linen Queen has reigned so long." I smiled and people laughed. "But it is time for me to pass the honor to someone else. I can't thank you enough for the support and respect you have given me. I thank you from the bottom of my heart. God bless you."

As I spoke, a lightness I had never known before came over me. I heard my voice as if from far away. The voice belonged to me and no one else. It was not Joel's voice, or Gavin's, or Rabbi Hurwitz's or Ma's—it was mine.

With that, I raised my hand and waved as I made my way down off the stage for one last time. I removed the tiara and the sash and held them out to a stunned Hannah McAteer.

"Go ahead, take them," I said. "It's what you've been dying for."

She grabbed them from me and clutched them to her breast as if afraid I might change my mind. But I had no intention of it. I had never been as sure of myself as I was now. I felt a tap on my shoulder and I swung around. It was Mr. Carlson.

"Miss McGee!" he exclaimed. "You can't be serious."

"Oh, but I am, Mr. Carlson. And I thought you'd be relieved. You wouldn't want a traitor representing your mill, now would you?"

He stuttered, as if he couldn't get the words out of his mouth quickly enough. "You're the most popular Linen Queen we've ever had," he said. "Won't you reconsider? You can have the title for as long as you wish."

I smiled with pleasure. "A generous offer, Mr. Carlson. And at one time I would have jumped at the chance. But that would have been the old Sheila McGee. I'm a different person now. Thanks all the same."

Mrs. McAteer glared at her brother and then at me.

"You're nothing without this, miss."

"Oh, you're wrong, Mrs. McAteer. I was nothing while I had it. Now I'm free."

She turned to her brother. "We can give it to Mary now," she said. "Mary's always wanted it."

Mary spoke up. "No, Mother, I never wanted it. It was your idea all along. I hated being in that competition. Do what you want with it," she said, nodding towards the tiara. "I'm going to marry George in spite of you and move as far away from you as I can."

A hand on my arm made me turn around. It was Gavin.

"Come on, Linen Queen, let's dance," he said.

I followed him out into the middle of the dock. Paddy Moloney's swing band, the same one that had played at the Linen Queen competition back in 1941, had struck up a slow tune, and Gavin took me in his arms.

"You couldn't resist, could you?" he said, smiling.

"What?"

"Enjoying the limelight one more time."

I laughed. "Well, the old Sheila isn't dead altogether."

ༀ

It was about six in the morning when Gavin and I arrived at the foot of the Flagstaff. We waved good-bye to the people who had given us a lift out from the docks, and hand in hand we climbed together to the summit just as we had done when we were children. We sat down on the damp grass, leaning against our favorite stone bench. Gavin lit two cigarettes and handed one to me.

A ship's horn echoed in the lough. Gavin stood up and walked to the edge of the land and looked out towards the horizon. I wondered what was going through his mind. Was he thinking of the *Ashgrove*, or his da? I left him alone with his thoughts. An image of Joel drifted into my mind. He appeared less often these days—only when I was in a place that held special memories. Like the Flagstaff. I glanced over at the big stone where he had played his fiddle. I saw him there now, playing a merry tune while children danced around him. I smiled.

Gavin came back and sat down beside me, stretching out his legs.

"I'm finished with the sea, Sheila," he said sadly. "I'm going to take up my teaching studies again—try to do some good in the world for once."

"Och, Gavin, you don't mean that," I said. "You belong on the sea."

"Not anymore."

The merrow poem Da had taught me came back to me. Creatures who belong on the sea never find peace when they are earthbound. I didn't want that to happen to Gavin. My heart went out to him.

"You'll change your mind someday," I said. "I know you will."

He smiled at me as if I were still the little girl he used to tease. "And what else do you know, Miss Sheila?"

I smiled back.

"A lot less than I used to think I did."

Gavin reached for my hand. "Jesus, you're freezing. Have you no gloves?"

I shook my head.

He pulled a pair out of his pocket. I sat up and put them on while he watched me. Then I placed my hand back in his and leaned against his shoulder.

The sun swelled in the sky, painting Carlingford Lough and the Clanrye River the color of marigolds. It set fire to the ruin of Narrow Water Castle and crowned the distant Mourne Mountains with a copper halo. As we sat without speaking, music drifted past us, carried on the breeze—fiddle music ancient as the stones that dotted this landscape. Overhead gulls circled and cried. Rabbits scurried in and out of bushes. A lone bird began to sing and then others joined in until their song reached a crescendo, reminding me of the spinners down at the mill. The beauty of this place stunned me into a belief in God. Once I had thought to leave it. Now I couldn't imagine being anywhere else in the world.

ABOUT THE AUTHOR

Patricia Falvey was born in County Down, Northern Ireland. She was raised in Northern Ireland and England before immigrating to the United States at the age of twenty. Formerly a managing director with an international financial services firm, she now devotes herself full-time to writing and teaching. She divides her time between Dallas, Texas, and County Armagh, Northern Ireland. Her first novel, *The Yellow House*, was published by Center Street in February 2010.